JUSTICE BETRAYED!

Justice tried to grab Merriman's arm, but he was clipped from behind by a rifle stock that took him to his knees. The fires began then, the village put to the torch as the screams of women being raped ripped like nails into Justice's head.

Through waves of pain he looked at Merriman. Merriman's .45 was leveled at him. "W-why?" he asked. "Why, you son of a bitch?"

"It's politics, that's all. This will be good for America."

"I'll k-kill you," he growled. "So help me God."

"Be a good trick, kid," Merriman smiled, then pulled the trigger.

Justice saw blazing light; then it was as if someone had hit him with a baseball bat across the chest. The shot turned him around, leaving him draped over the still-hot hood, his cheek searing, the smell of his own burnt flesh filling his nostrils. Merriman fired again.

Bantam Books of related interest
Ask your bookseller for the ones you have missed

Book of Justice by Jack Arnett
Book 1: Genocide Express
Book 2: Zaitech Sting
Book 3: Death Force
Book 4: Panama Dead

Eagle Force by Dan Schmidt
Book 1: Contract for Slaughter
Book 2: Death Camp Columbia
Book 3: Flight 666
Book 4: Red Firestorm

Overload by Bob Ham
Book 1: Personal War
Book 2: The Wrath
Book 3: Highway Warriors
Book 4: Tennessee Terror
Book 5: Atlanta Burn
Book 6: Nashville Nightmare

BOOK OF JUSTICE

#4

PANAMA DEAD

By
Jack Arnett

BANTAM BOOKS
NEW YORK · TORONTO · LONDON · SYDNEY · AUCKLAND

PANAMA DEAD

A Bantam Book / August 1990

ISBN 0-553-28774-5

Published simultaneously in the United States and Canada

Bantam Books are published by Bantam Books, a division of
Bantam Doubleday Dell Publishing Group, Inc. Its trademark,
consisting of the words "Bantam Books" and the portrayal of a
rooster, is Registered in U.S. Patent and Trademark Office and
in other countries. Marca Registrada. Bantam Books, 666 Fifth
Avenue, New York, New York 10103.

PRINTED IN THE UNITED STATES OF AMERICA

RAD   0 9 8 7 6 5 4 3 2 1

PANAMA DEAD

PROLOGUE

VOLCÁN BARÚ
22 APRIL 1978—1700 HOURS

William Justice bounced uneasily behind the wheel of the Panamanian National Guard jeep, the verdant, vibrant green of the jungle on either side of the dirt road turning darkly ominous as night crept in behind a diversionary light show of pale blue sky streaked with pastel pink. The man glanced quickly at the rearview to see if the deuce-and-a-half filled with Guardsmen was still pacing them before returning his gaze to the pitted and muddy dirt road that was the only access to this part of the Tabasara Mountains.

Frank Merriman sat beside him, all keyed up. He kept tapping his fingers like a drumbeat on his leg or on the seat between his legs as he chewed gum, head bobbing in syncopation to his imaginary beat. "We gonna make it before dark, kid?" the man asked, holding his arm up to read his watch in the dying light. "This'll be tougher in the dark."

"We're close," Justice said, once again checking the rearview, catching sight of the stoic, angry-eyed mestizo sitting beside the driver, the one referred to by most of his numerous enemies as *cara piña*—pineapple face. "How come the colonel's here? He wasn't a part of the original deal."

"He's Torrijos's boy, Will," Merriman said, turning to smile broadly at Justice. "He's head of NERI. Hell, he's entitled. What's the problem?"

Justice looked quickly at Merriman, trying to peg the

1

feeling that rolled off the man like noxious swamp gas. "I don't like him, Frank," he said, gearing down as the road began to drop sharply off, the jungle giving way to rocky hillside. "I don't trust him. Back in sixty-eight he was stationed out here. He ran the Chiriquí garrison."

"So?"

"So, the Guaymis hate him. He raped their women and stole their cattle. My contacts out here aren't going to be any too happy about it."

"Fuck it," Merriman said, going back to his drumming.

"Easy for you to say, fuck it," Justice replied angrily. "This Hate del Volcán warehouse is going to be a major bust, one that I engineered. I did it through establishing good relationships with the Indians out here in the mountains and by being as good as my word. I don't want *cara piña* screwing it up for me."

Merriman jerked his head to watch the truck behind them, no trace of the previous amusement in his wide eyes. "Don't you *ever* call him that," he whispered. "Jesus Christ, you'll get us both killed on the spot."

"I'm not afraid. . . ."

"Can it," Merriman spat, "and listen to me. You work for the Company, not those goddamned Indians. Since Noriega took over G-2, he's been our best source in the whole stinking country. We *need* him, Will, and if the man likes to play hide the stick with teenage Indian girls, by God, I'll help hold them down while he nails 'em."

"You're sick," Justice said.

Merriman just stared at him, Justice catching the man's look out of the corner of his eye. Merriman held anger in check, his tight lips slowly curling into a cruel smile. "Why, I'm just a poor white boy tryin' to make a buck in the cold, cruel world," he said in a fake accent. "I never did go to college like you, so you'll have to excuse me if I'm not up on all the social graces."

The road narrowed to the width of one car, the open drop-off beside Justice a straight plunge downward over a hundred feet to a narrow valley below where a score of scrawny cattle grazed on bright green grass. Large hills and small mountains cast long, fingerlike shadows across the open, rugged landscape, the sun setting fat and blood red between two hills, glowing like a monstrous furnace, stoking Justice's unease. And always they wound, a wide spiral around the hillside, circles and circles. Justice had never thought much about gut feelings before, but he had one now, and it scared him half to death. There was something about Merriman's eyes. . . .

"What's going on that I don't know about?" he asked, watching the curving roadway through the dirt-spotted windshield, his headlights defining the potholes far too late to avoid them.

"It's just politics," Merriman answered. "Don't worry about it. It's all in the best interests of the United States. Leave it at that."

At that instant they curved into the monstrous shadow of Volcán Barú, the extinct volcano dominating the landscape. Its first sight, as always, was a shock to Justice. It was simply too big, too massive, for the country around it. Like some alien anomaly it rose arrogantly into the heavens, many thousands of feet taller than anything within a continent of it. It was the pride of the Tabasara range, a boulder in the land of pebbles and, as such, was a holy place for the Indians of the region.

"There," Justice said, pointing toward the volcano's base. "Hate del Volcán."

The village sat at the base of the volcano, tucked delicately into its folds. It was a tiny hamlet of bamboo-and-thatch huts, a self-contained tribal unit. In class-conscious Panama, the Guaymis, descendants of American Indians, were the next-to-lowest rung on the social ladder, barely a step above the descendants of blacks imported from the West Indies to build the Panama Canal. Panamanian Indians lived in primitive conditions on the frontier, eeking out a living from the land, from trading and from cattle raising. The Guaymis of Hate del Volcán were no exception.

The roadway dropped sharply, descending at a sixty-degree angle to the mouth of the village. Justice could see people gathering in the dying light, pointing in their direction, several of the men mounting horses and riding toward them.

"All right," Merriman said, the excitement back in his voice. "The ball's rollin' now."

The man wet his finger, then used it to wash a small circle on the windshield before him. He took out his gum and stuck in on the spot, then reached inside his windbreaker, removing a nickel-plated .45 automatic and ejecting the clip into his hand.

"You're not going to need that, Frank," Justice said. "This'll be simple and straightforward."

"You sure the Cubans will be there?" Merriman asked, checking the load, then shoving the clip back into the butt of the automatic with a loud click.

Justice geared down to first to slow their descent, unable to take his eyes off the now treacherous roadway. "My people tell me they're always here the first week of the month. They take in a cocaine shipment from the Medellin cartel on a nearby airstrip, then sit on it for a week until American buyers fly in and take it from them. All Communist activities west of the canal are financed from this village."

"Must be a lot of nose candy," Merriman said, snapping a round into the .45's chamber and sticking it back in his belt.

"I estimate a good five hundred pounds a month," Justice replied. "Something over half a million bucks."

Merriman clucked his tongue. "It's a start," he said.

"What do you mean by that?" Justice asked, the hairs on the back of his neck bristling.

"Not a damned thing, college boy," Merriman said. "You just worry about getting us to the bottom of this hill alive."

The road was awash with mud, a perennial condition in Panama's breadbasket with its 150 inches of rain a year. It was all Justice could do to keep from sliding over the edge and making it to the valley the quick way.

By the time they made it to road's end, the valley had been swallowed by the night, only the barest hint of pink visible between the distant peaks. Two Guaymi cowboys, wearing straw hats and T-shirts, were waiting for them fifty yards outside the village. Justice recognized Mata, his village contact, the man smiling wide and dismounting when he saw Justice.

Justice was out of the car, the truck pulling up on Merriman's side, Guardsmen jumping quickly and silently

4

out of the back, their M16s off their shoulders and loaded with banana clips. They were Noriega's personal strike force, called Dobermans because of their viciousness.

"My friend," Mata called, meeting Justice with an extended hand. "We do good work tonight, huh?"

Justice shook the man's hand as his partner dismounted and joined them. Though Spanish and English were the official languages of Panama, the Guaymis retained their own Indian dialects. Mata was the only English speaker in the entire village, a job entrusted to one villager per generation.

"Are they there tonight?" Justice asked, Merriman coming around the rear of the jeep to join them.

"Yes . . . they are there," Mata said, pointing toward the darkened village, his own features nearly lost in the night. "They stay in a cave dug into Barú. Two nights ago they leave in their truck . . . varoom, varoom . . . go away, come back with the nose powder."

"How much . . . nose powder?" Merriman asked.

The man shook his head. "Lots. Whole truck full."

"Bingo!" Merriman said, turning to the deuce-and-a-half and jerking his thumb into the air.

It was only then that Noriega climbed out of the truck, barking orders quickly in Spanish to his men.

"Van . . . van! Apurate, hombres!"

The troops took off running, dark figures rushing past Justice, boots loudly trampling the underbrush as the colonel moved up to shove Justice out of the way and confront Mata, the Guaymi's eyes opening wide, standing out boldly in the rising moonlight.

"Cara piña," the man whispered urgently, his eyes, now accusing and filled with fear, turning to Justice.

The two men stared at one another for an instant, and in that eternal second Justice realized what a fool he'd been to trust . . . to trust . . .

Noriega grunted like an animal, a bayonet coming out of his uniform belt and whizzing past Justice's ear on its quick arc to Mata's throat. He struck home solidly, jamming the blade up to the handle in the man's neck, blood immediately gushing out of his mouth as he stumbled backward, weakly, a strange somnambulistic dance.

"No!" Justice yelled, Mata's partner turning to run as

Merriman, laughing, pulled out the .45, aiming at his retreating back.

Justice tried to grab Merriman's arm, but he was clipped from behind by a rifle stock that took him to his knees. And if he'd had the forethought to pray, he'd have prayed for the peace of unconsciousness that eluded him.

He hunched over weakly, his mind bright colors and slow motion. Merriman's gun exploded loudly beside him, a scream telling him the message had found a receiver. He tried to rise, fell again, Noriega and Merriman laughing beside him.

He crawled to the jeep for support, grabbing the rearview mirror to pull himself painfully up.

Then he heard it—gunfire. Gunfire all through the village, the screams of women and children telling him the massacre wasn't limited to Cuban infiltrators. They were slaughtering the entire village.

Through waves of pain he looked at Merriman, the jeep's support the only thing keeping him on his feet. Merriman's .45 was leveled at him. "W-why?" he asked. "Why, you son of a bitch?"

"Such language," Merriman smiled. "And directed toward a senior agent. I told you it didn't concern you. It's politics, that's all. This will be good for America."

The fires began then, the village put to the torch as the screams of women being raped ripped like nails into Justice's head.

"I'll k-kill you," he growled. "So help me God."

Merriman nodded thoughtfully, fires blazing magnificent red-orange behind him. "Be a good trick, kid," he said. "You see, it was unfortunate. We came out here to bust this operation, but the Cubans had already burned out the village. We took care of them bravely, after a huge firefight; but unfortunately, you didn't survive the battle. I hope you appreciate the fact that I'm doing you a favor here. You'll be a real hero. I'll see to that. Don't worry."

Merriman smiled, then pulled the trigger. Justice saw blazing light; then it was as if someone had hit him with a baseball bat across the chest. The shot turned him around, leaving him draped over the still-hot hood, his cheek searing, the smell of his own burnt flesh filling his nostrils.

Merriman fired again, then three more times, Justice not feeling any of the bullets. In fact, he couldn't feel anything. He assumed he was dead and that his hell was having to remain conscious to see the results of his actions. His eyes were open, staring at the windshield, at the reflection of the village fires, at Merriman's gum wad still stuck to the glass. His brain spun wildly, time losing all meaning as he was sucked farther and farther into a vortex of destruction brought on by his own naive innocence. Nothing in his experience prepared him for the sounds of burning, screaming death that surrounded him, all of it final, all of it his fault.

He heard the troops as they returned, laughing, drunken with animal passion. They were carrying bags of white powder, which they began loading into the jeep, Justice's eyes bearing witness to the price of human life. Then he saw Merriman moving to the passenger side to take his gum off the windshield and put it back in his mouth. Noriega walked up and embraced the man warmly.

"We are now partners, my friend," the colonel said. "The beginning of a lasting and beneficial relationship."

"I thank you," Merriman said. "The United States government thanks you."

"And our little agreement...?"

"Done and done," Merriman said. "My people will take care of Torrijos, and my government will back you as his successor."

"*Bueno*," Noriega laughed. "*Muy bien.*"

"We'd better get back and report the...battle," Merriman said, walking around to the driver's side of the jeep. "We wouldn't want to arouse any suspicions."

"This is my country," Noriega said, "my world. There will be no suspicions."

Justice saw Merriman's hands on his shoulders, then felt himself jerked off the hood to crumple on the ground. Within minutes all the cocaine was efficiently loaded, the vehicles departing without fanfare, leaving him alone to face his death.

He lay on the muddy ground, bugs crawling freely over him, accepting him as a new component of their environment. He could still hear the cries of the dying from the village, but after a few minutes, those stopped also, leaving only the night. His eyes stared straight up, the monolith of Barú a silent god standing watch over him. And as the vale of unconsciousness finally, mercifully, embraced him, he thanked whatever power it was that was removing him from the horror of life in the human jungle.

I.

1988

HAVEN ISLAND—FRENCH WEST INDIES
2 FEBRUARY—1023 HOURS

Charles Mandrake felt as if he were entering another world of out-of-place pastel hues and timelessness as the outboard-powered skiff, *Marie-Felin*, beached itself on the Caribbean side of Haven Island. His pilot was a dark-skinned Carib Indian who spoke only Creole French. The crystal-clear water lapping against the bright white boat was multicolored—from pale green to blue to vein traces of red algae. The sky was bright cerulean nesting a white-hot sun, and the beach—the beach—was black sand.

Mandrake stood, feeling silly in his pin-striped gray suit, and turned to the pilot. "Why is the sand black?" he asked, the man frowning at him and pointing to the water beside the boat.

"No," Mandrake said. "The sand. Why is the sand black?"

The Indian kept pointing, Mandrake finally realizing that he was supposed to be climbing out of the boat here, right into the ankle-deep water. He gazed sadly down at his Johnston and Murphy brogues, wondered for a second how this was going to look on the State Department expense voucher, then splashed into the surf, nearly dropping his briefcase as he tripped over the gunwale.

He stared at a long, vacant stretch of black beach that crawled up to serious palm trees and jungle, just like the

9

desert islands in the movies—except this island was far from deserted.

He turned back to the leathery-faced Carib, but the man had already pushed off and was drifting back into the current, leaving him alone.

Feeling the anger rising up his neck, he took off walking aimlessly, his feet sinking deeply into the sand, filling his wet shoes, covering them, his socks, and three inches of the pants leg with fine black grit. This was no way to treat the assistant secretary of state of the United States.

In point of fact, everything about this deal had been screwy from the start. From the eyes-only orders that had come down specifically for him from the White House, to the secrecy of the arrangements, to the mysterious boat trip from Martinique with a man he couldn't even communicate with. All to end up here on a deserted stretch of beach waiting to meet one William Lambert, the most brazen and successful terrorist the world had ever known.

The sound of a motor reached him, muffled by the tangle of jungle. As he scanned the tree line, straining to locate the sound, he realized there was much more to this place than black sand. Palm trees up and down the beach bristled with electronic equipment—radar guns, microwave transmitters, and occasional TV cameras—all aesthetically concealed within the large, undulating branches.

The motor sounds grew loud, whining. All at once he heard a war whoop, and a balloon-tired jeep came flying out of the jungle rise three feet off the ground. It bounced on the black sand, nearly throwing the driver out, then sped toward him, sand spraying wildly from all four wheels.

What had he gotten himself into?

The jeep careened toward him, grinding to a halt ten feet distant, the driver standing to address him over the top of the dirty windshield. The man was large and powerful looking. He wore khaki shorts with no shirt, dark glasses, and a tan cowboy hat soaked dark with sweat around the band.

"You that feller from the State Department?" he asked, spitting over his left shoulder

"Name's Mandrake, and I'd like to lodge a formal complaint about the method of my arrival, I . . ."

"You best climb in," the man said. "My name's Bob Jenks. Will'um wants to see you before his afternoon classes."

Mandrake moved to the jeep and climbed in the passenger side. "Afternoon classes?" he asked, leaning down to try to get as much sand off himself as he could.

"Yeah," Jenks replied, dropping the jeep into gear and taking off amidst another shower of sand. "He teaches history. Next time you oughta take off your shoes and socks and roll up them pants before jumping out of a boat."

"This is no way to treat the U.S. government," Mandrake said, grabbing the windshield to hold himself in the wildly bouncing vehicle.

"It's the way we treat everybody, partner," Jenks said. "Take it or leave it alone."

They reached the tree line, Jenks speeding into what looked like a dense section of jungle, only for the underbrush to give way within ten feet to a smooth asphalt roadway. Jenks geared into second, leaving rubber all over the road behind his fishtailing tires.

"Do you always drive this fast?" Mandrake yelled above the roaring wind.

The man looked at him as if he'd never heard the question before. "Sure!" he yelled back. "It's fun!"

The jungle went by in a blur beside them, big green bamboo and mangroves running together like a finger painting as large hills covered with sugar cane and banana plantations spread out all around. The area looked prosperous, not the brigand, outlaw empire stolen from the French that he had expected. He clutched his briefcase to him with his free hand, holding tightly to the paperwork that had brought him so far from the game and the rules of civilization that he had become accustomed to. He tried to occupy his mind with the scenery to keep from thinking of the crazy man beside him who was attempting to break the land speed record.

Jenks suddenly veered off the road, finding another hidden pathway in the inscrutable forest that led quickly to a small cement bunker in the middle of nowhere. Jenks screeched to a halt just outside the building and jumped from the vehicle. "Come on," he said.

"Are we there?" Mandrake asked, tentatively setting foot on solid ground again.

"First stop," Jenks said, walking to the unmarked door in the windowless structure and speaking into a grillwork beside it. "Robert Jenks."

There was a slight pause, then an audible click as the door swung open, Jenks ushering Mandrake into the bunker's dark recesses and turning on indirect lighting.

They were standing in a small interrogation and briefing room, Mandrake surprised at the sophistication of the equipment he found there. His first thought was that the place could be a torture room, but all the control devices seemed passive—lie detectors, EEGs, voice printers—electronic equipment designed for verification, not aggression.

"Why are we here?" Mandrake asked.

"Gotta check you out," Jenks said, smiling with his pale blue eyes and his crooked-toothed mouth. He moved up to Mandrake, going over him with a hand-held metal detector. "Everybody comes here first when they show up on the island."

"What are you afraid of?" Mandrake asked. "Resistance?"

Jenks stared at him for a moment, then bent to run the detector over the briefcase. "Protection for our citizens," he said. "We got people living here who wouldn't be *living* here if we didn't check. There's no weapons allowed anywhere on the island."

"Except for your people, of course."

Jenks straightened. "I said no weapons," he replied, pointing to a small booth in the corner. "Care to step in the X-ray? It won't hurt a bit."

Mandrake walked into the machine and stood. "How's this?"

"Face front," Jenks said, "and shut up for a minute."

Mandrake turned to face the opaque curtain.

"Hold your arms out to the side."

Mandrake complied, feeling stupid. He had dealt with a great many protocols during his ten years with State, but on Haven Island, things were done differently.

"Where'd you get the pin in your left leg?" came Jenks's voice from the other side of the curtain.

"The siege of Khe Sanh in sixty-eight."

"Marine?"

"Yeah."

"Figures," Jenks said. "Come on out. You're clean."

Mandrake moved out from behind the curtain. "What do you mean, by 'figures'?" he asked.

Jenks was already moving toward the door. "You just gotta understand Will'um. There's only certain folks he'll deal with. You should feel honored. Come on."

Honored wasn't exactly the word that had come to Mandrake's mind, but it would do for now. After all, he was here for delicate negotiation, and if he was somehow being complimented, he should accept it in the proper spirit. When he had expressed his initial reservations about coming here to the president, he was told to negotiate with the devil himself if it was in the best interests of the United States. So be it.

They moved out of the bunker and back into the jeep, Jenks's face lighting with joy as he dropped the thing into gear and squealed around the parking lot on two wheels before speeding back down the path to the main road.

They bumped up onto the roadway, passing a truckload of men going the other way, Mandrake surprised to find skin hues as varied as the colors of the Carribean. "Who are they?" he asked.

"Stockholders," Jenks laughed. "They're probably going out to work the sugarcane."

"So many nationalities..."

"Yeah...well, the Indians are from here, the French have been settling since the seventeenth century, Hindus and Africans came over as contract labor after slavery was abolished in the eighteen hundreds, and ever since Will'um liberated the island in eighty-five, people from all over the world have settled here."

"Liberated," Mandrake said. "A word of multiple meanings."

"Not here," Jenks said, his face hardening. "We mean what we say here. The revolution was the stockholders' idea, not Will'um's. It was accomplished peacefully, without bloodshed. Today Haven Island is self-determining."

"Lambert owns everything," Mandrake said. "Where does the self-determination come in?"

Jenks slowed the jeep down to a crawl. The smile had left his face. He turned to stare at Mandrake, his lips hard, his eyes lost behind the dark glasses. "Will'um is CEO and chairman of the board, that's all. The stockholders, all the

13

people who live here, *they're* the ones who own the company. Will'um doesn't even maintain a controlling share."

Mandrake didn't believe the man but turned and watched the scenery rather than argue. The jungle began to give way to small farms raising tamarinds and red pimentos. They were moving closer to civilization, the hint of a city visible in the distance. He wondered why he'd been dropped off at the most uninhabited part of the island.

"How long have you worked with Lambert?" he asked as they closed in on the city's outskirts, passing motorcars and buses painted bright, clashing colors.

"Since eighty-six," Jenks said, some of his good humor returning, along with his heavy foot. "I was sheriff of a small town in Kansas and got set up for murder when I tied some of the governor's men to a drug-smuggling racket. Will'um showed up and broke me right out of death row at Leavenworth. We been together ever since."

"I remember your case," Mandrake said. "You know, the president was thinking about giving you amnesty when you escaped."

Jenks laughed. "Fuck that," he said, shaking his head. "I know how that works. After you get fried, they come back and pardon your body. Fat lotta good that does. No sir, these past years have been the best of my life. I wouldn't trade them for nothing. Hey . . . here we are. Welcome to Schoelcher, our biggest and only city."

They entered what Mandrake could only think of as a metropolitan French town of about fifteen hundred. Gendarmes in khaki shorts strolled the narrow streets, weaving in and out of the French automobiles with yellow headlights and the outdoor cafés where old men drank wine and ate French cheeses and pâtés on crusty *baguettes*. Open-air markets filled the warm winds with sickly sweet pungency, island women wearing full multicolored skirts and bright head coverings swaying gently through the stalls, food baskets carried elegantly on their heads. The city was built on a hillside, most of the streets winding down to the harbor a hundred feet below them and dotted with scores of fishing boats plus a surprising number of large freighters. An old French fort sat in the mouth of the harbor, bleak and imposing amidst the colorful confusion of everything around it.

This was not the oppressed slave population of outlaws and boat people that he'd been told to expect. In fact he had begun to realize that he was being brought through town expressly to confound his viewpoint. Perhaps there was more to Lambert than he or Company Intelligence had suspected.

"The school's just outside of town," Jenks said. "We'll be there in a minute."

"This place... surprises me," Mandrake said.

"Will'um understands American intelligence gathering," Jenks replied. "He wanted you to see the truth before you met."

Mandrake was preparing to respond when he was caught completely off guard by two men he saw having coffee under a Cinzano umbrella at a café. They were both grave looking, their heads close together as they spoke. "Is that Henry Kissinger?" Mandrake said, confused.

"And Yasir Arafat," Jenks smiled. "And no bodyguards. Haven has become a popular spot for negotiating the last few years due to its nonaligned status. Will'um treats everyone equally."

The city gave way once more to flat farmland as they turned inland, rolling, forested hills rising to dull peaks all around in the near distance. Jenks pulled off onto a dirt road that led a hundred yards' distance to a rambling, one-story bamboo-and-thatch schoolhouse. They arrived amidst a dust cloud at a large palm tree set in the yard, a group of mixed-race children sitting cross-legged in the shade beneath the tree while a man dressed in a Panama suit and carrying a mongoose stood before them. Mandrake's mind flashed. *Greetings, William Lambert,* he thought, *or whatever your name is.*

Lambert was an imposing figure standing there in the glow of the tropical sun, the sleek, brown mongoose curling around his forearm. The white suit barely concealed a lean, hard figure and well-developed upper body. But this wasn't what attracted Mandrake's notice. It was the man's face. An aura of control and intelligence surrounded William Lambert. It physically oozed from the man's eyes, and for the first time in his life Mandrake truly understood the meaning of the word *charisma.* He was staring at a man who was, quite literally, bursting with life. It lit him up, even at a distance of thirty feet, and Mandrake had to physically force himself to stop staring. This was power in a very raw and organic sense.

"He'll be done in a few minutes," Jenks whispered, Mandrake amazed at the reverential tone the man's voice had taken. "You can slide a little closer if you want. Hell, you might even learn something."

Mandrake nodded, Jenks wandering back to the jeep and driving off, leaving him standing in the midst of a cloud of yellow dust. He brushed himself off and walked toward the man in the white suit, catching the tail end of a lecture, apparently about war.

"What's the point of these conflicts?" Lambert was saying as he idly stroked the mongoose, his students sitting in rapt fascination. "What is the real purpose of war?" He suddenly turned on his heel and faced Mandrake, acknowledging the man's presence for the first time. He smiled widely. "How about you, Mr. Mandrake... do you know the purpose of war?"

Mandrake moved to the outskirts of the group, smiling at the thought of trying to explain such a difficult topic to young children. "Ideological or territorial expansion," he said, shrugging. "Natural greed. In the case of the Russians, sometimes it's territorial paranoia as they search for a buffer zone to protect them from the outside world."

Lambert nodded, then turned to the children. "Does everyone agree with that?" he asked, nearly half of the thirty or so pupils raising their hands. Lambert pointed. "You, Yvette."

A small porcelain doll of a girl of no more than eight years stood shyly. After a look at Mandrake, she turned to the entire class. "Since the dawn of the industrial age," she said in French-accented English, "wars have basically been fought for the good of business. As business more and more asserts its domination over countries and their wealth of resources and workers, wars have been confined to the Third World, the still-undeveloped business zones of the planet."

"Right," Lambert said. "And the business wars are very definable. Business, like my mongoose here, operates on a set pattern always. The mongoose hunts the same trails over and over, keeping in cover of vegetation, just as business hides behind the meaningless ideologies of the governments

16

it controls. The mongoose eats away at all other predator species in its area, just as business chases away its competition. Once its area is totally defined, the mongoose will stay there, leaving other areas for others of its kind. Where does all this lead . . . Tan Phat?"

A Vietnamese boy, slightly older than the rest, dressed in short pants and a flower-printed shirt, spoke. "Ultimately peace will be the result . . . the flower of civilization that many wish for."

"Good," Lambert said. "And the problems . . . Andy?"

A freckle-faced American kid stood quickly, smiling at everyone around him. "Who's in charge and who's gettin' bossed around—that's the problem. If business runs everything, there ain't any laws to protect folks."

"Aren't, Andy . . . not ain't," Lambert corrected. "What is the solution?"

Andy frowned for a second, looking around for help.

"Think it through," Lambert said. "Be logical."

"Well . . ." the boy began, "it seems that you should either make sure you're the boss, or find a way to show that businesses run . . . humanely would actually produce more, because happy workers are good workers. The failure of the Soviet economy is probably a good example of how not to run a business."

"Right!" Lambert said. "Excellent. You're all dismissed for now. Our class after lunch will be how the pre–industrial age concept of Manifest Destiny helped lead to the business society that now exists. Enjoy!"

The kids jumped up, screaming with glee, and like small nuclear bombs exploded off in all directions, Mandrake smiling despite his discomfort and anger at the situation. He walked toward Lambert, the man handing the mongoose to a tall, stoic, exotic-looking man dressed in white trousers and a bright white Nehru jacket buttoned up to the neck. The man was extremely dark, Mandrake using his years of diplomatic travel to conclude he was from southern India. The dark man put the mongoose in a cage.

Lambert looked at him, and Mandrake felt as if the man were looking through his body, right at his brain and heart. He felt embarrassed, naked under the gaze of the mercenary. Lambert reached out a large hand. "Glad to meet you,

17

Mandrake," he said, shaking hands vigorously, his offered friendship seeming heartfelt and genuine. "Hope you don't mind my using you there in the class. I wanted my pupils to see how they teach people politics at Harvard."

Mandrake started. "How did you know I went to Harvard?" he asked.

"No one ever comes to this island without my first knowing about them," the man said. "I don't like bureaucrats, and I despise politicians and government flunkies. You're none of those. Besides, I'm sure you checked me out thoroughly before coming here."

"As thoroughly as we could," Mandrake said. "We traced back your name and birthplace. It seems you died at the age of two and a half in a house fire in Dallas, Texas."

"So I did," Lambert said. "I like a man who gets right to the point. You and I will do all right together."

"And I have to tell you that I thought your political analysis was a pile of garbage."

Lambert nodded, laughing. Mandrake looked surprised that his words elicited no apparent reaction from the man other than amusement. "Well, that doesn't surprise me either," Lambert said. "If you thought differently, you'd be living here with me on the island. But that's something we can talk about later. First, I'd like to introduce you to my associate, Mr. Sardi."

Mandrake moved to shake hands with the Indian, the man taking his hand firmly, but lightly. His face had a calm to it that he couldn't quite understand. "Pleased to meet you," Mandrake said.

"Likewise," Sardi replied, his voice soft-spoken, nearly a whisper. "We welcome you to Haven. I hope you haven't been too inconvenienced up until this point."

Mandrake was ready to complain, then looked at the men and thought better of it. What the hell. "Everything's been just fine," he said.

"*There's* the diplomat in him," Lambert said loudly. "Grace under pressure, huh, Mandrake?"

Mandrake just stared at him, deciding to avoid casual conversation as much as possible. Lambert was scoping him out too well already. He felt he had no secrets from the man, and that was no way to enter into negotiations.

"Well," Lambert said, "we have one more little trip to take before we settle down, but I promise it's a short one."

Mandrake looked around and saw no vehicle. "Jenks has already taken the car," he said.

"Don't need a car," Lambert said, pointing skyward.

Mandrake looked up in time to see the machine descending upon them from a hundred feet. "A chopper!" he said.

"Not just a chopper," Lambert smiled, while Mandrake strained his eyes to make it out.

"A Huey!" Mandrake yelled, smiling. "I haven't been in one of them since . . ."

"Since Khe Sanh," Lambert finished, as the chopper landed near them in a flurry of dust and heated air. He made a grand gesture toward the helicopter. "Your carriage awaits."

Instinctively ducking, the three men plus one caged mongoose ran to the open port of the Huey, its M60 mountings bare, its camouflage covering repainted in red-and-white stripes like a barber pole. As he scampered into the bay and grabbed a seat, Mandrake couldn't help but feel he had entered an asylum run by the inmates.

William Justice stared hard at the State Department's man sitting across from him in the Huey, Mandrake dividing his own time between returning the gaze full measure and looking uneasily at the blue-green water that lapped distantly beneath him. Justice liked the man, had known he'd like him when he ran his own security checks on State's negotiators, the computers kicking out Mandrake's name right away. So far he'd said what he'd meant and spoken honestly, backing it up with full eye contact. Had Mandrake not passed this visual check, they'd be turning north, back to Martinique and an end of this association with the U.S. government. He had no idea what they wanted from him, and he didn't much care, but he was willing to meet with almost anybody if he could feel they were addressing him honestly.

The fact that they'd cracked the Lambert alias meant absolutely nothing, except that he had again become a nonperson to the country he'd once served.

"Where are you taking me?" Mandrake said, shifting in his seat and staring out at the bay.

"Afraid?" Justice asked.

The man looked at him, his eyes hard. "Wouldn't you be?" he asked.

Justice shrugged. "Once...maybe. Your daughter, Mandy, graduates high school this year, doesn't she?"

"Where are you taking me?" Mandrake asked again.

Justice smiled and pointed to the southwest. "The people who live here call it Le Rocher du Diamant."

"Diamond Rock," Mandrake replied.

"You've retained your French since the old Paris embassy days," Justice said. "I maintain my headquarters off Haven Island. It seems safer for everyone."

"You mean you've simply kept a safe distance from all the thieves and cutthroats you've taken to your bosom," Mandrake replied.

Sardi spoke up, his voice gentle, barely audible over the beating of the chopper blades. "If you've driven in with Mr. Jenks," he said, "you already know that is not true. Haven Island is just that, a haven for people without a country...."

"Terrorists," Mandrake said.

"Intellectuals," Sardi said. "Experts in fields that governments are afraid of. Very few terrorists are ever deported and denied citizenship. They are either killed or they join the mainstream."

"You deny that convicted terrorists have gained asylum in your country?" Mandrake countered.

"What Mr. Sardi is trying to say," Justice replied, "is that the definition of terrorism is a very subjective one. If you choose to define it differently than we do, that's not my problem. If you don't like it, leave. I didn't invite you here, Mr. Mandrake. Quite frankly I feel there is very little of substance for us to discuss anyway."

"We want to hire your mercenaries," Mandrake said.

"You and everybody else," Justice said, then pointed. "Look again."

Mandrake turned and stared out at the bay. Diamond Rock jutted, monstrous and obscene, from the rolling waters of the Caribbean. "It's huge," he said.

"Six hundred feet from the waterline," Justice said. "The only rock ever commissioned into the British Navy."

"What?"

Justice smiled. "It was commissioned the HMS *Diamond*

Rock in 1804 and stocked with men and supplies. It took Napoleon's French eighteen months of heavy bombardment and assaults to dislodge the garrison. I think I could hold it for eighteen years."

"You're hardly the British government, Mr. Lambert," Mandrake said.

"Neither is the British government anymore, Mr. Mandrake," Justice answered, detecting amusement in the other man's eyes despite his attempts to hide it. Good. A man without a sense of humor is a man incapable of self-reflection.

They reached the rock, its bulk appreciable only close up, where size could be compared. They traveled up its shrub-covered height, circling about two-thirds of the way up. A section of the rock was sheared away flat and bulls-eyed; the Huey bounced down gently dead center, shutting down the rotors.

They climbed out onto the open rock face, the wind up high, whipping their faces with sweet salt air. Justice loved the wind's freedom, finding its assault invigorating. He looked at Mandrake, who was now staring around him in undisguised awe. "I'm a man who likes to be taken seriously," he said.

Mandrake nodded absently. "I've noticed."

"What would you like to drink?"

"An Old-Fashioned would be nice," Mandrake said, his own tongue planted firmly in cheek.

Justice bowed slightly and spoke to Sardi. "Would you take care of us, please? I think in the wardroom."

Sardi lowered his head slowly and moved elegantly across the makeshift landing pad to disappear through a metal door set right into the rock face, Justice and Mandrake following slowly behind.

"This is my fortress," Justice said, "my Keep, if you will. Anyone else but you, I would have met with on the island."

"Why am I different?" Mandrake asked as they reached the door, Justice opening it with voice activation, as Jenks had done at the bunker, the metal sliding open with a grating, hydraulic hiss, cool air rushing out to hit them in the face.

"One thing at a time," Justice said, leading the man into a dark hallway, dimly lit with red emergency lights. They moved to an elevator at the end of the hall. Justice pushed the button and waited for the elevator's return. "I want to show you my command center."

The elevator arrived quickly and silently, Justice ushering the assistant secretary into the triple-sized elevator, the doors closing to reveal eye-level windows. With a barely audible whoosh, the machine started down, hewn rock face sliding silently past as they descended into the rock-solid bowels.

"This is a war bunker," Mandrake said. "What the hell are you doing here?"

"I'm fighting a war," Justice said, "a war for the future of mankind."

He watched Mandrake turn to stare at him, could see the indecision on the man's face as he tried to decide whether or not Justice was insane. That was fine, too. One man's insanity was another's positive motivation.

"Who, then, are you fighting against?" Mandrake asked politely.

"I'm fighting against the jungle," Justice said. "I'm fighting against every son of a bitch who thinks that man's civilized leanings give him the right to take advantage and act like a jungle animal. I'm fighting against the darkness that has given humanity the means to destroy itself. I'm fighting to give people the chance to realize that this planet doesn't have to exist on a foundation of hatred and fear, that we are noble creatures with nobler possibilities. I'm fighting to give humanity a chance to live. And believe me, it's one hell of a battle."

"You *are* crazy," Mandrake said.

"Well, that's a start, isn't it?" Justice said.

"How can you fight human nature?"

"By reminding people they're autonomous and good," Justice said, as the elevator suddenly poured light through the cutouts, both men turning to stare at a huge room full of people and computers and electronic equipment. Justice pointed through the window as they slid past the room. "My research department. Not as big as the CIA's, but honed to a finer point. I'm able to keep track of nearly the entire world in here."

"The world?" Mandrake was staring in shock at him now.

Justice returned the stare with a tiny smile. "It's the world I'm trying to save, Mr. Mandrake," he said quietly. "If you're going to dream, you may as well dream big. By the proper manipulation of events and money, I'm able to... influence the world order. I do it through my mercenaries. I do it through my business interests, and I do it through education. For example, I've invested heavily in American elections, mostly at the local level where national leaders originate, though I am the sole backer of four U.S. senators and ten representatives."

They slid past Research, then another floor, a warehouse full of weapons. "The armory," Justice said. "As we walk out of the jungle, someone has to control the animals."

"So right or wrong is what you decide it is," Mandrake said.

"Exactly right," Justice said. "Very good. You worked it out right away."

"Where does that leave you?" Mandrake said.

"I hope to live long enough to see my usefulness come to an end," Justice replied. "Here are the living quarters."

They passed several floors that seemed to be filled with hallways leading to many doors, like apartments. "My people stay here, with their families, for three months at a time, at which point we rotate. Diamond Rock is really the heart of my operation."

After passing a food-storage floor, commissary, and cafeteria, they finally jerked to a stop before a long hallway from which other halls and many doorways branched out.

Justice led Mandrake down the hall, turning through several corridors before moving into the wardroom, the recreation area apparently set aside for the top brass. They walked though a large gym, complete with basketball and handball courts, and a weight room, before moving into a lounge containing easy chairs and conversation pits. The centerpiece of the room was a long table, upon which two cold drinks were placed.

The room was nearly dark, warmed by small ceiling lights that glowed the place to an ethereal dusk feeling. Justice picked up one of the drinks and handed it to Mandrake. "An Old-Fashioned, I believe," he said, picking up his own glass of orange juice and drinking it down with one gulp.

Mandrake lifted his briefcase to the table and opened it. "Perhaps now we can..."

"In a minute," Justice said. "Let's wait for Sardi first. Let me show you something."

Justice walked to the far wall and pushed a stud on the homey walnut paneling. There was a loud hum, the wall slowly sliding aside to reveal a ten-by-five-foot window overlooking the ocean from a vantage point of 150 feet. Bright sunshine poured into the room. Two miles in the distance Haven Island sparkled like a precious gem against the twin blues of sky and water. It was a sight that never stopped inspiring Justice, and he hoped that it would have some effect on Charles Mandrake.

The man walked up beside him, his face alight. "It's beautiful," he said low.

"My island used to be a leper colony," Justice said, putting a hand on the man's shoulder. "Maybe in a lot of ways it still is. I know you think I'm nuts for having a dream, but as one man to another, I want you to know that my dream, my only dream, is to make this a world where all people can stand up together and enjoy the civilization that is within our grasp. This is a world of pain and want and need. It doesn't have to be. It really isn't such an extraordinary thing when you think about it."

Mandrake looked at him. "I have no idea what you're trying to accomplish," he said, making hard eye contact. "Your vision, whatever it is, seems impossible." The man looked all around him. "But so does Diamond Rock. Whatever you are, I've never seen anything like you."

"Try looking in the mirror, Charlie," Justice said. "I can call you Charlie, can't I? You call me Will, everybody else does."

"What do you mean . . . look in the mirror?"

Justice's eyes darkened. "You were fragged pretty good in Nam, Charlie," he said. "And you paid your dues saving your buddies, not killing. I've talked to all three men you pulled out of the burning copter the day you nearly bought it. You're a man who cares. You just haven't learned how to dream yet."

Mandrake turned and walked away from the window, his hands in the air. "Now you're making *me* nuts. I came here to do a simple job. . . ."

"And we'll do it, too," Justice said. "In fact we're ready now."

At some point during the conversation, Sardi had come back into the room, Jorge Vanderhoff sliding in quietly behind. Vanderhoff wore a gray pin-striped suit, his short blond hair meticulously groomed, his deep eyes gloomy and baleful—the usual. All four men walked to the table and sat.

Justice looked at Mandrake. "This is my expert in matters legal," he said. "Jorge Vanderhoff. Jorge, this is the assistant secretary of state to the U.S. government, Mr. Mandrake."

Vanderhoff nodded without speaking, then pulled a small tape recorder out of his jacket pocket along with a notepad and pen. "We'll need nonreturnable copies of any paperwork you have," he said finally.

Mandrake sat before his open briefcase and pulled out two bundles of paper, sliding one to Vanderhoff and opening the other for himself. Justice watched him carefully, not so much wondering about his thoughts as his *feelings*. Having an ally like Charles Mandrake within the American government could have far-reaching consequences. Convincing him that loyalty had many different definitions would be the most difficult task.

"If you'll look at the agenda on page one . . ." Mandrake began, Vanderhoff raising a hand for silence as he speed-read the entire proposal.

Justice moved to stare out the window, several gulls flying just beneath him. He thought about time and he thought about dreams, but mostly he thought about death and his close association with it—the third partner in any deal he ever cut. Death was a physical presence to him, a traveling companion, like a great uncle left perpetually in his care. He trafficked in death but never knew it as anything but a responsibility he was stuck with. Like the unfortunate great-uncle, he wished death itself would die, knowing all the while that it would laughingly bury him.

"Will," Jorge said quietly, Justice turning to the sound of his name. "It's Panama."

Justice stared at him, his eyes traveling from an uncomprehending Mandrake to the compassionate face of Sardi. A deep stab of pain tore through his spine, the memory of pain. "Panama," he repeated, clearing his throat. He turned back to the window. "Tell me about it, Charlie."

"Quite simply," the man said in a professional monotone, "we're finding that the Medellin cartel is using Panama as a major jump point in delivering cocaine to the U.S. They operate out of a well-fortified base in the western mountains and can't be ferreted out without a large-scale military offensive on our part. . . ."

"And after what the U.S. government did to the people of Panama when they were trying to overthrow Noriega," Justice continued, flaring around, "you don't know if the civilian population would take kindly to a military offensive in their homes."

"Something like that," Mandrake said. "We feel that a small, highly trained mercenary force could go in there and perhaps break it up without having to commit U.S. forces. I want you to know something, Will," he said with sincerity. "Two-thirds of the nose candy coming into the country is run through the Medellin operation. With one swoop we could go a long way toward destroying the drug traffic in the United States. If you can handle the job, we're willing to pay your expenses, plus a million dollars in U.S. currency."

Justice stared for a long moment, his guts churning with Panama fever. His nightmares lay there, the root of his dreams and his insanity. But it wasn't right. "Tell him, Jorge," he said.

Vanderhoff slid the file away from him and sat back thoughtfully in his chair. "Our intelligence," he said after a moment, "tells us that, despite the uneasy truce you now enjoy with General Noriega, your State Department has been working closely with the Pentagon in attempting to work out a military overthrow."

"Whatever operations or suggested operations there may or may not be concerning Mr. Noriega," Mandrake answered, "it has nothing to do with the business at hand."

"This has everything to do with Noriega," Vanderhoff said sternly. "Ever since you failed to unseat him from power, you've been running through option after option, from your own Delta Force to Israeli Mossad, to nearly every free-lancer in the business, at all times trying to work out an assassination plan. Everybody turns you down because they know how firmly entrenched the man is."

"This is pure invention!" Mandrake said loudly.

"I believe that you believe that," Justice said. "But I also know that the problem of drugs has very little to do with the source and has been given less that devoted attention by the government. Noriega has traditional ties to the Medellin cartel. Don't try to tell me there's no connection with state on an operation like this. To begin with, the problem with drugs is on the user end, not the supply. Take away the desire, and you take away the problem. Leave the desire, and somebody will supply it. Too many U.S. politicians are taking too much money in the drug trade for an operation against Medellin to do any good. If you want to solve your drug problem, take away the desire or legalize the stuff. A military action in Panama will merely get a lot of people hurt."

Mandrake stood up, angry. "I can't believe after all your fine speeches earlier you're willing to let this evil persist without trying to stop it. Instead you give me a lot of political mumbo jumbo that every leftist has been proclaiming for forty years."

"Even leftists are occasionally right," Justice said. "Or do you believe that America has a lock on truth and justice?"

"We all have to believe in something," Mandrake said.

"Listen to me," Justice said. "Your government has only one thought on its mind right now: kill Noriega and regain control of Panama. This drug thing is just smoke screen. You boys are just trying to fool me into taking care of your problem for you. Drugs are not the issue here. Never have been."

"Do you want the job or not?" Mandrake asked. "To be honest with you, I voted against contacting you every time the proposal came up. The Marines strike me as the answer."

"Good for you," Justice said. "That strikes me as the answer also. What do you think, Jorge?"

Vanderhoff tightened his lips. "Suicide," he said. "It's a long, wild shot. The U.S. doesn't want to do it themselves because of the nearly impossible nature, but how easy to hire someone from the outside—throw a little money at the problem. If it works, it works. If not, nothing much is lost for them. No one even knows if Noriega's anywhere near those mountains. For us, of course, it's a disaster. I vote absolutely against such a proposal."

Justice looked at Sardi. "Your feelings?"

"You know my feelings," Sardi replied. "I don't want you within a thousand miles of those mountains, William. And my reasons are not unknown to you."

Justice nodded at the man who knew more about him than any other human being who ever lived. He walked up to the table, picking up the proposal and thumbing through the pages. "It appears that this particular deal isn't one that's going to..." He stopped at a photograph, a cold hand gripping his heart. He felt closed in, claustrophobic, and he forced himself to take deep breaths.

Turning abruptly, he strode away from the table, trying to mentally control the pain that was rifling through him. His left arm stiffened, and he began to rub it. "We'll make the deal," he said, his back to them.

"You will?" Mandrake said, incredulous.

He turned back to them. "Conditions," Justice said, and Vanderhoff began writing immediately as Sardi lowered his head and stared at the tabletop. "I will cut the deal, but not with you or any other flunky. The deal will have to be cut between me and the president himself over international TV hookup. And the price: ten million in gold, not dollars, half out front."

"No one will ever agree to that," Mandrake said.

"And I want something else," Justice said. "I want a seat at the United Nations, and I want *you* to arrange it for me through the resources of your government."

Mandrake stood abruptly, his chair falling over behind him. "You really *are* completely insane," he said, moving toward the door and shoving papers back into the briefcase.

"Just take my conditions back to Washington," Justice said. "We'll work out the arrangements by telex. Someone from security will escort you back to the chopper."

Mandrake pulled open the door and turned to face them. "Who the hell *are* you?" he asked.

"The man who's going to make a man out of you," Justice said. "Take it to the bank."

Mandrake walked out, slamming the door behind him. Justice smiled. He liked the man's style and forthrightness.

Sardi looked up then, his dark eyes searching Justice's face. "What did you see in that file?" he asked.

"My past," Justice answered.

"Your terms were unthinkable," Vanderhoff said. "They'll never agree."

"Noriega's a thorn in their side," Justice said. "The only thing that keeps Panama and the whole Canal Zone just out of their reach. They'll agree. It's just sneaky enough for them. It doesn't really matter, though."

"What do you mean?" Vanderhoff said.

"Don't you see?" Sardi answered. "It doesn't matter what they say, because we're going anyway. Isn't that it, William?"

Justice just turned and stared out at the wide and deadly ocean. You can run, he thought, but you can't hide.

II.

VA HOSPITAL—DALLAS, TEXAS
8 MAY 1978—1325 HOURS

William Justice lay, as he had lain for over two weeks, in total traction, his body trapped within the confines of a machine called a Stryker frame that resembled nothing so much as the clamping device he had used as a child to toast bread over an open fire. When he was done on one side, they'd flip him over to the other. He was currently facedown, listening to the murmuring voices in the hallway and the rustle of one of the nurse's skirts as she bustled around the room, doing God knows what outside the range of his vision.

He was only a mind now, a mind residing in a hulk of useless meat. All movement and feeling had fled at Volcán Barú, Merriman's bullets ripping the heart, if not the life, out of him. There was no pain—except for the raging headaches that the doctors had told him were a result of his blood pressure rising dramatically in response to the spinal injuries. For two weeks he'd known nothing but semiconsciousness and horror at the useless, pitiful thing that he'd become. He would have wished for death, had it not been for Merriman and Noriega and the Doberman Brigade. They gave him life—and anger—the reason for his life. A whole village had died because of him, and now there was no one but him to set it to rights.

And so he lay uselessly, plotting and hating, wanting to live only to bear witness to the horror and somehow expiate his own guilt in the matter. In the last two weeks he'd been in surgery seven times. Seven times they'd gone into his useless meat and tried to put it back together, and every time he'd gone under the knife he'd felt it was some kind of penance for his sins.

He was consumed by his guilt and by his responsibility. What else was there for a mind chained to a dead body? Life had been denied him. Even dreams of life couldn't exist in a brain that merely lived and relived the events of that night. He couldn't listen without hearing the screams of the women and children. He couldn't close his eyes without seeing the fire and smelling his own flesh as it burned on the hood of the jeep.

Why were they just standing out there in the hall? Why didn't they come in if that's what they intended to do? His eyes were staring straight down at the framework of the machine. Tongs had been inserted into his skull, a weighted pulley holding his head static. He had become intimately familiar with the shape and gauge of the Stryker framework, just as he had become expert at finding abstract shapes in the cracks of the ceiling tiles when he was flipped over on his back. Time had become meaningless, every minute an infinity of uselessness. He felt his eyes well up and saw a tear splash to the dusty framework below and trickle down its length.

He felt the door swing soundlessly open near him, outside noises rising slightly in volume. Several pairs of feet walked in.

"How are we feeling today, Bill?" asked a familiar voice.

"The same, Dr. Wexler," Justice rasped through dry lips. "Who's that with you?"

"Why don't we turn you over so you can see for yourself?" Wexler said, moving to the front of the Stryker and unhooking the skull tongs, Justice feeling a pressure on his neck. The doctor unlatched the catch on the frame. "Nurse. Help me with this, please."

"Yes, doctor."

Justice felt his framework revolve, his line of vision turning slightly to take in the rest of the room before settling back onto the ceiling. Turning the Stryker frame was the biggest excitement he had to look forward to on any given day—perhaps for the rest of his life.

Dr. Wexler stood beside him, peering down and smiling right into his face. "You'll be glad to know that the last operation on your lung was a complete success. You should eventually have nearly a hundred percent bodily function."

"Except that I'm paralyzed," Justice said.

A face came up to float next to Wexler's. It was unfamiliar to him.

"Good afternoon," the man said, smiling. "Name's Bignell. I'm here to debrief. Brought somebody along with me you might recognize."

Another face appeared on the other side of the frame, three full moons staring down, smiling stupidly. He hadn't seen this one since his training at the Company farm in Pennsylvania. "Gene?" he said. "Gene Tebbits?"

"Good to see you, Will," he said. "Rough about what happened."

"What are you doing here?" Justice asked.

Tebbits shrugged, the stupid smile still plastered on his face. "They just thought you might like to see a friendly face, that's all," he said, and it didn't ring true.

"You all are here to give me the bad news," Justice said.

"That's not the way to look at it," Dr. Wexler said. "I've told you that you'll recover nearly one hundred percent physically, and that was no easy task. Spinal injury such as you suffered leads to severe complications in your body response. Couple that with the damage caused by the other bullets, and it's practically miraculous that you're alive at all. But with proper care you could still expect to live a rich, full..."

"Hold it right there," Justice said, his voice weak as he tried to muster himself to conversation. "For the last two weeks I've been trying to find out exactly what's wrong with me."

"We haven't kept anything from you," Wexler said. "Your body went into total shock. Hell, the best you had was a bit of respiration. Everything else went. They were able to save your life at the Canal Zone base hospital, and we've been piecing you together ever since. It wasn't until the spinal swelling went down that we were even able to come up with any kind of prognosis."

"And what is the prognosis?"

The doctor straightened and cleared his throat. "Would you, er . . . like to talk to me privately about it?" he asked.

"They're going to have to know anyway," Justice said. "Just get it out."

Wexler nodded, all three men seeming to bend down a little closer. "There's a bullet," he said, pointing to the back of his own neck. "It entered your chest, just missing your left ventricle. It ricocheted off your clavicle and lodged in your spine at the C-5 vertebra, totally transecting the cord. . . ."

"Which means?"

The doctor grimaced slightly and wouldn't look at Justice as he spoke. "Your spine is, basically, severed, the electrical connectors to the brain shattered by the bullet. The bullet itself is lodged in such a dangerous place that we can't even try to remove it without causing you even further damage."

"You're saying I'm paralyzed for good," Justice replied, swallowing hard.

Wexler licked dry lips. "The spinal cord is a strange, fragile, nearly metaphysical part of the body, Bill," he said. "I can't tell you absolutely for sure what your future is, but I think it may be time to resign yourself to the fact that things may never get any better. You may find some small feeling return . . . I don't know. But I think I've studied your X-rays enough to know that the damage to your spine is, for the most part, profound and irreversible."

The impact on Justice was something like the sound heard from a distant explosion. He'd seen the devastation, knew what was coming, but still reeled under the sound of the blast when it reached him. His mind had become a large, open plain with no hiding places, and everywhere he turned he ran into the specters of the things he'd never do again. He stared up at the faces staring down at him, and in the pain and confusion that were tearing his soul apart, only one rock-solid beacon stood out from the horror. "Did you get my report?" he asked.

Bignell winked and pulled a cassette tape out of the pocket of his sharkskin suit. "Got it right here," he said, then looked up at Dr. Wexler, staring silently.

"Well... perhaps I'd better get on with my rounds," Wexler said, turning his gaze back down to Justice, who could see the man physically trying to keep the pity from his face. "I'll be around later so we can discuss your... recovery and the availability of physical therapy. Even without mobility, you're going to have to exercise those muscles."

"Sure," Justice said, forcing his mind from it, thinking instead of bright orange fire and screaming women.

"Nurse," Wexler said, straightening and motioning, Justice able to barely see a pretty red-haired nurse move from near the foot of the bed to follow the doctor out. Pretty girls were something else he tried not to think about.

When the door closed, Bignell shook the tape in front of his face. "You didn't need to do this," he said.

"I wanted to get it all out while it was still fresh on my mind," Justice said. "Obviously I can't write. The recorder..."

"Who turned it on for you?" Tebbits asked, face hard. "This is classified information."

"I don't know," Justice lied. "They left the room after turning it on. I had them address the envelope and put the tape in and seal it in front of me."

"Who?" Bignell asked, his voice tense, Justice feeling a strange vibration coming from him. "They could have looked at it after they left here."

"Just a nurse," Justice said. "It's all faceless uniforms to me here. I didn't pay attention. What about the information?"

"What do you want us to do with it, Will?" Tebbits asked.

"Do with it?" Justice replied, voice quaking. "I want you to arrest Merriman, Noriega, and the whole fucking Doberman Brigade and charge them with mass murder and drug running."

"Merriman's dead," Bignell said.

"W-what?" Justice said. "How?"

"Gunned down in the streets of Panama City," Tebbits answered. "Had five grand in his pocket and a forty-five with a full clip."

Justice found himself angry at Merriman's death, angry that he would be denied the right to spit in the man's face. "Then get *cara piña*," he said through clenched teeth. "The man's a butcher."

Bignell frowned, shaking his head. "It's not that easy, William," he said. "Colonel Noriega is an important ally of the United States. Now that we're having to give back the Canal Zone to the Panamanians, we need all the friends we can get down there. He's solid, you know? He hates commies almost as much as we do!"

Bignell laughed, Tebbits joining in as Justice looked in horror from one of them to the other. "This isn't a goddamned joke!" he yelled, then broke down, coughing weakly. "That man killed an entire village full of human beings."

"Look," Bignell said, harsh. "We're giving you the reality of the situation, take it or leave it alone. Noriega is our boy. He's in our pocket, and if he feels the need to shake up the Indian population, who are we to stand in his way? I'm sorry about what happened to you, but we have national interests to protect here."

"You son of a . . ."

"Wait," Tebbits said, glaring at Bignell. "Look, Will. You know me, and you know I look out for you. In fact I'll make it my personal job to make sure the Company looks out for you for the rest of your life. This deal in Panama . . . you know we understand it's not right, but it happened. One of those things. We can't compound the mistake by blowing our one chance to maintain our control in the Canal Zone. It's an area absolutely vital to our security. Noriega is second in command to Torrijos, next in line for the command of the National Guard. We just can't . . ."

"Torrijos is going to be killed," Justice said. "You guys are going to do it. And I'll tell you something, people are going to know about it, just like they're going to know what happened out there in the mountains."

He was immediately sorry he'd uttered those words. Both Bignell and Tebbits straightened, a look passing between them.

"I didn't mean that," Justice said. "I'm just . . . angry, I guess. Can't blame me for that."

"No," Tebbits said. "We can't."

"Look," Bignell said, bringing his wristwatched arm up to his face. "We've got to go. We'll send your report up through channels. Meanwhile, remember this is classified material."

"I won't discuss it with anyone," Justice said, fighting back the venom that threatened to roll from his lips.

Tebbits leaned down and patted him on the chest. "You just take care of yourself, buddy," he said. "I'll see that you're well taken care of."

"Thanks," Justice said. "I appreciate it."

"Hang in there, sport," Bignell said, turning and walking away. Justice couldn't move his head, but he followed the man with his eyes, watching as he wrote the room number down on a small notepad he carried in his jacket pocket.

The two men left quietly, Justice lying there, staring at the ceiling. Strong counteremotions were charging through him, zapping him like lightning, emotions so deep and profound that anything else he'd ever experienced in his life paled in comparison. This, in the midst of his greatest turmoil, was the moment of his life. The decisions he'd make now, today, would literally determine whether or not he'd even have a future.

He'd said the wrong thing, dropped the wrong name, and there was no doubt in his mind that for the good of the Company—and by extension the United States—he'd be killed sometime before the night was over. He had become a serious liability and, worse, a security risk. He couldn't even really blame them for killing him. There's nothing worse than a renegade agent, an open mouth that knew all the secrets.

The question was: Should he let them kill him? God knows, he had very little to live for. It would probably be a relief.

But he couldn't get Volcán Barú out of his mind. There was politics, and there was right and wrong. The two things, no matter how you define them, are very seldom compatible. Someone had to stand up for what was right. Someone had to treat human life with respect, or all of life would be a useless, cruel joke ending in mass destruction. Perhaps his removal from the animal needs of the body could allow him to be a mental force for good. Fat chance! At the moment he couldn't even control his own bowels.

"Would you like me to turn you back over on your stomach?" came a voice, startling him. He focused his eyes to see the red-haired nurse staring sweetly down at him. Her face was wide and innocent, her eyes filled with compassion, but not pity. She was there to help him and had no game plan other than doing the job she had been trained for—easing pain. People weren't all like Merriman and Bignell. There were ethics and happiness and love, and all of those things shone through the sparkling green eyes of the nurse who stared down at him.

"What's your name?" he asked, unable to keep from staring at her face.

"Allison Boyd," she said, leaning down to brush a stray hair out of his eyes. "My friends call me Allie."

"Are we friends?" he asked.

"I don't know," she said. "My friends smile at me."

He felt the laugh from deep inside, his lips breaking into the first smile he'd worn since Volcán Barú. "How's that?" he asked.

"We're friends," she said without hesitation. "Now, how about turning you over . . . ?"

"Will," he said, the woman nodding. "I want to talk to you first about something very important."

The woman looked at her watch. "I've got other patients," she said, "but a few minutes won't hurt."

"Thanks," Justice said, ideas tumbling quickly through his mind. If he was going to do this, there was an immense amount of details to take care of and not enough time. "Do you know who I am and what I do?"

Her eyes narrowed in confusion. "I think you do something with the government," she said innocently.

"I'm with the CIA," he said.

"You mean, like spies and stuff?"

"Yeah," he smiled. "Like that. I was shot up in Central America, and that's why I'm here now."

"I knew you'd been shot," she said.

"Those men who were just in here," he said, keeping his voice low, "they'd come for my report."

"Is it all right for me to listen to all this?" she asked, staring uneasily back toward the door.

"There may be some danger involved in this," he said, not wanting more innocent blood on his hands. "I can't guarantee you otherwise."

She stared in concentration for a moment, then suddenly

came to her decision. "We're friends, right?" she said. "I go a long way for a friend."

"I said the wrong thing to those men, Allie," he told her. "They'll send someone back tonight to kill me."

She laughed. "You're kidding. I mean, what could you . . . how could you . . . ?"

"I can still talk," he said. "And I can still see. I saw something inhuman, and I intend to talk about it."

"What?" she asked.

So he told her the story, leaving nothing out, changing nothing. He poured out his heart, crying as he did, spelling out the horror and the fears in bold detail, and when he was finished, she was crying too. "C-can't we . . . call the police or something?" she asked.

"Lady, they *are* the police," he said. "How far do you think I'd get if I tried to convince the police that the U.S. government's going to sneak into this hospital tonight and put a hit on a quadraplegic?"

She looked at the floor. "Then what could I do to help you?"

"There should be a bag of my personal items in the closet," he said. "Get it."

Allie Boyd went to the closet and brought back the brown paper bag.

"Look inside," he said. "Find my wallet."

She dug through the effects bag, quickly fishing out the black leather wallet. "Got it."

"There's a hidden compartment behind the billfold part," he said. "Pull it up and see if there's any cash in there."

She did it, pulling out a small stack of hundreds and holding them in front of his face. "Looks like a thousand dollars," she said.

"Good," he smiled. "It's yours."

She looked at him in shock. "What for?"

"You're going to go to the morgue and steal a body for me," he said.

Justice was nearly standing, and he liked the feeling. Allie had put him on a tilt board that could turn vertically and stood him just inside the door of the vacant room with the lights turned out. If anything happened to him at this point, he would at least meet his fate head on, like a man. There was no fear in him, though Allie was scared enough for the both of them. In fact he felt a sense of excitement, a realization that even though his body was gone, he could still scheme, still put his thoughts into action through others. It was a start.

The door opened, Allie slipping in, checking back out the doorway to make sure no one had seen her. "This is freaking me out," she said, putting a hand to her chest and taking deep breaths. "If I get caught putting corpses in the Stryker . . . well, no one's going to understand."

"I'll explain it to them," Justice said.

She rolled her eyes, only the whites showing up in the darkness. "Right," she said. "Are you sure you're not just trying to stir up trouble?"

"Did you have any problems staying over after your shift?" he asked.

She shook her head. "That was the least of it. They're always shorthanded. When I didn't leave, they simply assumed I was working a double shift on another floor. My biggest problem was sneaking you out of your room and into here. My second-biggest problem was getting the body into the Stryker all by myself. The poor man must have weighed two hundred fifty pounds. No wonder his heart gave out."

She moved to the doorway, peeking out in the direction of his room just down the night-darkened hallway. "What will he look like?" she asked, turning briefly to him.

"Like he belongs," Justice said. "What time is it?"

She held up her watch and read the luminous dial. "After midnight."

"I'll bet within the next hour," he said. "This is the slow, quiet time, he'll—"

"Shhh," she said. "Someone's coming."

"Can you get a look?" he rasped.

"A woman," she whispered, "wearing a lab coat, stethoscope around her neck. She must be new on the rotation. I don't remember seeing her before. Oh hell. She's going into your room. I'm cooked." She turned to Justice. "I got my last three cats this way. Why do I let people talk me into . . ."

"She went into *my* room?" he said.

Allie nodded sadly.

39

"Did she close the door?"

"Yeah, all the way, she . . ." The woman stopped talking, turning to stare hard at Justice in the darkness. "You don't think that . . ."

"You think a woman can't pull a trigger?" he asked. "Did she *look* like a doctor to you?"

Allie frowned. "Too much makeup. Her skirt was too short under the jacket. *Hmmm.*"

"What?"

"I think she's turning the light on and off. I'm seeing light under the door."

"Or a muzzle flash."

He watched Allie's shoulders hunch, sorry to be putting her through all this. She had a great deal to lose, and no real reason to help him. The thousand he offered her would do precious little for her if she lost her job. He was already worried about becoming dependent upon her. He'd need legs and hands. She had those. He wished there was someone else. He wished he had the money to make it worthwhile for her.

"She's leaving," Allie said, not turning to him, "walking fast."

"Go check it out," he said, the woman slipping quietly into the hall as soon as it was safe.

The minute she was gone seemed interminable. As he lay on the tilt board there in the dark, he realized just how vulnerable he really was. Anybody could take him anytime they chose. And plenty of people would want to take him. Unless . . .

Allie slipped back into the room, her face blanched pale, evident even in the darkness. "My God," she whispered. "I guess I didn't really believe you. Your friends don't mess around."

"What happened?"

Allie shook her head, looking down, shaking. "She must have really wanted to make sure, because she all but blew the man's head off. It's splattered all over the room."

"The face," he said, excited. "What about the face?"

She stared, angry. "I said it was gone for God's sake! What do you want, the gory details?"

"You can't tell the features anymore?" he persisted.

She shook her head. "At least now you'll have something to take to the police," she said.

"No," he replied. "I've just been murdered. Maybe it will be better to leave it at that for a while."

She walked up to him, getting right in his face. "What the hell are you saying?" she asked.

He met her eyes, shadows in the darkness. "I'm alive, Allie Boyd," he said with determination, "and I intend to *stay* that way."

III.

DIAMOND ROCK
5 FEBRUARY 1988—1617 HOURS

"One-third in advance," the president of the United States said wearily. "Your demands that the payment be made in gold puts a real strain on our covert operations budget. Not to mention the back doors we have to go through to keep that much gold secret."

Will Justice looked up at the president's image on the six-foot television screen that occupied the rock-face wall in front of him. He stood before his own TV camera at a lectern facing the screen, his board of directors occupying the ox-blood leather conversation pit just behind him. All around them the research department bustled with activity, employees occasionally stopping by to listen in on the negotiations that had already gone on for two hours. "Tell you what I'll do, Mr. President," Justice said, turning to wink at Bob Jenks, "you get me half in advance, and I'll pay my own expenses out of pocket. Probably save you close to two hundred thousand at this morning's rates."

"Just a minute," the president said, turning to face off screen.

The man was careful, Justice had to hand it to him. He bargained slowly and carefully, a lousy trait in poker players and race-car drivers, but the perfect stance for the negotiator. He thought through every decision he made as if he were actually making it for two hundred plus million people, and Justice admired that.

The president turned back to the screen. "All right, Mr. Lambert," he said, mustering a tired smile. "Five million in gold out front; you pay your own expenses. What's left?"

"Distribution of assets," Justice said, turning to Sardi, who pulled a sheet of paper off a stack of papers sitting before him on the low, round table and handed it to Justice.

He read the figures quickly, then set the paper on the lectern before him. "Here's the distribution," he said. "Of the five million in prepayment, two million will be brought directly here to Haven; a million and a half will go into an American bank account to be used for the establishment of my United Nations mission; and the remaining million and a half will be divided evenly between Lambert Enterprises' brokers in New York and Zurich."

The president wrote down the figures, looking off screen again and nodding before turning back. "You will furnish us with the names of the brokers, I presume?"

"Yes."

The president nodded again. "We'll have a military flight deliver the gold directly to your island before..."

"No," Justice said. "I'm sorry. I should have specified more clearly. First of all, no United States aircraft will be allowed to land on my island. House rules. The money will be taken to Martinique, then brought over by boat. And there will be no one, repeat no one, involved in dealing with me on money except for Charlie Mandrake."

"Mr. Justice," the president said sternly, "Mr. Mandrake is a very busy man. Surely you can't expect..."

"Only with Mandrake," Justice interrupted. "I trust very few people in this world. It's Charlie Mandrake or nobody. Same goes for work on the diplomatic mission to the UN. Nobody but Charlie. That's a deal breaker if you want it to be."

The president took a long, lingering breath. Justice smiled. It was almost wistful. He was wearing the man down. The president looked off screen, nodding from time to time before returning to him. "Do you want Mr. Mandrake to be placed on permanent assignment for you? That may be what it will take on the UN thing."

"No," Justice said. "I'm not trying to interrupt his career. I just want to know that he's running things for me and will be honest with me. It won't complicate his life that much. You should be proud that you've got somebody trustworthy on your staff."

"Uncalled for," the president said.

"Sorry," Justice smiled. "Do we have a deal?"

"Quite possibly," the president replied, donning a pair of half glasses and reading from a paper before him. "On our end, we promise to pay you five million in gold out front and five million in gold upon successful completion of the contract. Further, we promise to support and help facilitate the acquisition of a permanent seat in the United Nations General Assembly... all to be coordinated through the efforts of assistant secretary of state, Charles Mandrake. On your end..."

"On my end," Justice continued, "we promise to initiate covert activities in the Chiriquí region of Panama with the express purpose of infiltrating and terminating the organization known as the Medellin cartel, and shutting down all illegal drug operations of the cartel in Panama. We will be in the region as private operatives unconnected to any government and will not characterize ourselves as representatives of the United States. Only upon successful completion of the mission will the second half of the payment be secured in a manner that's timely and auspicious. Upon failure of the mission, all monies will be returned to the U.S. government, less one million dollars per man for every one of my people killed in the operation. Deal?"

"One more thing," the president said. "We want a representative to go in with you."

"No way," Justice replied.

"You've gouged us for a lot of money, Mr. Lambert. There's no way we can turn loose of that kind of cash without someone to observe your success or failure."

Justice stared hard at the screen. "You said the word *observe*. Did you mean that?"

"We just want to keep an eye on the money."

Justice looked back at his people, Robert Jenks shaking his head. "I don't trust 'em," the man said.

Justice turned back to the screen. "You may send someone along with us if you promise that he'll take all orders from me without a secret agenda and if his role is solely that of observer unless I specify differently."

"Done," the president said, and he smiled for just a second, Justice already sorry he'd made the deal. "Our operative will make contact with you in country."

Justice shrugged. "Looks like we've got ourselves an agreement," he said.

"Good. When will you get started?"

"As soon as Charlie shows up with the cash and I know that all other money has been distributed through the proper channels."

The president stared hard at the screen, and Justice knew the man was trying to size him up through the camera. "I don't know who you are," he said at last, "but you're one of a kind. Do you really think you'll get the UN mission?"

"I have great faith in the persuasive powers of the American government, Mr. President," Justice said. "Now if our business in concluded, I have a great many preparations to make. Good day."

Justice reached out and turned off his camera before the president had a chance to say anything else. "Tape!" he called loudly, then turned around to the small crowd gathered in the conference area with outstretched arms. "It's a go!"

The room broke into spontaneous applause and whistles, employees then returning to their workstations—the long banks of television screens and computers and microfilm processors that branched out all around. The research section was Justice's biggest expense and greatest triumph. In a world where information was king, he was a wealthy prince able to match wits and resources with even the largest of nations—all through the understanding of world events and the global zeitgeist. Knowledge was power, and if the research department ate up 75 percent of his resources, it gave him 99 percent of his tangibility.

His board of directors sat before him, some of them scratching notes on pieces of paper, others, like Jenks, shifting uneasily on the couch, ready to get out and *do* something. It was a group like none other, nearly all of them on the death lists of more than one country.

Jenks sat before him, dressed in shorts and a tank top, his bare feet up on the coffee table. Jorge Vanderhoff sat beside him, quiet and shifty. Vanderhoff had once been a free-lancer until running afoul of the SAS on a series of IRA hits. Sardi sat closest to Justice. Once a powerful minister in the Indian parliament, he was forced to emigrate because of too-vigorous anticommunist activities in a left-leaning government. On Jenks's other side sat Kim Bouvier, a computer expert forced to flee Vietnam when Saigon fell in '75. She'd also free-lanced for years before finally making her way to Haven in a speedboat, pursued by agents of the Syrian government who, needless to say, were able to chase her no farther than the black beach. The board was rounded out by true royalty, Prince Kiki Anouweyah, a tribal chieftain within the Kenyan Republic of Africa. He'd been forced to flee Africa after getting caught operating an antiapartheid guerrilla training base in South Africa; then was kept out by the duplicity of his relatives, especially his younger brother. The prince was an expert in urban terrorism: explosives, weapons, strategies, and hand-to-hand combat. He sat dressed in a multicolored caftan and fez.

He watched them as they watched him, knowing there were questions, and knowing they were good questions that he'd have a difficult time answering. "Okay," he said. "Talk to me."

"There's just a little somethin' I don't understand, Will'um," Jenks said, pulling his feet down and sitting up straight. "How come they went for a deal like that? You just ran 'em up the flagpole and ran 'em back down again and they thanked you for it. That just don't make no sense to me."

Justice looked at Sardi, the man's face unreadable. "You tell him," he said.

Sardi stood, his inscrutable gaze for just a second falling upon the man he'd tied his life to for good and all. "What was unsaid in the discussion was the name Manuel Noriega," Sardi said. He stood perfectly still, perfectly calm, as always a master of economic movement. "It is our supposition that the U.S. government will try to maneuver us into a position to assassinate the man who has turned his back on them. It leaves them clear to reassume the role of leader in that country once again, a country that is very high on their defense priority lists. I can't blame them for attempting this. It solves a great many of their problems in Central America."

Prince Anouweyah cleared his throat, his dark eyes intense as he spoke with the deep, melodious English accent he'd picked up at Oxford. "I know something of that region. In Panama, allegiance is owed to a person, not the state. Noriega's followers worship him as a god, all of them gladly dying to protect or avenge his life. What chance would we have in such a maelstrom?"

"Perhaps very little," Justice said. "On top of that, I have a history with the colonel. Given his proximity, I can't guarantee that I *wouldn't* try to kill him."

"Basically," Vanderhoff said in precise, clipped tones, "my original assertion is correct: You've just signed us on to a suicide mission."

"And to what end?" Kim Bouvier asked in her throaty, inflectionless English. She was dressed in jeans and cowboy boots, her waist-length black hair spilling down the back of a long silk shirt that was halfway unbuttoned. "Before, we've helped people to free themselves. If it is the yoke of oppression they wear in Panama, they seem to wear it gladly. This drug business is personal choice. Who cares if people in United States of America blow out their brains with cocaine? Not me. I'll take a good bottle of Scotch anytime, huh?"

"Yeah!" Jenks said loudly.

Justice felt a hand on his shoulder and turned to see one of his research people, a young African national, holding out a videotape. "Your contract with president," she said, Justice taking the tape and nodding. He set the cassette on the lectern.

Vanderhoff spoke up again, standing this time, his gray pin-striped suit unwrinkled, its creases sharp as razors. "The mercenary's job and obsession is to control every aspect of an operation in order to maximize efficiency and insure survival. Ten million dollars in gold means precious little if you're not alive to spend it. This whole job sounds like a cowboy operation, totally without control. It goes against the grain of everything I've ever believed in, or everything I've staked my life on."

"Good point," Justice said. "I have no answer for it."

"Will'um!" Jenks said, frowning deeply. "You're gonna have to do better'n that." He looked up at Vanderhoff, who still held the floor. "Sit down, Jorge. You're makin' me nervous."

"I'll sit down when you start dressing and acting like a grown-up," Vanderhoff replied.

"All right," Jenks said. "I'll play." He stood, then climbed on the table to command everyone's attention. "Now Will'um, I'd follow you just about anywhere, but it seems like you're askin' us to go straight to hell this time with no real reason."

Justice stared at them all, smiling at Jenks up on the table. The only one in the room, in his life, who knew about his background was Sardi, and it was going to stay that way. Part of his power was in his mystery, part of his mystery was rooted in the depth of pain and guilt he still bore. He was not an ordinary human being anymore. He'd elevated himself to another level, not for his own wants and needs, but because he felt the world needed what he had to offer. Had he any control over himself in this regard, he'd have run from the American offer as far and as fast as he could. But he was a legend now and not a man, and the demons within had been unleashed and demanded blood chit. He would go to Panama, with or without his people.

"All negative points are well-taken," he said, as Jenks climbed down off the table and sat, Jorge then free to sit also. "And in response I have absolutely nothing. The reason I've called all of you here is that I wouldn't—couldn't—ask anyone less close to me to go. This mission is very important to me, for reasons I can't go into. I can't do it alone but will try if I must. It is your choice to go or stay here, as you will. I *will* go to Panama. Those who choose to stay will possibly find themselves in charge very soon. To those people I can only ask that you continue the struggle. . . ."

A claxon sounded loudly through the room, its horn bleating out in loud pulses, research personnel scurrying to emergency stations. Justice looked down at the lectern and the control panel that sat there, a red "call" light pulsing in time with the claxon. He pushed the button, turning to face the wall screen.

A Frenchman with a turnip-shaped face faded onto the screen, lips pursed. Justice watched the red light on his own camera come on, then spoke. "What's happening?" he called to the screen.

"We've picked up a Mayday, sir," the man said excitedly,

the horn sound dying by degrees, "an ocean liner going down."

"Where?" Justice asked.

"Panama, sir. About a hundred miles to the northwest of the canal on the Atlantic side. It's a big one, five hundred passengers and apparently sinking fast."

Justice turned to Sardi. "Doesn't Lambert Enterprises have something in that area?"

"A fishing fleet, I believe," the Indian replied.

Justice snapped his fingers and turned back to the screen. "We've got a fleet that operates just off Bocas del Toro. Divert them to the area and get me somebody from Historical, okay? See about rounding up private choppers to help search for survivors . . . there's plenty of ex-GIs living down there who'd help. Get out standard assistance offers, and if we're first on the scene, claim salvage rights."

"*Oui*," the man said, blanking immediately, Justice turning back to the board.

"I'm telling you that there are no guarantees on this mission," he said. "There is a great deal of money involved, but as Jorge said, you can't spend it if you're not alive. I'm going and will welcome anyone who wants to go with me. If no one goes, I'll work it out myself, no hard feelings. On the positive side, Research is working diligently to provide us as much information as possible on the region, and we'll spare no expense in preparation and execution. I'm not going out to die, folks, but I'm not running from that eventuality, either."

The lectern buzzed, Justice punching up Historical on the screen, a small Creole woman with kinky black hair materializing. "You want something, sir?" she asked in a high, squeaky voice.

"I want some graphics on boats sinking after going through the Panama Canal," he said. "Just go back about six months. I know this isn't the first sinking."

"Give me a minute," the woman said, blanking.

Justice turned to the board again. "This one's for me, folks; I won't sugarcoat it," he said. "Are you in or out?"

Sardi stood immediately, walking to stand beside Justice, a loyalty that had been expected, so tied were the two men by ideals and emotions. "Mr. Jenks said you were leading us to hell," he said with a tight-lipped smile. "I've always wondered what it was like."

"It's a lot like Texas," Justice said, standing and hitching up his shorts, "only colder. I might as well go. I'm gettin' bored just hangin' around this old place. Ain't never seen that canal, no sir. Might be fun."

Justice nodded to the man as Kim spoke up. "I go with William always," she said. "I would have been dead anyway by now."

Justice and the woman shared a look, a chemical bond that in normal people would have long ago led to an emotional relationship. They were not normal people, and their bond remained strong and unspoken—almost a blood closeness. "Thanks," he said quietly, the woman tossing it off with a shrug.

The prince shifted uneasily in his seat, looking around uncertainly. "I owe much to you, William, but I also have a responsibility to my own people to stay alive for them."

"I understand," Justice said.

"But then again," Anouweyah continued, "was it not Aristotle who said that friendship is a single soul dwelling in two bodies? What good would I be without the other half of my soul? If we are booking passage to the hellworld, my friend, let us just make sure that we go first-class. But I must first say that it is not customary in my country to take the women along hunting."

He turned and stared cold fire in Kim's direction, the woman smiling sweetly in return. "Why is that, Your Highness?" she asked, a stiletto suddenly gleaming in her hand. "Afraid of being emasculated in your sleep?"

She slid close to him on the couch, delicately waving the blade before his face in a blurring pattern of white light, Kiki's face stoic, his eyes following the blur. "It is simply a matter of purity of purpose," he said, his hand suddenly streaking out to grab her wrist and hold it in a viselike grip. "The woman is unclean, not fit for the spiritualism of the hunt."

Kim dropped the knife, caught it in her other hand and jammed the point upward, stopping just short of the prince's neck. The man grinned broadly. "Of course, even in my country, the times are changing."

"Enough," Justice said, Kim pulling back immediately as Anouweyah made a show of straightening his robes and his dignity. "We're all board members here—equal. It's going to stay that way."

The Research light bleeped, Justice going to it immediately. He was looking at a map of the Canal Zone and its environs on the Atlantic side. A number of markers were placed out in the Caribbean, a large circle hand-drawn around them. The historian's voice rose over the map. "The markers are boats sunk within six months," she said. "They all went down in remarkably close proximity, as you can see."

Justice watched the graphic, the ocean represented in a pale blue color. All roads were apparently leading to Panama. "Seven vessels in six months," Justice said. "Give me their configurations."

"The first three were large yachts," the woman said. "The next four were of increasingly larger size and with more people, the last two being cruise ships."

"Have survivors given any indication of why that particular area..."

"There have been no survivors from any of the sinkings," the woman said. "Those waters are heavily infested with sharks and strong currents."

"No survivors?" Sardi said, looking gravely at Justice.

The news lights went on again, Justice switching back to the Frenchman. "You have something?"

The man nodded sadly. "We have put ships on the scene," he said. "The boat is already gone, along with the passengers. Only floating debris and an oil slick remain."

Justice grunted as if he been punched. "Okay," he said quietly, "send back all the boats but one. Let that one search the area for survivors. Call any choppers back in, too."

"Yes, sir," the man said, shutting down the screen.

Justice showed the board empty palms. A cloud had settled over the proceedings, the downed ship like a rumble of distant thunder moving closer. "Panama seems to be the order of the day," he said, then looked at Vanderhoff, the only one still uncommitted.

The man rose stoically. "I think all of you are being very foolish," he said, clipped, authoritative. "When I take a job, it is because I think I can do it. I cannot find any way that

51

this task could be accomplished. I'm sorry, William. Count me out."

"You son of a bitch," Jenks spat. "After all Will'um has done for you, you can't just..."

"No," Justice said. "It's his free choice and is probably a smart one."

"Thank you," Vanderhoff said curtly.

"Will you look after things here while I'm gone?" Justice asked, the man nodding. "Good, we'll draw up the papers and make it legal."

Vanderhoff took a long breath, Justice knowing, far better than the others, that Jorge's decision was not an easy one for him to make. Not that the knowledge helped any. It would be tough going without him.

Drawing himself up to his full height, Jorge turned without a word and walked with dignity from the room, everyone following his departure with their eyes and their doubts.

"Anyone else who wants to change his mind, do so now," Justice said, somewhat gravely. "Jorge's departure reduces our chances. Believe me, there'll be no hard feelings."

"Don't they have casinos in Panama City?" Jenks asked. "I sure ain't been on a crap table for years."

Justice smiled. "You'll be glad to know that our cover will make it essential that you spend time in those casinos. We're going to play dress-up this trip."

"You *do* have a plan," the woman said, sitting back to clean her nails with the tip of her dagger. "Why the mystery?"

"It's important to me that you be in this because you want to be," Justice said, "because you *choose* to be. You go because you're willing to *die* for me, and I can't give anybody good reasons for doing that. Sometimes life has to go beyond good reasons. Our bond is one that doesn't depend on words, a family bond. Now if you'll excuse me, I must drop this tape off at the vault. We'll leave within a week. Put your affairs in order."

He picked up the tape and State Department file and walked away from the lectern, Sardi standing to go with him. He looked at the man, saw the compassion in his eyes. "Not this time," he said. "I've got to be alone."

Sardi nodded understanding and backed away, Justice

moving past him without another word. He walked through the guts of the research department, the huge, rock-hewn room echoing the continual clatter of computer typers and printers, the whole area bathed in the bland whiteness of fluorescent lighting. He moved past long tables full of computer operators who spent three daily shifts, twenty-four hours a day, doing nothing but typing information into the computers, twenty-four hours a day spent increasing the knowledge and power of William Justice. Every click of a fingernail on the keys was another rung built onto a very high ladder of knowledge.

What he was doing wasn't lost on Justice. With all his control, with all his ideals and good intentions, he was ready to throw it away, along with the lives of those closest to him, on an obsessive dream of vengeance. Panama was his beginning and ending point, the measure of his heart and his folly. He moved through the complex that his control of reality had built, all the while out of control himself. He hadn't slept a night through since Mandrake's visit to Haven. It was as if the fires of Volcán Barú still burned, and within him they burned brightly indeed.

The vault sat in a natural antechamber adjacent to Research, the iron bars that closed it in set directly into the rock. He moved up to the bars, a khaki-suited security man hurrying to unlock the gate to let him in.

He passed the man without acknowledgment, walking directly to the vault librarian and handing her the tape. Beyond the librarian the cavern narrowed into a long hallway, steel shelving containing thousands of videotapes filling the rock wall along its entire length.

"File this in contracts," he told the woman, then held out his hand. "I want the key to the cage."

"Yes, sir."

The woman removed a chain from around her neck, a small gold electronic key attached to the chain. He nodded as she dropped the chain into his palm, then walked down the length of the vault toward the cage that defined its end wall.

The cage was made of titanian mesh and steel I beams. The lock was simply a tiny slot set directly into a beam, nearly invisible unless one knew where it was. Justice slid the gold card into the slot, the door buzzing and clicking open immediately.

Justice walked into the cage and closed the door behind him. Closed steel cases lined the inside walls of the cage. In its center sat a wooden table with a single chair. A TV screen and VCR sat on the table, along with a microfilm projector.

Justice sat, opening the file Mandrake had given him. The photo was on top, the one that had changed everything. He stared at the picture, at the man dressed in battle fatigues and Australian bush hat that American intelligence had identified as the cartel's ramrod in Panama, a man known only as Desechado—Outcast. He looked at the photo for a long time, drinking in the slim gray beard and the hard age lines around the man's eyes, but recognizing him just the same.

He shoved back his chair and stood, moving to one of the steel fireproof cabinets and opening it. His eyes quickly scanned the rows of titles set in neat black tape cases, finally settling on a box marked DOBERMAN, with the subtext GOMEZ.

He removed the tape and put in into the VCR, the tape coming on as he resumed his seat. He was looking at old newsreel footage of Noriega, the man whipping up the machismo of his people by waving a gleaming silver machete above his head as he spoke in Spanish from a dais before a large group of National Guardsmen. The camera held Noriega for a moment, then zoomed slowly in to take in a laughing general standing beside the man.

"Manolito Gomez," a voice-over narrator began. "Longtime Noriega confidant and supporter. Gomez had been a member of the feared Doberman Brigade, Noriega's private police force, and served as the colonel's private driver for over five years before a captain's commission moved him on to other duties."

Justice felt himself tightening up. The lines and the beard weren't there, but he had no doubt that Gomez and Desechado were one and the same person. The scene switched to shots taken from a slowly moving car at a man hurrying out of a restaurant. It was Gomez, dressed as a civilian in khaki pants and a wide-collared white shirt. He was hurrying to a chauffeur-driven Ford, looking suspiciously around him as he climbed into the vehicle. The narration continued.

"These shots, taken in early 1984, are the last known

pictures of Gomez. He retired from the military in 1983 and dropped immediately out of sight. His whereabouts and profession are unknown, though it is unlikely that Noriega would allow a man of his loyalty and confidential knowledge to get far from his control. Gomez was apparently a key subject of investigations into Panamanian human-rights violations by Amnesty International in 1985, which lists over two hundred confirmed eyewitness reports of his personally conducting the interrogation and torture of political dissidents, many of whom died during these sessions. The book is still open on Colonel Gomez."

The tape went in close on the man's face, freezing a front-view picture of him that held on the screen and burned itself into Justice's brain. The U.S. had talked about Desechado as an unknown commodity, not tying him to Noriega at all. Did they really not know, or was it part of a setup? He stared at the screen, his mind picturing fire behind the driver's head. He could hear the laughter, smell his burning flesh and the charred wood of the village, his mind filled with screaming and with automatic-weapons fire. And the screaming, burning faces all turned into the face of Allie Boyd as he felt the cold sweat rolling down his face.

The screen went white, then filled with static, Justice picking up the photograph again. He looked at it, staring hard. There were men in the background of the picture, barely focused and inconsequential—except for one. Just on the edge of the photo, just a hair's breadth from being out of the frame, was a face he saw every night in his dreams and nightmares—Frank Merriman. The son of a bitch was alive. He looked down to find all his muscles tensed painfully. His hands were clenched into white-knuckled fists in front of him. Blood ran from his palms.

He took a deep breath, trying to slow down his body and its out-of-control adrenal surge. Death filled his mind, unreasoning, jungle passion beyond his control. He closed his eyes, trapped in his past.

Dying again—a thousand times over.

IV.

VA HOSPITAL—DALLAS, TEXAS
9 MAY 1978—0342 HOURS

Justice lay on his back on the gurney, his eyes accustoming themselves to another ceiling as Allison Boyd hovered over him, her concern divided between his plight and the incredible situation she had placed herself in.

"We'll never get out of here," she whispered from the supply-room door as she peeked out at the uniformed cops who traversed the dark hallways in a futile search for a killer who'd done her business and been gone for hours.

"They won't stay long," he said weakly, the night's ordeal of movement and excitement leaving him drained and barely conscious. "They already know they're wasting their time. This is just routine."

"Mr. Justice . . . I'm scared," she said.

"We haven't done anything wrong," Justice replied. "You've saved a life. Don't worry. And please, call me Will."

"Will," she breathed, almost a laugh. "You were well named."

Justice was holding onto consciousness as he'd hold onto life itself. The woman was barely in control at this point, and any chance at all that he had of staying alive depended absolutely on his being able to keep her pumped up and on his side. It was maddening. As he lay there, his mind soaring and plotting, he was able to continue living only through the kindness and tenacity of someone he didn't even know. For the woman's part, she saw herself going up against everything she believed in *plus* the medical establishment that fed and sustained her. And the only thing that kept her tied to Justice's plans was her concern for the life of another human being. For that she was risking everything, and Justice couldn't help but wonder at what exact point self-preservation would take over Allie Boyd's mind and cause her to run at breakneck from the crazy quadraplegic.

He was living right on the edge of the razor blade right now. One misstep and he was gone. For his own survival, he *had* to hold the woman to him. There was no one else.

She turned to him from the doorway. "The hall's clear," she said.

"Okay," he replied quickly. "Move while we've got the shot. Get me out in the hall and head us toward the emergency room."

"What happens if we run into someone?" she asked, her voice high and frightened.

"Listen to me," he whispered harshly. "You will do what you have to do and get me out of here. I'm dead if you don't. Do you hear me?"

She stood over him, her hands on either side of her face. "Yes, I hear you. I just don't . . ."

"Please," he said. "Allie . . . please. Look, you're a nurse and you're pushing a hospital bed. Why should that cause you any problems? Don't think, just do it. Do it now!"

She looked at him, and he saw the fear in her eyes. He summoned his reserves and smiled at her, winking. "Come on, honey," he said. "I'll get you a presidential citation when this is all over."

She rolled her eyes but smiled beneath it all. Taking a deep breath, she moved around to the head of the gurney. "Okay, hotshot," she said. "Here goes nothing."

She pushed, the door banging open at the foot of the gurney. He was in the hallway then, the ceiling and light fixtures rushing past his line of vision. "Slow down," he said. "Easy . . . easy. You don't want to attract attention."

"Okay, okay," she whispered nervously. Then, "There're police by the nurses' station!"

"Act normal," he said. "Be casual."

"They'll know. They'll be able to tell."

"Hell," he said, "they'll look at your face and your body. They won't even notice that you're pushing a bed."

"I think you've just flattered me," she said, voice quavering.

"Say thanks and move on."

"Thanks," she said, and the lights got brighter overhead, Justice knowing they'd reached the nurses' station.

Two blue uniforms drifted past, Allie having slowed to a leisurely pace.

"Evening ma'am," one of the cops said. "Can you handle that big old thing all by yourself?"

"N-not really," he heard her say, his heart sinking. That was it, she'd hit the wall. "Could you give me a hand?"

"Sure," the cop said, and Justice saw the man move to take Allie's place pushing the gurney. "Where we going?"

"Down to emergency," she said, voice firmer. "He had prostate surgery a little while ago and is going to convalesce at home."

He looked up to see her staring down at him, an almost bemused expression on her face. "Rest easy, Mr. Ritter," she said, patting his hand. "We'll have you home before you know it."

"Thank you, nurse," he said, holding back his own smile. The woman had joined into the spirit of this a bit more quickly than he would have hoped. What had he gotten hold of? This was obviously the perfect solution. No one was going to challenge a policeman pushing a man on a gurney.

They made the elevators and took the ride to floor one. The cop pushed the whole time, making small talk with Allie Boyd, Justice surprised at his own reaction to the whole thing. It made him uneasy and more than a bit jealous. In his private fantasy situation, Allie Boyd was free and unattached and had nothing to do in her life but take care of him. The walk reminded him that he wasn't a normal man and that he couldn't offer her any of the things a normal man could offer a woman. And what was her life like outside of work? Was there a husband, a lover, a casual partner? He'd never thought to ask. He'd been too busy trying to control the reality of the situation. He found the thought depressing. It was all he could do to keep his spirits out of the gutter, so thin a thread he hung by.

They arrived at the ER, the cop working Allie quickly to

get her phone number and vital statistics, though much to Justice's relief, she sidestepped the man easily.

The ER was noisy, raucous, with people pushing by his bed continually. "What's going on?" he asked.

"Must have been a wreck or something," she said. "Lots of people are moving in and out. What do we do now that we're here?"

"Are there ambulances outside?" he asked.

"I'll see."

She moved away, leaving him to be jostled by groups of relatives and friends and bleeding victims. They seemed young. Teenagers. He found it difficult to muster sympathy for them, as he was so tied up in his own troubles. He forced himself to care, to think about someone else. Self-pity would not serve him well. He'd already decided that he was going to live. But there's a great deal of difference between living and being alive, and Justice realized that his attitudes were going to have to remain strong and positive. There were no insoluble problems, only setbacks. His father had told him long ago that a person could accomplish anything—anything—in life he wanted, as long as the attitudes were strong and righteous.

Allie was suddenly there, staring down at him. "There are three or four ambulances outside," she said, "the attendants just waiting for reassignment."

"Wheel me outside," he said. "Do it now."

She pushed the gurney through the crowds in the fake marble halls, then through the electric-eye double doors and into the balmy Texas spring night. For the first time in weeks he was looking up at stars instead of ceiling, and the stars were infinite and distant. It gave him some heart. He remembered lying on the ground at Volcán Barú, listening to the cries of the dying long after the Dobermans had gone, knowing he'd never see the sky again and praying for the guiltlessness of death. Tonight the sky was hope for him. He was the sole survivor of a massacre, the witness to inhumanity, and in the vast reaches of the universe there would have to be room for him and his brand of retribution. No matter what he had to do, no matter how difficult—he would accomplish it. And under the infinity of stars, he quietly made an oath that would see him through the dark nights of despair.

Reality was his for the making, as long as he believed in himself and his goals.

"Now what?" she asked.

"Push me to the closest ambulance," he said. "Offer the driver a hundred bucks to get us out of here. Tell him the same thing you told your friend in blue."

She smiled. "How'd you like that?" she asked. "Pretty gutsy, huh?"

"Yeah, they broke the mold with you all right," Justice said, then smiled. "Go on. Let's get out of here."

"Where do I get the hundred bucks?"

"I gave you a thousand earlier. Where is it?"

"You said that was mine!"

"For God's sake, we'll work it out later," he said, exasperated. "Just get us out of here."

She disappeared, returning a moment later with a large black man wearing an Afro and a goatee. "Now, I don't have much time," he was saying as he opened the back doors of the ambulance. "They call me on something, and I'm gonna have to go."

"No problem," Allie said. "Help me get him loaded up."

The two of them hoisted the gurney into the back of the ambulance, the wheels folding flat onto the bottom of the thing. His view now was of oxygen hoses and dangling blood-pressure cuffs and stethoscopes. Allie climbed in next to him, kneeling by his side. She immediately took his wrist and found the artery, counting the blood pressure as she looked at her wristwatch.

The ambulance lurched forward, the driver pulling out of the emergency room lot and into the flow of traffic. "Where to?" he called back to them.

"Where to?" Allie asked, folding his arm back over his chest.

"I'm open," he said. "How about your house?"

"*My* house?" she said. "You mean you don't have anyplace to go?"

"Lady, I've never been in this city in my life," he said. "If you've got any other ideas, I'd be happy to listen to them."

"But what am I supposed to do with you?" she said. "You need care, constant attention..."

"Where to?" the man called from the front again.

She looked down at him. He met her eyes and held them. She looked hard, searching. He let her see his own fears and his own need, and she sighed deeply.

"Go out to Irving," she said. "The King's Gate addition on Grauwyler."

"Got it!" the driver called.

She turned back to Justice. "You can stay the rest of tonight," she said, "but tomorrow you've got to find something else. You're still a critical-care patient. You're going to have to have someone with you twenty-four hours a day."

"What about you?" he asked. "Can't you do it?"

"You don't want much do you?" she asked, angry now. "Believe it or not, I've got to work for a living. I've got a mother to support. If I don't lose my job over everything that's happened so far, I don't intend to do anything else to jeopardize it. You don't understand how bad off you are right now."

"Believe me," he replied, harsh. "One thing I do understand is how bad off I am. Everytime I want to jump up and walk across the room I remember."

"Sorry," she said. "It's just that you need to start making plans that don't include me. I'm no guardian angel. I'm just a nurse trying to make ends meet."

"I don't mean for you to do it for free," he said. "I'll pay you."

"With what?" she said loudly.

"I'm working on it!" he returned.

Her hands went into the air, and she sat back on the side bench. "Like I said, champ. You're out tomorrow. I have some sick leave coming to me. I'll stay home with you, work out your transportation, or whatever else you want. But by tomorrow night, you're gone, okay?"

"We'll talk about it," he replied.

"Talk about it? Don't you understand anything? You can't even eat right now without someone standing by to keep you from choking...."

"Insurance," he said.

"What?"

"Insurance...that's the answer."

"On top of everything else, I think you're insane," she

said, shaking her head. She leaned back, taking a deep breath, and he realized that she'd been at the hospital for over sixteen hours straight, most of that time running around doing things for him.

"I want to thank you for everything you've done," he said. "I know that I haven't exactly been easy to work with."

She waved it off. "Don't hit me with gratitude," she said, tired. "I'm confused enough as it is."

"Will there be any problem with the dead guy?" he asked.

A light smile just ran across her lips as she sat, eyes closed, head tilted to the side. "I hate to admit this, but I've maybe got a larcenous heart," she said. "When I heard about the guy dying in the ward, I checked him out and found he had no family, no one to claim the body. I signed him out of the morgue myself, told them he was being picked up for burial. He's gone for good."

"Just like that," Justice said. "Kind of sad, isn't it?"

"We see a lot of it in the VA," she replied. "Lifers who were married to the service . . . you understand."

"All too well," he said. "What would you consider a decent living wage for full-time nursing care?"

"You couldn't afford me," she said.

"Go on," he answered. "Give me a number."

"Oh, let's see," she said wistfully. "I think sixty-five thousand a year would probably cover it, with three weeks off in the summertime, paid of course, plus at least one night off a week."

"I'll give you seventy-five thousand," he said.

"Great," she answered, shaking her head sleepily. "You do realize that hallucinations are symptomatic in paralyzed patients."

He started to answer but noticed that her breathing had become regular and even. He lay quietly, listening to her sleep, listening to the occasional crackle of the two-way in the front. It amazed him at what a little resourcefulness could accomplish. Here he was, a free-floating brain, trapped and immobile, yet able to move life in the directions of his choosing by careful manipulation of others. World leaders understood this. What was politics but manipulation of emotions? It wasn't any different from his playing to Allie Boyd's altruism.

It was an awesome realization, and one that carried heavy responsibilities lest he become like those who were out to kill him. Manipulation, yes, but ethical. He'd blindly accepted the truth of others until Volcán Barú. From now on he'd only follow his own conscience. No one else could tell him what was right and true. He had a mind. He would follow his own path.

The outer road lights flashed past the windows, mesmerizing, Justice taking in everything, his brain a funnel for every sight and sound and smell. God, how he wished he could move—even an inch, a millimeter. So much that was human was lost. What was a brain without a body to control? No, he needed to keep himself together. He would have a life, some kind of life.

Some kind.

The ambulance slowed onto residential streets, Allie waking instinctively to guide the driver to her door. By the time they'd lowered him from the back of the vehicle and wheeled him up to her house, he'd already fallen from his lofty manipulative perch to feel like a helpless baby again, dead, useless meat. Sometimes it was all he could do to hold himself together.

From the limited amount he could see there on his back, the King's Gate development was misnamed. The houses were small, nearly ramshackle, reminding him of the tar-paper-and-shingle frame houses built for the GIs returning from World War II.

The house was dark when they entered, Allie whispering to the attendant as she turned on a living room light. "I guess we'll bring him back here," she said, pointing to a room just off the small living area.

They wheeled him into what must have been her bedroom. It was tiny and filled with the kinds of things that teenaged girls like to keep around—stuffed animals, lacy pillows, and stacks of magazines.

"Let's get him on the bed," she said.

"But this is your place," Justice told her. "Where will you sleep?"

"The way I feel right now, I could sleep anywhere," she answered. "Don't worry about it. The couch is comfortable."

They lifted him onto the bed with professional expertise, Allie making sure that the bottom sheet wasn't wrinkled, a cause of bedsores and discomfort for a body that couldn't move.

"You got everything here?" the driver asked. "I'd better be getting back."

"Sure," she said. "I appreciate it. Could you take the gurney back with you?"

"Got it," he said.

"What's goin' on in here?" came an old voice from the doorway.

"Go back to bed, Mama," Allie said, her voice taking on a practiced cadence. "Sorry we woke you up."

"Who's this Negro man?"

"He's a friend, Mama. Please, you need your rest."

"How can anybody rest with all this racket going on?" the woman asked, and he could hear her shuffling into the room.

"So long," the driver said, Justice listening to the song of the gurney wheels as it was pushed out.

The old woman was looking down at him, her hair stringy gray, her face like a withered cantaloupe. If he watched her out of the corner of his eye, he could see her leaning against a walker. "Who's this?" she cackled.

"That's Mr. Ju . . . Brown," Allie said. "He's a patient of mine and will be staying here until tomorrow."

"I never heard of no nurse takin' her work home with her before," the woman said, sticking out a bony finger to prod him. "What's wrong with you young feller?"

"Can't move," Justice said, smiling at her. "My name's Will. Pleased to meet you, Mrs. Boyd."

"You'll have to get your own food," the woman said. "You're not eatin' mine."

"Mama!" Allie said.

The woman shook her head. "Give them your food and first thing you know, they want to move in permanent."

Allie laughed. "I heard that," she said. "Now you go on back to bed. We'll talk about it in the morning."

"All right," the woman said, shaking her head and turning from him, "but I never heard of no nurse baby-sittin' her patients before. What's this old world comin' to?"

Allie had left with her mother, Justice alone in the room, feeling her presence, smelling her smell. What a strange road had brought him to this bedroom in the middle of the night.

She was back in quickly, a stack of towels in her hand. "If you're going to live away from the hospital, you'd better begin thinking of how to take care of yourself." She set down the towels and began rolling them up, then lifted his legs and placed the towels underneath them. "This is called the Trelenberg position, your head lower than your feet. We'll have to constantly move you...turn you over. Your own Stryker frame would probably help. You'll need massages and passive range-of-motion exercises to keep your extremities from deteriorating. You'll need physical therapy and..."

"I need a telephone," he replied.

"What?"

"A phone. Could you make a call for me?"

"Now?"

"Yeah...it's important."

She moved a phone from her night table, holding the receiver up to his ear. "Give me the number."

"Okay, it's a two-one-two area code...."

"Long distance!"

"We'll work it out," he said. "Please."

She relented, dialing the number for him. Even though it was past four in the morning, Paul answered on the first ring, his voice tensed and cracking.

"Yeah?"

"Paul, it's me."

"Will! I-I just got off with the government. They said you were...were..."

"I'm okay, little brother," Justice said, then laughed at his own choice of words. "But I'm in a lot of trouble."

"What's happening?"

"I saw something I shouldn't have seen," Justice answered. "They tried to whack me tonight."

"The Company?"

"Yeah."

"Oh no. What can I do?"

"Two things," Justice said. "First, leave me dead. I'm a lot safer that way. Second, I'll need cash."

"You know I'll do what I can," Paul replied. "I'm tapped out right now, but maybe I can get a loan or something. How much do you need?"

"You're going to be rich very soon," Justice said.

"What do you mean?"

"I took out an insurance policy in your name, Paul. It's worth three-quarters of a million dollars."

"My God."

He glanced up at Allie, the woman trying unsuccessfully not to listen. "Will you split it with me? I'm p-paralyzed. I have no way of making a living."

"Paralyzed? Oh, Will, I . . ."

"Not now, Paul," Justice snapped. "I don't need pity. I need money."

"Let me come to you. I'll help."

"Like hell you will," Justice answered. "You suddenly showing up would only arouse suspicions. What I need from you is routine. Do what you always do . . . don't change anything. You'll fly the body up to New York and bury it with Mom and Dad. . . ."

"Will!"

"Just do what I tell you," he said, harsh. "I'm trying to stay alive here."

"Sorry. How do I get in touch with you when the money arrives?"

"I'll give you a number, but don't ever call it from your home or your work. Use a pay phone and ask for William Brown. That's the name I'll use from now on if I call you. And Paul, don't tell anybody I'm still alive."

"This will really hurt Aunt Jo," Paul said.

"I can't help that right now," Justice replied.

"I've got to tell Joanie and the kids," he said.

Justice thought about that for a moment. "Tell your wife," he said, "but leave the kids out of it. What they don't know won't hurt them. This isn't a game. We're playing with the Bigs now. They don't take prisoners."

"My God, what have you gotten yourself into?"

"The deep stuff, Paul," he answered. "Play your part to the hilt and everything will be fine."

"I understand. I'll call you after I hear from the insurance people."

"Yeah," Justice said. "And little brother . . . give me a decent send-off."

"I'll cry the loudest . . . take care of yourself."

"You, too."

He heard the phone click in his ear, feeling bad, realizing the pain that he was causing his family and friends. He stared up at Allie, the woman nodding and hanging up the phone.

"You heard?" he asked.

"I heard."

"My offer is seventy-five thousand dollars a year," he said. "Do we have an arrangement?"

The woman turned from him and walked several paces before turning back. "This is so damned nuts," she said. "What in God's name is this all about?"

"It's very simple," Justice said, mustering himself to some authority. "I'm alive, and I fully intend to stay alive. Not only that, I intend to walk again, to regain my life and to take revenge on the people who put me here, for the sake of that village. I will do these things. I will not fail. I'll pay you the seventy-five thousand in advance. Do we have a deal?"

She walked to the door. "I'll be right out here on the couch," she said. "In a couple of hours, I'll come in and move you around a little. If you need anything, just holler. You seem pretty good at that."

"Do we have a deal?!" he demanded.

She nodded. "We have a deal," she said softly, then turned and walked out of the room.

He breathed deeply, easily, for the first time that night. This was a start, a lot of bold talk, but the insurance money wouldn't last long considering his needs. He had to figure out a way to make a living, and he needed to do it soon.

He closed his eyes, but visions of fire and the smell of burning flesh kept him wide awake.

V.

DIAMOND ROCK
12 FEBRUARY 1988—0900 HOURS

The sun was up just over the crown of Diamond Rock as Mandrake's boat approached from the Martinique side, the spectacular backlighting polishing the rock to high luster, glinting the edges in a million brilliant pinpoints of light that sparkled like the diamonds that gave the small island its name. And he had to fight the feeling that such a magnificent day and spectacular view had been ordered solely for his benefit by the rock's master.

Once again he was surrounded by people he'd never seen, a small unmarked cargo freighter the unlikely repository for two million dollars in gold bullion. Three swarthy-looking men with skin like aged, cracked leather were the ostensible protectors of the sizable fortune, and once again, they spoke only Creole. It had taken a major negotiating effort on his part just to talk the lieutenant colonel in charge of the shipment into loading it onto the boat at all.

They lapped closer to the small series of docks that formed the western side of the monolith. The wind was up and the water choppy, and God help him, he found himself churned up with the water, excited about returning despite the kind of news he was bringing to Lambert. There was something untamed, yet civilized, about the mercenary, a simplicity in approach to life and unerring belief in himself that made him unlike any other man Mandrake had ever met. Where most statesmen and politicians always got gummed up in bureaucracy and definitions of terms, Lambert moved directly to the heart of the matter and measured it against the yardstick of his own ethical system, taking steps accordingly.

How many times during his tenure in national government had he wished for the simplicity of that approach to life and politics? How many times had he found himself disgusted by the equivocation and expediency of the petty bureaucrats around him? And to make it worse, it seemed that Lambert instinctively understood that about him, playing him like a prize bass on a twenty-pound line.

A man stood on the end of the pier, watching, waiting for them to dock. At first he'd thought it was a statue of a man, so solidly it stood there, but as they closed in, he realized that it was Sardi, patiently performing his duties to Lambert as he had once performed them for much larger governments and more famous heads of state. The man was dressed as he had seen him last, in a white raj suit, a small gold ankh around his neck. His dark lips broke into a smile as the boat bumped up to the pier, the deckhands hurrying to throw ropes on the pilings and snug them up. There were several fishing boats docked around them, plus what appeared to be a racing yacht being tended and loaded for departure.

"Welcome, Mr. Mandrake," Sardi called, moving to the gangway and holding out a hand for him. "We have been most anxiously awaiting your return."

"Beautiful view," Mandrake answered, shaking off Sardi's hands and climbing out himself, his legs feeling shaky after the choppy ride. "Will you supervise the counting and unloading of the gold?"

Sardi smiled widely, then gestured expansively toward the end of the pier. "We trust you," he said. "We will not count the money. I've come to escort you to William."

"I have papers to be signed, documents to . . ."

"Time enough for that," Sardi said, cutting him off, and they walked down the pier together, Mandrake turning once to look furtively at the unguarded boat and its scruffy crew before moving on.

"Did you receive the videotape we sent you about our island and its history?" Sardi asked.

"Yes," Mandrake replied, loosening his tie and getting

into the slow pace of things. "I watched it last week, then sent it on to the considerations committee at the UN."

"How did you like it?"

"Enjoyable propaganda," Mandrake said. "I don't know how much of it is to be believed, however."

Sardi laughed. "William has no reason to lie about any of this," he said, opening his arms wide and laughing again. "You should know that by now. Life here is just as we've told you."

They'd walked off the pier, passing a forklift going the other way, and moved into a natural cave entrance that was bolstered on the inside by several sets of hydraulic steel doors. "It's difficult to think of Mr. Lambert as anything but a hired gun who controls Haven like a dictator," Mandrake said. "There's not much room in the modern world for Robin Hood myths."

"You don't believe that," Sardi said.

"Not completely," Mandrake replied. "Tell me different."

Sardi turned and stared at him, his eyes deep pools in the dim light of the cave. "It becomes very simple when you modify your definitions. Mr. Lambert is a businessman, whose business is people," he said slowly. "Power means nothing to him, nor does money. They are only a means to an end. He measures wealth in terms of service."

"The end being?"

"The end being... utopia, I suppose," Sardi said, stopping them at the first vehicle in a line of golf carts and pointing to the passenger side. "There may not be an end, you see. Life is a journey whose end never comes. The trick, as always, is to make the journey as meaningful as possible. For William, as for me, the journey's magic comes in giving to others, in realizing that only in total concert with our fellow man are we truly happy, truly free. It's the secret of life, Mr. Mandrake."

Mandrake climbed into the passenger side of the cart, Sardi starting them off with a jerk. The cave walls had given way to smooth cement hallway, Sardi pinging along at a good clip, occasional carts passing them going in the opposite direction. "You'll have to excuse me if I find it difficult to merge the two images of the man in my mind," Mandrake said.

"It's quite all right," Sardi replied easily. "William is an enigma, a man of flawed righteousness. When you've known him longer, you'll understand him better."

"I get the impression that nobody really knows him."

Sardi nodded. "Perhaps true, though to me he is the greatest man I've ever known."

Mandrake turned in shocked surprise. "But, sir . . . you've worked with Ghandi himself!"

"You've been checking up on me," Sardi said, turning a corner at an intersection of halls. "I'm flattered. But I still hold to my original statement. Ghandi was a great man, but he did not possess William's insights into the soul of modern society, nor did he possess William's acumen for understanding the global state that all of us live in but none fully appreciate. But that's not what I want to talk to you about."

"Oh?"

The hallway walls suddenly disappeared, the floor turning into a catwalk suspended above a huge bank of generators and transmission equipment, the beating heart of the operation, all conversation ceasing until they had passed over the machinery and its loud, insistent whine.

The hallway immediately branched off into several crossroads, Sardi pulling up near another parking area marked by red lines on the floor, and stopping among a number of carts.

"You've never seen William as you're going to see him today," Sardi continued, climbing out of the machine as Mandrake followed suit. The man walked toward a set of stairs carved right into the rock wall. He stopped at the bottom and looked gravely at Mandrake. "You may find him somewhat insane."

Mandrake laughed. "I wasn't expecting to hear that," he said. "What do you mean?"

"Crazy wisdom," Sardi said. "He's not like other men. He doesn't . . . act the way other men act. He's exercising now, and when he exercises, he does it religiously, meditatively. His mood becomes altered."

"You mean like runners when they become exhausted and get high on their own endorphin flow?" Mandrake asked.

"Most perceptive," Sardi said, raising an eyebrow. "It's more than that, but that will do for now. Also he is mentally gearing up to the mission. It also . . . changes him."

Mandrake shrugged. "I was a soldier myself," he said. "No problem." He started up the stairs, Sardi stopping him with a hand on his chest.

"Remember what I've said when we go in there." Sardi didn't so much speak the words as burn them into Mandrake's soul through eye contact. With that, he took his hand away, leading the man up the stairs to a red metal door set in the rock face.

Mandrake's heart was jumping in his chest by the time they went through the door, Sardi's attitude just contributing to the off-balance feelings he was already living with on this trip. If Lambert's idea was to keep him off balance, he was doing a hell of a job.

The red door led into a small arena that was actually a natural cavern. They were at the top, looking down, twenty rows of seats defining the edge of the semioval bowl. The arena itself was circular, surrounded by a ten-foot chain-link fence. Its diameter was about fifty feet, its floor deep sand from the black beach, bathed in a bright white light. Beyond it, the natural bowl shape of the chamber leveled off, fronting a wide expanse of open, well-lit cavern that contained pistol and rifle ranges, mock war-zone ruins, and obstacle courses. It was the most serious and sophisticated guerrilla training school he'd ever seen.

But he didn't have time to dwell on the amazing place, for his eyes were drawn to the sight of William Lambert, stripped to cutoff jeans and no shirt, standing in the middle of the arena, sweat glistening under the harsh lights. The man's body might as well have been chiseled from granite, so rigid and hard were his muscles as he half crouched, arms opened wide, and stared at the edge of the arena. Intensity radiated from the man, his eyes fixed, almost crazed. A small crowd sat scattered around the bowl, speaking in hushed tones.

Lambert was talking loudly to the Dutchman, Vanderhoff, who stood near the arena fence, taking notes. He kept trying to speak above a low, roaring sound that echoed sporadically through the cavern. ". . . and authorize counsel to continue the Union Carbide investigation in Bhopal until further notice."

"William," Vanderhoff said patiently. "You've already spent . . ."

"I don't care," Justice said, clipped, a command. "Just do as I say."

"Let's move closer," Sardi said. "Watch your step."

He took Mandrake by the arm and helped lead him down the rock-hewn stairs, closer to the bright arena floor.

"Hey, Charlie!" Lambert yelled, though he hadn't looked even once in Mandrake's direction. "How's it going?"

"Going fine!" Mandrake called back, wondering what it was that so involved the man.

"No it's not," Lambert called back. "Something's bothering you!"

"Jet lag, maybe," Mandrake replied. "I'm tired out."

Lambert straightened and stared at him for a long second, his brow furrowed, and Mandrake knew the man was looking into his soul.

All at once something jumped at Lambert from the edge of the arena, a streak flashing, a . . .

"My God!" Mandrake yelled. "That's a tiger!"

Lambert dived to his right, rolling, then coming back to a standing position. The tiger, snarling, missing with his leap, had already recovered, twisting to pounce again as the man regained his feet.

Mandrake shuddered as the huge animal, nearly twice Lambert's size, fell upon the man, its roar echoing through the chamber like thunder.

Lambert threw himself at the animal, somersaulting over it as he used its back for a springboard. Incredibly, he landed on his feet, then turned back to the animal and went to one knee as the tiger pounced again. Mandrake jumped as the tiger landed upon the man, but Lambert rolled backward with the beast, his feet planted in its stomach, and levered the creature's weight against it, throwing it behind him, the beast scurrying back to its feet and retreating ten feet to prepare for another go at the man.

Lambert jumped up quickly to face the tiger again, both of them crouched and sizing the other up, the tiger pacing slowly back and forth, its ears pinned back.

"And Jorge," Lambert said. "We need more people on the banana harvest. Talk up some overtime to the pimento farmers. They might be willing to subcontract for awhile."

"Got it."

The beast sprang again, Lambert impossibly sidestepping at the last second, then spinning away as the tiger made its quick second pass.

"Bring the money, Charlie?" he called, as Mandrake and Sardi reached the fence, standing near a barely hooked gate.

"Got it," Mandrake said, wondering alternately how Lambert knew something was eating at him and how he'd escape getting eaten by the tiger if it got out the gate.

The tiger pounced again, knocking Lambert to the sand. But as it tried to pin him, he started rolling away, just out of the creature's grasp, its long, flashing claws futilely digging empty air. When it tried to gauge his roll, he fooled it and rolled the other way.

"If the dollar goes down any more," he said, jumping up and once again sidestepping, "sell twenty million and invest in yen. But wait until close of business on Friday...." He collapsed on the floor, the tiger jumping over him. "I don't want to start a panic."

"Okay, William," Vanderhoff said. "Swiss francs are solid right now, too."

The animal sprang onto its hind legs, Lambert meeting it head on, his own head buried in its chest, as his arms tried to hold back the claws. Mandrake watched in morbid fascination and horror, sure he was about to see Lambert's death. But the man began spinning, taking the off-balance tiger with him. They twirled, almost a dance.

"Go half yen, half franc," Lambert called from his death dance. "If the dollar climbs again, buy it all back."

The tiger's growls turned to whines, Lambert releasing the animal which collapsed dizzily on the ground. He jumped on it immediately, planting a knee softly on its chest as he began to gently massage the flank. The tiger's whines turned to purrs, then contented rumbles as it fell rapidly to sleep, its legs defenselessly splayed wide open. Lambert stood quietly and walked away from the tiger.

He moved up to the fence, wiping sweat from his face, thin parallel lines of blood crisscrossing his arms and chest, attesting to just how close the tiger had come. His eyes were still wide and glazed, his breathing deep, controlled. He locked eyes with Mandrake.

"What are you doing," Mandrake asked, "trying to kill yourself before you earn all that money?"

"Practice," Lambert said. "Just keeping up the reflexes." He took a deep breath, then laughed loudly. "Gets the blood up, doesn't it?"

Mandrake heard a door creak around the far end of the arena, another tiger springing into action. "Another one!" he yelled, Lambert backing into the arena center to meet it as its companion slept peacefully nearby.

"Nine feet long, Mandrake," Lambert said, as the animal slowly stalked him. "Five hundred pounds...and he eats mammals!"

The tiger sprang, Lambert rolling away. "Tell me about the UN mission!" he yelled as he sprang to his feet.

Mandrake looked at Sardi, the man shrugging slightly. "I warned you," he said.

"It may not be an impossibility," Mandrake called as Lambert dived away, again and again, from the rampaging tiger, the man's own animal screeches mixing with the cat's guttural growls. "Your real problem, as you figured, is going to be the French. They have the potential of denying you if they work at it. And they're still angry about the loss of Haven."

"Throw some technology at them," Lambert said, springing to his feet and facing the tiger with rapidly changing hand movements, misdirection.

"What do you mean?"

The tiger leapt, Lambert grabbing the thing in midair and shoving it away.

"Help them out on their space program," the man said, the cat shaking its head and squaring off again. "There's lots you can give them. In return, they may even let you share in their liquid electricity research."

"Why should they do that?"

"I've got a few dollars invested in their project," Lambert replied, he and the tiger walking a slow circle around one another. "I can help."

"You think of everything, don't you?"

"Not everything," Lambert said. "I don't know what it is that you're keeping from me right now."

Justice watched the man closely for response, careful not

to turn his attention totally away from the tiger. Mandrake took a long breath, Justice knowing the man wouldn't be callous enough not to admit the problem. "I've done some checking," he said.

The tiger leapt, roaring, Justice moving instinctively, pain shooting through his arm as he just escaped wildly flailing claws. The thing came back again, heartened by the smell of blood, Justice throwing himself down again and rolling. He was tiring, the cat fresh and ready for the kill. He rolled, rolled, the tiger desperate and pouncing, the arena going around in a blur. He snaked out a hand, grabbing the cat's hind foot and flipping, the creature falling away, retreating to stalk again.

Justice jumped to his feet and faced the animal. "And what did you find out?"

"Look, you've put me in an untenable position," Mandrake said. "I mean, we're talking national security areas here. . . . I just want you to know that you were right to fear the real reasons that you're being sent to Panama. I just want to say I'm sorry about selling you on this deal under false pretenses."

"What *exactly* did you hear?" Justice asked, prodding, moving the man subtly in his direction.

The cat charged, muscles rippling. As it pounced, Justice went into it, throwing himself shoulder first into the cat's barrel chest, thudding to the ground with a groan from the impact, the cat going down next to him. They both scrambled up and distanced themselves.

"Give me a break!" Mandrake called to him. "I'm a representative of the United States government. I can't give you classified information."

The cat charged, anger slapping Justice like a punch. "No!" he shouted savagely, then leapt to the fight, banging into the tiger, then slamming his hands over the beast's ears, knocking it to the ground, dazed and disoriented, its inner ear devastated.

He swung immediately in Mandrake's direction and pointed at him. "No! Tell me exactly what they said, Charlie. Tell me now, or are you prepared to piss our lives away, with your ethics of discretion, for the people who lied to *you?*

Some things are more important than government and rules. Make your stand . . . now!"

Mandrake met his eyes and traded fire with him. The man was silent, Justice knowing that he instinctively realized that he either had to say the right thing or walk away. It was a moment of truth. Charles Mandrake was being forced to confront his beliefs.

He cleared his throat and spoke in measured, even tones. "I read some memos," he said, "that had filtered back and forth between my boss and the director of the CIA. All discussions were geared around the notion of a mercenary force not connected with the government whose sole mission is to assassinate Manuel Noriega. The operation was never sold to me that way, but that's the way it germinated. I'm sorry."

"Not your fault," Justice said amiably, smiling. The tiger still lay at his feet, quaking slightly. The other tiger was just shaking himself awake. He moved to the gate, opening it and extending a hand to Mandrake. "Good to see you."

The man shook hands with him. "I don't feel right about telling you that," he said.

"Really?" Justice said, raising an eyebrow. "I'll bet you're wrong. I'll bet you sleep a whole lot better tonight than you did last night."

Mandrake shook his head. "How did you know I didn't sleep last night?"

Justice winked at him and gestured toward the tigers. "What did you think of that?" he asked.

"The only thing that surprises me is that it didn't surprise me," Mandrake replied. "What kind of a maniac are you to take on tigers bare-handed?"

"Tell you the truth," Justice said. "They just kind of help keep me in shape. I did it the hard way to get the exercise."

"The hard way?"

"Sure," Justice said. "The easy way is to control them with your eyes."

Mandrake laughed. "With your eyes," he repeated.

"Sure," Justice said. "Try it."

With that, he grabbed Mandrake's hand and jerked him into the cage, then stepped outside and barred the gate.

"You're crazy!" Mandrake screamed. "Let me out of here!"

"Now watch out, Charlie," Justice said through the fence. "That one waking up doesn't look any too happy right now."

"Let me out of here!"

"Don't look at me, Charlie!" Justice called. "The cat...watch the cat! Get eye control and keep your fear under wraps. He'll charge right away if you don't."

Justice watched the man, watched him turn his attention to the tiger, which was up and stalking. Mandrake spoke, forcing his voice to an even timber. "So help me God, you've got to let me loose. This thing's going to kill me."

"Just stay calm," Justice said, voice smooth. "Stick with it. Remember the eyes."

"If I'm killed..."

"Stop thinking that way," Justice said. "Listen. There's a man up in the seats with a rifle...just in case. You're going to be all right. Just use your eyes. It'll work out."

"A rifle?"

"He's a crack shot," Justice said. "Believe me. The eyes."

He watched Mandrake's intensity increase as the man crouched and established eye contact, the tiger growling low, threatening. Mandrake ad-libbed, growling back, circling tighter.

"That's it," Justice said, coaxing. "You overpower your enemy with intelligence and confidence. The human being is the ultimate animal. Nothing is like him. Move closer."

Mandrake grunted, taking a step toward the tiger. It backed up a step, then snarled, lashing out with a large paw.

"Let him see the power of your mind," Justice purred. "Let it pour through your eyes. Your eyes say power. Nothing is like you in the jungle—nothing. Move closer."

Mandrake took another step, then another, the tiger backing away, matching the steps, then breaking off, crouched low to the ground, its ears pinned against its head in defeat.

"I did it!" Mandrake yelled. "I really did it!"

The audience applauded. "Great!" Justice called. "Now come on out of there. We've got things to do."

Mandrake waved, laughing to the crowds, then did a

little dance around the still-fallen cat before moving to the gate.

"Don't press your luck," Justice said. "Come on out of there."

Mandrake laughed and moved through the open gate. "Sorry," he said. "Knowing the guy was there with the gun . . . I guess I got carried away."

Justice looked hard at him. "What guy?" he asked. "What gun?"

"You're kidding," Mandrake said, his eyes widening comically.

Justice shot a smile to the man, clapping him on the back. "Come on, Mandrake. Let's go look at my boat. It's a beauty."

They started up the stone steps, Justice turning to Vanderhoff. "Join us, Jorge," he said. "I have something else to show you."

The four of them walked up and out of the arena, leaving the same way Mandrake had entered. At the motor-pool area, Sardi left them and headed back to the docks while Justice drove in the other direction. He had Mandrake on the hook now. All he had to do was play him right and he would land one of his biggest fish to date. Vanderhoff was another brand of salmon altogether. He didn't go for the big, shiny lures. He'd have to be teased gently into the boat.

"When will you leave?" Mandrake asked as Justice drove them deeper into the caverns, toward the only restricted area in Diamond Rock.

"Any time, buddy," Justice said loudly, turning to clap Mandrake on the shoulder again. "We were just waiting on you."

"Do you have transportation for me back to Martinique?"

"Could if you wanted. Do your people expect you back today?"

"Not necessarily," Mandrake said. "They're supposed to wait—"

"Say no more," Justice replied. "I have a deal for you. You'll spend tonight in my villa on Haven. I've set up dinner for you with a U.S. senator, an OPEC negotiator, a politburo member, and three Asian film stars who speak no English but are fluent in . . . French."

"French?" Mandrake smiled.

"*Oui, oui*," Justice replied. "We'll have a boat waiting to take you back to Martinique in the morning, no sweat. My chef is preparing a special meal of local delicacies, and you'll have the chance to do a little exploring of Haven Island on your own. What do you say?"

"Well . . ."

"Good. It's settled then," Justice said, turning down a narrow hallway that had armed guards on either side of it. He waved to the guards as he passed, then stole a look to the backseat and Jorge Vanderhoff. "You're in charge now, Jorge. I hope you'll see to Mr. Mandrake's needs."

Vanderhoff looked up at him, his eyes betraying no emotion. He didn't respond to Justice's statement. Good. It was eating away at him. Justice hoped the next few minutes would turn the tide.

The hallway was a hundred feet long, an open steel door at its end. They drove through, into another cavern. Justice turned to watch Mandrake's reaction as he drove in.

"My God," the man whispered reverently.

"Welcome to the First National Bank of Haven," Justice said, and chuckled as he watched Mandrake stare around him with wide eyes. The chamber was filled with gold bullion in six-foot stacks, all of it gleaming brightly under white lights, a forklift moving a full pallet around, the gold from Washington. There were areas of bundled paper money and coins also.

"There must be billions here," Mandrake said.

"A billion is a lot . . . even a billion in gold," Justice replied. "Our official currency here is the French franc, but we've a smattering of all currency. We obviously use the gold standard, though. Jorge . . . I want you to do me an audit in here."

"An audit?" Vanderhoff replied.

"If anything happens to me this trip," Justice said, "you'll be acting CEO and chairman of the board. A good, solid accounting will set you up well with the stockholders. You know more about the operation here than anyone left behind. I want you to be able to continue."

"William, I . . ."

"You might want to start now," Justice said, motioning Vanderhoff out of the cart. "You've got a lot to do."

"If you're trying to make me feel guilty," Vanderhoff said, stepping out of the vehicle, "it won't work."

"People make themselves feel guilty," Justice countered. "Isn't that right, Charlie?"

Mandrake just looked at him.

"Guilt is simply a symptom of responsibility, Jorge," Justice continued, starting off the cart with a jerk. "It's totally self-sustaining. See you!"

He drove off, circling the "bank" once before driving out, Mandrake turing in his seat to flash a catlike smile. "You're a devious man, Lambert," he said.

"You don't have to call me Lambert anymore," Justice said. "You can use my real name—"

"I didn't want to know it," Mandrake said. "If you told me, I'd have to tell my superiors. Do you really want them to know?"

"No, I don't, Charlie," Justice said. "And I don't want you to tell them."

"Now you're asking me to keep secrets from my own government!" Mandrake said, as they drove back down the long hallway. "It's bad enough that—"

"Justice."

"What?"

"My name . . . is Justice, William Justice."

Mandrake looked angrily at him. "I told you not to tell me!" he said, exasperated. "Now I have to tell the government."

"No, you don't," Justice said. "You don't have to tell anyone anything. Did they tell you what they really intended when they sent you all the way over here to negotiate with me? You see, there's right and there's wrong. There's lies and there's truth. They lied to you. *I* told you the truth."

"Dammit, it's not that simple."

They had reached the end of the hall and turned back the way they had come, heading back toward the docks. Justice hit the brakes, skidding them to a stop. He turned to Mandrake. "It's *exactly* that simple," he said. "There's no justification for lies, no matter what anyone tells you. And I'll tell you something else—you already know that. Deep down inside you already know it. You've been conditioned to accept some governmentally rationalized view of life that is antihuman and probureaucracy. But down beneath all the crap and all the mumbo jumbo, you know that there's a right and a wrong that isn't open to definition."

Mandrake leaned back, rubbing his face with his hands. "Everything is so black and white with you," he said.

Justice started off again, passing the entrance to the arena, moving toward the generators. "Life is black and white. Gray areas were invented so that people could do wrong and not feel bad about it."

"I feel like a traitor or something," Mandrake said.

"No," Justice answered. "You're a good man who knows another good man when he sees one, that's all. Governments by their nature are immoral because they take on their own kind of unethical life. It doesn't have to be that way."

They crossed the catwalk above the generators, all talk stopping until they'd reached the other side. "You're denying over two hundred years of American patriotism," Mandrake said.

"I guess I am," Justice replied, speeding through the rest of the cavern and bringing them out into the bright sunshine. He drove up to the pier where the yacht was being outfitted, and stopped. "Let me show you how we're going into Panama."

They climbed out of the cart and walked down the forty-foot pier, Sardi at its end, watching the loading of provisions. Justice felt his blood rise with the refurbishing of the *Lutine*. She was an exciting boat, sleek and sultry, her taming a difficult, loving exercise uniting man and nature. Justice loved the primal challenge of the sea. There were no attitudes to be understood, no egos to stroke, no lies to gum up the works—there was only honest survival. To tame the sea was to tame oneself, to *know* oneself. There was nothing more enervating.

"Yo, Will'um!" Jenks called from the mainmast. They looked up; the man was at the top of the sixty-foot pole, wrapped around it like a monkey, checking lashings.

"How's it looking?" Justice called through cupped hands.

"Got some dry rot!" Jenks called down. "You don't take this puppy out enough."

Justice laughed loudly. "We'll be sou'westin' it today,

mate. We'll check and see if your sea legs have dry-rotted, too."

"This is quite a ship," Mandrake said as he watched a number of Mac-12 submachine guns being packed into fake baffles beneath the gunwales.

"My pride and joy," Justice said. "Fifty-five feet of fiberglass heaven right here on earth. It crews six, will do ten knots in the right wind, and when her sails unfurl, she's the best-looking woman I've ever seen."

"The name's familiar," Mandrake said. "*Lutine* . . . *Lutine* . . .*"

"Bought her from Lloyd's of London," Justice said, climbing aboard to pull on the rigging, testing for rot. "It's named after their bell."

"My God!" Mandrake exclaimed. "The *Lutine!* You won the America's Cup several years ago."

"So I did," Justice said, then turned to a heavily tanned man who was loading plastique into a secret compartment in the main mast. "Careful with that. It's C-four, highly volatile . . . and keep the detonator separated from it."

A small grin straining his lips, Mandrake climbed on board, moving aft to swing the tiller. "Spent a lot of summers on Martha's Vineyard in boats like this. God, I almost envy you."

"William," Sardi called from the dock. "You must soon replace Jorge on the crew list. Someone must be prepared to take his place. We sail in two hours."

Justice frowned. "Just hold it open for now, huh?" he said, walking up to sit beside Mandrake, whose hand was still on the tiller. "You know, Charlie. I've been thinking about those friends of yours in the State Department. I knew from the start why they were sending us to Panama. But what I'd really like to know is if they intend for us to leave again after we're through."

"You talking about assassination?" Mandrake asked, surprise lacing his voice.

"Jorge will not be coming," Sardi said. "He's too locked into his principles to change for you now."

"Everybody who works with me is a certain kind of person," Justice answered him. "Leave the spot open for now." He looked at Mandrake. "Yes, I'm talking about assassination. I don't trust the Company man we're supposed to meet over there."

"I never heard anything along those lines," Mandrake answered.

"Could you . . . find out?"

The man turned to him in righteous horror. "Are you suggesting that I *spy* for you?"

"I don't think I stutter," Justice said. "You've already made your stand, haven't you? You know, in for a penny, in for a pound."

"William," Sardi called. "We really need to fill that spot."

"Not now!"

"I c-couldn't do that," Mandrake said. "Protecting you is one thing. . . ."

"So, if you had access to the information that could save my life and the lives of my people, you wouldn't tell us?" Justice asked.

"Why do you always put it that way?"

"Because that's the way it is."

Mandrake angrily slapped the tiller. "What are you trying to do to me?"

"Help you to reach your full potential, that's all."

Mandrake took a breath. "You asshole."

"Maybe," Justice said, then stood, pointing back down the pier, past Sardi. "Looks like you can stop worrying about that extra crewman."

Everyone turned to see Jorge Vanderhoff drive right down the pier, veering close to the edge, then skidding sideways to a stop right before Sardi.

Justice climbed out of the boat to greet him.

Vanderhoff jumped out of the cart and stalked, frowning deeply, right up to Justice. "You're a son of a bitch, you know that?" he said.

"I know," Justice replied.

"You got an extra spot for me in your damned cowboy operation?"

"Does it rain on weekends?" Justice replied, then turned to look at Mandrake. The man rolled his eyes and raised his hands in surrender. *Got him.*

VI.

LEWISVILLE, TEXAS
23 MAY 1978—HIGH NOON

The van bounced along the plow ruts as Allie took them out to the meet, every bump jostling Will Justice as he lay on the folded gurney in the back of the thing, every jerk of the wheel a nightmare of pain. He'd learned about pain only in the last week when the diaschisis, the cord shock, had worn off, leaving him with limited use of his right arm, the ability to turn his head, and a pain like constant fire, his body's payback for the abuse he had caused it.

He held his hand up in front of his face as he struggled against the almost unbearable pain to slowly open and close the fist. He had no power, no strength, but the sight of a moving limb attached to his body, even a limb that throbbed in agony, was a matter of total absorption and fascination to him.

"Are you doing okay?" Allie called back to him, something she had asked him every quarter mile or so.

"Yeah," he said, mustering his voice, not wanting her to know how much even this short trip to the outskirts of Dallas had tired him out. "We almost there?"

"I see the tree you were talking about," she called loudly, above the constant rattle of the bouncing vehicle. "It's about a quarter mile ahead. A car is already parked there...."

"What sort of car?"

"I can't tell," she called. "A small one... maybe a foreign job."

"That's him all right," Justice replied. "My brother always was a cheapskate."

"You're terrible," she said, clucking her tongue.

Justice smiled. She really meant it. Allie Boyd was one of those genuine individuals who saw nothing but the good in people and would no more think of talking behind someone's back than she would of causing physical harm to them. That was Allie—lost puppies and homeless waifs. He supposed that he fell into the homeless-waif category.

He could feel the sweat running down his face and found it the greatest liberation in the universe to be able to reach up with his usable hand and wipe it off himself. The pain came again, excruciating, pulsing like a beating heart. He consigned it to an unused part of his brain and breathed deeply to relax. He'd been working his mind, visualizing with the only intact tool he still possessed, and even after just a few weeks, he'd found that the brain was a tremendous instrument of control. He'd never really told Allie about the pain, figuring to control it with his mind and save her the worry. Slowly, imperceptibly, it had begun to work. And Justice figured that if it worked in this, it would work in other things. If mental power was all he had, then, by God, his mental power would be astounding. He'd begun to exercise his mind like a muscle, limbering it up, forcing himself to hold great amounts of information consciously—and most important, he'd begun to visualize, to try to eliminate the barrier between thought and action.

The inside of the van was hot and bottled up like an oven. There was a strong, almost reassuring mechanical odor about his cocoon of heat and green-painted steel, his gurney creaking along with the machine as if it had become a part of it. His senses were acute, and he enjoyed the atmosphere surrounding him right now.

The bright light pouring through the back windows suddenly darkened, the van and its creaking coming to an abrupt halt.

"We're there," she said, and he heard her pull up the hand brake. "There's a man walking toward us...."

"Tall ... with a moustache?" Justice asked.

"Yes."

"That's him! Don't introduce yourself."

"Don't worry," she replied, and climbed out of the truck.

He lay there, listening to his own sweat roll down his face. Then he heard several seconds' worth of muffled voices before the back doors swung quickly open. His brother's large form blocked the opening for just a moment before...

"Oh God, Will," the man practically cried, as he climbed in on hands and knees, sliding right up next to him. "Oh no, look at you."

"Don't pity me, Paul," Justice choked out, forcing his mind to control. "Not in front of me. Please. I don't have time for that."

"I-I'm sorry," Paul said, the tears in his eyes telling more than words ever could. "I guess I just wasn't p-prepared. . . ."

"Forget it," Justice said. "I'm just glad you're here. Come on. Help my friend get me out of here."

"Sure," the man said, sliding back out. He and Allie, taking opposite sides of the gurney, pulled it into the north Texas afternoon.

They were under the leafy branches of a huge elm tree, a light southern breeze mixing with the shade to make the heat enjoyable. The sky was a bright, clear blue overhead as the sun burned away like a huge light bulb. A scissortail called loudly from the branches of the elm, angry that unwanted visitors had ventured so close to her new nest and family. Justice felt good as they wheeled him up closer to the trunk, the sight of his brother a reminder that he wasn't totally alone and without a past. It was somehow reassuring.

"Joan and the kids okay?" Justice asked when they'd stopped.

"The kids are devastated," Paul replied without disguising his feelings about that subject. "I'm sorry I ever made that promise to you."

"Let's just keep it this way for a while," Justice smiled. "After all, if they should let anything slip, you'll probably do jail time for insurance fraud."

The man took a long breath. "Guess I never really thought of it like that. I don't want to give them that responsibility."

"Good. You brought the money?"

"Yeah . . . after the taxes, your share comes to slightly over three hundred thousand."

"No trouble with the insurance people?"

"Not a bit," Paul said, almost surprised. "I think the government must have put the lid on everything and called it national security. They froze out the insurance people, and it was paid up almost immediately."

"I think this damned cart comes apart so I can get into a better position," Justice said. "How about giving me a hand?"

"Best we're going to be able to do is fold it down," Allie said.

"Fold it down and lean it against the tree," Justice answered, anxious to get as close to vertical as possible. "I'm strapped in."

They did as he asked, Allie hovering the whole time, watching with practiced eyes, saying "careful" whenever he was jostled too much. Within a couple of minutes he was leaning against the elm tree and looking around like a real person.

They were way off the highway, its concrete ribbon evident in the distance as it carried tiny vehicles at high speeds, their sounds like the murmuring of insects. A field stretched far around him, flat and level, like a pool table made of red earth. He could see for miles in either direction. To the east he could see a farmer plowing amidst a billowy cloud of dust, a small flock of blackbirds following in his wake, occasionally dipping down to the field for worms. It was quiet and peaceful, Justice feeling totally removed from the ebb and flow of normal life.

He slowly, painfully, extended his right hand. "Shake hands with me, Paul," he said.

His brother approached and their hands met, Justice barely feeling the pressure of his touch. It wasn't much, but it was something.

"What's this all about?" Paul asked, his face sagging every time he looked at Justice.

"It's not about anything," Justice said. "How did the funeral go?"

"A lot of people turned out," Paul said. "A *lot* of people, including several of your old girlfriends." The man looked at Allie. "You haven't introduced me to your friend."

"And I won't," Justice said. "I'm not sure how seriously you've taken all this, but believe me when I tell you that the less you know, the better for all of us." He looked at Allie, at the apprehension in her eyes, and knew what would do the trick. "Let's take care of the money first. We'll get that out of the way."

"Let me get it," Paul said, turning and hurrying the short distance to his car.

"I need to exercise your legs," Allie told him as soon as Paul was gone. "It's past time."

"Not now."

"There's nothing worse than getting off your physical therapy schedule," she said in a clipped, professional tone. "Let me see to..."

"I don't want him to think you're a nurse," Justice said. "He's a wild card in this. We can't give him much. Besides, I kind of like him thinking you're my girlfriend."

Allie blushed easily, and did now. Justice was always amazed at how pretty she could look without doing anything to herself. Today it was jeans and a floppy shirt with rolled-up sleeves, her red hair fixed up in a ponytail. Tomboys didn't come in packages like this when *he* was a boy.

"Okay," she said in her stern warning tone. "But we're going to do double duty when we get back."

"Okay, warden," he said, just as Paul returned with an attaché case.

"Here it is," he said, opening up the case.

Allie gasped, a hand going immediately to her mouth.

"Like I said," Paul continued, "a little over three hundred grand. We can count it...."

"It's fine, thanks," Justice said, reaching out a tentative hand to touch the stacks of hundreds and fifties. He looked at Allie. "Take it to the van and bring back lunch, okay?"

The woman smiled, and he realized that for the first time she actually believed that he'd come through with the cash he'd promised her. It touched him to know that everything she'd done for him had been for reasons other than a sure and easy dollar. Her seventy-five grand would be the best money he'd ever spent. In fact he decided on the spot to give her a ten-thousand-dollar bonus.

"Lunch?" Paul said.

"It's lunchtime, isn't it?" Justice said. "You don't think I'd bring you out here, then not feed you? Mom and Dad raised me right."

Paul laughed. "Mom and Dad never put on a lunch in their lives," he said. "They were always too busy building churches and preaching."

"And civilizing, Paul," Justice said. "I think their greatest trait was their sense of civility... their politeness. God, I miss them now. I wish they were here."

"I'm not sure that Mom would have approved of your choice of careers, Will," Paul said, eyes twinkling. He turned and watched Allie walk up with a large brown paper sack and a six-pack of beer in pull-off plastic rings.

"Looking at it now," Justice said sadly, "I think that my choice of careers had something to do with their death. I felt so... I don't know, responsible, that I wanted to do something, get even somehow..."

"It just happened, that's all," Paul said. "You were off at college. What were you supposed to do? You can't control the world, you know. What is it the kids say—shit happens?"

"Should I go away and come back later?" Allie asked.

"I'm just dredging up some ancient history," Justice said. "Come on, let's eat before I get all melancholy. Have I told you, Paul, that it's really good to see you?"

Allie pulled a beer off the ring and handed it to Paul, who bent back the pull tab and took a long drink. "Listen, big brother. When I heard your voice on the phone after they'd told me you were dead, I felt like I'd gotten a reprieve from the electric chair. Tell me the truth, how are you doing?"

Allie had pulled a blanket out of the sack and was spreading it on the ground. "I'm alive and want to be," Justice said. "That in itself is something incredible. Beyond that I'm not completely sure." He looked at Allie again. "Hey, how about one of those beers for me?"

She narrowed her eyes. "That's *all* you need," she said. "With the liver damage you..."

"One won't hurt me," Justice said flatly, chastising with his eyes.

Allie frowned for a moment, and he could see the wheels turning inside her head as she weighed the thought. Finally she opened a beer for him and placed it carefully in his good hand. He took a long drink, the beer slightly warm, pungent. It burned and felt good, and he couldn't have been more excited if he'd won the Pulitzer Prize.

"Come on, let's eat," he said.

"It's not much," Allie told Paul as she pulled a number of convenience-store sandwiches out of the sack. "Will insisted on it at the last minute."

"I want the ham and cheese," Justice said, excited just to feel somewhat normal. "And open me up a bag of those greasy chips."

Allie tightened up but took it all with relatively good humor. For the last two weeks she'd hand-fed him vitamins, proteins, fiber, and health. He was ready to junk out. Things hadn't been easy. His system had gone through incredible turmoil, with bowel and bladder dysfunction the most annoying aspect. But today, right now, he determined not to worry about it. He was going to have a lunch of junk food with his brother, and by God, if it killed him, he deserved to be dead. It was time to stop thinking like an invalid.

Allie opened a sandwich for him and switched it for the beer in his good hand. He took a bite, loving it, watching her watching him for signs of choking, another problematic aspect of his condition. She and Paul sat themselves on the blanket and began to eat.

"Now that we're sitting out here in the middle of nowhere," Paul said, "I'd kind of like to know what happens now."

"Now I put the pieces back together," Justice said. "I get myself well and healthy, make some money, then go after the motherfuckers who did this to me."

Paul looked confused. He turned to Allie, the woman staring down at her sandwich. He looked back up at his brother. "I don't mean to be crass," he said, "but wasn't your spinal cord transected?"

"That's what they tell me."

"I studied up on that a little bit after I found out," Paul

said, taking another long drink. "From my reading... your condition is permanent, your paralysis complete."

"You shouldn't believe everything you read, little brother," Justice said. "I intend to get back on my feet and retake control of my life."

"But that's impossible!" Paul said, too loudly, his voice breaking at his brother's fantasizing. "You can't put a spinal cord back together."

"I can," Justice said. "I intend to do it with my mind. It may take a long time, but time is something I've plenty of."

"How will you live, Will?" Paul asked, upset. He stood and paced. "You need constant attention and special treatment. That money I gave you won't last long at that rate."

"I certainly will need to make a living."

"But... how?"

"He's been reading," Allie said. "Every day, *The Wall Street Journal*, *The New York Times*, books on real estate and money markets and stock speculation."

"I'm learning," Justice said. "I realized that it may take time to get me back on my feet, so I looked around for ways that a man could make a living without leaving his room. Outside of running a clipping service, my best bet is investments and realty. With the money you just gave me I can begin my career as a stock speculator or..."

"God, Will," Paul said. "You don't know anything about investment. You need to take that money and figure out a way to stretch it over the years...."

"Would you stop trying to make me a cripple!" Justice shouted. "I will not be a cripple. I will have my life, and I'll have my vengeance! I don't care what the doctors say, and I don't care what *you* say."

"Your blood pressure," Allie said gently.

Justice nodded, breathing out. He didn't need to take his frustrations out on his brother. "Look," he said. "I know you don't think I can handle this. I can live with that. If I believe in myself, that's enough. I've been studying up on healing imagery. I will make my mind the master of my body, that's all."

Paul walked up to him, wrapping his arms around him, gurney and all. "I love you, Will," he said, choking back tears. "What happens if your scheme doesn't work?"

"You don't understand," Justice said. "It's not a scheme. It's my reality, and I *will* control it. I've learned more about myself and life in the last three weeks than in all the years that went before. I can have what I want. It won't be easy, but I won't back down from it either."

Paul stepped back from him, Justice studying his brother's eyes, realizing that the man was looking at the old Will Justice, not the man strapped in the gurney. "I wish you luck," he said softly, then turned to Allie. "Both of you. What can I do to help?"

"Forget about me," Justice said.

"What?"

"A connection to you will be dangerous for both of us. I wanted you to come down here to Texas and meet me because I needed to tell you this in person. I'm going to get myself a new identity so I can become the businessman I need to be. I'm going to change residence. Don't try to call anymore. We've already cut off the phone and reconnected it under another name. I don't expect you to understand the danger here. . . ."

"Will, I . . ."

"Let me finish, dammit," Justice said. "Please. My every waking moment I'm reminded of the duplicity that's left me as I am. But it's kept me sane, reminded me of the depths the human animal is capable of reaching. They'd think nothing of killing you and your entire family if they thought you were a threat to national security."

Paul stared at his beer can, then drained it all at once. "So, I'm supposed to just write you off, forget about my own brother. We've always looked out for each other."

"You've already buried me, Paul," Justice said softly. "Leave it at that. One day when I'm well, when I've got things under control again, I'll come walking up to your door and ring the bell. We'll laugh about all this."

Paul stared sadly at him. "Okay," he said quietly. "I won't pretend to understand or agree with everything you're saying, but I respect you, just as I've always respected you. If cutting yourself off from me is what you want, I'll go along with it."

"It's not what I want, Paul," Justice said. "It's the way it has to be."

The man turned to Allie. "I don't know who or what you are," he said, "but please, take good care of him. He's the only brother I've got. I'm going to leave a lot of my heart behind when I drive away from here."

Allie walked silently to Paul and hugged him, and Justice knew that she was acting as his proxy. Paul clung fiercely to her, then abruptly broke the embrace, swiping at his eyes with his hand. "I-I think lunch is over," he said, turning from both of them. "I guess we both have things to do."

"I guess we do," Justice said.

Allie had already bent to the remnants of lunch and begun to pick things up. "Here, I'll help you," Paul said, substituting rote work for thinking.

Justice watched him, knowing the man understood nothing of what he'd been told. He had to distance himself from Paul, because he wasn't about to put those closest to him in proximity to the fire that was sure to surround him. Paul carried the paper bag back to the van, Allie right behind with the blanket. They disappeared around the side of the vehicle, out of his sight, and he knew that Paul wasn't finished talking.

He looked around. The farmer and his audience of birds was gone, but the never-ending highway to the west rolled on perpetually. The scissortail had quieted, no longer fearing their presence. The world rolled on, with or without him. How easy for life simply to plow him under, as the farmer did his field. How easy it would be simply to give up, roll over, and end it. He had chosen the path of greatest resistance, and he wouldn't necessarily be the better for it. But he had a mission, a reason for being alive, and it kept him going.

He would succeed. Whether or not that would bring him the peace he craved, he didn't know. But it was the only path for him, and not Allie or Paul or the Company or the rest of the bleeding world would stop him. Of that he was absolutely sure, because he understood something that most people never even guessed at—the entire world and everyone in it is a plum waiting to be plucked. All it would take would be the right mind, the right mental direction. Individuals had controlled the destinies of nations and peoples since the dawn of time. No reason in the world why there couldn't be a little place for Will Justice.

No reason at all.

He watched Allie and Paul walk back around the van, neither of their faces betraying any emotion. Paul looked up, saw Justice watching him, and turned his lips into a false smile.

They put the legs back down on the gurney and rolled him back to the van, loading him in silence. When they were done, Paul climbed in beside him as he'd done when they'd arrived.

"Will," he said softly, taking his brother's hand. "I'm not sure what all this is about... all you're talking about, but I want you to know, whatever it is that you're doing, I'm always there for you. And if you need money—"

"Paul, don't."

"Listen to me," Paul said, sharing a quick look with Allie, who hovered by the doors. "I'm putting my half of the insurance money into savings. I'm not touching it at all. If you ever run really short of cash, it's there for you."

"I won't need it," Justice replied. "Spend it. Have a ball."

"And take care of yourself," Paul continued as if he hadn't heard Justice's words. "I worry about you."

"I won't do anything foolish," Justice said, then laughed. "At least not anything any more foolish than I've ever done."

"*That's* what I worry about," Paul said, both of them sharing a laugh, and Justice realized that was the place to end it.

"I'd better go," he said quickly, shaking Paul's hand again.

Paul looked down nervously. "I don't know how to leave you like this," he said.

"Easy," Justice replied. "Turn around and take off. Don't look back. I'll be all right."

Paul stared hard at him, his eyes softening seconds later. Without a word he nodded once, climbed out of the van, and hurried to his rental Toyota, Justice watching him through the still-open doors, swallowing any feelings into his great, sucking whirlpool of growing mental control.

He heard Allie climb into the driver's seat and close the door. "Seems like a nice guy," she said as she started up the engine and dropped them into gear. "Why did you send him away like that?"

"Do you think he'll keep his mouth shut?" Justice asked, ignoring her question.

"Probably," she said low, and they started off, bouncing through the plow ruts again as they returned to the civilized highway.

"What did he tell you before?" Justice asked loudly.

"What?"

"What did he tell you before?" he asked again. "When you two put up the food, what did he talk to you about?"

Her answer was slow in coming, but when it did, he knew it was the truth. "He said that he was afraid you were going insane," she said. "He pleaded with me to get you some kind of mental help and to put you back in the hospital. And I'll tell you the truth, I'm not sure that I don't agree with him. All that talk about controlling reality and walking again . . ."

"I *will* walk again," he said flatly. "And if you doubt my ability to control reality, just open up that briefcase and take another look at all the money you just made. By the way, I've decided to give you eighty-five thousand in advance instead of seventy-five."

"What's this about getting a new identity?" she asked, the bouncing of the van shooting the really bad pain through his arms and neck again.

"I can't operate in the open with my real name," he said, refusing inwardly to acknowledge the pain. "You're going to help me become someone else."

"I'm a nurse, dammit," she said, then excused herself for the expletive. "I don't know anything about . . ."

"I'll tell you what to do," he said. "It'll be easy for someone with a larcenous heart."

"Touché," she replied.

They drove in silence for several minutes, Justice's mind dwelling on the possibilities now that he had some capital. All at once the rumbling stopped, and they were on smooth pavement again, the pain in his arm subsiding to a knife edge.

"Are you doing all right?" she asked.

"Fine," he replied, but the emotional drain of controlling so much pain was beginning to take its toll. He was physically and mentally exhausted and close to depression, but he fought it back, determined that he would handle himself no matter what.

"Physical therapy double session when we get home," she said. "It'll make mother's day."

"Really," he replied. "She just loves to see someone in worse shape than she is."

"That's Mama," Allie laughed. "Did I understand right? Your parents were preachers?"

"Missionaries," he said. "I spent my first eighteen years living outside of the U.S.A. In seventy-one I decided it was time to see my native land and came back here to go to Boston College. My folks had been working in Vietnam since the midsixties. . . ."

"Vietnam?"

"Crazy, isn't it?" he said. "I lived there for years. The closest thing I ever saw to the war were occasional B-fifty-twos overhead on their way to bomb Hanoi. It was all very distant. But right after I left, Tet of seventy-two, the NVAs swept south, catching my family right in the middle of things. My brother got away; my folks didn't. I should have been there but wasn't."

"You can't blame yourself for that," she said. "That's when you went to work for the CIA?"

"I was a Marine first," he said. "But I was so gung ho and angry that the Company recruited me and put me in the field. It was good for me at first. I felt as if I were helping people and stopping the bad guys at the same time. That was before I understood that you can't tell who the good guys and bad guys are. When I look back now, I guess I was preaching in my own way. That was a month ago. It seems like a lifetime."

"Vengeance doesn't suit a preacher," she said simply.

"I'm not a preacher anymore," he returned, barely awake. "I'm a wide-open realist."

"You're a very special man," she said. "You should celebrate your own uniqueness, not mire yourself down in animal passions."

"The world's a jungle, lady," he said, fighting to retain consciousness. "Animal passions are all there is."

"Then why do you care about what happened to the people of Volcán Barú?" she asked, voice hard. "Good cannot spring from bad. If you're a civilized man, you've got to learn to behave that way, or all you do is make things worse. Please don't poison yourself with hatred."

"You sound just like my mother," he said, the civilized, mechanical rumble of the highway lulling his senses, deadening his conscious brain. Moaning, he gave up and let his eyes close, his mind giving over to rest. For a while, just a while, he'd put himself in Allie's control.

So he slept, dreaming dreams of burning villages and screaming children. Jungle dreams.

VII.

PANAMA CANAL—MIRAFLORES LOCKS
18 FEBRUARY 1988—1446 HOURS

William Justice stood fore with Kim Bouvier, watching the lock walls rise around them as water was pumped out of the second tier, effectively lowering them to the height of the Pacific Ocean. He turned once to look at the canal pilot astern as he stood watching the tow line and drift with a practiced eye from the wheel. They had picked the pilot up on Limón Bay, near Cristóbal on the Atlantic side, canal rules dictating that any skipper must give up his vessel to a canal pilot for the duration of the eight-hour trip through the locks. Justice hated to relinquish control for any reason and would be glad enough after they'd passed this last lock and they could leave the pilot at the entry to the Bay of Panama, near Panama City.

It had been an interesting five days at sea for him and his crew of nonseamen. The inexperience of the crew had added an extra day to the trip, and seasickness had made it seem even longer for most of them, with Kim the exception. The voyage had heartily agreed with her, and she stood now, smiling and relaxed, in a small black bikini and sunglasses, the pilot unable to keep his eyes off her. Inexperience in a sailboat, however, always gives way quickly to the necessities of surviving the waves and the wind, and his crew had learned quickly. On the final day of the trip they had pulled together like a team, a sustained speed of twelve knots for a portion of the morning and afternoon the cause for celebration.

It had been a raucous bunch that had entered the canal

that morning, but that had given way quickly to the awe of moving through the greatest technological achievement of the Victorian Age, the massive system of locks and pulleys, a marvel that had yet to be improved upon. And the nine-mile-long Gaillard Cut through the heart of the Continental Divide was an engineering feat the likes of which hasn't been attempted since. Unfortunately the canal had also been the burial ground for its builders, thousands perishing from malaria and yellow fever. The French had been the first to attempt the dig. Two out of three of its many thousands of workers died before the project was ultimately abandoned.

It was always the same with Justice. He looked at the Pyramids and saw the suffering of slave labor, visited the Great Wall and saw nothing but the workers buried within its massive bulk. Apparently "civilization" was not possible without construction. Somehow he missed the point.

"So much water gets pumped in and out of here," Kim said.

"Believe it or not," Justice replied, "they pump through fifty-two millions gallons of fresh water for every ship that passes the locks."

"Where does it all come from?"

"Nine hard months of rain a year," he said, "and gravity to pull it down here."

A sharp horn blast sounded, the signal that the lock had drained to the proper level.

"Here we go," Justice said, feeling the excitement rising within him. He looked at Kim. "It's show time."

The woman smiled and, standing on tiptoes, kissed him lightly on the lips. "I'm ready," she said.

The massive lock gates began to swing slowly open, each one, laid on its side, taller than the Eiffel Tower. He looked starboard; the small train, the *mule* that had towed them through the canal, had started up, the towline growing taut as it moved down the steep incline and pulled them toward the gates.

"All right!" he heard from behind, Jenks bounding up from belowdecks, followed by the others, all of them trading the bright yellow slickers they had worn during the trip for sport clothes. Jenks walked up and slapped him on the back.

"Man, I don't know. Not sure anymore whether or not I'll be able to walk on something that ain't movin'."

"How're you and Jorge getting along?" Justice asked.

"Fuck Jorge," Jenks said. "He ain't had two good words to say the whole damned trip. He's just a holier-than-thou shit as far as I can see."

"That's what I like about you, Bob," Justice replied, smiling. "You're so nonjudgmental."

Jenks spit over the side of the boat. "Life's too short to spend with assholes," he said.

"I'm going to go below and change," Kim said, moving off.

"Change into a man," Prince Kiki called to her as she hurried aft and disappeared below. He was dressed all in white, looking almost like an American sailor except for the wide-brimmed hat and blue topsiders he wore.

"Looking good, Your Majesty," Justice called to him, the man smiling wide and turning a full circle as he walked fore, nearly losing his footing and falling overboard, Sardi right behind to help steady him.

"I wish to dress in the style and custom of the native population," Kiki said proudly, Justice not having the heart to tell him he wasn't even close.

As the two men joined him, he saw Vanderhoff standing aft, his back to them, smoking a cigarette.

"Ah," Sardi said. "Our companion."

Justice turned and looked forward. The lock had opened, giving them a view of the large passenger liner they had played tag with the entire trip through the canal. The ship was a huge one, the words *Norwegian Princess* painted on the hull just above the waterline aft. The *Princess* had a mule pulling it, too, and not one canal pilot, but four. Every ship, even warships, passing through the canal had to abide by the same rules.

"Are you doing all right?" Sardi asked him low, so no one else could hear.

"Don't worry about it," Justice replied too quickly, Sardi turning slowly to stare at him. "It's just another job, that's all."

"That's not true, and you know it," the man said. "Everything you were is buried here. Just remember the new man, not the old one."

"I have to put them together sometime," Justice answered as he watched the gates slide past them, the open channel that now faced them their brief remaining passage to Panama Bay.

"Don't close yourself off, William."

"I won't," Justice said, but he knew what Sardi was getting at. His agitation had increased with every wave that had broken upon the *Lutine*'s bow, with every trade wind that had blown him closer to his destiny. Sleep had been fitful, the dreams more real. He felt like a high-wire performer who, having fallen and broken his back, was having to climb back up and face the same wire again lest he lose the heart for it.

It was all a question of heart. A man either had it or he didn't. The world was run by people with heart. Everyone else existed to serve. Life was that simple.

"Meester Lambert!" the pilot called from the wheel, and Justice turned to see him waving.

He left Sardi and Jenks, moving back along the port gunwales that all of them had walked often enough in the black of night that they could do it now with eyes closed. The pilot, a mestizo, was smiling as he approached.

"This is fine vessel," he said. "You come down here to race?"

"Just sightseeing, Mr. Garcia," Justice said. "Should we unfurl the sails?"

The man frowned and shook his head. "Only a few miles to Thatcher Ferry Bridge," he said, pointing off the port at the small fishing village of Balboa. "My country much troubled. Not good for sightseeing now."

Justice reached into his back pocket and pulled out his wallet. "I haven't been here for ten years," he said, then searched through the wallet, pulling out a hundred, American. The dollar was accepted as currency everywhere in Panama. "I hear the Canal Zone is different now, too."

The man eyed the bill. "Everywhere trouble," he said. "The *nationales* hate the *élites* in their American towns, want control of everything yesterday, you understand?"

"Yes, I do," Justice replied, handing the man the hundred. "I really appreciate the job you've done. Do you live in Panama City?"

Garcia shook his head. "Colón."

"Well maybe this will help you get through the long night," Justice said, nodding toward the money.

The man shrugged. "Do yourself favor, Meester Lambert," he said. "Stay in Panama City, don't go to interior. Leave soon. This no good for you."

Justice laughed. "I wish I had a dollar for everybody who ever told me that," he said, then watched the man's eyes go wide. He turned to see Kim come up from below, dressed in an extremely low-cut white sundress and matching floppy hat. She moved up and took his arm.

"Do I look like the concubine of rich American businessman?" she asked huskily.

"Call it girlfriend," he said. "Americans are genteel about their labels. Go fore. I want to talk to all of you."

The woman moved along awkwardly in her heeled sandals, the hot wind billowing her dress up around her legs, nearly driving the pilot crazy. Justice moved past him, walking up to Vanderhoff, who had just chucked his cigarette overboard and was watching it float away from them.

"Hot enough for you?" he asked the man, who turned to him slowly, thoughtfully.

"I dreamed we all died last night," he said, eyes half-lidded, soporific.

Justice grunted. "Probably wishful thinking after the way you handled the crossing," he said.

Vanderhoff smiled despite himself. "I'm more the mountainous type," he said.

"Good," Justice replied. "Then you should enjoy the last leg of our journey. How about heading fore? I want to talk to all of you."

The man nodded curtly and walked off, dressed as usual in a loose-fitting suit, his topsiders the only concession to conditions at sea.

Justice turned once more to the pilot. "Mr. Garcia," he said. "Do we drop you at the bridge?"

The man nodded and waved, his eyes still fixed on Kim. Justice moved up to join the group. They were all unusual people, accustomed to privacy and control over their own lives. Despite the personality clashes that always characterized a dynamic group, they had handled life in closed quarters well enough. And if camaraderie wasn't the right word to describe their condition, working as a team was. It was a start.

He stood before them, looking at the people who had agreed to enter his nightmare with him as they stood or sat on deck, Kiki, as was his custom, smiling widely as if life itself were some huge, laughable irony.

"We're here," he said. "You've come with me out of loyalty alone. I don't intend to let you down. We have been drawn here by devious minds for desperate purposes, but we have intelligence and insight and talent, and will prevail. Remember our cover. I'm a rich bastard, taking my racing yacht and crew out for a little excursion. . . ."

"How about that?" Jenks laughed. "Will'um's playin' himself."

"We're staying at the Hotel Continental," Justice continued. "Sardi, Kim, and I will be staying in an upstairs suite. The rest of you will have single rooms. And yes, Bob, they do have a state-operated casino."

"Why are we so out front?" Vanderhoff asked. "Wouldn't it be better not to call attention to ourselves?"

"We're going to go at it head-on, partner," Justice said. "Straight up, straight out."

"Whoo-ee!" Jenks shouted.

"I *want* to attract as much attention as we can," Justice said. "That's the only way to flush out everything into the open."

"What do you mean by everything?" Kim asked.

"If I knew that, I wouldn't need to flush it out," Justice replied. "Remember, the entire country may be our enemy." He shook his head. "Hell of a way to make a living."

"You can say that again," Jenks replied, pointing off the port bow.

They were sliding past Albrook Air Base, United States territory for as long as there was a canal to defend. The entire ten-mile-wide Canal Zone had once been a U.S. possession, but all that had been turned back to the Panamanians in the 1977 treaty, of which the death of Volcán Barú had played a part; but the U.S. still had the rights in perpetuity to "defend the neutrality" of the canal. Justice wondered exactly how that would really work out in times of war.

At the moment the streets around the outskirts of the base were filled with thousands of chanting protesters, banners waving, their voices floating across the waters of the canal like human thunder, and maybe that's what it was. They wanted the Americans out. They wanted the canal for themselves. Life was a continual negotiation between those who had and those who wanted, with violence the unit of currency.

It was always violence. The only difference Justice could see between Man and the animals of the jungle was the symmetry of the dwelling—civilization once again defined as construction. His father had preached from the Bible about what Jesus had called whited sepulchres—monuments beautiful on the outside, filled with the rotted decay of death within. Maybe it was civilization *he* was talking about.

The surroundings had become familiar to Justice, and with the familiarity came the feelings of rage. He had been to Albrook many times, had gotten drunk with Merriman in its officers' club the night he'd told him about his progress with the people of Volcán Barú, and about the drugs that had been stored. When he'd seen the man's eyes light up, he'd assumed it was from indignation. It was only long afterward that he'd realized he'd been looking into the heart of pure greed.

"Towboat!" Vanderhoff called, a rowboat oaring gently toward them from the edge of the channel, just before it widened to the bay. A hundred yards ahead of them, the canal pilots were being lowered into a similar boat by bos'n's chair, deckhands throwing down the towlines a hundred feet above. Since the completion of the canal in 1913, the routine had never varied. Rowboats always brought out the towlines and pilots, and returned for same at the end of the journey, fifty miles later.

"Your ride's here!" Justice called back to the pilot, Garcia waiting until Sardi hurried back to the wheel before walking away from it.

The man hurried fore, all smiles, probably getting creative with his thinking about what he could do with a C-note fifty miles from home. He walked up to Justice, shaking hands warmly. "Immigration docks starboard," he said, pointing. "Right near the bridge. You'll need passports, passenger and cargo manifests."

"We're carrying no cargo," Justice said.

The man smiled a tiny smile, then looked overboard, watching how low they rode in the water. He straightened and shrugged. "Immigration people very stupid," he said, pointing to his head. "American passports give you free passage. . . ."

"Our passports aren't American," Justice answered.

"Then you need visa," the man said, then rubbed his thumb across his fingers in the universal gesture. "This is what you need for visa, understand?"

"Loud and clear," Justice said, helping the man over the side and into the rowboat, a swarthy mestizo with a slash mouth and thin mustache giving him a hand on the other end.

The oarsman pushed off immediately, Garcia waving as he receded. "Good luck," he called, his face frozen between a smile and a frown.

Justice turned to call back to Sardi. "Follow the *Princess* to the docks," he said through cupped hands; Sardi waved and, expertly spinning the wheel, took them in on inboard power.

Thatcher Bridge loomed ahead, large, spanning the canal. It was also called the bridge of the Americas and was the point of origin of the Pam American Highway traveling west. It was the route that he and Merriman had taken the last time he'd been here.

Sardi took them into port, the Pacific, up that day, raising them almost to the level of the small craft docks. They were slipping among a number of yachts and sailboats, fitting in. Fifty yards distant, at a large pier, the *Norwegian Princess* was still trying to get tied down, the mammoth ship dwarfing them to insignificance.

Jorge and Bob Jenks got them secured, Justice and Kim climbing the three rungs up the ladder to dockside. A military jeep was racing down the dock toward them, skidding to a stop twenty-five feet away. A Panamanian National Guardsman, a captain, jumped out of the jeep and strode resolutely toward them.

"Looks like the fuzz," Kim said in a put-on American accent.

"And he looks unhappy," Justice replied, reaching into his back pocket and pulling out the manifest and passports.

The driver of the jeep got out of it slowly, an American Canal Zone policeman, and ambled toward them.

The captain was a small man, of slight build and light complexion. His eyes were small and too close together, and his lips wore a permanent pucker and frown lines. He seemed to move, even to breathe, in agitation. "You cannot land here," he said quickly when he reached them. "You must untie your lines and shove off."

"Now, what's the problem, General?" Justice said, keeping his voice casual. "Did I do something wrong?"

"At Colón, when you paid passage, you listed your passport as being from a country called Haven," the man said, shaking his head in short, jerky motions. "We do not have records of any such country. You'll have to..."

"Well, just the same," Justice said, handing him the small stack of passports. "That's where we're from. See here? You from the interior, General?"

"I'm a captain, Mr. . . . Lambert," the man said as he shuffled through the passports before coming to Justice's. The American had stopped a short distance from the proceedings and seemed to be enjoying himself. He smiled and shook his head every time the captain jerked his body, which he seemed to do often. "And this makes no difference. We recognize no such country. You cannot be allowed into Panama without a valid passport unless you are a United States citizen."

Justice cocked his head. "Well, that seems pretty final, all right," he said, watching as another jeep came rolling down the pier, this one full of Panamanian soldiers. "Did you say you were from Almirante?"

The man stopped vibrating and looked up in surprise. "Close... I'm from Bocas del Toro, across the channel." The men in the jeep behind were climbing onto the dock, small assault rifles slung over their shoulders. The captain darkened again. "Now you will kindly untie and leave port. Now."

"You know," Justice said, putting an arm around Kim, who smiled sweetly at the captain, "I own some businesses in Bocas del Toro. Got a fishing fleet and a hatchery and a pretty big cannery. Own some land there, too. What did you say your family name was?"

The man just glared at him.

"Why that's Captain Ortiz," the American said, grinning through a west Texas accent.

"Now, Captain Ortiz," Justice said. "I'll be needing visas for myself and my whole crew. A month would be sufficient, I think."

"You must leave port now!" Ortiz said loudly, then motioned behind him, the men with the guns moving up closer. Justice looked down, the others stood on deck just below—waiting.

"Sure," Justice said amiably, turning to Kim. "Let's go, darling." He moved to the ladder, then stopped, turning. "You know, I believe I have an Ortiz working for me at the cannery. Now...what's his name...Guillermo, that's it. Guillermo Ortiz, he's my plant manager. Any relation to you, Captain?"

The man swallowed hard. "My uncle," he said low.

Justice walked away from the ladder, smiling in turn at each of the soldiers. He'd noticed that the American cop had walked off and was talking on the two-way in his jeep. "Isn't it a small world?" he asked. "I want to tell you, Captain, that your uncle is one of my best workers. I'll just bet he's a real mainstay for your whole family." He laughed loudly. "Hell, I pay him enough to support any six families. Next time I talk with him, I'll tell him that we met. A shame it couldn't be under better circumstances."

He looked hard at the man, his agitation growing.

"I'll bet a *lot* of your relatives work for me or live in some of my housing," Justice said; this time he kept his face hard, playing body language with the man.

Captain Ortiz took a long breath, looked down at the passports, then smiled widely. "Welcome to Panama, Mr. Lambert," he said. "It is a great honor to meet the owner of Lambert Enterprises. Did you say that thirty days would be enough? We could extend it to sixty, if that would be more convenient."

"Thirty's fine," Justice said, smiling. "Where can we get some transportation?"

The man initialed the passports, then handed them back. He pointed to a long building at the end of the pier. "Take these through Immigration. They will give you your visa.

Because of the arrival of the passenger boat, a great deal of surface transport will be available."

"That's a pretty long walk with our luggage," Kim said, Justice chuckling. "Do you think your big, strong boys could help us with the bags and give us a lift?"

Ortiz jerked as if he'd been slapped, then looked at Justice who was holding up another hundred. "For your trouble," he said, and within ten minutes the jeeps had been loaded with luggage and people, driven to Immigration, and unloaded again.

They flew through Immigration, just beating hundreds of passengers from the *Princess* and soon found themselves in a Hotel Continental shuttle bus, waiting for a full load to take across the bridge.

It was hot in the small bus, stuffy, Justice wiping dust off the inside of the window to get a look out. Nothing much had changed here in the last decade. It was still small-town America transplanted to a foreign shore, the fantasy life that expatriates build to keep their worlds intact. But there were palm trees, too, and a sweltering sun and ghettos for the descendants of West Indian blacks who'd built the canal. And soon they'd go by the ruins of Old Panama, destroyed by Henry Morgan, the pirate, in 1671. They'd pass through the neighborhoods of the élite, the pretend American royalty that lorded it over the country, and drive through the squalor of Panama City to reach the splendor of the Hotel Continental. The haves and the wants.

"Bill Lambert!" came a startled voice, Justice looking up to see a familiar face standing in the aisle.

"Good God," he said, standing and extending a hand. "Ed Barkes. What the hell brings you all the way down here?"

"Billy!" screeched a young woman from behind Barkes. She shoved past the older man, breaking the handshake to throw herself into Justice's arms, her heavy gold chains and bracelets jangling like a tinker's cart. He rolled his eyes over her shoulder, the man smiling back through crystal-clear blue eyes. He was lean and hard and didn't look a day of his seventy-eight years.

"Marti and I are on our way to Rio," he said. "You know... something different."

"Are you going to introduce me?" Kim said from the seat beside, her left eyebrow arched high on her forehead.

"Sorry," Justice said, forcibly extricating himself from Marti Barkes and her ton of jewelry. "Ed and Marti Barkes, this is my friend, Kim Bouvier. It was Ed who taught me how to sail in Lake Michigan a number of years ago."

"Charmed," Kim said.

Barkes smiled easily at Kim. "I didn't so much teach him as turn him loose. Though it didn't seem to stick. He won the cup, then retired from competition." He looked at Justice. "We haven't seen your like since, my friend."

"Nobody's *ever* seen anything like Billy," Marti Barkes sighed, her husband shaking his head, smiling just a touch.

"You'll be happy to know, then," Justice said, "that we're down here with the *Lutine*, getting the cobwebs out."

The old man nodded happily. "A ship like that needs to be exercised, pampered like a beautiful woman," he said, looking at Marti. His voice turned sad. "We've missed you, Bill. Where have you been keeping yourself?"

"I live on an island," Justice said. "Guess I've gotten kind of reclusive."

"Come on, let's go!" came a voice from behind, and he could see that they were blocking up the aisle.

"You staying at the Continental?" Justice asked.

"Just for tonight," Barkes said. "We leave tomorrow morning."

"How about dinner?"

"Yes!" Marti said.

Barkes shrugged. "There you have it, Bill. The boss has spoken." They began to move on, toward the back, everybody waving as they passed down the aisle, Marti blowing him a kiss.

He sat back down and looked at Kim.

"Billy," the woman spat, imitating Marti Barkes. "Billy. You old enough to be her father and he old enough to be her grandfather. Shame on you, bad man."

Justice smiled and patted her hand. "Lighten up, darling," he said. "We're on vacation, remember?"

She frowned, looking once down the aisle. "Barracudas don't take vacations," she said.

He could hear Jenks laughing from farther back. He had

struck up a conversation with one of the women from the cruise ship and was in the process of sincerely explaining to her all the details of some imaginary adventures.

The bus filled slowly, a young mestizo boy in shorts and a dirty white shirt slipping on with everyone else and standing in the front, peering intently at all the passengers. Justice watched him because he seemed to be looking for something. Just then the driver came up the steps and chased the boy off, Justice observing through the dirty window as the boy scurried across the black asphalt parking lot to a red Mercedes sports car with dark-tinted windows. He watched the boy knock on the driver's window, which came down only far enough for him to reach in and take something from the unseen driver.

"You ever sleep with her?" Kim pouted from the seat beside.

"Ed is one of my dearest friends," Justice said. "I wouldn't..."

"You tell me truth," she said, taking his arm hard, digging her nails into his flesh. "You sleep with girl?"

Justice looked her straight in the eyes and smiled. "None of your business," he said, then yelped as she dug her nails in farther.

The bus roared to life, starting off with a jerk. They circled the parking lot once, then drove off, taking the short block to the bridge entry and starting across. Before they were halfway across the bridge, Vanderhoff was beside him, down on one knee, his voice lowered.

"William," he said softly, "I think we're being followed by a jeep full of Canal Zone police."

Justice nodded. "I know," he said. "They're not the ones who interest me, though. It's the red Mercedes behind them that I wonder about."

Vanderhoff narrowed his eyes and stood, looking back through the window of the back emergency door. "Are you finished flushing yet?" he asked.

"I've just begun," Justice said. "Welcome to the hornets' nest."

VIII.

DALLAS, TEXAS
12 AUGUST 1978—1105 HOURS

Will Justice lay, eyes closed, trying to visualize the bullet lodged in his spine—.45 cal, 3.2 ounces of lead, flattened by shattering contact with his clavicle and reflattened by its angled burrow into the gristle of his spinal cord. He pictured it as a tiny heart, beating within him, wanting to help him. Lead, he reasoned, conducted electricity, and what was his spine except electrical conduits lined in sync? He intended for the bullet to help make him whole again, backing his intention by hours of visualization day in and day out.

He was chucking medical science, starting from scratch. He had obtained the records from nearly a hundred mental institutions, checking death rates and causes, and had come to the inescapable conclusion that the mentally retarded died from different causes than their "normal" counterpoints. He had seen in supposedly normal people a sudden deterioration of body and mind when exposed to a negative diagnosis by a medical "expert." And in study after study, he kept coming up with the fact that people controlled their own bodies, life and death, with their mind. Cancer is nearly unheard of in mental hospitals—the patients simply don't understand the concept and refuse to give it substance.

How much the human animal controls its own body with its mind! How incredible the power of suggestion to people when they feel they are hearing the advice of an expert,

112

someone who knows what they don't know! It was all there in the mind. It was the place where God dwelled, and God could do anything, even heal paralysis—especially heal paralysis.

And so he visualized the bullet, visualized it as a healing instrument instead of a destructive one. He would be the God of his own mind. He would dispel his own doubts and make his wishes real. He would control the world of his body and force it to respond. He would . . .

"Yeah . . . Bill," came the voice in his head, breaking his concentration. He opened his eyes, reaching up from his hospital bed to adjust the volume on the telephone headset he wore. All around him the small medical clinic he had bought gleamed antiseptic white, a slight ammonia smell still lingering, but evident only to his heightened sense of smell.

"What's it look like, Ed?" he asked. "Did you find those companies I asked you about?"

The man hesitated only slightly before answering, and Justice knew that he would get an honest appraisal. He'd stumbled upon Ed Barkes by chance while looking for brokers, and the man, already retired, had just been too honest and straightforward to let off the hook. "They're on the New York boards," Barkes said, "but they haven't moved in a year and a half. I mean, I know that the Japs have whipped up on the car market, but the electronics have evened out, I think."

"Look, I did some research," Justice said, " and I really believe that the next big pull is going to be in the area of home videotape."

"People can't afford that shit, Bill, I . . ."

"Just listen to me," Justice said. "Hear me out. The cost of home video will go down quickly as soon as more people get into the act and start buying it. That, plus what the Japanese are doing with integrated circuits and microchips, makes this the best buy I've ever seen. The damned things will just keep getting smaller and cheaper. Look, if the technology takes off, everybody over here is going to have to go to Japan to get their tape players made anyway. We simply don't have the production facilities over here because we farm everything out to them already."

"IBM is still good," Barkes said. "Why don't you just stick with that if you're interested in electronics?"

"Because I'm speculating, dammit!" Justice said loudly. "Speculating on the future. Isn't that what it's all about?"

"You said you've done research?" Barkes asked.

"I'll tell you the truth, my friend," Justice replied. "I did more homework than you can imagine. I've got my whole life riding on this, and I'll tell you that I can't afford to take a bath on it. I'm *sure* of this one."

There was a quick knock on the door, Allie entering a minute later wearing a gray wig, old-lady makeup and a bulky dress. She was holding a social security card in the air. "I've got it!" she mouthed silently, pointing to the card. Justice waved her over to the bed.

"I've never done this before," Barkes said, "but you're a persuasive man. I'll not only buy you into those microprocessor companies, but I'm going to put a bundle of my own scratch down on it. I hope you know what you're talking about."

"I do," Justice said. "But even if I didn't, I wouldn't feel responsible for *your* investments."

Barkes chuckled. "I guess you can't buy security," he said.

"Ain't no such animal," Justice said. "Everything's transitory. And on that subject, I have a confession to make. You remember I gave you my social security number a couple of weeks ago when we started all this?"

"Sure."

"Well, I was mistaken. I thought I remembered the number, but I didn't. I just found it . . . you want the real number?"

"Of course I do."

Justice read him the number, then handed the card back to Allie, who had taken off the wig and was shaking out her red hair. "We're going to be spending a lot of time on the phone in the next few weeks," he said. "I think the Repubs are going to win in eighty, and I want to invest heavily in armament manufacturers for a couple of years. I also want to get out of dollars. I think the Republican answer to the balance of trade will be to let the dollar drop worldwide."

"Not in a million years," Barkes said incredulously. "The strong dollar is what holds this country together."

"That's certainly the conventional wisdom," Justice said, winking at Allie, who was lighting the room like sunshine in cutoff blue jeans and a bright red halter top as she shucked the dress she wore over them. "We'll work on that. Talk to your chums at Fed, okay? Gotta go, Ed. See you."

He reached out his hand without pain and shut down the phone at the source on the nightstand beside him. He pulled off the headset and looked at Allie. "No trouble?" he asked.

She shrugged, wiping at the makeup on her face with a large towel. "I used the dummy IDs you had made for me and just walked into the social security office and told them my retarded son was getting his first job, and I needed to help him with a social security card. None of this has been difficult since getting the duplicate birth certificate from the name on the tombstone."

"Good," he said. "Next we'll need credit cards, library cards . . . I really want to build a life for Mr. William Lambert. Besides, I need to have all this to take the test for my real estate license."

"Real estate!"

"There's only so much land, Allie," he said. "That's where the real value lies. Wipe the mascara off your nose."

"You're doing all right," she said, narrowing her eyes and flicking the towel over her nose. "You've already begun to have some luck with your investments. Why push it?"

He turned dark. "You don't want to hear me say it."

"You've been having nightmares again, haven't you?" she asked.

"It's my problem," he answered.

"You're my patient," she said. "Your mental attitudes are as much my problem as yours. And if you continue to eat yourself up with hate, all of this will come to nothing. Now, let's roll you over. It's time for your range of motion."

He dutifully allowed her to pull down the covers and begin the laborious task of rolling him over. At least he was able to help her with his good arm somewhat. Somewhere off in another part of the clinic he could hear Jan, her mother, singing tunelessly. "I saw the bullet today," he said, flopping over on his stomach. "I mean really saw it in there. I think it's in a pretty good place."

"Don't get too caught up in that," she said as she went

over his back and pulled down his pajama pants to check for developing bedsores, his worst problem at the moment. "You're just setting yourself up for disappointment."

"I thought that health care professionals were supposed to encourage their patients," he pleaded.

"Teaching them to face reality is what we do," she said. "Oh damn. We're going to need to take these pants off for a while. You're getting a bad rash around the band."

"Whose reality?" he asked as she slipped his pants off. "I've been learning about a lot of different kinds in the last couple of months, and it seems as if everybody makes his own, including doctors and including nurses."

"William," she said sternly. "Severed spinal cords don't heal themselves. Get used to it. You've made a wonderful life for yourself here, and you're astounding me with your ability to make money. Be satisfied with who, with *what*, you are." She began bending his left leg at the knee, flexing it, working the hamstring to keep it from constricting. He wondered why she went to so much trouble if he wasn't going to walk again.

"I'm sorry," he said, "but I won't accept it and I won't get used to it and I won't be satisfied with it. I don't believe you or the medical establishment. *I* choose my reality, and it will come to pass."

"Damn, you're pigheaded," she said.

"I'm just trying to survive as some sort of a man," he said, too loud. "Can't you understand that? I'm not going to live my life in this fucking clinic."

She looked at him for a long moment, then sighed. "What am I going to do with you?" she asked.

"Just stay with me," he whispered, choking up. "Please just don't leave me."

"Oh, Will," she said, her own voice husky with emotion. "You're so torn apart by so many feelings. Sometimes I think you're a nasty old man, and sometimes you're just a scared little boy. I'm not going anywhere. I work here, remember?"

"How could I forget?" he said, sniffling, regaining control. "You're the best deal I ever made."

She began working the other leg, massaging the calf muscles. "Mother seems to be adjusting well to her new surroundings," she said. "She keeps thinking she's visiting someone in the hospital and can't remember who. But it keeps her happy somehow, almost as if being healthy in a hospital is a kind of power over sickness, or death."

She moved down and began to work on his feet, massaging and bending at the ankles.

"I think I feel something down there," he said.

"No, you don't," she replied. "How's your bladder been working since we took the catheter out?"

"Fine, Mommy," he said. "I can pee with the best of them now."

"Don't get tacky. It looks like your wounds are pretty well healed back here, though you look kind of like a road map with all the scars. Bet you can't wait to show all that off to the other boys."

"Now, don't you get tacky," he replied. "I think I might need a little percussion."

"Good," she said. "Let's roll you over and see what's what."

They repeated the lengthy process of turning him onto his back, Allie forcing him into a sitting position, then pulling the bronchodilator off the nightstand and getting it into his mouth. "Okay," she said, sitting behind him and wrapping her arms around his stomach, "take deep breaths. I'll help you."

He breathed deeply, feeling the fluid in his lungs gurgling. The fear of pneumonia had been his biggest problem since the shooting, as fluid insisted on pooling in his lungs because of reduced respiration.

Halfway through the procedure he began gagging, Allie reaching up to jerk the respirator out of his mouth as he choked up the congestion. "Damn," he said between fits, weakness spreading through his whole body. "Why do I bother with this? I never..."

"Don't say it," she warned. "You're recovering well. Keep your spirits up. You've been to hell and back. It's going to take some time."

"You really think I'll be okay?" he asked, ashamed of the cowardice that raged through him at times like this.

"Sure you will," she replied, helping him to lie down again. "You have to. They take away my nurse's pin if you don't."

"Sometimes . . . it's so . . . difficult," he said, taking deep breaths, consigning the emotion to his mind's back alleys.

"I know," she said quietly and began to massage his arms. "Is feeling still increasing in the left arm?"

"A little more every day," he said, not telling her about the pain, always the pain.

"Things could be a lot worse," she said. "At least you'll have good, usable arms."

"Not enough," he replied. "I want *everything* to work. Everything, Allie."

"I know," she said, and moved down to his legs.

He stared straight up at the ceiling, taking ragged breaths, trying to build emotional scar tissue around his heart so he could stifle self-doubts. And then, in a small, surprised voice from far away, he heard her say, "Well . . ."

"What is it, I . . ." He looked down at her as she worked his naked leg, amazed to see his penis erect, rock hard and bouncing against his stomach with the movement.

She quickly moved up to face him. "It doesn't mean anything," she said, face pained. "It's simply a reflex spasm, like the severe muscle contractions you had a month ago."

"It may be a reflex to you, but it's a hard-on to me," he said excitedly. "I didn't think this could happen again."

"It's not happening," she said. "It's just a muscle spasm."

"Listen to you!" he said excitedly. "Let's talk reality. You're standing here denying that I've got an erection when it's obvious that I do!"

"I'm *not* denying it," she said angrily, then turned and grabbed his penis. "See? I know the goddamned thing's there, I'm just saying it doesn't mean anything."

"It means I'm horny, for Christ's sake!"

"It just means that the equipment still works, that's all."

"How do we know it works until we try it out?" he said, smiling wickedly.

She released him, jumping back with wide eyes. "What are you suggesting?" she said, horrified.

"Look," he said. "You're a young, healthy woman. You've locked yourself in here with me for two months, no dates, no friends. Hell, you've got to have an itch, it's only natural. And honey, for once in my life I'm in the right place at the right time."

She turned her back to him. "That wouldn't be ethical," she said.

"Dear God," he pleaded. "Don't you know how much I've suffered thinking I'd never be a man again? What if I never get it up after this?"

She turned and walked back to him, leaning down and kissing him gently on the mouth. "You don't understand," she said. "You wouldn't feel anything. There'd be no pleasure, no sensation at all. It wouldn't do anything for you."

"It'd make me feel like a man," he said, his voice breaking. "Please Allie. I know that it would be too much to think that you c-could have any . . . feelings about me. You're so beautiful and I'm . . . I'm . . ."

"You're one of the most wonderful men I've ever known," she said. "And it hasn't got anything to do with that. In fact . . . the opposite's the problem."

"You mean . . . ?"

"I'm your nurse, Will. It just wouldn't be right."

He looked at her, his eyes sinking deeply into hers as he tried to pour out all his frustrations and feelings in the eye contact alone, desperate to let her know exactly how he felt and knowing it couldn't be done with words.

She stared back at him for a long moment, her lips trembling. She took one look down the length of his body before returning to his eyes. "God help me," she whispered.

"Kiss me again," he said. "Make it a good one."

With only slight hesitation she leaned over him, kissing him deeply on the mouth, her lips soft and yielding, his hard and insistent. The sensuous contact jolted him like electricity, his heightened senses sharp and aware. The kiss lingered, progressed, and she relaxed against him, her hand gently caressing his chest.

"Oh my," she whispered once, breaking the contact, then went right back at it again, his right hand coming up to stroke her hair. His hand slid down her neck, touching her lightly, Justice reveling in the contact. His fingers found the knot that held her halter together and untied it, pulling the material down and exposing her pale, pendulous breasts.

He fondled her, her large nipples hot points against his palm as she began to moan down deep in her throat and move slightly against the bed.

Breaking the kiss he stared into her eyes. "Take your pants off," he whispered, voice hoarse. "Straddle my face."

She straightened, her pale complexion flushed deep red with excitement. She quickly shinnied out of her clothes, more beautiful than he had imagined, and climbed up on the bed with him, her hand reaching back to stroke his erection for just a minute before she moved up his body and knelt over his face.

He pulled her down slowly to this mouth, drinking in her smell, smiling at the heat and wetness there. And he kissed her vagina, long and slow, moving the tongue in and out, just as he had done when he kissed her mouth. Her moans turned quickly to grunts as she moved herself against him.

Somewhere inside he realized that she'd been saving herself for him, not consciously, not knowingly. Somewhere deep inside she was so emotionally tied to his lot in life that she was unable to do anything but empathetically live his celibate life-style with him. This was the coming out for both of them.

"Oh God," she whispered loudly, her hips bucking against his face, and he had to force himself away from her to speak.

"Take me inside," he said. "Please . . . now."

She stared at him with glassy eyes for a moment, too lost to comprehend, then she shook her head and slid back down his body, squealing as she sank down onto his rigid staff. She sat quietly upon him for a moment, eyes closed, biting her lower lip. Then she began to rock, slowly, dragging it out.

At first there was no sensation for him, no bodily hint that he was sharing such intimacy with a woman he cared about so deeply. He closed his eyes, listening to her guttural growls, and pictured his spine, pictured the bullet lodged there. With his mind he traced an electrical pattern through the bullet, an erotic pattern right to the brain. He traced it across the bullet over and over.

She was moving faster, her breath coming in great, sobbing gasps as she let out pent-up denial and frustration. He desperately retraced the electrical patterns of the bullet, willing himself to feel, demanding performance from his ravaged body.

And as she screamed through the final seconds of her

release, he felt it. It build slowly within him, an anticipation, a pushing toward something. The feeling built, the need for release becoming desperate. That the equipment would work was not the issue. *Feeling* the equipment work was.

She fell across him, her orgasm a jolt to her denied system and he heard himself groan loudly, his hips bucking just the slightest touch with his release as he emptied himself into her, a wave of satisfaction cresting both physically and mentally through him.

She lay crushed against his chest for a moment, their loins still united, breathing hard. Then she rose on her elbows and stared uncomprehending into his eyes. "You *felt* that, didn't you?" she said in awe.

He was smiling, his lips straining involuntarily across his teeth as the tears streamed out of his eyes and rolled down his face. "I really did, Allie," he said. "God in heaven, I really did."

She began to roll off him, but he held her fast. "Not yet," he said.

She smiled. "Fine with me," she said, and sat up, his eyes and mind filled with her beauty. She shook her head at him. "You know that what just happened is impossible."

"Nothing's impossible," he said. "Impossibility is a word invented by a closed mind. I can and I will control my reality." Her face had taken on an odd, almost frightened look as she stared at him. "What's wrong?"

"What kind of a man are you?" she asked. "These kinds of things don't happen in real life."

"Get used to it," he said. "They're going to happen more and more often now that I have the confidence to do it right."

But the expression never left her face, and he knew that she was finally beginning to believe his dreams and accept his reality. It was happening, just as he knew it could happen. Anything—*anything*—could be his. He'd crossed the pale, had defied logic and scientific reality, to re-form life in *his* image. The world was now his for the taking.

"Oooh," she said, eyes widening.

"What is it?" he asked.

She smiled, kittenish. "Something is growing big again inside me," she said, wiggling her eyebrows. "Guess I'll have to do my nursely duty one more time."

Slowly she began to rise and lower herself on him as he reached out his good hand to massage her breasts. He needed a couple more things to really get rolling again. One would be a plastic surgeon to change him just slightly. The other would be a gun. She'd get the doctor for him, but the other he'd have to take care of himself. He'd have to work something out.

But that was no big deal.

IX.

PANAMA CITY—HOTEL CONTINENTAL
18 FEBRUARY 1988—2330 HOURS

Justice leaned his chair back on two legs and puffed gently on the long green cigar. He didn't inhale, he just rolled the smoke into a ball in his mouth and eased it back out again as he listened to Kim hold open court right there in El Pescador restaurant. The hotel's formal dining room spread around them, all white linen and tinkling crystal, but to-night's crowd was being treated to a little more than polite dinner conversation.

Kim sat up on her chair back, her shimmery blue Bill Blass original gown jammed between her widespread legs, her three-inch heels balanced on the chair seat, ripping at the fabric as she told her story in punctuated rhythm, her dark eyes set deep, staring intently at nothing.

". . . So he punched me in the mouth . . . *Bam!* Then he did it again . . . *Bam!* I mean I tell you I was bleedin' like some fucking pig . . . and he picks me up and *throws* me down on the table . . . *Bam!*"

Justice smiled over at Ed Barkes, the man saluting with his own cigar and smiling in enjoyment at the kind of time only William Justice could have given him. The remnants of dinner lay scattered on the table, most of Marti Barkes's untouched as she leaned up close to Kim, listening, horrified and enrapt. From the casino entrance at the far end of the huge room, the commotion that had started several minutes earlier continued unabated, several large bouncers hurrying in that direction even as Kim continued her story. Sardi hovered protectively around the table, refilling champagne glasses and refusing to let anyone else wait on Justice and his guests.

"Then he *jumps* up on the table with me," Kim said, reaching out to grab the champagne bottle from Sardi as he passed and tipping it to her lips, "and he said, 'You're mine now, you little bitch,' and he starts trying to fuck me right there."

She stopped talking, tilting the bottle way back and drinking deeply, the wine overspilling her mouth to drain down her chin.

"What'd you do?" Marti Barkes asked breathlessly, several more bouncers running past them toward the casino as two others were taken out, bleeding, one on a stretcher.

Kim looked at her, then wiped her mouth on the back of her hand, Sardi sneaking the bottle away from her and continuing with it around the table. "I reached up and grabbed that motherfucker by his fucking throat, and I told him, 'Ain't no fucking *Cuban* cock ever gonna go inside a' me!'"

She suddenly jumped up off the chair, her hand snaking out to grab a sterling silver knife on the table and raise it high in the air, a woman screaming from the other side of the room. "Then I pulled my K-bar out of my boot and I *nailed* that motherfucker's hand to the table!"

She brought the knife down hard on the tabletop, jamming it in halfway, Marti jumping back with a shriek as Justice and her husband laughed.

"My g-goodness!" Marti said, swallowing hard, a hand to her milk white chest. "Whatever did you do then?"

"What did I do then?" Kim whispered hoarsely, getting right down in the woman's face. "What did I do then?"

Marti nodded continually.

"Ha!" Kim said loudly, straightening. "Why then I went out and *got laid!*"

Kim and the men began laughing, Marti looking incredulously from one to the other, as people at the other tables applauded, Kim turning a complete circle and bowing deeply.

The commotion at the casino entrance had reached riot

proportions as more bouncers hurried by, Justice frowning and looking at his watch. It was awfully early for this. He motioned Sardi to him, the man bending his ear to Justice's mouth. "Go take care of that," he said, Sardi nodding and moving quickly off.

Justice watched him go, leaned up to knock ash off the cigar, and spoke to Barkes. "Glad to see you getting away like this, Ed," he told the man. "You always worked too hard."

"You know the consortium worries about you, Bill," the man replied. "We've had no direct word from you in years."

"You guys are doing a fine job with Lambert International," he replied. "You don't need me around checking up on you. Besides, there's nothing goes on that I don't know about."

Barkes took a long drag on the cigar, a small barrel of ash tumbling onto his white tuxedo jacket. "It's not that," he said. "Hell, Bill, we just *miss* you, that's all. This is the first exciting day I've had in four years."

Justice looked around. "What excitement?"

Barkes shook his head. "You need to think about rejoining the human race," he said. "It's been a long time since..."

"Don't say it," Justice said, his eyes flashing darkly. "Let's don't talk about it tonight."

Barkes frowned deeply, and Justice hated the sadness he saw in the man's eyes. There was going to be enough auld lang syne on this trip without asking for it.

The commotion in the casino had quieted, Marti leaning toward Justice and taking his hand. "Our lives are just plain dull without you around, Billy," she said breathlessly, bringing his hand to her chest and clutching it there.

"Billy," Kim mumbled gutturally, staring at the knife still vibrating in the tabletop. "Billy. Sound like Old MacDonald farm around here."

Justice extricated his hand and flicked ashes onto his plate. "I'm doing all right," he said sincerely. "Let's leave it at that."

"You're the boss," the man said.

Justice looked hard at him. "Yeah," he answered, harsh. An end to that line of conversation.

A crowd had poured out of the casino doorway and was

spilling into the dining room led by Sardi. They were carrying two squirming men above their heads.

"Some people just never get to have any fun," Barkes said, chuckling, as the crowd edged its way toward them.

The procession stopped at their table, Sardi shrugging helplessly at the sight of Bob Jenks and Kiki Anouweyah being carried away.

Jenks looked down at the table, his clothes torn up, blood running from his nose. "We could 'a' taken 'em Will'um," he said, words slurring slightly. "But we didn't want to hurt nobody, ain't that right, Kiki."

The prince looked down regally from his prone position. "That is correct, Robert," he said drunkenly. "We did not wish to hurt any of this fine, indigenous population. And call me Your Majesty, please." The prince smiled widely, then threw up all over his bearers.

"What should I do with them?" Sardi asked.

"Get them to their rooms," Justice said. "And pay all these nice people off."

"In American?"

"Give them Balboas," Justice answered. "We don't know how much longer the dollar will be used as currency here." He looked up at the human parcels. "See you in the morning, gentlemen."

"Bye-bye," Jenks called as the procession moved off, Jorge Vanderhoff passing the small parade without a look as he came in, moving in a direct line toward Justice's table.

"Looks like business," Barkes said, pointing to the man. "I'm beginning to think you're not as reclusive as you pretend to be."

"Sometimes you think too much, Ed," Justice returned, gesturing to a waiter for the check. "I'm the kind of guy your mother warned you about when you were young. Excuse me for just a minute."

Jorge moved up to the table, the knot on his tie slightly loose and askew, a detail that told Justice there was enough trouble brewing to shake the man. "My apologies for interrupting your dinner," he said, nodding curtly to the table.

"What's up?" Justice asked, Jorge leaning over near him to speak quietly.

"Things are going crazy," Vanderhoff said urgently. "I just checked on Noriega. The public information office says that he's gone for a month . . . doing an inspection tour of the western garrisons."

"Chiriquí," Justice said, feeling the noose tightening around his neck. "Volcán Barú."

"You've got an urgent message from Diamond Rock at the front desk," Vanderhoff continued. "You need to get in contact with them immediately."

The waiter walked up with the check, Justice signing it and adding a large tip. "What about the canal police?" he asked as the waiter walked away.

"Surveillance at all exits," Vanderhoff replied, shaking his head. "They don't want you out of their sights for some reason."

"Strange," Justice said. The cigar had turned stale in his mouth. He removed it and stubbed it out on his plate, a meal of fish from a country whose name, best translated, means "land of abundant fish." "How about the Mercedes?"

"Checked into the Hilton across the street," he said. "It's a woman. The name on the register is Alice Smith."

"Smith?"

The man shrugged. "Room two-thirteen," he said. "Has a balcony facing streetside."

"Same as us," Justice replied. "Interesting."

"The game is getting complicated, William," Vanderhoff said intensely. "I believe there are layers of meaning here that we don't know about."

Justice picked up his glass of champagne and took a sip. "Not yet we don't," he replied. "Maybe I can find a few answers out for myself."

"You need me?"

Justice shook his head. "Go to bed, Jorge. Get a good night's sleep. I appreciate your work tonight."

"I'd have done it anyway," he replied. "What does tomorrow bring?"

"Who knows?" He smiled at everyone at the table, then raised his glass high. "A toast," he said loudly. "To tomorrow, and to its surprises."

"Tomorrow!" everyone echoed, raising their glasses and drinking.

Vanderhoff straightened, his unlined face a mask. "Have a pleasant evening," he said politely. "Once again, my apologies for interrupting your dinner."

"He worries too much," Kim said, finishing her own glass and taking Justice's from him.

"Maybe *you* don't worry enough," Justice replied, taking the glass back from her and pouring it out in the ice bucket.

"So," Ed Barkes said genially. "Now that things have calmed down a touch, perhaps we should repair to the casino."

"Not for me," Justice said, standing. "I only bet on sure things. I probably need to turn in anyway."

Kim's eyes lit up. "Yeah," she said. "We need to turn in."

Justice moved over to shake hands with Barkes. "It's been great seeing you," he said. "Will you be around tomorrow?"

Barkes shook his head. "The *Princess* sails in the morning. I can't take *that* much time off. Thanks for jazzing up my life a little, Bill. That always was your strong suit."

Marti moved past her husband to throw herself into Justice's arms. "Please don't be a stranger," she said, then pulled his face down to hers, giving him a long kiss.

"Yeah," Kim said, walking up to Ed. "Don't be a stranger." She jammed the old man up close to her and kissed him deeply, moaning as she did, raising a leg to rub up and down the outside of his thighs.

When they parted, Barkes's face was sunset red, and his wife's was chalk white. They looked like a barber pole.

Kim picked up her handbag by its long strap and slung it over her shoulder. "Thank you for a lovely evening," she said, then turned and wobbled away on her high heels.

"Have a good trip," Justice said. "And Ed . . . don't worry about me."

"For once, Bill, I'm not going to take your advice," the man replied, putting an arm around his wife. "If you need anything . . ."

"I won't," Justice said, "but thanks anyway."

He turned and walked away, hurrying to join Kim. Why did he have to run into Ed and his old memories? He was having a difficult enough time dealing with the ghosts of Panama—why did it *all* have to come back? There was only so much emotion he could bury, only so much he could live with before exploding and screaming at the moon.

He reached Kim and took her by the arm. She turned and smiled at him with her wide, full lips. Her face was comforting. It held no sadness or pity. In Kim Bouvier's life there was no time for any of that, and he envied her that direct approach to life. If there had been demons eating at her, she'd slain them long ago.

"What you like about that woman . . . Marti?" she asked. "Betcha I fuck better'n her. I *know* I drink better'n her."

"Jealousy doesn't suit you, darling," he said, stifling a smile. "Your eyes have turned green."

Kim put a hand to her face. "What that mean?"

They moved past the maître d' on their way to the lobby, the man visibly sighing with relief at their departure. The lobby was wide open and luxurious, full of potted palms and rubber trees, Victorian design and furnishings giving it an unspoken elegance. People tended to whisper in the lobby as if they were in a library.

Sardi was moving quickly across the room toward them. He checked the proximity of other guests before speaking. "I think we have plainclothes DENIs all over the lobby."

"DENIs?" Kim asked.

"Panamanian G-2," Justice said. "Army intelligence. Well, I guess the gang's all here then. Did you attract a lot of attention getting Kiki and Jenks to their rooms?"

The man smiled. "I think they enjoyed their roles tonight."

"Good. You and Kim go on up to the rooms. Get the transmitter out; I want to call home."

Sardi's eyes narrowed. "You're not coming?"

"In a minute," Justice said. "Something I want to take care of first."

"But . . ." Kim began, but Sardi took her by the arm and directed her toward the elevators.

Justice watched them go, feeling many pairs of eyes on him as he stood in the lobby. He walked to the long darkwood registration desk, a huge crystal chandelier hanging above it, glittering that area bright white. A freestanding cylindrical ashtray with trash storage beneath sat in front of the desk. Justice felt around in his pockets until he came up with a pack of matches.

"Can I help you, sir?" asked the desk clerk, a white man of some authority.

"My name is Lambert, in six-seventeen," he said. "Are there any messages for me?"

"Yes, sir!" the man said, turning and hurrying back to the beehive behind the desk. "There have been a number of urgent messages for you."

As the man went through the cubbyholes, Justice lit a match, then lit the entire pack of matches, dropping the small blaze into the front aperture of the ashtray.

The clerk came back to the desk, setting a whole stack of messages before Justice. "It seems terribly important," he said.

Justice winked at him. "Thanks," he said, then slid over to a bank of easy chairs to go through the papers. They were all from various shifts of computer control; they were all marked urgent and called for immediate response, mentioning nothing else, as was customary with intelligence or security issues.

"Fire!" somebody yelled. Justice looked up to see smoke pumping into the lobby from the fire he'd started in the ash can. People began running everywhere, while Justice stood and walked to the door casually in the smoke and confusion. Outside, several people stood on the streets, coughing and talking excitedly. It had rained sometime earlier, making an already hot night even hotter, muggier. But the streets were slick with rain still, reflecting the lights of Vía España, called Panama's Wall Street because of its profusion of famous banks and expensive high-rise apartments. The Continental was located at the top of a high hill overlooking the rest of Panama City. Justice moved into the center of the street and looked down at the thousands of lights stretched out around him. It was so peaceful on the surface, so calm. Then he looked the other way and saw the army jeep parked half a block up, in front of the Hilton.

He took a look back at the Continental. A group of about thirty people stood mulling around its entry as smoke trickled out from the revolving doors in front and dissipated into the oppressive night sky. He heard sirens from a distance and getting closer. The fire department.

His dinner jacket glowed bright white under the streetlights. He took it off and turned it inside out, exposing reversible black. He put the jacket back on and continued across the wide expanse of Vía España, toward the jeep.

He'd gotten almost all the way up on them before they saw him, an American in plain clothes jumping out of the passenger side, followed within seconds by the driver. Justice stood in the roadway, sparse traffic picking its way around him, the conspicuous magnificence of the Hilton rising majestically before him.

Both men were big, both, he figured, cops. Most Canal Zone cops were retired military police who decided to stay in country when their tours ran out. Justice had always wondered if they'd kept their jobs after the Zone went back to its rightful owners. Now that he had the answer to that question, he wondered—why?

"Good evening, gentlemen," he said pleasantly. "I assume you're out here to keep an eye on me. Just thought I'd drop over and tell you that I'm fine."

The driver had eased out wide from the vehicle and had circled back around behind him. The man was wearing jeans and a T-shirt, a shoulder holster stuffed with a .357 magnum dangling under his arm.

"He don't look like so much to me, Luke," the passenger, a wiry-looking black man said. "Maybe we ought to soften him up a bit."

"Luke . . . is that your name?" he asked, turning to the man circling him. "Let me give you some advice, Luke. That magnum you're wearing is a pretty gun, and I'll bet it's a real hit when you practice your quick draw in front of the mirror . . . but buddy, do yourself a favor and get something easier to handle. . . ."

The man lunged at him. Justice sidestepped and tripped him neatly, sending him into the arms of his friend.

"Now me," Justice continued, "I use a twenty-two automatic—light, accurate . . . quiet."

Both men came at him, Justice throwing himself low, rolling. The men tangled up in him and went down as Justice somersaulted back to his feet.

"You see?" Justice said. "You need to decide whether the gun is a tool to be used, or just an extension of your dick." He fell on the man, ripping the magnum out of his holster and stepping back a pace, pointing it down at the two men still on the ground. He hefted it a time or two, then lowered it. "Naw ... this isn't for shit. Too cumbersome. Maybe you could use it like a club."

He took the gun by the barrel and made a hammering motion in the air with the butt. "You can stand up, by the way," he said. "How about telling me why you're following me?"

The black man threw himself at Justice, who twirled and brought the gun butt slashing in a wide arc to crack against the man's skull from behind, dropping him immediately, unconscious. The other man hit him from behind and tried to grab the weapon, Justice slashing back with the barrel, burying it in the man's stomach.

The man wheezed once, like a concertina, then fell down gasping for breath.

"Maybe this isn't such a bad gun," Justice said, turning the thing around in his hand. "Now, tell me what's going on."

"Fuck you," the man groaned as he rose to his knees, still doubled over.

Justice's hand flashed down between Luke's legs, grabbing him by the balls and squeezing, the man falling on his side in the fetal position, whining loudly. The fire engines arrived at that moment, flashing lights flooding the street like a carnival.

"Now, my friend," Justice said quietly to the man. "You've got about three seconds to tell me what I want to know, or I rip your fucking balls off and stuff them down your throat." He squeezed harder just to make the point. "Why are you following me?"

"D-don't know," the man gasped. "We're h-here to keep you from l-leaving."

"What?"

"That's w-why we impounded your ... fucking boat."

"My boat!" Justice strained to control the anger, then rasped, "Why?" He straightened, jerking Luke's arm, the man screeching as another fire engine charged down Vía España, siren blaring.

"I s-swear to G-god," he said. "We were j-just told to w-watch you."

"Who do you work for?" Justice asked. "The U.S. or Panama?"

"B-both," the man said, and Justice released him to roll around on the wet asphalt.

Justice stepped back from the man, looking down at the nickel-plated revolver in his hands. "You can always tell a crooked cop," he said, "by his fancy guns. I want you to get your friend up and put him back in the vehicle. Then I want you to go tell your people that I intend to get my boat back. Hard or easy, it's mine. I don't care how we play it."

The man dragged himself up, using the jeep for support. Justice moved to his still-unconscious partner and picked the guy up, slinging him over a shoulder. As the driver climbed in, Justice stuffed his bundle through the open passenger window, the legs still sticking out.

The jeep fishtailed away, and Justice looked up to the sound of a single pair of hands clapping. A woman wearing diaphanous white stood on a second-story balcony. A highball sat on the ledge before her. She picked up the drink and saluted.

"Very good, Mr. Lambert," she said. "Bravo."

Justice stared up at her to see long chestnut hair, a perfect figure backlit and just visible through her nightgown—a dream?

"Good evening," Justice said. "You seem to have the advantage over me, Ms. . . . Smith, is it?"

"Good," the woman answered. "Very good." Then she turned and disappeared through the billowing veranda curtains into her room.

He thought about making the trek into the Hilton to ferret her out, but he was worried about the calls from Haven. Ever since Mandrake's initial visit, he'd been waiting for the other shoe to drop. He had to take care of the call now.

The show was about over at the Continental. A fireman was standing on the sidewalk, directing a huge jet of water toward the battered remnants of the ash can as it bounced around on the sidewalk under the torrent. Justice stuck the gun in his belt and moved back across the street, going into a side entrance and taking the stairs up to the second floor to avoid the confusion of the lobby.

On the second floor he took the elevator up to the ambassador suite, knocking on the door. Kim answered it in a minute, her mouth opening in surprise. "You don't go to Marti room?"

Justice rolled his eyes and moved past her into the spacious suite. The rooms were wide open and decorated as elegantly as the lobby. A long veranda stretched across the entire length of the place, Panama City's magnificent view twinkling like a ground-hugging star field.

"Where you go?" Kim asked, following him in.

"Had to talk to a man about a gun," he said, reaching into his belt, pulling out the magnum, and holding it out to her. "Here. Just for fun tomorrow have Jorge run a registration check on it."

She hefted it, frowning. "Too big," she said, wandering off in the direction of the east bedroom.

Sardi was out on the balcony, adjusting the small microwave dish on the wide, sculpted cement railing. Justice walked to the wet bar and fixed himself a whiskey before joining the man outside.

"I heard sirens below," Sardi said as he used a screwdriver to attach the lead wires to the base of the dish.

"False alarm," Justice replied, walking to the edge of the balcony and looking across the street at the Hilton. Ten stories down, the light was still on in Alice Smith's room.

"I've heard that the U.S. Navy is furnishing escorts to all ships traveling into the Atlantic side of the canal."

Justice grunted. He turned back to Sardi, hoisting a leg up to sit on the balcony rail. "Noriega's in Chiriquí."

He watched Sardi tense slightly as he stretched the lead wires back through the balcony to the transmitter set just inside the suite. "History is repeating itself, William," he said, Justice drifting back inside to watch him with the transmitter. "You're being drawn into a whirlpool of your own device."

"Tar-baby syndrome," Justice replied. "The more you fight it, the more it sucks you in. I can't help but feel there's some manner of destiny at work here."

Sardi threw some switches, the small unit humming to life. Outside, the dish revolved on its base until it locked onto their Comsat with a small clang. "You have a much greater responsibility to the world than to die here," he said.

"I can't walk away from it now," Justice answered, working at his tie, loosening it. "I think I've got to deal with this inside myself. Besides, we're stuck here. They've impounded the boat and won't let us go."

"What about the ordnance on board?" Sardi asked, pulling a small microphone out of an accessory bag and unwinding the cord.

"We'll get it if we can," Justice said. "Hell, we've improvised before."

"They're boxing you in. There must be a reason."

"Yeah," Justice said, walking to the transmitter. "And I'm afraid we're going to find out about that right now."

He picked up the mike, Sardi plugging it in and adjusting the cycle to their shortwave band. This was going out unscrambled. It could have been a mistake had anyone been eavesdropping, but there seemed to be no secrets anyway.

"Diamond Rock control," he said. "This is Big Bear, over."

He repeated the entry several times before a woman's voice crackled through the speaker too loud, Sardi hurrying to turn down the volume. "Big Bear, this is Diamond Rock control. . . . Stand by for an urgent message, over."

Sardi picked up a pad and pencil, prepared to take anything important down. "Standing by, Diamond Rock. Over."

The message got right to the point. "Baby Bear reports that the U.S. Sixth Fleet . . . repeat, the U.S. Sixth Fleet, is presently under way for regularly scheduled military exercises in the French West Indies. . . ."

"Son of a bitch," Justice said. "Stand by, control. Over." Baby Bear was Charlie Mandrake. His information was from the horse's mouth. He looked at Sardi. "There wasn't anything scheduled in our area, was there?"

The man shook his head. "I think they're going to make a grab for the island."

"Those sons of bitches are looking to get me out of the way," Justice said, laughing. "I'll be goddamned. We got Charlie's number, right? What time of the day is it in Washington?"

"Same as here," Sardi said.

"Good," Justice said. He hoped Mandrake was sound asleep. He pushed in the mike button. "Control... listen carefully to me. I want you to put your own surveillance on the Sixth Fleet upon their arrival. I want to know exact locations and numbers, over."

"Message received, over."

"Inform me of everything that goes on in regard to this," Justice said. "Over and..."

There was a yell from the direction of the bedrooms, Justice up and moving with the sound. A mestizo was charging across the living room, bundled money falling out of his pockets, a gun in his hand.

"Hey!" Justice called, charging, putting himself between the man and the door.

Without hesitation the man fired, Justice spinning away, anticipating the shot. He dived forward with the second shot, doing a half somersault and pushing off with his hands to slam his feet into the man's chest, the gun discharging again as it flew from his grasp.

The mestizo stumbled backward but didn't go down. Justice sprang to his feet and smiled at the man. "Finally, a little activity," he said.

A large knife came out of the man's belt. He motioned as if he were going to charge Justice but instead turned the other way and grabbed Kim, who'd come running out of the bedroom after the guy. He twisted her before him, sticking the knife into her throat.

"Let me through or she's dead," the man said through clenched teeth.

"Don't hurt him," Justice told Kim.

"The bastard was hiding in the bedroom," she said casually. "Nearly scared me to death."

"Quiet!" the man yelled. "Get out of the way... now!"

"I've been waiting for him," Justice said. "I want to talk to him."

"Okay," Kim said, coming down hard on the man's foot with her spiked heel.

He screamed, loosening his grip for just a second, Kim driving an elbow to his gut, then levering him hard to the floor as he doubled over. With a liquid motion, she twisted the knife hand, disarming him, then swung over his body to plant a spiked heel firmly on the man's right eyeball. "You move even an inch, and I drive my shoe into your brain," she smiled down at the man, who stiffened immediately, not even breathing.

"We sure flaunted it enough," Justice said, moving up to the man. He began pulling stacks of bills out of his pockets and throwing them in a pile on the floor. "Been waiting all day for somebody to try and get my cash. Maybe people just aren't as quick as they used to be."

"Can I kill him when you're finished talking?" Kim asked.

Justice shook his head, retrieving the man's gun from the floor and checking it. "Now this one isn't too bad," he said. "Thirty-two automatic, lady's gun, but serviceable, easy to carry." He knelt to the man, whose one eye not occupied with Kim's heel was opened wide and frightened. "I mean you obviously carry this for business, not ego. I salute you on that. Too many people carry guns for the wrong reasons."

Justice pulled back the hammer, sticking the gun to the man's head. He glanced at Kim. "You can take your foot off now," he said. "Besides, he's getting a great look up your dress."

Kim grunted. "You a dirty man," she told him, moving away from the mestizo, who sagged with relief.

"Oh no, my friend," Justice said, grabbing him by the front of his shirt and pulling him to his feet. "It isn't over yet. We have to talk now."

Justice stood before the man and planted the barrel of the .32 right in the center of his forehead. "Now, my man," Justice said quietly. "I don't want to have to go through a lot of trouble. Let's just understand one another, okay? You know what a bank is, don't you? Though you probably never use one during business hours."

The man nodded briskly.

"Well, let me tell you something," Justice returned. "I want some information from you, and I want it now. If you aren't going to give it to me, just say so, and I'll blow your miserable brains out now and get it over with, and you can take that to the bank, *comprende?*"

He stared coldly at the man and jammed the gun barrel

a little harder against his head. "I u-understand," the mestizo said.

"Good," Justice said. "Kim . . . get my friend a drink. We're not being very hospitable."

"Okay," Kim said, moving to the wet bar.

"Now," Justice said. "I know you're just a petty thief, but the gun and the knife . . . well, that tells me a little more . . . that maybe you're connected up with something a little larger, *hmmm?*"

"I work with Medellin," the man said. "Everybody works with Medellin."

"Good," Justice said, "we're making progress." Kim walked up and handed him a glass full of whiskey. He reached out and gave it to the man. "Go ahead . . . drink it down."

The man took a sip, the gun still lodged in his forehead.

"No," Justice said. "Drink it all down."

The man's eyes narrowed, but he drained the glass, gagging, and handed it back.

Justice gave the empty glass back to Kim. "He's thirsty. Give him another."

"Waste of good booze," the woman pouted, but walked away.

"I want to buy some cocaine," Justice told the man.

"Meester . . . I don't . . ."

Justice poked his forehead with the gun. "Stop," he said. "The next time you try and bullshit me, it's over. No more bullshit. I don't have time to fuck with you."

Kim arrived with another drink, the glass filled to the top. She gave it to the man.

"What's your name?" Justice asked.

"Enrique," the man replied. "Enrique Cazorla."

"Drink that down, Enrique," Justice said. "Enjoy."

The man drained the second glass, a glaze settling over his eyes. He was beginning to relax, even with a gun to his head. Justice gave the glass back to Kim.

"Give him another." The woman walked off, Sardi moving over to sit on a sofa and watch the proceedings. Justice looked hard into the man's eyes. "I want some cocaine, Enrique. A lot of cocaine."

"I can get you some," the man said, his words slurred

badly, "but not a great quantity. I'm just a little part of the wheel. That's why I have to rob hotel rooms."

"Ah, my man," Justice said. "I believe we have reached the beginnings of understanding. Can you hook me up with someone who might be able to furnish a quantity?"

"How much?"

"Half a million dollars' worth," Justice said, a large grin spreading across the man's face.

"I can do that," he said.

Kim arrived with another drink, Justice forcing this one, also, down the man, who was listing badly by the time he'd finished it.

Justice lowered the gun, letting the man slump into an easy chair. "They're goin' to want to see your money first," Enrique said. "They can afford to do bi'ness that way."

Justice nodded. "I want a meet set up tomorrow at a place of mutual agreement," he said, dropping the magazine out of the butt of the .32 and tossing the weapon back to the man. "I'll be happy to show the money then."

"Then you can maybe make a deal," Enrique said, quickly pocketing the .32. "But I can't make no promises."

"Promises are for weddings," Justice said. "I make deals. And here's my deal for you." He moved to the pile of money on the floor, picking up a bundle of hundreds, then retrieving the man's knife from the floor.

He dropped the bundle of money on the coffee table, pulling two hundreds off the top of the stack and handing them to Cazorla. "This is for your trouble tonight," he said, then held up the knife, "and this is for later." He set the bundle of money in a neat little pile, then began hacking the pile in half, sawing through it with the man's knife. He smiled. "Should be five thousand here... *hmm*, sharp knife."

"I'll say," Kim said, rubbing her neck. "Why don't you just let me kill him?"

Justice took a breath, explaining carefully, slowly. "Because, Mr. Cazorla is now our partner. He's going to make a major deal for us, aren't you, Enrique?"

The man nodded dumbly as Justice picked up one stack of halved bills and handed it, along with the knife, to him. "Here's the arrangement," Justice said. "You set up the meet, that's all you have to do. When I arrive, the other half of the five grand is yours. What do you think?"

Cazorla smiled drunkenly. He had just died and gone to heaven. "I think, my friend, that we will make very good bi'ness partners together."

"Excellent!" Justice said, standing, Sardi walking over to help the mestizo stand on wobbly legs. "You may get back with me early tomorrow. If no one is in the room, just leave a number with the front desk."

"The front desk?" Cazorla said as Sardi helped him walk to the door.

Justice shrugged. "Why not? If you prefer, you can wait for me in the lobby. I'll stick close."

"Sounds like a deal . . . partner," Cazorla said, moving to embrace Justice, who returned it with gusto.

"Looking forward to working with you," Justice said, as the man stumbled into the hallway. "Maybe we can do a lot of business together."

Cazorla stared down the hall, weaving badly. "You a very perceptive man," he said over his shoulder. "You see Enrique's strength of character."

"Absolutely," Justice said, and closed the door. He looked at Sardi. "Make the connections to get Mandrake on the line."

"Isn't it risky to call him unscrambled?" Sardi asked.

"Who knows?" Justice said. "We don't have any time or any choices."

Sardi moved to the transmitter, searching the orbital schedules in order to pinpoint an AT&T satellite, Kim taking Justice's arm to stop him. "Why you play that game with the thief?" she asked.

"Seems like the easiest way to get into the fortress at Volcán Barú is to be invited," Justice said, "and it seems to me that at this point Senor Cazorla thinks he's fallen in with American Mafia. It's just expeditious business."

"You should 'a' let me kill him," she said, wandering to the bar and fixing herself a drink.

He heard Sardi whistle, a high-pitched screech, and knew he'd found a line and was whistling in the 800 code for a free call. He moved over to the transmitter and picked up the mike, the sound of a ringing telephone coming through the tiny speaker.

Mandrake's voice, heavy with sleep, came on after six rings. "Wha—?"

"Good morning, Charlie," Justice said. "You seem to be sleeping soundly."

"I'm not sleeping," Mandrake said. "I'm passed out drunk...and you should be, too. They're going to chop your fucking head off. And what the hell are you doing calling me at home?"

"Do you think your phone's tapped?" Justice asked.

"Yes...no! Hell, I don't know anything anymore."

"Wake up enough to give it to me straight," Justice said. "I'm extended out to the edge here."

"What's happened?" Mandrake said quickly, concern lacing his voice. Justice smiled. The man had grown very attached in a very short time.

"Don't worry about it," Justice returned. "Just tell me what's coming."

"They've told me some," Mandrake said. "I've heard some; I've...sneaked some and figured some of what wasn't there to see. Near as I can figure, they don't expect you to make it out of Panama alive. At that point they move in with the troops and take over your island, saying there was a mutual defense treaty between the two countries that gives them the right to defend it. That will put them at Castro's back door with air bases and missiles. It's a deal for them, Will. Not only strategic to Cuba, but a great jumping-off point to the Middle East, where, as you know, they've had a rough time getting permission to land their aircraft."

"What if I don't die in Panama?" Justice said, his mind spinning, working with the possibilities.

"I think they'll move in anyway," the man said sadly. "Christ, I'm sorry. I've served this...government for nearly my whole life, I...I just assumed that I was on the right side. I can't decide whether to kill myself or them."

"Ah," Justice said lightly. "Don't be too hard on yourself or the American government, Charlie. It's just a bureaucracy moving under its own steam, and bureaucracies don't have souls. American government is still one of the best around. At least it doesn't institutionalize the physical repression of its population. You'd be surprised at what a civilized concept that is."

"Will," he said, "they intend to kill you!"

Justice laughed. "Well, all we need to do is think of a reason for them not to. Go back to sleep, Charlie. Let me handle the worries."

"You're a cool one," the man said. "I'll give you that."

"Just a businessman," Justice responded, smiling wanly at Sardi, who was rubbing his forehead in concentration. "Keep me posted."

"Yeah."

The phone went dead, Justice setting the microphone down leadenly. "Woof," he said.

"All shoes have dropped, William," the man said. "What are you going to do?"

"Get some sleep for now," Justice replied. "We'll be a lot better at answers in the morning. The Americans can afford to wait for the best positioning on this. I don't think they'll try anything as long as I'm alive."

"For the moment," Sardi replied. "You need bargaining power before anything happens. The U.S. has no idea of what would happen if they attacked Haven."

"I know," Justice said, thinking of the hundreds of millions he'd spent in state-of-the-art coastal defenses, from missiles to microwave radiation. He'd lose to the Americans eventually, but could exact a toll on them far greater than they could comprehend. "Go on to bed. We'll worry about it in the morning."

Sardi stood and began disassembling the transmitter. "You need rest yourself," he said.

"I'll be along," Justice told him, picking up his forgotten drink and walking out onto the balcony. "Just leave that stuff. I'll take care of it."

Sardi looked at the man but said nothing. Instead he moved quickly around the room, turning off lights before disappearing quietly. Justice sat on a lounge chair on the veranda. The night was still hot, but a pleasant, salty breeze made it enjoyable. He had settled into the eye of the storm for the moment, the place of calm before the conflagration. It wouldn't last long.

"There you are," came Kim's voice from the sliding doors. "I need zipper help."

She proceeded out onto the balcony with him, moving sensuously without her high heels. She walked up to him, turning her back, and holding up her long, sleek hair. "I can't get the goddamned snap," she said. "Lady clothes made for crazy people."

Justice reached up and undid the snap, then rasped the zipper down until it ran out of room in the hollow of her back. "Done," he said. "I wish all problems were so easily solved."

"Thanks," she replied, and pulled the dress up over her head right there on the patio. She stood before him, naked except for black panties, her unblemished olive skin glowing warmly, bathed in moonlight. He stared at her. She was quite beautiful and sometimes, when her eyes were round and misty, like now, quite innocent.

"You'd better turn in," he said. "We'll need a lot of rest for the duration."

"You come in and sleep with me?" she asked in a child's voice.

"No," he said simply.

"You don't like the way I look?"

"I love the way you look," he said. "But this is business."

"It's business with me and the others," she said, "but not between us. I know you care about me."

He turned from her and stared out over the city, taking note that Alice Smith's light was still on. "That's just the trouble, isn't it?" he replied.

She moved to him, pulling his face around to hers. "What wrong with you?" she asked. "Sometimes I think I go crazy I want you so much."

"Me, too," he said, swallowing hard. "Me, too."

She straightened. "Then why?"

"Just go to bed, okay?" he said. "Please."

"You have me now, or you never have me," she spat, hands on hips.

"Please go to bed," he said, looking back out over the city.

She turned and walked away, moving partway through the suite before turning and coming back to the doorway.

"William," she said, husky. He turned and watched her leaning forlornly against the door. "I didn't mean what I said."

"I know."

"The trouble around here is that it's just too damned quiet."

He nodded, smiling sadly, and she was gone. He turned back to the city, putting his feet up on the railing and making sure he had a clear view of Alice Smith's room. It was all coming back, every bit of it. Sardi had called it history repeating itself. All the emotion he had stored and hidden in order to control his life was all coming back now to kick him in the teeth, the years of denial a cruel joke.

Every step brought him closer to Volcán Barú and Frank Merriman, every turn brought him in contact with serious, killing emotion, the kind that crippled most of the world's population. His life, his empire were based on one concept— absolute control over his mind, and hence his world. But that control was slipping away. He was making choices with his heart and not his head, and already he was in more trouble than he could handle. He hadn't destroyed the emotion, he had just shut it out for a time. But it was coming back now. He was beginning to realize that he really hadn't come that far from the man who'd been gunned down along with an entire village in 1978. He was having to face the toughest opponent of his life—himself.

He took a long drink, the whiskey burning a line down his throat. He wanted to get drunk but knew his body wouldn't let him. His internal controls were too well tuned. He wanted to go in and make long, slow love with Kim Bouvier, but he wouldn't do that either. Most of all, he wanted to hide, to chuck everything and go underground and forget about it. He called his island Haven, but it wasn't one for him. All that it was, was more responsibility, more guilt karma for what he'd done to Volcán Barú.

He uncoiled his lanky frame and stood. In the morning he'd exercise for a couple of hours before getting things started. If nothing else, he could lose himself in the selfish physical, the only place where he could hide while still awake.

He stared down at the light in Alice Smith's room. Another loose end. Perhaps in the morning he'd pay her a little visit. For now, she was just another piece in a tantalizing jigsaw puzzle of life and death. He saluted her, then finished the whiskey.

The place was dark and quiet when Justice walked off the balcony. Kim had said it was too quiet, and despite the intensity of the evening, he couldn't help but agree. That she was running from life just as hard as he was had been a foregone conclusion of his for years. The only difference between the two of them was that he realized consciously that he was running, and she simply accepted her life at face value.

It was time to go to bed, but he feared the dreams. He'd been able to smell burning flesh the night before on the boat. That hadn't happened for a long time. But sleep couldn't be escaped for long, so he had to try.

He passed the transmitter, remembering that he'd promised Sardi that he'd take care of it. He followed the lead wires back out onto the veranda and picked up the microwave dish, idly looking back down at Alice Smith's hotel room as he did.

Her light was off.

X.

DALLAS, TEXAS
15 NOVEMBER 1979—MIDMORNING

"What *is* that noise?" squeaked Ed Barkes's voice over the conference speaker. "It's driving me crazy."

Will Justice spun his wheelchair 180 degrees, dribbled once more, then shot at the hoop on the far side of the room, the basketball spinning three times around the metal ring before finally dropping through the netting to bounce on the floor. "Don't worry about it," he called back to the speaker on the desk, then rolled quickly back to the ball, circling it, dribbling it back to control. "Just tell me why you don't think I should sell now."

He dribbled again, still sitting under the basket, taking a quick shot backwards over his head, the ball swishing through, dropping back into his lap. He wheeled out—fast—his upper arms rock hard, three hours of upper-body-muscle work a day setting him on a taut, quivering edge. His body gleamed with sweat, soaking his muscle shirt dark. His hair hung wet and dripping over his headband, covering his plastic-surgery scars, as he jerked himself around the former medical clinic that had been transformed into a workout gym of unequaled sophistication and equipage.

"Why?" Barkes said loudly. "Why? Everything's straight up. Your speculations have paid off like nothing I've ever seen. I ask *you* why. Why cut the head off your prized chicken?"

The far wall was taken up with a long row of hand-over

146

bars set at six feet, four inches—exactly his size. He dropped the ball and jerked his wheelchair in that direction, building up speed. His chair hit the bumpers in front of the bars hard, spilling him out as Justice propelled himself with his arms, his fingers just grasping the first of the handholds. He swung, pectorals bulging as he pulled himself along the wall. "I'm a fundamentalist, Ed," he said, puffing slightly with the exertion. "I've been studying the long-term indicators and see a bear market looming."

"Come on, Bill," Barkes said. "Very few modern analysts find anything but random factors in indicator study. . . ."

"That's what makes horse races," Justice said, straining himself to the end of the bars, then turning and coming back. "And what makes people like me rich. The world is full of fools, Ed. Most modern analysts don't study the history of the market, just current trends. We're going to sell short, my man. I predict a five percent market drop. If I'm right, we'll save ourselves about fifty million. I'm really not into negotiating this point."

"What do you want me to do with all that money?" Barkes asked.

Justice reached the end of the bars; his wheelchair lay on its side beneath them. Grunting loudly, he began swinging back and forth, his body arcing higher with each swing. When he reached optimum, he released the bars and fell, landing on his hands, his legs folding up atop him. Off balance, he teetered across the floor on his hands, finally getting control and hand-walking back to the chair.

"We're going to invest it in business," he said. "It's time to start creating on our own instead of subsidizing the labor of others."

"What kind of business?" Barkes asked.

Justice balanced himself on one hand, using the free hand to pull the chair back upright and roll it away from the bars. He set the brake on the wheel. "I think a number of different kinds," he said, positioning himself in front of the chair. "As you know, I work with a number of different brokers and advisers. For those that are willing, I'm going to set up a consortium of partners, a brain trust, if you will. These partners will meet and make decisions regarding the businesses, their potentials, their directions. I will reserve final decisions, of course, for myself; but I look at that as only a passing phase. Once we all totally understand one another, I eventually want to work myself out of the operation and let you guys run it."

"A consortium," Barkes said guardedly. "You know, Bill, speaking for myself, I'm a damned fine broker but know next to nothing about business administration."

"It's not administration I'm concerned about," Justice said, lining himself up carefully with the chair. He began twisting his body slowly, trying to turn it while still balancing on his hands. His muscles strained visibly as they tried to hold the bulk of his useless limbs, but they succeeded almost until reaching the chair seat, at which time Justice gave out, his body falling into the chair. He straightened and took a long breath. "Administrators are a dime a dozen. It's creativity in outlook I'm looking for, creativity in direction. Administrators don't have the mind for that. In fact, I'm hoping you'll take the position of general secretary to the enterprise. I want to leave most of this in your hands."

"I'm no young man," Barkes said, Justice wheeling up close to the speaker on his desk, the only piece of furniture in the wide-open gym. "I'm sure there are others. . . ."

"The position starts out at a quarter of a million dollars a year, Ed," Justice said. "And there's nobody but you to do it. And I already have our first investment lined up."

The fifty-pound dumbbells sat on the floor near the speaker. Justice bent to pick them up, one for each hand, and began flexing.

Barkes laughed. "You and I have never met face-to-face, yet you've made me rich and are now trying to make me richer. I think we're best friends, but with you, I'm not sure of anything."

"I trust you, Ed," Justice said simply. "That's all there is to it. You don't have to meet somebody to trust them. I've never met any of my people. What do you say? Want the job?"

"Tell me about the first investment."

"This one will be purely money-making," Justice said. "Later, once we get the consortium rolling, I want to branch out into other things. But this one will build liquidity. I want to invest about one hundred million dollars in movie rights."

"What?!"

"I want to buy up the videotape rights to every motion picture we can get our hands on. Within a couple of years, those rights will be worth their weight in gold."

"You want to go into video production and distribution?" Barkes asked. "I'm not sure the investment would be large enough to..."

"No," Justice said, holding the barbells out from his body at arm's length, until he was straining, his arms shaking. "I just want the rights. We'll resell them when people realize how valuable they are. It'll roll itself over in a couple of years—real short-term stuff. What's your answer?"

His arms fell to his sides, the barbells dropping with a thud to the floor. He sat back in the chair for a minute, breathing deeply.

"You know, I already retired a while back, I..."

"Come on, Ed!" Justice said loudly, smiling. "We're talking about getting out there and mixing it up, life on our own terms, control over our world. This doesn't have anything to do with money, and you know it. You're not the kind of man to sit back in your solarium and wait for the meat wagon to cart you off to the graveyard. You're alive! You're healthy! Take your shot!"

"You ought to be a preacher, William."

"I am," Justice said. "What's your answer?"

"You know my weaknesses, my friend," Barkes said. "No, I'm not ready to roll over. The whole thing sounds like a kick. I'll do it, but only if I get stock options, too. I trust you to make anything you touch a success."

"Of course, stock options," Justice said. "There's enough to go around for everybody. Welcome aboard!"

"Thanks," Barkes said, then added quietly, "Thanks for believing in an old man."

"Old is in the head," Justice said. "Now I believe you have some stock to dump."

"I do indeed," Barkes said. "This is going to cause a little excitement on the floor. You know, you could be the cause of that bear market right now, today."

"That thought has occurred to me," Justice replied, smiling. "See you, Ed."

"See me? I'll believe it when it happens. Check you later, partner."

Justice reached out and cut off the conference speaker, taking a minute to let his breathing return to normal. He looked around his domain, with its center posts that had replaced clinic walls as his condition had gone from purely medical to purely rehabilitative. Nautilus equipment was scattered around, along with a large variety of weight-room paraphernalia. He'd discovered the internal power of exercise to dull the senses, the euphoria of endorphin secretions; the so-called "runner's high" was the state of mind he lived for, the only time he wasn't overburdened with the guilt, vengeance, and debilitation of his own condition. For whatever else he had accomplished—and it had been remarkable—in the year and a half since his tragedy, he still couldn't use his legs.

Walking, the simplest of human activities, was still beyond his ken. No matter how hard he had tried his imaging techniques, no matter how desperately he wanted himself well and healthy to avenge the people of Volcán Barú, his legs were denied him. He'd prayed to a God he no longer believed in; he'd cursed and sold his soul to an equally distant devil; he'd cried and sworn oaths, threatened bodily harm to himself, and utterly given up more times than he could count. Nothing helped.

Allie had tried to console him by telling him that he'd come back further and faster than anyone she'd ever seen, but all that did was make him angrier. He wasn't just anybody. He was Will Justice and *control* was his to command. In everything but this.

He reached into the side pocket of his wheelchair and pulled out a towel, rubbing himself down with it. At the old front entrance to the clinic, he saw Allie and her mother come in carrying groceries.

"Need any help?" he called.

"No thanks," Allie waved back, moving off into the alcove that had once been a break room and was now a kitchen.

He wheeled the chair in that direction, picking up speed as he went, the air in his face making him laugh. He skidded to a stop right in front of the alcove kitchen area, Allie rolling her eyes, her admonitions about safety always lost on him.

"You're gonna scuff up my floor doin' that!" Mrs. Boyd said, shaking a finger. "You young people and your toys, always getting underfoot. It's getting so a person can't have any peace and quiet anymore. Where's Jerry? I haven't seen him all day."

"Jerry died in the war, Mama," Allie said, as she put up the groceries. "That was a long time ago."

The old woman laughed loudly. "Oh, lordy!" she said after a moment. "You sure don't know a thing. I saw Jerry just this morning. He and your father went fishing up to Skilman Lake."

"Getting cold out there," Allie told Justice. "Pretty early for Texas. I'm afraid we're going to have a long winter."

"Got a job for you," Justice said.

She stopped what she was doing and looked at him. "Oh?"

"I'm starting up a kind of a company," he said. "I want you to sit on the board of directors to be my eyes and ears."

She laughed and went back to her groceries. "Right," she said. "Your own eyes and ears look okay to me, even with a new face."

"I can't face people . . . like this," he said.

"Why not?" she returned. "You've got a handicap. So what?"

"I don't know why your father fishes," Mrs. Boyd said. "He sure doesn't like to eat them."

"Papa's dead," Allie said.

"I'm not a real man, Allie, I . . ."

"Oh stop," she said. "I'm getting a little sick and tired of the self-pity. Look, if you don't want to go to the meetings, put a tape recorder in there."

"I don't want a tape recorder," he said, angry. "I want you."

She stopped what she was doing and stared fire at him. "Well, you can't have me."

"I pay you good money," he spat. "If I tell you to jump, by God, you'd better jump."

She stiffened, and he regretted his words immediately. What had begun as a close and loving relationship between him and Allie had somehow degenerated into something distant and petty in the preceding months, and he couldn't put his finger on it.

Allie took a deep breath and looked at her wristwatch. "It's getting on noon, Mother," she said. "I think your television shows are coming on."

The woman's eyes lit up. "Ooh," she said. "I want to see who that nasty old Erika's sleeping with now. I swear, these young people." She walked past Justice and moved toward the back of the clinic where the rooms were still intact. She called back over her shoulder. "If you see Jerry or your father, tell them that we won't have fish for dinner."

"Okay, Mama," Allie called, then waited until the woman was out of sight before speaking to Justice. "If you ever say anything like that to me again, I'm walking out and never coming back. Am I making myself clear?"

He looked down and tightened his lips. "Look, I'm sorry," he said. "I'm just trying to help you out. You could stand to make a lot of money in this deal."

"You're not trying to help me out," she said. "You're just trying to lock me tighter to your side. You don't feel like you're man enough to hold me with love, so you think you can do it with money. It's all part of your control game, and it doesn't work with me."

"Everybody wants something," he said. "I just try to give it to them."

She frowned and sat down, her tan wool skirt and sweater complimenting her light complexion. "You want to give me what I want?" she asked. "Okay... give me you, the real you, not the mindless ape you're trying to become, not the megalomaniac who controls everything he touches. There's no humanity there."

"That's just ... me, Allie," he said, his eyes wide.

"Stop it!" she said. "Stop playing the self-pitying game. It doesn't mean anything to me. You've gotten so good at manipulation that I don't think you can see the truth of things anymore."

"I don't understand what I've done to make you angry with me," he said. "God, Allie. I *love* you. All I want to do is make you happy."

"I think you really believe that," she said. "I think

you've lost touch so much that you're mistaking what you feel for real emotion. I love you, too, Will. I love you so much sometimes it hurts, especially when I see what you're doing to yourself. But love doesn't cover everything. There's more, much more."

"Like what?"

"Like ideals, ethics," she said. "I've got to respect the man I love. Lately you've turned into all the things you used to hate. You think you can make all your own rules. . . ."

"I know I can," he said with authority. "Reality is mine to create."

She shook her head slowly. "No. In every man's life there must be something greater than himself, some considerations that go beyond his ability to act on his impulses."

He made a toss-away gesture. "I don't have any idea what you're talking about," he said with finality.

"You don't?" she said, standing and glaring down at him. "You don't? Well, I'll show you. I'll spell it out for you."

She moved past him, her skirt slapping his arm as she went by. He spun the chair around and followed, her body held stiff and rigid as she walked all the way across the gym to his desk. She moved around to the business end of the thing and jerked open the drawer, reaching in. Within seconds she withdrew the .45 automatic he'd put there.

She dropped it heavily onto the desk. "This is what I'm talking about."

"I got that for protection," he said. "If somebody came in here in the middle of the night you'd . . ."

"It's not the gun, dammit!" she said. "It's what it stands for—the hatred, the revenge, all the dark thoughts that you use to pump yourself up—that's what's driving us apart."

"I've known great evil . . ." he began, but she cut him off.

"Spare me the great evil speech," she said. "My father was beaten to death in an alley behind a bar for three dollars. My brother was killed by friendly fire in Vietnam. My mother's been unhinged for ten years because of it."

"But none of it was your fault. . . ."

"Stop it!" she screamed. "Just stop. I can't stand any more! Don't you see? You're a good man eaten up with hatreds and bad motivations. You're not the first person to be affected by inhumanity in this life, and you won't be the last.

You have a great gift, Will, but your outlook is going to be your downfall."

"My outlook is all that's kept me alive!" he shouted back. "What can you know about it? You're walking around on two good legs, doing what you want to do."

She moved around the desk and leaned down close to him. "I know that hatred can tear a person apart and make him inhuman," she said low. "I know because I'm watching it happen to you. Why do you think I didn't accept this year's salary in advance? It was because I didn't want to be committed to you that long. I wanted to be able to bail out and move on anytime it got too rough around you. Your imaging has worked miracles, but you know what? It won't help you in the end!"

"What are you talking about?" he said, nearly irrational because of the closeness of the subject matter. "My imaging has been the only thing helping me to progress."

"And now your imaging is taking away your legs," she said.

"What are you talking about?"

"You've got some feeling down there," she said, pointing to his legs. "Other stuff works. At this point there's no reason for your legs not to be coming along. It's your own head that's stopping you. Your body refuses to get well in order to do wrong."

"You're fucking nuts," he said, turning the chair away from her. "A year ago you refused to believe that imaging helped at all. Now you say it's helping in the wrong way. You don't have any idea what you're talking about. I know what it takes to control . . . I know!"

She moved around to face him. She leaned on the chair rests on stiff arms. "Then tell me what it takes to control me," she said. She looked at him hard for a minute, then stood up straight. "Because I'll tell you, if things don't change in a hurry, I'm walking away from here. You don't need a lover or a therapist anymore. Maybe your money would be better spent on a psychiatrist."

She turned and walked off.

"Come back here!" he shouted, but she ignored him and kept walking. "I didn't say you could leave! You still work for me until I say different, you fucking bitch! Who needs you anyway?"

She disappeared into the back of the clinic, Justice clenching his fists at the side of his head and shaking them wildly, his face reddening. He swung the chair around, banging into the desk. Growling loudly, he tipped the desk up on two legs and shoved it over to crash loudly on the floor. "I'll show you!" he yelled. "You fucking bitch, I'll show you!"

He wheeled the chair around and pointed it toward the Nautilus equipment and the parallel walking bars. He reached the end of the ten-foot walkway and stared down its length. His mind, already filled with darkness, slipped easily into the Volcán Barú mode, the screams and the gasoline smell of the fires filling his head.

The bars sat before him. He grabbed them with powerful hands and pulled himself out of the chair, holding himself straight on stiff arms, his dead legs dragging uselessly on the rubber runner.

He visualized the bullet in his back, thought the electrical connections through it. And then he pictured Noriega and Merriman, laughing at him, backlit by a tremendous fire. Their men were throwing people into the fire, and they laughed louder each time a screaming child went up like a torch. And he pictured himself closing the distance between them, taking a step, then another. He pictured himself reaching them, his powerful hands ripping out their throats, choking the laughter right out of them. And it was real, so real—the smells and the sights filled his head to overflow until all that existed was Volcán Barú and the two steps it would take to reach Noriega and Merriman.

His legs came up firm on the runner and he released his pressure on the bars—falling in a heap on the walkway.

"No!" he screamed, pulling himself up again, picturing the scene again, building its reality. And as he tried to take those two steps, he fell again.

"Dammit to hell!" he screamed, fists pounding the walkway. "Goddammit!"

He was vibrating wildly, his body out of control, his face strained in emotional agony.

Suddenly she was beside him, touching his sweating, straining arm. "Try it my way," she said low.

"Fuck you!" he yelled. "Fucking hell!"

"Try it," she urged, and he turned to her in cold anger.

"All right," he said. "You want it, Miss Stuck-Up Bitch, I'll give it to you."

He reached up and grabbed the bars above him, pulling himself to a standing position. He stared momentary hatred at her, then closed his eyes.

"Breathe out the anger," she whispered. "Take it the other way."

His mind was spinning, picturing Volcán Barú again, the fires raging, Noriega laughing. But this time he looked past the two men, looked to the fire itself. It took on reality, the reality creation that he'd spent a year and a half perfecting minute by minute. He saw the village—burning, saw a small child at the window of a burning hut. He was no more than three years old, his little eyes wide, shaking with fear. He wanted to reach the child but couldn't. So close . . . so close, just two steps away. But he just couldn't . . . get . . . there. And the fire reached the child, Justice watching in horror as the boy's shirt burst into orange flame right before him. The child screamed, pleading with him, little arms reaching forward in pitiful supplication, and as the fire rose to consume him, Justice stumbled to the window, grabbing the child and pulling him away from the flames.

He heard crying, loud, unchecked.

He opened his eyes. He was at the far end of the walkway, Allie sitting near him on the floor, her face buried in her hands, her tears like soothing rains from heaven as she wept out her passion and her happiness.

He stared back down the walkway in stupefication. He had done it.

He had walked.

XI.

PANAMA CITY—HOTEL CONTINENTAL
19 FEBRUARY 1988—0713 HOURS

Will Justice stared down at the street twelve floors below, watching as the Canal Zone surveillance changed shifts. The cement railing was rough on his hands as he traversed it, feet in the air, working the stiffness out of his system and getting the blood circulating in his head. Walking on his hands had been, for several years, his only means of self-propulsion, and he began each day in its repetition, the beginnings of his morning devotion to life and motion—his religion.

He watched the new jeep pull up near the Hilton, the low hum of Sardi's mantra insistent in his ear from the far end of the patio. Two plainclothes Americans were getting out and conferring with their predecessors, the whole act then turning in his direction and looking up, pointing. He carefully pulled a hand off the rail, balancing on one arm, and waved to the men beneath. They turned immediately and got into their cars, the one from the night before riding away.

Jorge and Kim walked outside to join him, a cup of room-service coffee in each of their hands. Jorge was dressed in a suit, but in deference to the tropics and relaxation, had taken the jacket off. It was quite a step for him. Kim was looking scrubbed clean and well rested in tight jeans and a Harvard University T-shirt. The .357 that Justice had taken away from the cop the night before was stuck in the waistband of Vanderhoff's trousers.

157

"What's the story on the Zone police, Jorge?" he asked, hand-walking quickly—hand-*running* perhaps—up and down the length of the rail. "Know anything about the infrastructure?"

Vanderhoff walked to the rail and looked down at the jeep far below. "We studied up before we came," he said, "but the dynamic was difficult to understand. The Canal Zone police had traditionally been retired American servicemen, but after the seventy-seven treaty, their positions became unclear. As the U.S. turns over more and more of the Zone and the canal operation to the Panamanians, the Zone police have been caught in the flux, losing power that had been traditionally theirs. Right now they seem to coexist with the Panamian military that has control over the area, but it's difficult to say who controls what or just how much power they have anymore."

"Or whom they work for," Justice replied, crumpling to somersault on the narrow rail, then springing to his feet. "I want to see the registration on that gun. It might tell us something. I haven't been able to figure those guys down there, and it's starting to get to me. What's their stake in all this?"

"Maybe they work for U.S. government," Kim said. "Make sure we don't leave until we do the job."

Justice squatted Asian style on the rail, looking down at the jeep. He hated random elements that he didn't control. "Maybe," he said. "But I have to wonder. If I ran their territory and suddenly found myself with a new boss, I'd figure pretty quickly that if I didn't work with the new kid, he'd replace me soon enough. The Zone would be a hell of a place to live if you didn't carry the hammer."

"What about our weapons?" Kim asked.

Justice suddenly sprang, a back flip, turning a double gainer and landing on his feet. "It keeps coming back to the Zone," he said. "If we can't work this out with those sons of bitches pretty soon, I believe we're going to have to shake the tree a little bit and see what flies out."

"That could be a dangerous game," Sardi said, unfolding himself from the lotus position and standing. "The Canal Zone has traditionally been a position of real power to its rulers. The trees may not so much shake as fall on top of you."

He walked up to join them, folding his hands in front of his face. "*Namaste*, Kim," he said, bowing slightly. "*Namaste*, Jorge. I think that my assessment of the situation would be much like William's. The Canal Zone police are in an untenable position. There must be at least some service to their new masters."

"But that still doesn't explain why they're keeping tabs on us," Jorge said.

"No," Justice replied. "And it doesn't tell us who that woman in the Hilton is. But I believe I'll take care of that particular piece of business right now."

"Be careful, William," Sardi said. "She seems to enjoy constructing her own reality as much as you do."

"A gamer," Justice smiled. "My feeling, too."

"I'll go with you," Jorge said, but Justice waved it off.

"Go get that gun started through our system," he said. "Then make sure that Kiki and Bob are in some kind of shape. I think things will begin moving a great deal faster at this point. There's something in the air."

"That DDT," Kim said. "They spray this morning."

Justice went back to his bedroom and changed into slacks and a sport shirt, then walked out of the suite, taking the elevator to the lobby. He'd had the dreams again last night and had awakened at three A.M. with cold sweats, afraid to try to move, afraid he was paralyzed. He had lain like a statue for nearly an hour before finding the courage to move. Sometimes he thought he was crazy, and, the whole-world's-crazy-and-isn't-it-funny; but sometimes he could get a real glimpse of just how close to that edge he really was, and it wasn't funny. It wasn't funny at all.

"Meester Lambert!" the deskman called as he passed registration. He turned to see the man holding up a manila envelop. "This just come for you sir!"

"Thanks," Justice said, moving over to take the envelope. He heard the distant blare of a shrill whistle and looked in perplexity at the deskman. "What's that?"

The man's eyes lit up. "When the wind is right, we can hear the whistles from the docks. Is pleasant, no? That's probably the *Norweigan Princess* saying good bye to us."

"Very poetic," Justice said, smiling at the man. He opened the envelope while heading for the door. It was the information about the Bocas del Toro sinkings that he had asked for from Research. He closed the envelope, folded it in half, and stuck it in his back pocket.

The day outside was clear and hot, much hotter than his breezy perch up on the twelfth floor. Vía España was bursting with traffic, mostly Japanese cars with a mixture of Chevrolets from the fifties and sixties. A janitor sat on the small set of steps leading down to the wide sidewalk, banging away with a hammer at the ash can that had gotten so battered up by the fire department the night before. He was trying to knock it back into shape, a task that struck Justice as a lot like trying to put out a gasoline fire with water.

He looked down the block, to the west, and could see the harbor way off in the hazy distance. The *Princess* was indeed getting under way, another large liner of the same general configuration all ready to take its place at the docks. *So long, Ed,* he thought, wishing the man well. He was thankful that the *Princess* had come through the locks on the Pacific side, an ocean away from the sinkings.

He picked his way across Vía España, then moved along the sidewalk toward the Hilton. As he got closer to the ubiquitous Canal Zone police jeep, he waved heartily and called out to them in greeting. In response the jeep started up and rolled farther down the block before parking again.

He went into the hotel, walking through its ultramodern lobby, all peach colors and large prints of paintings that shouldn't have been painted to begin with, and pushed the up button on the high-chrome elevator station, his reflection distorting up and down the length of the chrome.

The elevator arrived and he took the ride to 213, walking quietly down the last bit of hallway to Alice Smith's room. He looked both ways down the vacant hall and bent to the lock. The maid's ingress button was out, the door not thumb-locked from the inside. He reached into his pocket, pulled out a number two burglar's pick, and worked it into the lock, the door opening easily in his hand.

He moved slowly inside the room, closing the door and putting his back to it until he'd gotten the feel of the place. He closed his eyes and let the smells play on his nostrils: a whiff of perfume—Charlie, if he wasn't losing touch—a hint of soap, the stale odor of cigarettes, and Scotch whiskey.

The closet lay just to the left, in a small hallway that led ultimately to the bathroom. He checked both of them first, finding the tub and shower curtain still wet, then moved into the room itself. The bed was unmade, the perfume odor heavy there, along with the cigarettes. A full ashtray sat on the nightstand. The odors were fresh, especially the soap smell. He concluded that the room had been occupied as little as five minutes before.

Then he turned and saw the message on the mirror, written in lipstick. He smiled and read: GOOD MORNING, MR. LAMBERT. YOU'VE JUST MISSED ME. WHY DIDN'T YOU COME LAST NIGHT? I WAITED FOR YOU. —A.S.

He turned to the patio door. It was ajar. Her escape route. While he'd been fiddling with the lock, she'd been going over the side. He moved onto the veranda, looking up and down the street, just in time to see her Mercedes screeching off in the direction of the docks. Strange.

He went back inside, used a washcloth to smear his name out of the message, and left. The mystery lady would have to remain a mystery for a while longer.

He crossed back over to the Continental, the janitor still working with the ash can, Justice beginning to feel a little guilty about all the man-hours he had created with his little fire. Then he simply realized it was the basic nature of a capitalistic society.

He saw Enrique Cazorla the moment he walked into the lobby, the man, God bless him, trying his best not to look suspicious and failing miserably. Justice made the lobby, seeing one man he was sure was watching him, another he suspected. As Cazorla caught sight and moved in his direction, Justice waved him off and pointed toward the elevators.

They entered an open elevator and rode it up with a boy of about nine in a swimsuit who was dragging a beach towel and dripping water all over everything. The boy got off on six, and when they started up again, Justice cut the power, stranding them between floors.

"Good morning, my friend," Justice said, shaking hands with the man. "I hope you had a successful evening."

Cazorla rolled his eyes. "I was so drunk that they didn't believe nothing I said."

"Until you showed them the money, right?"

"That's right," Cazorla replied. "They say they meet with you today at two o'clock...but you must come alone and bring the money."

"You say I'm to come alone," Justice repeated, "carrying a half million dollars."

"Yes, that's right."

He looked at the man, wondering if Cazorla really thought him that stupid. Well, what the hell? He could play, too. "Will you go with me?" he asked.

"Sure," the man said happily. "I want to collect my share."

Then Justice realized that Cazorla didn't think him stupid. From Cazorla's tiny perch on the world, stupid was too lofty a concept for him even to appreciate.

"Where's the meet?" Justice asked.

"Not far," the man said. "At the Old City, Cathedral Tower."

"It's a deal," Justice said. "Meet me out in front of the hotel at one-thirty."

"Okay!" Cazorla said excitedly, and Justice couldn't believe that the man didn't know when he was being set up. How had he stayed alive this long?

Justice pushed the button for seven and turned the power back on. When the door opened, he eased the man out of the lift and told him to wait for another. Then he rode up to twelve to tell the others the good news—he was going out to the Old City to be killed. It looked as if the tree shaking was about to begin.

"No," Justice said emphatically. "You're the one who doesn't understand. That's my boat, and I'll board it if I want to."

"You'll stand aside," the American Zone cop said, a hand on his uniform gun belt. "I have orders to shoot anyone who tries to board."

Justice looked past the man and down the long pier. Two more American Canal Zone police stood on guard at the boat itself, both of them looking with interest at the altercation. Justice had to get all of them out of the way.

He reached into his pocket, pulling out a wad of bills. On the pier occupied yesterday by the *Princess,* another cruise ship, the *Crystal Queen,* rocked gently in its moorings. He began peeling off hundreds, the man's eyes wide as he watched. "I just want to go on for a few minutes," he said. "Perhaps an arrangement..."

"No," the man said, forcing himself to look the other way. "You will stand aside... now!"

"And what if I don't?"

The cop's eyes flashed, and he jerked the .45 from its patent leather holster, Justice twirling and kicking out, connecting the nickel-plated automatic jerking from the man's hand and skittering across the pier to plop into the waters beneath. He twirled the other way, cracking the man's jaw with the blade of his foot.

The man went down hard, the other two guards charging back down the pier, M16s up and ready. Good. He smiled widely at the men and figured that if he was wrong about them not shooting him, he'd find it out now.

"Put your hands behind your head!"

They were ten feet from him, the assault rifles shouldered, live rounds in the chambers. The man doing the talking was the one who'd been with the Panamanian captain when they'd arrived yesterday.

Justice put his hands behind his head. "So many guns," he said.

The cop on the deck rose to his knees, moaning, hands clutching his face. "Shoot the son of a bitch," he strained through clenched teeth, the effort hurting his jaw even more.

The cop with the M16 ignored his partner's probably sound advise. "Keep the hands up, friend," he told Justice. "Jesse... frisk him."

Jesse, a corporal, handed his rifle to his partner and moved to Justice, patting him down roughly.

"Watch out," Justice said. "I'm ticklish."

The man's face twisted into a hard grimace, and he lashed out, punching Justice in the stomach, the blow landing on muscles long conditioned to physical pressure.

"Didn't hurt," Justice taunted, and past his assailants he could see Bob Jenks quietly pull himself out of the water and onto the deck of the *Lutine,* ducking behind the mainsail jib.

"Damn you!" Jesse shouted, and cocked a beefy fist.

"No!" his partner said. "Not yet."

Jesse swung around to the man. "Dammit, Nathan! Can't we just..."

"Shut up!" Nathan snapped, the man on the pier finally getting to his feet and staggering to lean against a pylon.

"Would it help," Justice asked, "if I told you that it hurt a little bit?"

Kim slipped on board, fifty feet down the pier, her small form visible for only a second as she ducked down, helping Jenks remove some of the contraband from the hidden gunwale storage.

All at once emergency horns began sounding up and down the docks.

"What's that?" Justice asked, fearing the answer.

"You just worry about yourself," Nathan smiled. "Cause you just brought all the trouble in the world down on your head."

He nodded past Justice to the road behind. An old Cadillac convertible was rushing toward them, dust kicking up behind it, three men in uniform in the front seat. The car sped past Immigration and screeched up onto the pier, jerking to a stop near Justice.

Two of the three men got out of the car, the driver staying behind the wheel, a magazine coming up to his face no sooner than he'd put on the parking brake. Of the two men striding toward him, he recognized Captain Ortiz from yesterday. The other man was far more imposing, a chill knifing through Justice as he watched the man stride forward.

He was a lieutenant colonel in the Panamanian National Guard, wearing full-dress uniform, including the fruit salad over the heart. He was meticulously well-groomed and would have been handsome, except that an aura of cruelty hovered precariously around his eyes, leaking out over everything he came in contact with.

"What's going on here?" he asked, his voice quiet, controlled, his English of textbook quality. He stared hard at Justice, trying to wither him with a glance.

The horns still bleated loudly, activity beginning around the canal, helicopters taking to the sky from the air base, moving past them toward the Pacific.

"I've come to board my boat," Justice said. "Are you the man who's holding it?"

The man smiled with thin lips. "Mr. Lambert," he said. "My name is Colonel Portilla. And I am, indeed, holding your boat. I see you have injured one of my men." He looked at Ortiz, motioning him toward the injured man. "You are not behaving yourself very well. Perhaps you have forgotten that you are a guest in my country."

"What are the sirens?" Justice asked, a navy cutter steaming past them, also moving through the bay toward the Pacific.

"An unfortunate occurrence," Portilla said, the smile still fixed on his unlined face. "A passenger ship has issued a Mayday and is going down." Ortiz had taken the man back to the Cadillac and was walking back to stand with his boss.

"*Norwegian Princess?*" Justice asked, feeling a gnawing in the pit of his stomach.

The man still held his eyes. "Just so," he said quietly. "Now you tell me why I shouldn't have you arrested and thrown into jail for assaulting one of my policemen?"

"*Your* policemen?" Justice returned coldly, his insides churning.

"This is my canal, Mr. Lambert," Portilla said, "*my* territory. I am the law here, and you are breaking that law."

"And why the hell are you standing here flapping your fucking jaws when you should be out doing something about those ships?" Justice said, unable to keep the calm in his own voice. He pictured Ed and Marti, going down, disappearing just like all the rest of them.

The man smiled again. "You don't ask the questions, Mr. Lambert. Your job is only to answer to me. You don't understand the serious nature of your transgression. Perhaps a jail term would be more to your liking."

"Sounds like a deal at that," Justice said, shooting in the dark. Portilla didn't look like a man to waste words on anybody. If he was going to do something to Justice, he would have already done it. "Go ahead and arrest me. You're holding my boat illegally, asshole, and I'll be damned if I'm going to let you get away with it!"

Portilla started but held himself back. Why? It was beginning. Some sort of ball was rolling, and try as he might, he couldn't get the fix on it. And the horns blared, Justice knowing that at that very moment Ed could be drowning, dying, while he stood here arguing with this idiot.

"You will leave this area at once, Mr. Lambert," Portilla said. "There is no more to be said."

The man turned sharply and began walking away. Justice, his blood up, felt his control slipping. "Not this time," he said, walking in front of the man, blocking him off. "What the hell is going on here? What kind of sick game are you playing?"

"Get out of my way," Portilla said, drawing himself up.

"No," Justice said. "Not until you tell me what's happening to the boats going through the canal. What are you doing with them?"

The man shoved him, trying to knock him aside, Justice responding with a hard right to the man's chin, sending him backwards into Ortiz's arms. He took another step toward the man, stopping at the sound of the bolts being pulled back on the M16s. He looked up at the other two men, knowing they were too distant for him to do anything about.

Portilla straightened, tugging his dress jacket down, a hand coming up to wipe a line of blood from his mouth. He tasted it. "Any other man would be dead right now," he said.

"And why not me?" Justice asked. "Why don't you kill me?" He opened his arms and turned a full circle. "See? I'm an easy target."

"It's unfortunate," Portilla said, unholstering the Uzi pistol strapped to his belt and pointing it at Justice. "You see me not handling this situation. You perceive weakness in me. I am a very sincere and strong man, Mr. Lambert. You must understand that."

"What I understand about you," Justice said, "is that you're a punk all dressed up in khaki and braid. The public toilets are full of assholes like you."

"You strike me as a decent man," Portilla said, priming the pistol, "maybe even a good man. Perhaps I can get your attention some other way."

Justice should have seen it coming. In his mania over Ed Barkes and his desire to push for answers, he'd failed to appreciate the hardness of the man. Almost in slow motion, he saw Portilla turn to Captain Ortiz and fire point-blank at the man's chest.

Ortiz went down hard, blood gurgling from his mouth and the gaping wound in his chest. His arms vibrated wildly, banging against the rough wood of the pier.

"No!" Justice yelled, running to the man, bending to him. His bloody lips tried desperately to speak as he fixed Justice's eyes with his own, fear and questioning oozing out along with the life force.

Justice tried to apply pressure to the wound, but it did no good. The artery had been severed, Ortiz bleeding out within a minute, his body stiffening at once, the questions in his eyes turning to a marbly glaze as he died. Justice closed the man's eyes and stood, his fists clenched to bloodless white as he stared cold fire at Portilla.

"Do you have more questions for me?" the man asked. "There are many more people on the docks." He looked down at Ortiz, shaking his head. "An unfortunate terrorist attack, don't you think?"

Justice turned and looked at the Canal Zone cops. Their weapons were still trained on him, their faces hard on the stocks. And he knew that there was nothing else to say, that he had said too much already. He looked once at the boat, just in time to see Jenks go back over the side. He had won the battle but lost the war. Without a word he turned and walked silently off the dock, his mind lost in darkness. The wheels were turning, grinding everything into grist, and he was caught up on the wheel just like everybody else.

Salt air and the stench of dead fish assailed him as he climbed into the rented Volkswagen van he'd left parked in the Immigration lot. He dropped it into gear and drove east along the pier access road, stopping a mile down, next to the black English Ford parked behind a small snack bar set up for the dockworkers. The smell of frying peanut oil drifted heavily through the entire area, gulls circling continuously, occasionally dipping down to buzz the trash cans.

Sardi got out of the Ford, his eyes narrowing when he saw the look on Justice's face. "What happened?" he asked, Vanderhoff getting out of the passenger side, looking across the top of the car in concern.

"I just got a man killed," he said. "A poor little guy who hadn't done anything."

"Why?" Vanderhoff asked.

"Why," Justice repeated low. "Why!" He banged the front of the van with a heavy fist. "Because some swaggering bastard wanted to show me he was tough. Because for some reason I'm untouchable, and he needed an example. Because... there's no because." Justice turned from them, pain shooting through his back. "Because I pushed them too far."

"Why wouldn't they go after you?" Vanderhoff asked.

Justice took a breath. He'd take care of Portilla when the time was right. At the moment he had to keep his mind clear and engaged in the business at hand. "I'm sure of it now," he said. "The Canal Zone police are in this party up to their eyeballs. They're connected somehow, and I'm going to nail them along with everything else."

"They're back," Sardi said, pointing.

Kim, Jenks, and Kiki were walking toward them from the dock area, all of them wet and dripping, large waterproof sacks slung over their shoulders. Vanderhoff hurried to open the Ford's trunk, the sacks going in quickly.

"*Mon*," Kiki said, face shining darkly. "What goes on at the dock?"

"The game," Justice said. "The damned game. The *Norwegian Princess* is down."

Kim walked up, concern on her face. She wiped wet hair out of her eyes and took his arm, looking up. "Your friends..." she said, compassion welling up in her face. "Maybe they won't be dead."

"Yeah, maybe," he returned, not believing it. He cut it off—battle losses. "How much did you get?"

"Enough to frag up a minor revolution," Jenks said, wiping his wet hair on a towel handed to him by Sardi. "So the killin's started."

Justice looked at each of them in turn. "It's started," he said, "and I'm afraid it's going to get real messy. Whatever happens, save that son of a bitch, Portilla, for me. You know what to do. It's time to do it."

His people climbed into the Ford, Justice wandering, alone, back to the VW. He opened the door and felt a hand on his arm. He turned to see Sardi staring at him, his brown eyes murky, swirling liquid. "It wasn't your fault," he said.

"Of course it was my fault," Justice countered. "I pushed too far."

"Remember the dharma," the man replied. "Appropriate duty and morality. Your dharma is as a just warrior, and your duty is clear. You cannot feel yourself responsible for the actions of others."

Justice nodded. "You'd better get going," he said, Sardi nodding and walking away.

"Sardi!" he called after him, the man stopping, turning slowly. Justice smiled. "Thanks."

"Thank me when it's over," Sardi replied, then turned and continued walking.

Justice climbed up into the driver's side and slammed the door, leaning his head on the steering wheel. He heard the Ford start up and drive off, leaving him alone. He looked at his watch. It was time to go to the hotel and pick up Cazorla; the man was probably jumping up and down in anticipation of his own demise.

He started the van and turned it around, heading back toward the Thatcher Ferry Bridge. He couldn't get Ortiz out of his mind. Innocents died in war all the time, and war was what he waged—war on all levels: political, social, economic, and military. And the purpose of his wars was to free people like Ortiz from the tyranny of people like Portilla. When it worked the other way, it hurt him, physically hurt him, and the pain in his back had been severe.

Panama Bay sparkled like a jewel with a million facets as he drove across it, trying to separate his duty from his desires. The steel structural span of the bridge crisscrossed his vision like jail bars, and it could have been the prison of his own mind locking him into a scenario of his own creation. Panama had already turned into a dark and dangerous dream to him, and as he approached the time of contact with the Medellin people, he wondered if the dream would override his reality. Innocents had already died, and he mourned Ed and Marti Barkes, all the while knowing that their deaths were somehow a part of the larger pattern that he had yet to discern.

The city traffic was heavy, but he had luck with the lights and took the hill up to the Continental with time to spare. As he'd suspected, Cazorla was ready and waiting for him, excited. In the arena of users and the used, Cazorla definitely fit into the user category—the enemy. He had no qualms about walking into a firefight with the man at his side, unarmed, of course. He looked at the situation as natural selection in action, nature weeding out the less-deserving members of the species.

Cazorla climbed into the van, his face lit up as if he had just won the lottery. He was eating an ice cream bar, the thing melting rapidly down the stick and onto his hand. "You got the money with you?" he asked.

Justice smiled, realizing that the allure of money was enough to turn anybody stupid. "Don't you worry, partner," he said. "I've got everything taken care of."

Justice geared the van and moved on to Vía España, past the Hilton. He had lost the Zone surveillance jeep when he'd gone to the docks, but they were back waiting for him again. He looked at his watch. There wasn't a great deal of time left to lose them again.

"I'm gonna buy me a car with my money," Cazorla said. "A new one, maybe seventy Chevy, bright red with big chrome headers. What do you think?"

"I think I'm going to take a right on Brazil, then try to lose our tag," Justice said.

"What tag?" the man asked, face falling as he turned to watch the jeep several cars back. He turned to Justice, all worked up. "What we gonna do?"

Justice ignored his question. "Will Vía Israel get us to the Old City?"

"Yeah, yeah," the man said, watching behind them as the ice cream dripped on his pants in huge, runny gobs. "It's five miles away . . . five miles."

They rushed the light at Brazil, still in the financial district, and took a right, the jeep following. He was just getting ready to make a move on the Zone police when a familiar sports car roared up beside him, Alice Smith waving, then falling back.

He watched in the rearview as she put herself between him and the police; then at the next light she slowed, blocking the jeep, and when it tried to go around, she jerked the wheel, smashing into the fender. Justice smiled, shaking his head, watching in the mirror as she ran around, screaming and pointing to the two burly men, attracting a crowd as they argued over the wreck. Within another block they were lost from sight.

"Ah," Cazorla sighed. "Lucky for us, huh?"

"Yeah," Justice replied. "Lucky."

The rest of the trip went quickly, both men quieting and settling into their expectations and fears. He took a left on Vía Israel and followed it as it wound its way down to the Pacific. The ocean rolled to their right, boisterously free, as they passed the statue of Father Morelos, a national hero of the Mexican Independence, the Old City visible in the distance.

Justice submerged himself into the warrior's mode as they skirted the ocean and pulled up to the gaming ground, his eyes slowly roving the landscape first one way, then the other. The old city, or Casco Antigua, as it was called locally, seemed to glow with mystic portent. It lay before them in skeletal remains of gray stone walls and roofless dwellings, a vague echo to past lives lost, past dreams dashed. Games had been played here before. In 1671 Henry Morgan's fleet had laid waste to the town and its inhabitants as he searched for the Portobelo treasure house where the Spanish stored their own plundered Peruvian gold. Senseless violence and injustice screamed from every rock as they lay, still in the same positions the ancients had placed them, foolishly attesting to the civilization of construction, even in the epicenter of extreme folly.

"You'll need to park the bus," Cazorla said, pointing to a flat area on the city's outskirts that was geometrically marked by the foundations of long-dead dwellings. Justice pulled in next to several other cars, his senses on edge, tingling, as he tried to clear his mind of everything but caution and awareness.

They climbed out of the van, Cazorla still carrying his decomposing ice cream bar, Justice going around to the sliding side door to remove the steamer-size aluminum trunk carrying the half million in cash. Cazorla reverently watched him handle the bag, Justice reflecting on the quasi-religious value most people placed on money. To him it was only a means to an end. He could lose the whole suitcase and give it very little more than a passing thought; but to somebody like Cazorla it represented a life value, something that would perhaps make him a worthwhile person. Him and every-body else. Fat chance. A rich punk is still a punk.

They entered the bones of the city through the remnants of a stone gate, bright green grass poking up through the rows of stone and half walls, life forcing itself out of death.

"The cathedral is this way," Cazorla said, pointing in the direction of a seventy-five-foot tall stone structure in the distance. "We'll cut through the plaza."

He moved to the right, Justice following. They walked to a series of high, thick, deteriorated walls, interconnecting at right angles with long tunnels cut through them. Two dark men, perhaps Indians, stood at one tunnel entry, both of them carrying Remington twelve-gauge pump shotguns. They eyed Justice darkly as he passed them, the man smiling in return.

They entered the tunnel, Cazorla laughing nervously, the sound echoing eerily through the breezeway. They exited onto what had at one time been a narrow, twisting street and walked it, more men with guns surveying their path from the tops of ragged walls all along the roadway. Justice counted nine of them before the street ended at the front door of what had once been a large church—what the Spanish had referred to as civilization while they were robbing and killing the local populations of their conquests.

They entered the church, the Compañía de Jesús, a mammoth stone structure with no roof and no glass in its double tiers of windows, grass and wildflowers growing abundantly in the huge atrium. Justice watched Cazorla make the sign of the cross when they walked in, the man walking quickly now, leading him forward, in the direction of the sacristy. Three more guards casually kept positions near the walls, none of them hidden, all of them comfortable on home ground.

The bell tower sat outside the church proper, its mono-lithic presence commanding the high ground overlooking the Pacific, having once served its military purposes excellently during the Spanish conquests. Two burly men with primed Uzis stood at the door; another man, dressed in a white silk suit, stood casually in the doorway, leaning against it. He smiled when he saw them approach.

"You must be Mr. Lambert," he said, moving forward

out of the shadows to extend his hand, his eyes on the suitcase the whole time. Justice shook the man's hand. "My name is Victor Ibanez. It is so good of you to come under these less than ideal circumstances."

"Just business," Justice said amiably. "I take it you know my associate, Mr. Cazorla?"

Ibanez turned his eyes briefly on Cazorla, his lips curling up at the sight of the ice cream dripping on the man's hand and arm. "Only slightly," he said.

Cazorla turned to Justice. "Mr. Ibanez is a very important man," he said.

"I see," Justice said, "Well, then, he must be the man I want to see."

"Yes," Ibanez said. "I hear you may have a mutually beneficial financial arrangement to offer my superiors."

"I do, indeed," Justice said, holding up the suitcase. "And my good intentions are right here. I want to tell you that I also appreciate all the people you've brought with you to help protect my investment."

The man smiled. "A trifle," he said. "It was nothing. Now if you will hold your arms out straight, I fear there is one more formality we must observe." The man nodded to one of the big guards, who put down his weapon and moved to Justice.

Putting down the suitcase, Justice held out his arms, the man patting him down expertly, not finding anything. The punk moved away from him, shaking his head at Ibanez, who seemed to relax, his face settling into a silly grin.

"Very good," Ibanez said. "You are an honorable man."

"As are we all," Justice replied. "Shall we get out of the sun now?"

"Most assuredly," Ibanez said, pulling a handkerchief out of his pocket to wipe at the beads of sweat on his forehead. He motioned Justice through the doorway of the tower, following him in as Cazorla tagged along, happy as a kid with a new toy.

A spiral staircase made of stone curved around inside the inner walls of the tower, leading to a loft high above, sunlight slanting in through the many cutouts in the wall at odd, surreal angles. Justice took the steps, lugging the suitcase with him. If Ibanez was in the Medellin hierarchy, he was just barely in. He didn't appear smart enough to exercise real authority over much of anything, though Justice figured he could still be a valuable link to the real power. No doubt he was somebody's brother-in-law or something, entitled to a slice of the pie by the thinnest of luck and acting as if that minor authority were his God-given birthright.

He made it to the loft, dragging the suitcase up behind him. He was in a tiny room, perhaps ten feet square, with a plank floor. Three-quarter window spaces were gouged through the stone on all four surrounding walls, the wooden bell cradle hanging in the middle of the small space, dominating it, the church bell long gone.

"Privacy, no?" Ibanez said, his head poking up through the floor as he climbed up, looking like a cat toying with a cricket. He stepped into the loft, then began meticulously brushing dust off his fancy suit. Cazorla followed, his ice cream nearly gone now, most of it residing on his right arm.

"So," Justice began. "My friends in Chicago told me that you people might be able to handle all my business. I've been very unhappy with my Middle Eastern connection."

"We are a very large operation," Ibanez said, placing himself strategically near one of the cutouts. "We have many satisfied customers in the United States of America. But before we can talk freely about it, you must show me the good faith you say that you carry."

"With pleasure," Justice said, placing the suitcase on the floor and snapping it open. Cazorla gasped loudly when he saw the pile of bundled cash within, even Ibanez craning his neck to get a good look.

"*Madre de Dios,*" Cazorla said, Justice watching carefully as Ibanez made a great show of wiping his face with the handkerchief as he stood by the window.

"Now," Justice said. "Let's do it like we do in the States. It's called show and tell. I've shown you mine, now you show me yours."

"I will, indeed," Ibanez said with self-satisfaction. He reached into his pocket and withdrew a short-barreled .38, the kind once called a police special. He pointed it at Justice.

"What are you doing?" Cazorla said, amazed. "We had a deal. . . . You told me we had a deal!"

Ibanez shrugged. "There's another expression you have

174

in the States," he said. "A fool and his money are soon parted, no? You were a fool to come in her alone with all that money."

"What makes you think I'm alone?" Justice asked, fixing Ibanez with hard eyes, giving the man a dose of pure, unattenuated power, the man buckling slightly, backing up a step.

Several loud cracks were heard outside, gunfire, popping like a string of firecrackers, excited voices mixing with the sounds.

"What's happening?" Cazorla screeched, eyes wide, the ice cream finally giving up and falling off the stick and onto his shoes.

"Just business," Justice said quietly, then looked at Ibanez. "You want to give me the gun?"

"No!" the man said, backing all the way against the wall, sweat now running freely down his face, the gun shaking slightly in his hand. "You couldn't . . . you . . . you . . ."

"I could and I did," Justice said, pointing out the windows.

His people, dressed in the gray of the stone walls, were moving fluidly through the ruins all around them. A life-size chess game, they pushed like a machine through the various blocked-off areas, making of each one a gaming place as they came to it—surrounding, setting up cross fires, choking off.

"But I've still got you," Ibanez said, mustering himself, but Justice knew he didn't have the heart for it.

"This is crazy!" Cazorla shouted, moving from window to window. "Crazy!"

"You've got one chance," Justice said. "Give me the gun right now."

One of Ibanez's door guards at the tower charged across the yard below, withering fire cutting him down before he could get fifteen feet, the man crumpling hard, his body spitting blood.

"I just wanted to get your attention," Justice said. "We can still do business."

Ibanez's gun hand began shaking, fear quickly supplanting all other emotions in his eyes. There was gunfire from below, the last of the guards taking refuge within the tower, his assault rifle exploding loudly in the hollow space, Ibanez jumping with each shot.

Then the man screamed, the sound swallowed in the huge explosion that rocked the floor, almost knocking Ibanez out the window.

Justice looked at the man silently, then held out his hand. Whimpering, Ibanez handed him the gun.

"Now," Justice said. "We both understand each other, right?"

Ibanez swallowed hard, nodding quickly as Justice pocketed the .38. "You won't . . . k-kill me?"

"My man!" Justice said genially, walking to put his arm around the shaking man. "Why would I want to kill you? We can get rich together. We'll be partners."

"Partners?" Ibanez said, desperate hope clinging to his words.

"Yeah!" Cazorla said. "We're all partners."

"Will!" came Jenks's voice from below. "You okay?"

"Yeah," Justice called back down. "Me and my new partner are just having a little chat up here. Gather up the bodies."

"Already started," he called.

"Now," Cazorla said. "About my money . . ."

"What money?" Justice asked, taking the .38 back out of his pocket and pointing it at Cazorla. "Seems to me you set me up pretty good here."

"But, I didn't—"

"Shut up," Justice said, pulling back the hammer and pointing at the man's head. He toyed with it, flirted with ending the man's miserable excuse for existence right there. Instead he said, "You wanted a car, Enrique. Mr. Ibanez certainly has too many cars right now, don't you, Victor?"

"Too many," Ibanez said quickly. "And nobody to drive them."

"Pick a car," Justice said. "Pick a car and take it. Either hot-wire it or go through the dead men's pockets, but do it now, because I'm done with you one way or the other."

The man looked at him, understanding, and ran. Within fifteen seconds Justice saw him charging out of the bell tower, running toward their impromptu parking lot.

He turned back to Ibanez. "Can we do some real business?" he asked.

The man swallowed again. "For this size of an operation,

my bosses are going to want to meet with you themselves," he said. "They are very fair people, and you will be able to work out an equitable arrangement with them. We will have to take a journey together to the west. I will call them and set it up."

"To Volcán Barú?" Justice asked, bending to the suitcase and taking out a stack of bills.

"You've been to school on us," Ibanez replied, taken slightly aback. "We will probably leave early in the morning."

"This time my people come with me," Justice said, peeling ten hundreds off the stack and handing them to Ibanez. "For funeral arrangements."

"Of course," the man replied, pocketing the cash. "For you, Mr. Lambert, anything."

Justice smiled. "That's the boy. Shall we join my friends below?"

The two new "partners" climbed down the stone stairs, the body of the last guard still lying, in pieces, on the bell tower floor. They skirted it without comment and walked into the sunshine, a pile of bodies laid out in a neat row near the door, Justice's people, their faces blackened, sitting in the wall shade. The smell of death permeated the entire area. He could just make out Sardi in the distance, moving through the ruins of the Old City like a tourist, examining.

Justice counted off the bodies, stopping at the end of the line, then looked at Jenks who was going through a pile of weapons on the ground in the hopes of finding something salvageable.

"Anybody hurt?" Justice asked.

"Naw," Jenks said, not even looking up. "They wasn't even a good warm-up."

"I made fourteen coming in," Justice returned. "There's only thirteen here."

"I got him!" Kim called from across the wide yard, a body slung over her shoulder as she weaved slightly underneath the weight of it. "He's a fat one, too!"

She staggered up, dropping the body at the end of the line. Justice turned to Ibanez, the man staring in numbed silence at all his men on the ground. "Victor," he said, "these are my associates. You can meet us all in the morning at the Balboa monument. Got it?"

The man nodded gravely. "Mr. Lambert," he said, "what am I supposed to do with these dead men?"

Justice shrugged. "Do whatever you were going to do with me," he said, turning to the others. "Let's get the hell out of here."

They started off, Justice studying the dead again, taking the full measure of death upon himself. While dispassionate to death, he never wanted to be cold to it. He had taken life in the service of humanity, but he had taken it nonetheless, making him a part of all that he hated. Such was the everlasting pain of William Justice.

As the others drifted off, he was drawn magnetically to one of the bodies in the middle of the pile. Dead meat, he was, like the rest of them, his face frozen in a painful grimace. But there was something about the man...something, different. He couldn't put his finger on it.

"Is there trouble, Mr. Lambert?" Ibanez asked.

"Who is this man?" he asked, pointing.

"Just a man who works for me sometimes," Ibanez said without emotion. "A local man, that's all. Nobody special. You know him?"

Justice looked at the man, then turned and walked off, his path merging with Sardi's as he retraced his steps out of town. Sardi hadn't participated in the firefight, as was his usual custom. The two men walked silently side by side for a moment on one of the narrow cobbled pathways that led back through town.

"You're troubled," the man said after a few moments.

"Just thinking," Justice replied. "Trying to place somebody. It's a go to Volcán Barú in the morning."

"I suppose I should congratulate you," the man said.

"I have to do this. You know that."

"I know the lines of worry on your forehead," he replied. "I know the circles under your eyes. I know how you cry out in the middle of the night. But about your emotional return to this land of death, I know nothing. This isn't normal for you, William. You're playing someone else's game under rules you don't understand."

"I understand plenty," Justice countered. "A path once walked is marked with my footprints forever. I can't cover those tracks. I've got to learn how to live with them."

"Or die trying," Sardi said. "Do you wish company on the ride back to the hotel?"

Justice shook his head. "I've got some thinking to do. Go ahead. I'll be along."

They'd reached the edge of the ruins and crossed to the vehicles. The others had already discarded their camouflage clothing and stashed the weapons, Jenks putting the Ford into reverse and backing out, driving over to pick up Sardi.

"Best not to hang around here," he said, someone opening a back door. "You coming with us?"

"Yes," the man said, looking once at Justice before climbing in, the car taking off immediately.

Justice walked to the van and climbed in, his mind clicking, picturing faces. Where had he seen that dead man before? Warning bells were ringing loudly in his head, but he couldn't quite place it.

He started up the van and headed back out on Vía Israel, the Pacific on his left now in beautiful, untamed panorama. It was water that he kept associating with the dead man, water and hard eyes—the canal!

That was it. It was the same man who'd come up in the rowboat on the canal to take back the pilot and the towrope, those same eyes, already dead even when the punk had been alive. Those rowboats had access to every vessel that came through the canal. How easy to plant an explosive charge just below the waterline on a well-chosen craft, then simply follow it in another boat, detonating the charge by remote control when the target ship was in unprotected waters.

The dead punk worked for Medellin, but nothing went on at the locks that Portilla wasn't a party to. He had to assume that the colonel had a part in everything, which made proceeding from this point difficult. His first thought was for the safety of the passengers on the *Crystal Queen*, the liner that had followed Ed's ship into the docks. Because of the navy escorts on the ships exiting into the Atlantic, Medellin had simply decided to take it the other way, which made the *Queen* the logical choice for the next target.

Police headquarters was in the Court of Justice building on Balboa near the Thatcher Bridge. He remembered that from the old days. He gunned the engine, staying on Vía Israel until it turned into Balboa. The Pacific still at his left, he hurried along the coast until running into the small peninsula of Avenida Central and turning oceanward. His drive took him through the teeming public market, its outside stands colorful, the sickly sweet odor of ripeness and rot carrying far beyond the marketplace itself.

He drove into Plaza Independencia, the park at the historic district, racing past the busts of the founding fathers and the famous Central Hotel with its iron grill balconies that had once housed the French and American engineers who built the Panama Canal.

The Court of Justice was a vast government building of centuries-old design. He skidded up to the curb and jumped out, charging into the place, the POLICIA sign beaconing him in immediately.

He ran into a high-ceilinged room, a central foyer that led off into hallways in many directions. Ceiling fans hung down on long poles, circulating the hot air that stifled the atmosphere in there.

A uniformed National Guardsman sat behind a caged counter watching him with dull eyes as he approached.

"My name's Lambert," he told the man. "I need to speak with someone in authority."

"Concerning what?" the man asked slowly.

"I have some information about what's happening to the boats going through the canal."

The man stared at him but never changed expression. He turned, slid his wheeled chair up to another counter behind him, and picked up a phone, speaking softly into it. Then he swung back around. "Lieutenant Rowena will be with you in a moment," he said. "He asks that you please wait."

Justice looked hard at the man. There was something about his demeanor—something different from the expression he wore before he made the phone call. He went with the feelings. "I've got to leave," he said. "Tell the lieutenant I'll get back with him."

He turned and started for the door, the soldiers pouring in before he reached it. He swung quickly back the other way, the man in the cage ducking down as more uniformed troops hurried into the room, their M16s up and ready.

"Going somewhere, Mr. Lambert?" came the voice of

one of the nameless faces that he'd seen staking him out at the Hotel Continental.

Justice turned a full circle. He was surrounded by soldiers, all of them drawing down on him.

"I have to talk to you," he told the lieutenant, an overweight, genial-looking man with a moustache.

"Excellent," the man said. "You see, I want to talk to you, also. You have saved me the trouble of coming to find you. You will please raise your hands, Mr. Lambert. You are under arrest."

XII.

LOS ANGELES, CALIFORNIA
27 JUNE 1981—1100 HOURS

William Justice stood staring out at the Pacific Ocean from his back deck, uncomfortable in his white tux, the glass of champagne in his hand turning warm even as he held it. He leaned heavily on his ebony cane, the pain in his back and legs intense today with the stress and the length of time spent on his feet, but he didn't care. This was *the* day of his life, the culmination of every other day that had gone before, the beginning of a new chapter for him. And he couldn't be happier.

The deck was thirty feet above the beach, supported by pylons the size of telephone poles. It spread out all around him, tables piled high with food and drink, a trellised canopy adorned with white roses featured prominently on its south side. The sky was fragile blue above, no clouds anywhere on the horizon, and for the first time since '78, he really believed that he'd done his time in hell and that things were going to get much better.

Allie had been his salvation. Allie and her goodness and her intelligent approach to that goodness. She'd replaced the bitterness and self-pity that had motivated him with the concept of service to humanity. What had been anger became devotion to cause, and with every positive step she'd instilled within him he'd gotten better, both physically and emotionally, until finally, over three years later, he was ready to rejoin the human race as a functioning human being.

The dreams had stopped over a year ago, the memories of Panama dimming as he controlled them with his mind. The guilt had never left him, but there were some things a man deserved to live with. His thoughts of revenge had been shuttled away, marked off as part of ancient history. With so much to give, there was nothing he wanted to take away. And if the beauty of the day was a trade-off between Allie's goodness and his responsibility to the people of Volcán Barú, he chose the goodness gladly, knowing that the dead could never truly be brought back.

William Justice was getting married today.

"Will!" came her excited voice from just inside the house. "The bus is here!"

He turned to smile at her, the sun rising twice today— once in the sky and once in her eyes. She wore white lace, but of a sensible length, a dress she'd wear again. Her face glowed with just a touch of tan to highlight it. "Let's greet them," he said, hobbling toward her, the cane bearing most of the weight on his left leg. His therapy still continued, his body still a long way from recovered, but he could walk now, could face the world head on, and the rest would come.

She moved up to him, and he put an arm around her, drinking in the barest scent of patchouli. God, it was good to be alive.

"You need to sit down for a while," she said. "You're really favoring the leg today."

He turned and kissed her on the forehead. "Stop playing nurse," he said. "I'll rest the leg later. It's okay."

"All right," she said. "You'll get your way . . . today."

He reached down and slapped her on the butt, Allie laughing and skittering away from him, disappearing inside the house.

He limped through the sliding glass door and into the first toy he'd bought himself since he'd become rich. He'd spent a million and a half on his house in Malibu on a whim, simply because Allie had once told him she'd never seen the ocean. He chose the Pacific so that they could sit on the deck and watch the sunset together.

The house was huge, designed by one of those California neoclassicist architects who did movie-star houses that were supposed to look like the Taj Mahal. The place was glitzy and quirky, with overhanging lofts and skylights that turned the sunshine lime green. It wasn't Allie's kind of place, but she made do because it had a separate apartment for her mother, who seemed to flourish under Southern California neon while she played mah-jongg three days a week with her lady friends. Feeling uncomfortable in the art-deco fast lane, Allie refurnished the place in solid Early American, which seemed to tame the wildness and, parenthetically, started a small decorating revolution when their house was featured in *Southern California Living*.

He followed Allie through the breakfast room, then through the multitiered living room with the mauve carpet, to the big double front doors. She was already outside, waving to the fancy charter bus that had pulled up in their circular drive. He joined her with a sense of anticipation. He was going to meet his partners for the first time.

"Gentlemen and ladies," he called as they stepped curiously off the bus. "My name is William Lambert. Welcome to my home."

There was recognition and laughter as Justice introduced himself, no one on the bus having any idea why they were there.

"We'll all visit in a little bit," he called. "Right now, let's go on out to the back deck. I have a few words to say to you."

There were twenty-one of them, people he had come in contact with through his business dealings, people who he'd instinctively felt were his kind of people. Some, like Ed Barkes, had been with him from the beginning. Others had joined in the last several months as his business interests continued to expand in different areas, calling for different talents to manage them. Some had already been successful and important; some had been lower-management people he'd simply plucked out of dead-end jobs when they'd handled something minor for him in an honest and dedicated way. Justice worked from his intuition, and it never seemed to let him down.

He brought them out to the deck, smiling at the appreciative noises they made at the offered amenities. As they made themselves comfortable with food and drink, he moved purposefully through the crowd, shaking hands with each person in turn, reserving a special, close welcome for Ed

Barkes who, more than anyone, had made Justice's dreams a reality.

Once he had met everyone, he moved off to the side, smiling, watching the interaction of good people. He could feel the warm and genial atmosphere, and it made him happy. "My friends!" he called, silence settling over the group. "I'm sorry to bring you all here on such short notice, and so mysteriously, but I think you should be more than happy when you find out what's going on."

"Who's minding the store?" someone called, the crowd laughing.

"First of all," Justice said. "It is truly wonderful to meet all of you. Some of you know one another from previous board meetings of Lambert American, but most of you have never met." He smiled. "For example . . . Mary Goddard, where are you?"

A woman raised her hand. "Present!" she called, everyone laughing.

"Well, Mary," he continued. "Over there, standing forlornly in the corner with the big Scotch in his hand, is Joel Cohen, who helped you close the Pacific Lumber deal."

"Oooh!" the woman squealed. "We made the front page of *The Wall Street Journal* with that one, photos and everything. Are you married?"

The crowd applauded, Justice raising his hands for silence. "We'll do more of that later. First of all, though, there's a few things you ought to know. I've brought all of you on board for certain reasons. All of you are intelligent, gutsy, aggressive . . . maybe except for Ed Barkes . . ."

Everyone laughed again.

" . . . and open to new ideas."

"Malleable, you mean," Barkes called out to more applause.

Justice smiled, Allie disappearing to answer the doorbell. "We won't quibble over definitions," he said. "Well, we're going to be dealing with a great many new ideas at this point, and I think you'll be excited by the possibilities. First of all, Lambert American is going public, which will make every one of you a multimillionaire going in. . . ."

There were gasps, especially from the newer members of the team.

"Next," he continued, "we're changing the name from

Lambert American to Lambert International . . . folks, we're going multinational. I want to deregionalize our approach."

"Why?" someone called.

"Humanitarian reasons," Justice said. "I want the tone of our businesses to be humanist and honest and planetwide. From now on we're going to be very careful about where we invest. It will already make many of you happy to know that we are pulling money out of all armament manufacturing. . . ."

Again, scattered applause.

"Our business is going to be a life giver, not the other way around," he continued. "We can still get rich, but we're going to do it by reaffirming the quality of life, not destroying it. I know all of you. I picked you carefully, and I don't believe there's a person here today who won't welcome those changes."

This time the applause was loud and sustained. Many of the board members had tears in their eyes. Good people, all.

"Also, one of our recent acquisitions has been a modest newspaper chain," he said, a loud groan coming from among the guests. Justice grinned. "That's Marty Grossman, one of our accountants who thinks the newspaper chain was a waste of money. Well, maybe it was. But as always, I don't do things without reason. I want to start a paper . . . to be called the *Watchdog*. We're going to use the paper to call attention to human-rights violations all over the world . . . but not just political violations. I want to go after every industry, regardless of its size or geographical boundaries, that pollutes the skies and the streams. I want to expose industrial slave-labor conditions. As many of you well know, I believe that it is big business that really controls the world. Well, it's time somebody took it to task."

"The giant killer!" a woman called, raising her glass, everyone joining in the salute, Justice once more putting up his hands for silence.

"Two more things," Justice said, watching Allie return to the deck with a severe-looking man in a dark suit. "First of all, Lambert American's net worth has recently been computed by *Forbes* at just over five billion dollars, in the incredible span of a little over three years. This is a tribute to all of you, and you have my thanks. You may or may not know it, but I conducted all business from a small room while recuperating from a debilitating illness. You guys have been my legs, my eyes, and my ears. Which leads me to the most important announcement of all and the real reason you were all called here. I'm getting married to the most wonderful woman in the world today, and I want all of you, my good friends, to share this happy moment with me. My hermit days are over. I hope from this day on that I will get to share much more than phone calls with all of you."

They flocked to him and Allie then, some crying, some complaining that he didn't give them time to get a wedding present, many of them knowing that their mysterious boss had done things this way for precisely that reason. And he loved them all; they had achieved the American dream without compromising their personal values, and they deserved to be rewarded for it. How simple and good life could be if it was approached in a communal way, with the good of the species the overriding concern.

And so William Justice Lambert and Allie Boyd were married then, under the canopy, the justice of the peace Allie had hired keeping the ceremony brief, the minimum legal requirement. Allie's mother, looking tiny and cute with a garland of flowers in her hair, was the matron of honor, only holding the ceremony up once as she tried to find her husband. They brought no religious formality to the occasion, their ideas about life and its purpose something close and personal that didn't seem to need public display. And when it was over, and he crushed Allie to him in a long, meaningful kiss, he knew that he had made the prize catch of all time. A woman of substance, a woman of deep and abiding love for all humanity—she was his joy and his conscience—and if he was able to change the whole world, it wouldn't be enough thanks for all she'd done for him.

When it was over, and everyone had toasted the lovely bride and the lucky husband, Justice called for their attention one last time. "There is a brief ceremony Allie and I would like to perform," he said. "And we would like all of you to help us witness it. If you will follow me, ladies and gentlemen, we will repair to the beach."

Laughing and chatting, the entourage followed Will and Allie as they slowly made their way down the length of wooden steps to the beach below, Allie carrying a large wooden box in her hands.

They reached the sand, people stumbling and laughing in their good shoes as they tried to navigate the shifting ground, Justice having no problem, as handling the beach had been an improvised part of his physical therapy. They led the group under the deck, into the forest of dead trees that supported it. A large shovel leaned against one of the pylons. Justice picked it up.

"Today is a new beginning, not only for the company, but for me as a man. As with all new beginnings, there must be endings." Allie held up the box while he continued speaking. "The past will be buried here, and here it will remain."

He began digging, going down several feet, people backing away from flying sand.

"What's in the box, Bill?" Ed Barkes called, Justice shaking it off.

"It's not important," he said, and kept digging.

It became a game, then, people calling out possibilities, everything from a little black book to photos of a first wife.

When he was through digging, he and Allie together placed the box in the ground, both of them covering it back up. And as they all climbed the stairs back up to the party, many people were probably surprised at the effect the burial had on Allie. She glowed as if on fire, her spirit so high she could have been floating. And her reaction kept them guessing; for days and months and even years afterward, Justice continued to receive strange phone calls and letters from his people, all of them still curious about the box, all of them still making guesses as to its contents.

And not one of them ever guessed that the box contained a .45 automatic and a box of shells.

XIII.

PANAMA CITY—COURT OF JUSTICE BUILDING
19 FEBRUARY 1988—1943 HOURS

The overweight cop sat sweating and watching from his desk as the Cuban circled slowly around Justice, the circles getting ever closer, tighter, like a vulture staking its prey. The cop's name was Arroyo, and he seemed a decent enough sort, a typical policeman, all rules and no thought. The Cuban, though, he was another story. Nameless and humorless, he was a product of the politburo, a good commie at war with the world. He was a thinker, that one. In fact he thought too much, and all in the wrong directions. The direction he was thinking in now was how to frighten Justice, an exercise in futility if ever there was one.

"You may as well cooperate in this matter, Mr. Lambert," the Cuban said. "You see, we know all about your arrangement with Miguel Porras. It could only be to your advantage to confide in us now. Perhaps we could be convinced to spare your life, if only..."

"I don't know any Miguel Porras," Justice said for the fiftieth time, twisting uncomfortably on the wooden chair, his hands cuffed behind him, the severe metal cutting into his hands and wrists. "I came to tell you about the canal... I know what's happening there. You must take..."

The Cuban came around with a hard right, catching Justice on the side of the head, knocking him onto the floor, pain flashing. Justice immediately consigned the pain to the

189

back of his brain, and rose. "Touch me again and I'll kill you," he said.

The room froze, the only sound the insistent propeller noise of the overhead fan. Both men stared at him, harsh lighting giving their faces a sinister twist. Beside him a window cut in the wall looked out over the muted shadows of the vestibule where he'd first been taken.

"There's no need for that kind of talk," Arroyo said quietly, wiping his wide forehead on his shirt sleeve.

The Cuban walked right up to him, his dark face strained with rage. He brought a penknife out of his pocket and slowly opened the blade. "I would kill you right now," he said, "but I would rather bleed the information out of you first." He brought the blade up and laid it against Justice's nose. "I know that you are conspiring with Miguel Porras to overthrow General Noriega. I want the details, or I begin to cut. Now!"

Justice stared the man down. "My man," he said, hard. "Excuse me. Maybe you didn't hear me right. Use that pig sticker if you want to, but if you don't kill me, *you're* dead. I'll rip your balls off and stuff them down your fucking throat and take a picture to send to your mama. You understand? I don't say something unless I mean it."

He watched doubt creep into the man's eyes and knew that his heart went only so far. He'd been foolish not to stop at the hotel and tell Sardi where he was going. Now he was caught in serious politics and could almost bet that his present predicament could be traced to a leak in the State Department.

The Cuban backed away from him. "You're going to tell us what we want to know one way or the other," he said, but the bravado was gone. Maybe Justice could use *him* for information. "Make it easy on yourself."

"I'm here on vacation," Justice said. "I've discovered a conspiracy between the Medellin cartel and Colonel Portilla to . . ."

"Portilla . . . Portilla," the Cuban said, banging Arroyo's desk, the lieutenant making a face. "I've had enough of this Portilla!"

"Maybe he's telling the truth," Arroyo said. "Perhaps we could check. . . ."

"This man is a political provocateur!" the Cuban screamed, taking his wrath out on someone who wouldn't argue back. "He is somehow connected to Miguel Porras in a plot to overthrow the general. That's why I am here, you idiot!"

Whoever this Porras was, he certainly had everybody in an uproar. Justice felt like the jilted husband... always the last to know.

There was a commotion out in the entry, Justice turning to look through the window. A nun had just come through the front doors with a large group of ragged-looking children, maybe twenty in all. The kids scattered everywhere, yelling and laughing, running at the offices and the Guardsmen, their hands out looking for charity.

"What now?" Arroyo said, standing to look toward the window. "I've *told* them to keep those children out of here!"

Several soldiers had come up to the nun and were talking loudly, trying to convince her to take out the children, their ruckus truly a sight to behold.

"Never mind that!" the Cuban yelled.

"How can you never mind?" Arroyo replied, his hand over his ears.

All at once smoke began pouring through the vestibule, from an unknown source, and Justice knew the hand of God when he saw it.

"Excuse me," he said, "that's my ride."

He fell backward, rolling into the fetal position and pulling his hands over his legs, getting them in front of him. He sprang to his feet as the Cuban ran toward him.

He sidestepped the man, grabbing him by the uniform jacket and spinning him around, Arroyo, gun drawn, following the action in jerky motions.

"Stop!" he yelled.

"Okay!" Justice called, and slung the man away from him, right into and through the plate-glass window, shattering glass popping loudly over the children's voices.

Justice dived out right behind the man, gunfire following him from the office. He came down hard atop the bleeding Cuban, the man whining loudly.

"I'll be going now," Justice said, jumping up and charging into the thick, choking smoke.

He took the lobby on a dead run, vaulting children and

knocking down Guardsmen just for general principles. "Thanks, Sister," he called as he ran past the nun.

"Wait for me, asshole!" the nun screamed, charging after him, and he smiled when he recognized the voice.

They ran together through the Court of Justice, the habit coming off as they went, the headpiece flying, landing atop a bust of Simón Bolívar. Alice Smith smiled at him as they ran, looking far more natural in jeans and tie-dyed T-shirt. "You get yourself in more shit!"

"How'd you know I was here?" he yelled as she pulled on the rosary beads that made up the cinch, the beads flying, bouncing all around them on the fake marble floor.

"Cazorla's one of my informants!" she yelled. "I was there at the Old City. Pretty nifty."

"Thank you," he said. They banged through the front doors on a dead run, Justice's van long impounded. "Where you parked?"

"I couldn't fit all those kids into a car!" she yelled. "I'm a couple of miles away."

"Damn!"

They charged across the street, just missing traffic, a long line of soldiers and smoke trickling out of the building, giving chase.

"Cut through the park!" she yelled.

They ran into the twilight park, past the busts of the patriots and the benches filled with young lovers. It was nearly dark, long shadows angling across the forested acre.

"You Company?" he said, several shots ringing out behind them.

"Yeah! Name's Gail Compton!"

"Lambert!" he called back, shaking her hand as they continued running. "You're in pretty good shape!"

"Thanks!" She shook his hand, a volley of shots spurring them on, a bullet whizzing past Justice's head to bury itself in a China elm.

They exited the park on the far side, zeroing in on the smells of the outdoor market. It was closing down. Right on the outskirts was a large truck being loaded with melons, the motor running, but no driver.

"You see what I see?" he called.

"Like the man says," she returned, "any port in the storm."

They reached the truck, a beat-up flatbed, Justice taking a look back to see behind them. Soldiers were charging through the park in large numbers, several military vehicles filling the streets on both sides of the park.

She jumped in the passenger side, Justice pushing past the truck owners and climbing behind the wheel. He slammed the door, a man yelling in Spanish jumping up on the running board. Justice was ready for him. He held a wad of cash up in front of the man, all hundreds, then tossed it onto the ground. The running board cleared immediately, Justice grinding the ancient gears with his cuffed hands until the thing, complaining, wheezed off down Avenida Central, hundreds of melons slipping off the bed to bounce down the street, smashing themselves everywhere as Justice grabbed the wheel.

"They're still coming," Gail Compton said, turning to look through the small back window.

Justice checked the rearview. The army trucks were relentless, plowing through a block of mashed melons to continue after them. The streets on both sides were filled with people going home from work and the market. Justice looked at the woman, then at the cuffs on his hands.

"Put your hand in my pocket," he said.

She raised her eyebrows. "I don't know you that well."

"Just do it," he said. "I can't drive and reach at the same time. There should be money in there. There's always money in there."

"My God!" she exclaimed, reaching into his pants and coming out with a large wad of bills. "Do you print this shit up or what?"

"Stop ogling it and toss it out the window!" he said. "We'll never outrun them in this heap."

"Your paper," she sighed, kissing the stack. Turning, she leaned halfway out the window and began calling to the people in the streets. "Free money! Free money! The ship of fools has just landed with money!"

She tossed it out in three bundles, the hundreds floating streetside, scores of people charging out to fight over it.

"That got it!" she squealed, Justice checking the rearview

to see a fast-flowing river of people separating them from army jeeps and covered deuce-and-a-halfs.

Justice turned the truck immediately, hacking side streets, just marking time. "You were about fifteen minutes early getting me," he told her, Compton still watching behind them.

"What are you talking about?" she asked, indignant. "If I hadn't shown up when I did, *you'd* have never come out of that fucking place. It's just a good thing that one of us is alert."

"Hell, I knew what I was doing," he said. "I had them right where I wanted them. And I got *you* to finally show yourself didn't I?"

She turned and slipped down to a sitting position. She glared at him through narrowed eyes. "You didn't set that . . . naw, you didn't. . . ."

He winked at her. "Who the hell is Porras?" he asked.

She hesitated just a second, Justice's trust in her dropping a notch. "Minister of the interior," she said.

"Is he a U.S. flunky?"

"*Flunky* is a pejorative term," she said.

"Well, that answers my question."

"Where the hell are you going to go now?"

He shrugged. "I just figured that you'd take care of that," he said.

She sank, dejected, farther down into the seat. "You know you weren't hired to come out here and start a giant uproar."

"No?" he asked. "Why *was* I hired?"

"Don't you ever let up?" she replied. "Boy, a person could get tired of you in a hurry."

"We need to get these cuffs off me," he said. "You got a gun?"

She frowned at him. "What are we going to do . . . shoot them off?"

"You got a better idea?"

The back road they were driving had narrowed and taken them into a shantytown of rusted tin roofs and abundant palm trees, the black ghettos occupied by the descendants of the Africans imported to build the canal, and still the most discriminated-against group in a multiracial land. Justice pulled the truck onto a dirt side street and parked it beneath a stand of palms.

"You can't be serious," she said, as he climbed out of the truck.

"Stop arguing," he said without humor. "We don't have the time. The first place they're going to go is back to my hotel to arrest my group. We've got to be mobile. I wonder if there's a phone around here."

"I don't think so," Compton said, gazing around her at the plank-and-mud shacks that made up the neighborhood. A small crowd of children had gathered around the truck, eyeing them suspiciously under the pastel pink of the ever-darkening sky.

Justice moved to the back of the truck, anxious to get his hands freed. "Hey, kids," he said, smiling all around. He reached into the back of the flatbed and began pulling out the remaining melons and handing them to the children, who'd run off, yelling happily.

"You'll have the whole neighborhood here in a minute," the woman said, shaking out her hair, hand combing it.

"We'll be gone in a minute," he said. "Get out your gun."

She frowned and bent over, pulling up the leg of her jeans to reveal cowboy boots beneath. A stainless-steel .22 automatic protruded from the top of her boot. She pulled it out.

"Ruger Mark II," he said. "Good weapon . . . means business. It's what I use."

"I'm so glad you approve," she said rolling her eyes. "Now we've got two problems—the report and the ricochet."

"Not to worry," Justice said, as he pulled several of the large, dark melons toward him, piling them into a mound. "Come here."

He grabbed one of the melons with both hands, the handcuff chain stretching tight across the skin. "Put the barrel right on it."

"You're the boss," she said, and stuck the long Ruger barrel up against the chain. "Ready?"

"Go to it."

She pulled the trigger to a muffled splat, melon flying

everywhere, getting all over both of them, Justice jerking his hands free with a loud grunt.

"That's it!" he said. "Let's go find a phone."

He raced for the driver's door, an ominous sound stopping him as he opened the door—a piercing whistle, just like the one he'd heard that morning from the *Princess* as it pulled out of port.

"What is it?" she asked, as he hovered at the cab door.

"The *Crystal Queen*," he said. "It's getting under way."

"So?" she replied, watching him through the open cab as she stood with her own door swung wide.

"So, we've got to stop it!"

"What about—"

"No time," he said. "Quick. Let's go."

He jumped into the truck, grinding it to life, anger washing over him as the adrenaline rushed through his system, energizing him. He pictured Ed again, dying—for what? So that someone could strip the watch from his lifeless arm? Gail Compton jumped in beside him, and he took off, the squalor around him darkening his mood even further. Jungle passions and desires always seemed to outstrip the human's capacity for community and peaceful coexistence. Well, this time it wasn't going to happen. This time *he* was going to do something about it, fuck the system and fuck everybody in it.

"Would you please tell me what's going on?" she said.

"When we get to the docks," he said. "I want you to find a phone and warn my people. Sardi will be in the ambassador suite."

"What's happening?"

"I've got to stop that boat," he said. "It's going to be sunk."

"How do you know?"

"A hunch," he said, bumping out of the ghetto dirt roads and up onto the wide expanse of Avenida des los Mártires. "The operation is being slowly squeezed off by the U.S. government. I think they're trying to jam in as much as they can before that happens."

"I have no idea what you're talking about," she said, exasperated. "Who is going to sink the *Queen?*"

"Medellin," he said. The street name changed to Amador,

Thatcher Bridge visible in the distance, along with the liner, still sitting in its berth. Still time. "And I think they're working with a Colonel Portilla, who apparently runs the Canal Zone."

"Portilla?" she said, a strange tone to her voice.

He turned to stare at her. "You know him?"

"Of him," she said. "He's a tough son of a bitch."

"*I'm* tough," Justice said. "Portilla's sadistic. You're not holding anything back from me?"

She looked him in the eye. "No," she said unconvincingly.

They'd reached the bridge and started across, the sun nearly set in the west on the Atlantic side. As they moved across, the canal lights came up carnivallike in the distance, twinkling bright yellow, stationary fireflies stretched out in military precision.

When they reached the west side, Justice took the truck quickly off the bridge, jerking onto the access road in a cloud of yellow dust, the last of the melons bumping off and suiciding on the roadway beside them. He briefly wondered if the Guard could follow his impromptu bread-crumb trail and find him.

They reached the pier, Justice watching lines being cast off, as dockworkers began to taxi the stairway ramp away from the ship. The deck rails were jammed with vacationers, waving and watching the sunset that undoubtedly had been promised them in the travel brochure. A cold chill went through him as he jumped out of the truck.

"Make that call!" he yelled, then took off running down the length of the pier.

Someone told him to stop as he jumped onto the up ramp and began vaulting stairs, but he had no time. He was up the landing in seconds, fifty feet above the pier. Deckhands were already closing the shipboard gate, a gap of five feet between the ship and the landing. He jumped blind, slamming into the closing gate, sending it and two deckhands flying.

He went down in a heap on the deck, someone smashing onto him almost immediately. Gail Compton.

"I told you to make the phone call," he said, scrambling to his feet.

"My job's with you," she said. "That call would have been too late, anyway."

"What the hell are you doing?" one of the deckhands said as he sat against the bulkhead, rubbing the back of his head.

"My wife and I are a little late," Justice said sheepishly. "Sorry."

He reached down and took her hand, pulling her to her feet. "We'll deal with this later," he said. "Right now we've got to find the captain."

The ship had already cleared the dock and was heading out to open sea as they ran the main deck, looking for stairs up. The ship was huge, hundreds of people filling the decks to say good-bye to Panama. The shrill whistle blew again, and to Justice it may as well have been a death knell.

They found stairs and moved up a deck, coming out by an unoccupied swimming pool and fenced tennis courts. Running back the way they'd come, they found more stairs. Each deck up was smaller than the one before, the fourth deck the last that passengers were allowed on. The stairs up to the fifth deck were barred with a chain that carried a sign saying: CREW ONLY.

They unhooked the chain and went up, only to be greeted by an air force SP with an M16.

"Am I glad to see you," Justice said.

The man shouldered his weapon and pointed it. "You are in an unauthorized area," he said loudly. "Stand at attention and put your hands behind your heads."

"Look, my man. . . ."

"Now!" the man shouted, and Justice could tell from the man's eyes that he was pumped up enough to use the automatic. He straightened and put his hands behind his head, Compton following suit. His handcuff pieces stood out prominently. Great.

"I've got to see the captain," Justice said. "I have some very important news for him regarding the sinkings."

"You're wearing handcuffs," the man said.

"My name's Lambert, son," Justice said. "You may have heard of Lambert Enterprises or Lambert International. I've been held by terrorists and have important information regarding the threat to shipping in the canal. You've *got* to let me see the captain. The safety of this entire ship depends on it."

"Glib," Compton said low.

"We'll go to the bridge, sir," the SP said, "but I can't guarantee that the captain will see you."

"That's all I ask," Justice said.

The man marched them toward the bridge, Justice turning to him as they walked, darkness total now, the decks flooded with artificial cabin light. "You here to protect the ship?" he asked.

"After what happened this morning," he replied, "they decided to put men on every ship going either way through the canal."

"Any word on the *Princess?*"

"Gone," the man said, nervousness evident in his voice. "Sunk without a trace."

"What happened to the escorts?"

"Don't have that many ships to spare," the man said. "Just keep moving."

"How many of you on here?"

"What's it to you?"

Justice turned to look at the kid. "You got me, see? We're all in the same boat. There's nothing I can do with the information."

"There's five of us, sir."

"Not enough, Sarge," Justice replied. "Not nearly enough."

They arrived at the bridge, a darkened, windowed cabin, instrument lights throwing ghostly illumination on the five-man bridge crew within. The SP knocked lightly on the door; a distinguished-looking man with a gray Vandyke beard and intense eyes poked his head out.

"Captain Bergman," the SP said, "I caught these people in unauthorized space. They insist on speaking with you about the sinkings."

Bergman looked at Justice, narrowing his eyes when they fell on the handcuffs. "I don't have time for this," the man said.

"This boat's going down as soon as you reach open waters," Justice said, harsh.

The man continued to stare at him. He spoke after half a

minute. "Make it quick," he said, opening the door wide, the SP moving in behind as Justice and Compton entered.

"I have reason to believe that a bomb has been planted just below the waterline on this ship," Justice said, his eyes adjusting to the blinking red and green lights spread out fore and the pale haze of the sweep radar screen. "It will be detonated by remote control when you reach open waters, and then you'll be boarded by brigands who will kill and rob you and send this beautiful ship to the bottom."

"How do you explain the handcuffs?" he asked.

"Never mind about the fucking handcuffs," Justice said with intensity. "Just turn this vessel around and go back to the safety of port until you've checked the hull."

"It's not that simple," the man said, his white uniform glowing in the pale lights. "Time is money, and the wasted fuel . . ."

"Then shut down the engines and sit for a minute while you decide."

The man shook his head. "The tidal waters are too tricky," he said. "Give me your wallet."

"What?"

"Train your rifle on him, Sergeant," Bergman said, the atmosphere growing tense as the rifle was primed and raised. "Now, sir, you will give me your wallet."

"You're making a mistake," Justice said, bringing out the wallet and handing it over, "endangering the lives of your passengers."

"By not listening to a madman who comes running in here with handcuffs on, Mr. . . . Lambert?" the captain asked as he looked in the wallet. "Are you a passenger on this vessel, sir?"

"No."

"And a stowaway to boot," the man sighed, then looked at Compton. "Are you with him?"

The woman shrugged. "My mother always warned me about bad companions."

"Mr. Stimmis," Bergman said with authority. "Raise port authority and tell them that I am holding a Mr. William Lambert here in the bridge who has some story about a bomb planted on board. I will await word from them on disposition."

"Yes sir," the radioman said, tuning to port frequency.

"You're making a terrible mistake," Justice said, checking out the small room. It had doors on either end and an infinite dark ocean all around. He slipped himself into the combat mode.

"Got 'em, sir," Stimmis called from the radio.

"Turn it up," Bergman said. "Let's hear what they have to say."

"*You've* got Lambert?" came a confused American voice from the other end. "Well, hold onto him. He's an international criminal wanted here for the assassination of Miguel Porras. We've been tearing up the port looking for him."

"Porras!" Compton said, shocked.

Bergman stared hard at Justice, then stretched out his hand for the microphone. Stimmis gave it to him. He thumbed the juice button and spoke. "This is Captain Bergman of the *Crystal Queen* speaking. Do you want me to return to port with him? Over."

"Good," Justice said.

"No," the radio squawked. "Just hold him and continue on. We'll send a cutter to pick him up. Over."

"I appreciate that," Bergman said. "Over."

"Our pleasure," the voice returned, then quickly added, "Out."

The captain handed the microphone back to the radioman and stared hard at Justice in the dim light. "There you have it, Mr. Lambert. As sole authority on this vessel, I am hereby placing you under arrest. You will be incarcerated until such time as I can turn you over to shoreside authorities."

Justice smiled once, then kicked back while shoving the captain with his hands. His foot connected with the SP's chest, the man falling back, grunting, as his gun discharged into the ceiling.

"Come on!" he yelled to Compton, then charged to the cabin door, throwing it open just in time to see the butt of a rifle coming toward his face like a freight train. He thought about ducking, but the thought got suddenly frozen in a black, fuzzy void where everything changed and nothing mattered.

XIV.

MALIBU BEACH
9 APRIL 1983—2200 HOURS

Justice loved running at night. It was as if he were a shadow flitting just above the ground, disassociated from any concept of mind or body. Tonight he ran with Ed Barkes, visiting from Chicago, but whether he ran with people or alone, the feeling was the same. Exercise was a high to him, an addictive drug that he partook of obsessively and on a daily basis. Too long had he lain an invalid, too long the prisoner of a broken, mangled body. If he had a religion, it was the religion of mental and physical freedom. Perhaps in that was the denial of what he had been before, but Justice couldn't be burdened with the past. He always looked forward now. He dwelt in the land of power and service, and if he took his pleasure from the physical denial of his past, what harm was there in that?

Barkes had dropped slightly behind as they ran along the shoulder of California Highway 1, the lights of Los Angeles twinkling seductively in the distance to the south. "Come on, Ed," he chided. "How do you expect to keep up with that sweet young thing you're seeing if you don't get into shape?"

"I *am* in shape," Barkes said, puffing, moving up to pace Justice. "It's just that *you're* a maniac."

Justice laughed and ran several circles around the older man, their sweats soaked through in the muggy night. "Come on, Ed. Get with it."

"Enough," Barkes said, slowing to a walk. "You win. If you want me out, I'll quit. Just don't run me to death."

"Okay," Justice said, slowing. "I'll tell you what. Tomorrow we'll take out the *Lutine* and forget about jogging."

"Let's take out something smaller, okay?" Barkes replied. "Using two of us to run a boat made for six is worse that this."

A car zoomed past them in a whoosh of air, Justice turning to watch his friend. "When are you going to get around to telling me what you came down here to tell me?" he asked.

"When I've got you in a good mood," Barkes replied.

"This is as good as it gets, my man. Let's hear it."

"It's about that damned newspaper. . . ." Barkes began, Justice cutting him off.

"There's nothing to discuss about the *Watchdog*," he replied.

"Twenty-seven lawsuits is nothing to discuss?" Barkes said. "Dammit, Bill. Seven of those suits are in international court. We're keeping thirteen law firms busy just defending us."

"I don't care if it's twenty-seven hundred lawsuits," Justice said. "I'm not going to back off." He stopped running for a moment and stood. The beach lay a distance below them down a long, rolling hill, breakers foaming up white as they crashed loudly against the sand. His house sat quietly a half mile distant, an unfamiliar car parked in the drive.

"You know why I keep the paper going," he said quietly, staring at the slightly puffing man through the span of darkness. "The last time I looked, the paper was responsible for the passage of over two hundred antipollution and antitoxic dump ordinances worldwide. There's got to be more, Ed."

The man looked down, frowning, kicking at the loose gravel. "To tell you the truth, Bill," he said, "I'm beginning to get scared."

"Scared?"

"You're pissing off everybody," he said. "Hell, you said yourself that government and big business are fuck buddies. There's not a major corporation you haven't gone after, and now it looks as if the government is retaliating by singling out *our* businesses. They're going through everything with a fine-tooth comb, looking for violations of government regs, making them up if they can't find any."

"I don't mind being scrutinized," Justice said. "We're subject to the same rules as everybody else."

"That's not it," Barkes explained. "I'm afraid of just that. If they can't get us on rules violations, they may turn in other directions, more . . . nasty directions. Your sheer invisibility protected you before you went public, but now you're out front and vulnerable. The best we can expect, I fear, will be some kind of crazy indictments or something against you. A man can't stand alone against a force as powerful as the one you've taken on. You wouldn't be the first individual broken by the system."

Justice smiled and cuffed him on the shoulder. "Well, don't put me in the pen yet. I have a great deal of faith in the system, and more faith in people's basic honesty. The people will stand behind me."

"What about the people who worked in that strip-mining operation you stopped in Greenland, Bill?" he asked. "You're telling people they have to sacrifice now. Nobody, and I mean nobody, wants to hear that."

"Ahh," Justice said, "you worry too much."

"I hope so," Barkes replied, and they started moving again, closing on the house and the strange car parked there.

As they came closer, Justice's senses began to tingle. He fought it off, chalking it up to Barkes's fears. He fixed on the house, watching. All at once the car backed quickly out of the drive, its tires screeching as it skidded onto Highway 1.

"What the hell—"

Justice turned it on, charging toward the house as the car banged into gear and squealed out, fishtailing in their direction.

"Watch out!" Barkes called, grabbing Justice and shoving him off the hillside as the car swerved, nearly hitting them as it raced past.

Justice jumped up and charged down the road, again toward the house, an explosion going off in the back, orange fire shooting fifty feet into the air.

"No!" he screamed, as another firebomb went up in the front, then another on the side, engulfing the entire house in flames.

He charged the flames, the image searing his brain as images of Panama kept crowding out the reality around him. He made the front yard, the sounds of screaming piercing the night as he ran right up to the flames, his eyebrows and hair burning off as he fought for entry.

Barkes was pulling on him. He stumbled backwards, falling, picking himself up as something came flying through the picture window in the front. It was Allie's mother, her entire body on fire. She staggered to her feet, screaming, running with outstretched arms. He tried to catch her, couldn't, then turned back to the house that had become Volcán Barú, Allie's screams the screams of the dying come back to haunt him.

He ran at the house again, this time determined to die with the villagers, to accept his full measure of guilt as the orange fire soared majestically, the house a giant half-million-dollar torch.

A hand grabbed him. He turned to it. "Get away from me, Merriman!" he yelled. "You son of a bitch!"

"God!" Barkes screamed, trying to pull him away from the flames. "God help me!"

He turned and slammed Merriman in the mouth, the sound of sirens now loud in his ears as he charged the fire, the roof collapsing with a roar as he kicked open the door to an inferno.

And then it happened. Pain scorched through his back like a poker, his body going numb. He fell, paralyzed, unseen hands dragging him helplessly away from Volcán Barú. Faces were looking down at him—Merriman, Noriega—and they were laughing, laughing as the women and children screamed out their pitiful lives, and orange cinders floated heavenward to join in harmony with the distant starfield.

And in that insane, delirious moment, William Justice knew that he could never, ever escape his past, that it was a memory tattoo destined always to rise, like the molten lava in Volcán Barú, to erupt the fabric of his restless life. He was mortgaged to yesterday, body and soul, a zombie condemned to walk with the living, though his heart lay dead. And the cinders floated gently upward, carrying with them what had once been a human being named William Justice into the cold, unfathomable void.

XV.

SOMEWHERE ON THE PACIFIC
20 FEBRUARY 1988—0314 HOURS

In the hazy vision Allie's mother stood before him, her body in flames, chastising him as her flesh fell off in great, black, smoking chunks.

"You did this!" she screeched. "It's all your fault! If my husband were here right now, he'd thrash you!"

He sobbed into his hands. "No... please. I didn't know, I didn't... want it to happen."

"You broke my heart when you killed my little girl!" the woman screamed. "Here! You might as well take it!"

The woman tore open her own chest and reached inside, coming out with a heart-shaped picture frame containing a picture of Allie. He reached for it, but when he touched it, it burst into flame, the woman in the picture screaming, screaming....

"Aaah!" he awoke with a start, jumping, the pain searing his head and knocking him back to the bunk.

"Well, good morning," Gail Compton said, leaning down from the bunk above. "I was beginning to have my doubts about the hardness of your head there for awhile."

Eyes closed, he reached up and touched his forehead to discover a bandage there. He opened his eyes to pain, then sat up slowly, a hand on either side of his head. A bulb in the closet-sized bathroom threw dim illumination through the room. "How long have I been out?" he asked.

"A long time," she replied. "Hours. It's the middle of the night."

"Great."

He swung his legs over the side of the bunk and stood shakily. They were in a small stateroom, bare except for two bunks and attached plumbing. Heavy iron bars replaced a regular cabin door. A small porthole looked out into the black night. "What about my head?"

"You took a good shot," she said. "Five stitches across your forehead and a small concussion. You've drifted in and out all night long. You don't remember? The doctor wanted to leave you in the infirmary, but Bergman insisted you be brought here."

He shook his head to flashing pain. Moving to the bars, he grabbed them hard and held on, sinking himself down into the alpha state, where he could reassign the pain. He worked with it, breathing deeply, pushing it deeper and deeper into the brain cage where he kept all the slithery demons of pain and bad memories. It was a full room with no vacancy, but he made do, jamming the pain in somehow. And when he opened his eyes, if he wasn't better, at least he was somewhat functional.

He turned to her. "Have I missed anything?"

She shrugged. "A midnight snack," she said. "I ate both our shares. I hadn't had any dinner."

"We need to talk," he said, crossing to the porthole and looking out. Though the night was black, the beginnings of morning traced a glowing, fuzzy line across the horizon. When the devil came to cart them away, they'd be able to see him. "You know that everyone on this ship is going to die soon."

"I've heard you say that," she replied, "but I couldn't swear by it."

"I don't suppose you've still got your gun?" he asked.

She shook her head. "A very nice nurse did a strip search. I hesitate to say that she enjoyed it too much."

He walked to the bunks, staring up at her as she reclined on her side, her lovely head supported with an open palm. He got eye to eye with her. "I want some answers from you, and I want the truth."

"Sure," she said.

"Dammit!" he spat. "Don't give me 'sure' and then fuck me off. Our lives depend on this. You're a gamer, I know that. So am I. Well, this time the games could get us both killed. I've been down some trails, lady. Take my word for it—we're screwed this time."

Her expression never varied. She was a pro, and therein lay the problem. She may never really tell him the truth about anything.

"What do you want to know?" she said with appropriate solemnity.

He crossed to the cell bars, reaching through to the locking mechanism. He'd left his burglar's tools at the hotel, not figuring he'd need them at Casco Antigua. "You got a bobby pin?"

"*That's* your question?"

"Have you got one?"

"No."

He pushed against the door, testing. There was no give at all. The cell framework was apparently sunk deeply into the ship's bracing. Frowning, he walked back to face her. "We'll start with Porras," he said. "What's his story?"

Her expression still didn't waver. "You already guessed it," she said. "He is, or *was*, our boy. The government wanted to promote him as new leader if they ever succeeded in dumping Noriega. You think he's really dead?"

"Judging from the way the Cuban at the police station was jazzing me about the guy, I'd say they probably did go over and finish him off just to end the controversy. Noriega's people must have gotten wind of something. What about Portilla?"

She sat up, tightening her lips. "He's Porras's National Guard support," she said, the words coming a little harder. "As you well know, the Guard runs the country. You've got to have trumps to play in the National Guard if you want to run the show. Very few people know what I've just told you."

"Am I playing the fall guy?" he asked. "Is there something set to go down that I don't know about?"

"Nothing that I know of," she said, then jumped off the bunk when she saw the disbelief in his eyes. She put a hand on his arm. "Honestly. I've been down here since seventy-eight and have watched the contacts slowly grow once we

208

went on the outs with Noriega. We support Porras, but I haven't heard anything about any action. Noriega controls most of the Guard. He's supplemented that with loyal Cuban troops. Add that to the drug money he's pulling from his association with Medellin . . . and it looks to me like he's here to stay."

"Unless he was to die," Justice said. "You say you've been here since seventy-eight?"

She smiled sadly. "Yeah," she said. "It was my first big assignment. I thought I was going to go out and whip the entire world after a small training period." She laughed, shaking her head. "I've been stuck here ever since."

"Whom do you work with?" he asked.

"Mostly a rotating pool of agents who move in and out," she said. "I'm the one fixed point in an ever-changing universe."

"I could have told you that the Company discriminates," he smiled. "Murder and mayhem are traditionally thought to be the man's domain."

"Cheap shot," she said.

"Maybe," he returned. "Wasn't there some trouble down here in seventy-eight before you came in?"

"Now you have walked into areas that are none of your business," she said. "If you want the truth from me, you'll have to stick to the topic at hand."

"I appreciate the warning," he replied. "Now tell me exactly what your orders are concerning me."

"Watch you into the Medellin operation and watch you out," she said. "State is looking for a way to break Noriega's back economically. If you put a dent into his drug profits, he may find it more difficult to pay his army, which may make things easier for a takeover. The Guard is still the key. Where they go, so goes the country."

"What about Noriega?"

"What about him?"

"You know that he's in the western provinces right now," he said, not a question.

"Coincidence," she said. "It doesn't mean anything."

"It does if he's at Volcán Barú."

She looked at him for a long moment. "So it does," she said darkly, her eyes narrowing. "Look. I'm the hired help same as you. I swear to you, Lambert . . ."

"Call me Will," he said. "And you don't need to say anything else."

"Then let me ask you a question," she replied. "What the hell is going on here?"

A rumble, like thunder, rolled through the ship, the deck pitching, both of them hurled to the floor, the woman falling into his arms.

"It's started!" he yelled, jumping up and running to the porthole, the ship listing starboard. He cupped his hands to the window and stared into the night. Sure enough, an old converted minesweeper, still bearing navy insignia, was pacing them on the port side—a shark ready to rip into the exposed, tender flesh of the *Queen*.

"What's happening?" she asked, grabbing his arm and spinning him around.

"We're sinking," he said calmly. "And unless we come up with something quickly, we're fish food."

Terror edged her eyes, but it was quickly supplanted with professionalism. "Maybe they'll come let us out."

"Yeah, maybe," he said. "Would you?"

She stared at him. "Give me a kiss," she said, smiling wickedly.

He took her into his arms, crushing her to him in a long, lingering kiss that promised more. "You got heart, lady," he said, then moved back to the porthole.

The sweeper was close enough to make out men on the decks dressed in Canal Zone police uniforms, yet the deck was strangely lacking in external light sources. Screams were beginning to filter down the hallway toward them as the passengers panicked. The floor was tilted at a thirty-degree angle, Justice having to lean way out to look through the port.

A bullhorn squawked form the deck of the sweeper, Justice unscrewing the porthole and opening the glass to get a better listen. The sky continued to lighten, the sweeper's gray color edging out of black.

Several people charged past the brig, yelling, dressed in nightclothes.

"Smoke!" Compton said. "We must be on fire."

"Incredible," Justice said, anger welling up within him as the screaming became louder, shriller.

The man with the bullhorn spoke: *"Crystal Queen, we*

have firefighting equipment on board. Abandon ship. Lower your boats. We will pick up passengers. Your mayday is being disseminated. Prepare to be boarded by firefighters."

"Sons of bitches," Justice said. "No wonder the Maydays never come. They're pretending to help."

"Are you sure they're not?" Compton said, rushing to squeeze up to the porthole with him.

"That's not regular navy," Justice said. "They're Zone police. This is bullshit."

Another explosion rumbled through the hull, Justice grabbing the window cutout to keep his feet. Lines were being fired from the sweeper by small cannons as people, screaming, flew past the window, plunging to the choppy sea below.

He ran back to the cell door, throwing himself against the uncompromising bars. It was useless. The only way they were going to get out of there was if they were let out. More people came charging down the hall, rushing past them. Compton ran up beside him, reaching through the bars, imploring.

"Please," she called to people running past. "Please. Have somebody get us out of here!"

Justice watched people turn to them, staring uncomprehendingly as they rushed past, smoke rapidly filling the hallway, animals scurrying away from a forest fire. They'd get no help there. Perhaps death by fire was his destiny.

Back to the window. Dawn slowly creeping over the far horizon, the water filled with bobbing heads. A boat was lowered right past their window, Justice watching a mother trying desperately to calm her crying children as the fires roared the waters to flickering life all around them. Men with guns began sliding across the lines holding the two ships together. They weren't in uniform—Medellin bandits.

The party was about to begin.

Gail Compton moved up beside him again. Frenetic activity juiced everything around them to intensity, yet within their little prison all was calm. They watched more boats go into the water, an unbelievable number of people abandoning ship, filling the sea around them as the smoke got thicker, drifting through their cabin in a foglike haze. The *Queen* was listing badly now, the brig a steep incline.

She moved up and slipped into his arms, Justice holding her tightly as he tried to maintain balance. "We're going to die here, aren't we?" she said softly.

"Perhaps," he said. "There's got to be more."

"Like what?"

"Like what's left on this ship," he said. "If they're going to let it go to the bottom, it won't be until they've taken everything of value off first. That's the whole point of this."

Machine-gun fire rattled the night, loud, louder than the screams of the passengers. Justice tore loose of the woman and stared through the porthole. A large group of men lined the port side of the sweeper, all of them armed with automatic weapons, all of them firing.

They blasted away, laughing, at the people in the lifeboats and the people still in the water, a chain rattle of machine guns tearing at Justice's brain and gut, their muzzle flashes like mini–lightning bolts tearing the life out of the poor bastards who thought them their salvation. He watched animals caught in the bloodlust, emptying their clips on full auto, then reloading, laughing, and doing it again.

And the water frothed red with blood, bodies floating, clogging up the area between the ships and beyond, the still living screaming out of the crucible for mercy and receiving a death sentence instead. Justice's knuckles turned white with strain as he held the window space, shaking with rage, and he felt he could almost rip out the hull to get to them. He wouldn't—couldn't—let go this easily.

Then he heard firing on board, getting closer. There had to be resistance from the SPs. The sound of footsteps, charging headlong in their direction. Justice ran to the bars as the SP who had taken him to Bergman hurriedly arrived with keys in his hand. His face was black with soot, blood soaking the left side of his uniform. All the boyhood had gone out of his eyes.

"You were right," he said to Justice as he leaned against the tilt of the ship and tried to get the key in the lock. "Those bastards, they . . ."

The hallway growled with machine-gun rattle, the SP's chest and head exploding as he spun away from the bars, slamming into a wall and, already dead, falling heavily to the deck. The sound of footsteps approached cautiously, Justice gluing himself to the wall beside the cell. He stared at Compton who stood before the bars, her jaw set hard.

"They'll check the body," he said low. "Get them in here."

"How..."

"Whatever it takes," he said, the woman straightening, slipping into the gaming mode.

Justice watched her, unable to see through the door space. She had made her face wide and innocent, and looked years younger.

He heard shuffling, then a startled voice—American. "Well, what have we got here?" the voice said, low and full of swaggering humor.

Gail ran to the bars, holding them tightly. "Please," she said, breathless. "They said I stole that jewelry, but it was... it was already mine. Just because you get a divorce doesn't mean..."

"Jewelry?" the voice asked. "What jewelry?"

"I hid it, though," she said, and if Justice hadn't known better, *he* would have believed her. "They couldn't make me tell."

"Hid it where?" the voice asked.

"Please let me out," she pleaded. "I'll show you, I swear I will."

"Tell me now."

She backed away from the bars, her hands going down to tug at the hem of her T-shirt. "If I tell you, you won't let me out."

"Then fuck you!" he spat.

"Okay," she said in a little-girl voice. "I'll do that, too." She pulled the T-shirt up and over her head, baring her breasts in the pale light. She stood somewhat shyly, partially bent over, her hands occasionally bringing the shirt up to cover herself. "But don't hurt me."

There were several seconds of silence, Justice desperately hoping the punk wasn't gay. "How would I get in there?" he said.

She pointed. "T-that man... on the floor. He has the key."

Justice heard the man curse under his breath and begin

fumbling with the body. Gail shot him a glance, shrugging. He nodded in return, giving her the thumbs-up.

"You sure you got jewelry hidden?" the man asked, Justice listening as the key rasped in the lock.

"Oh please hurry," she said, running up to the bars, the man's hand coming through to fondle her.

"There," he said, his voice husky.

Justice heard the door squeak open on tight hinges, Compton backing up several paces, the punk in uniform following her in, walking uphill with outstretched arms, a Mac-12 SMG in his left hand.

"My man," Justice said quietly from behind him.

The punk turned quickly, staring with open mouth.

"You've done so much bad," Justice said, shaking his head, his words like ice.

The punk swung around with the automatic, and to Justice it was like slow motion. He was living in the land of adrenaline and endorphins now, his senses honed like a diamond-tipped scalpel.

His right hand snaked out and grabbed the cop's gun hand, his left streaking out to take him by the throat with fingers steeled by years of exercise during a time when his hands had to do the work of his whole body. He squeezed hard, the man's larynx collapsing under his probing fingers.

The man gagged, grabbing with his free hand, his other tightening on the trigger, the gun blasting harmlessly into the wall. His eyes bulged, the gagging more strangled, the throat constricting under Justice's hand.

He let go of the man, stripping him of his weapon. The cop stumbled backward, hands to his throat as he fought, unsuccessfully, for breath. He fell to the floor, rolling down the tilt to bang against the wall. He was clawing at his throat, Justice moving up to take extra clips from his gun belt as he lay, kicking wildly, frantically, on the floor.

He looked at Compton. She had already put her shirt back on. "Let's go," he said.

She nodded once, and they were out the door. Justice bent to the dead SP and rolled him over. The man's M16 was gone, but a standard-issue .45 was strapped to his belt. He took it, along with an extra clip, and stood. To the right was thick smoke, layering down the hallway toward them in thicker and thicker strata. To the left came the sound of a firefight. Justice smiled and jogged down the left hallway.

Compton ran beside him, the Mac-12 in her hands, her pockets bulging with clips. "Now what?" she said.

He looked at her in amazement. "Now we start killing those fuckers," he said, coming to a crossroad hallway and bearing to the left again, charging uphill.

They came to a door that led to the outer deck. Through it he could see a line of punks sending full bags back along the pulley lines joining the ships. They were moving quickly, expertly. He could have taken several of them, but he didn't want to—yet. If there was still fighting somewhere on the ship, that meant there were still passengers or crew alive. When he made the big sweep, he'd need all the help he could get.

They retreated slightly from the door and made their way down a long, carpeted hallway. This one was wide, a major thoroughfare. The firing came from farther down the hall.

"Make sure you've got a full clip," he told her as they moved down the darkened aisle, walking at a severe angle, lines of gift shops, a beauty parlor, and the infirmary on either side, the glass already smashed out and the shops ransacked. There was no smoke up here, the fires still apparently confined to the aft sections.

The sounds of a skirmish grew louder, emanating from a room at the end of the hall facing it—the dining room. They moved up cautiously, an open breezeway to the outer decks cutting a swath in front of the place. They charged across the breezeway and planted themselves on either side of the double doors, peeking in.

A mixed group of Medellin punks and Zone cops had taken up positions within the room, tables knocked over, white linen and centerpieces spilling everywhere. They fired and moved up a table, closing the noose. They were concentrating a pattern of fire toward the bandstand at the far end of the room, where two SPs protected fifteen or twenty people up on the stage. The SPs had dumped over a grand piano and piled up drum sets and guitar amplifiers for cover, and bullets ripping through the fabric of the piano played a discordant melody on the strings as children screamed and the SPs shouted warnings to each other.

He turned to her, the door space separating them. "You ever killed before?" he asked.

She understood what he was asking for immediately and nodded. "I'll do my share," she said. "Don't worry."

He nodded. "I count ten of them," he said. "I've got nine shots in this magazine. If you can take out the three on the far side of the room, I should be able to get the rest."

"You're kidding," she said with wide eyes.

"We'll know in a minute," he said. "Ready?"

"Lambert . . ."

But he wasn't listening. He had become the right hand of God, the gun in his hand an extension of the mind and heart. He was retribution, the jungle coming back to reclaim its own, and nothing—nothing—could stay the power of his wrath. "Now," he said calmly, and walked into the room, raising the weapon like a pointing finger.

In the crystal clarity of his directed brain he focused on two thoughts: first, that he'd have only one shot per man; second, that he wanted the biggest target with the greatest result—the chest.

The men were scattered around the large room, none of them looking his way. He picked the one farthest from him, took a relaxing breath, drifted with his intuitive nature, and fired casually at the man's exposed upper back.

The man jumped with the hit, then sagged like an animal, Justice already moving to the next-farthest man, firing immediately, without conscious thought, taking him at the neck, the punk pitching forward across his table as Justice moved on.

The third was just turning around, the shot catching him sideways on the chest, knocking him comically on his butt, where he sat, looking stupidly down at himself, and Justice was already picking another target as he heard Compton firing beside him on full auto.

They were turned to him now, and he took out the fourth as the man was trying to bring his M16 to bear, his chest exploding at the heart, death instantaneous, and Justice was still moving, still the roving hand of Fate.

The others had begun to fire, Justice taking them all in

at a glance and taking out the closest this time, spinning the man around with a shot just off the mark, a second shot, head high, taking him all the way out of the action as bullets began to eat away at the floor and wall beside him.

He dived sideways, rolling quickly down the tilt, then jumping back to his feet and firing at the dead-center middle of the sixth man, knowing that the seventh was already drawing a bead on him. As he swung, though, the guns rattled from the bandstand, the Zoner going down in a withering cross fire, the whole exchange taking place in less than twenty seconds.

Justice turned to Compton's group, two of them down, a third, wounded and on his knees, still trying to return fire. He aimed chest high, then brought his finger up a notch and fired, taking off the top of the man's head, knocking him forward to roll down the incline and bang into a table.

"You're a maniac," Gail Compton breathed beside him, and he ejected the clip from the butt of the .45 and inserted the extra he'd taken off the dead SP.

The people on the bandstand, tentatively at first, then with greater urgency, swarmed toward him, the SPs leading them. He watched the crowd. There were a number of men within the group. They were all shell-shocked by this time, some in pajamas, others in hurriedly thrown-on pants and nothing else. Another man wore jockey shorts. Maybe it was better this way. Their lives were going to be altered for good and all tonight and too much thought would only lead to mistakes.

"What do we do?" one of the SPs asked.

Justice looked hard at him. "All able-bodied men," he said loudly. "Take the weapons from this meat on the floor and arm yourselves. Take extra clips. If you want to survive, you've got to kill the men who have taken the ship. You and your families will all die unless you kill your enemies. No quarter, no discussion. Kill them and do it quick. Do you understand me?"

They looked at him strangely, some in amazement, others without comprehension. He spoke again. "This ship is going down with you on it. Almost everyone else is already dead. Look at your families. If you want them to live, we've got to take the other ship. They won't give it to us. We must kill them, or we die." He looked at the SPs. "It's your job to make sure every male is armed and knows how to use his weapon. You will take all orders from me, understood?"

A tall, blond airman, no older than twenty, looked hard at him. "Mister, I don't know who you are, but I'd follow you into hell right now."

"Good," he replied. "We're there."

As they gathered up the weapons, Justice called to them, "Take their clothes and put them on. We'll need a ruse to get aboard their vessel." He looked at Compton. "How're you holding up?"

She smiled at him and ejected the clip from her SMG, jamming another hard in its place. "Just getting warmed up," she said through clenched teeth. "You sure know how to show a girl a good time."

"I aim to please," he replied, and watched as the young airman gave rapid-fire instructions on the care and handling of instant death.

The task was completed within five minutes, Justice fixed up with a squad of eight, not counting him and the woman. He worried a touch about the killer instinct but hoped that the desperation of their families' plights would spur them on.

There was still firing coming from the upper decks forward, Justice figuring that there was resistance on the bridge, thanks to the remaining SPs. "We'll go up on the blind side," he said. "Take them quickly. We don't have much time."

He led them out of the dining room, uphill along the breezeway until they came out deckside on the port. The *Queen* was riding low in the water on this side, waves washing up onto the first deck, the tilt always trying to take them over the rails and into the choppy sea.

The area was quiet now, the only sounds the sporadic firing on the upper deck. The ship was minutes away from its own death rattle, activity now concentrated on the starboard side as the brigands prepared to move on.

The group moved quickly and quietly, Justice in the lead, taking the outer stairways up higher and higher. He looked aft. A monstrous fire was raging through the back third of the ship, black smoke bleeding profusely into the dark crown of the night, the sight of fire sinking Justice deeper into his own mental pit.

Several men occupied the upper deck starboard, laying down a pattern of fire at the bridge door on that side. They hid behind bulkheads, just dipping out to fire, then duck back, Justice realizing they weren't so much trying to mix it up with the bridge crew as simply keep them pinned long enough for the ship to be abandoned. At that point they'd leave the crew to their fates on the sinking ship.

"They're going to be tough to get out of there," the blond SP said, coming up behind Justice as he crouched on the last set of sets, occasionally craning up for a view.

Justice looked at him. The SP had taken a Zone cop uniform and looked more than passable. "Maybe not so tough," he said, smiling. "You're one of them. Just walk on up."

A smile spread across the man's face, and he turned back, all of them lined down the stairs, and picked three men.

"Wish me luck," he told Justice, the man shaking his head.

"No luck involved," he replied. "Just keep picturing those bastards belly-up. What's your name?"

"Miller, sir."

"Give 'em hell, Miller."

Miller motioned his people forward, Justice letting them go to build up their confidence. Just in case, he was crouched there, ready to come to their aid.

"Don't shoot," Miller called to the pirates as they made the deck. "It's just us."

One of the punks leaned out quickly from the bulkhead, then motioned them over. Miller and his people moved along the tilting deck, holding the handrail, and disappeared around the bulkhead. The area exploded in blazing light and sound seconds later, one of the punks rolling out onto the deck, then over the edge, his body bouncing on each deck as it made its inevitable trip to the Pacific below.

Miller poked his head out and waved at Justice, then turned toward the bridge. "Jerry!" he called. "Jerry . . . it's me, Bob! We've got it secured out here!"

A head peeked tentatively out the broken window space,

Miller waving to the SP, calling him out. "Hurry!" he called, Justice jumping up to move toward them.

The door opened, five more men, including Captain Bergman, coming out. The captain saw Justice and moved up to him, the ship exploding aft again, everyone grabbing a rail to keep from being pitched into the raging waters.

"I should have listened to you," he said, a large cut on the side of his face dyeing his beard red. "Who the hell are those people?"

"You don't want to know," Justice said. "Arm your men, and be prepared for the bastards on the other side of the bridge."

They didn't have to wait long. As soon as the punks on the other side realized the bridge was empty, they came charging through the open doorway and onto the starboard deck, Miller happily waving to them. "Got 'em!" he called, the rest of them coming through the door, Justice's now formidable force cutting loose, chopping the four men to pieces.

The ship was shuddering beneath them and not long for the world. Justice looked over the side to see the main deck they had walked just minutes before completely under water, as the fires raged even worse aft. Whatever was going to happen had better happen quickly.

"I tried to raise port on the radio," Bergman said. "I couldn't get through."

"They're probably jamming you from the sweeper," Justice said. "The damn thing is bristling with electronic gear. What a racket."

"What'll we do?"

Justice spoke loudly, so that everyone could hear. "The *Queen* will be history in a matter of minutes," he said. "We've got to take the sweeper, or we're dead. To do that, we're going to have to use the rappelling lines they've already sent over. It means getting right up on their asses and surprising them."

"How do we do that?" Miller asked.

"The way anybody gets in anywhere," he replied, "by acting like we belong. I want two of you to round up any survivors you can find. We've got to be fast. Don't think . . . just act. Kill them all and take their fucking boat. Gail . . . they

220

didn't bring any women over, so you're the logical choice to lead the survivor party, okay?"

"Got it," she said, picking two men and hurrying them back down to the deck below.

He looked at his remaining force of ten men. "It's show time," he said. "There's no plan except getting as close as we can before they figure us out. Got it?"

He stripped one of the dead Medellin people of his camouflage jacket and bandolier and put them on, the coat too small. He led them back through the bridge and straight out onto the deck, the sight that greeted him tensing his muscles involuntarily.

He listened to the others groan and retch as they walked out onto the deck. The waters below were filled with the dead—five hundred, maybe six—as the mammoth ship burned beautiful violet and orange, out of control. An orgy of violence and senseless brutality had erupted out of nowhere in this island of peace, and Justice's head held nothing but death wishes for the slime who labored below, still sliding large bags of personal effects across the fifty-foot gap between the two ships. He made twelve men, five on the *Queen* and seven still aboard the sweeper. He assumed that someone was skippering the pirate vessel, but didn't want to include him in the body count—yet.

They were spotted from below as they walked casually, Miller waving down to them.

"Hurry!" a man called up to them, and made an exaggerated gesture of pointing to his wrist, telling them they were out of time.

Miller waved again. "All secured up here!" he called. "We're coming down."

"They want us to hurry," Justice told the group. "Let's oblige them."

They moved quickly to the stairs down, the ship's tilt throwing them up against the cabin walls, the angle of tilt nearly impossible to walk now. They moved to the lower deck, weapons ready, everyone silent as they played out what might be their last moments in silence, each lost in his own thoughts, his own fears.

As for Justice, he couldn't wait to get down there.

They traversed the third deck, then the second, picking

up the pace even more before recognition became a factor. Practically running now, they hit the main deck just as one of the Zone cops turned narrowed eyes to them, the light dawning slowly.

"Now!" Justice yelled, cutting loose with the .45, blasting a third eye in the Zoner's forehead, the man stiffening, then tumbling sideways over the rail and falling atop the bodies already choking the blue-green waters in the early morning light.

A firefight erupted in the confined space of the deck with nowhere for anyone to hide or run, muzzle flashes punctuating the early morning as shells zipped and ricocheted loudly, sparking the cabin walls and decks, Justice stoic amid the screaming carnage, picking targets, firing methodically.

It was over in thirty seconds that seemed like thirty years, the bandits dead on the red-stained decks, several of Justice's people down for good also, including Miller, the brave one.

"Let's go!" Justice cried, no time to think. He ran for the tethers, even as he watched the men left on the sweeper hurrying to sever themselves from the death ship.

He threw away the empty .45, prying an M16 from a dead punk's hand, the thing still primed. A sack was hanging from a metal hook on his end. He grabbed it, jumped to the liner's rail and dived into space, firing at the man trying to undo him at the other end, dropping him, then turning on others.

The wind rushed at his face as his weight bore him quickly, the nylon line whining loudly, the sweeper's deck a good thirty feet lower than the *Queen's*. The rattle of machine guns followed him as they tried to pick him off, his own people taking to the ropes also. He blew a punk off the deck, even as he rushed up on him, raising his feet and letting go as he reached the sweeper.

He hit and rolled, nine-millimeter death chewing up the deck all around him as he jumped back to his feet and fired back, the deckhands now caught in a cross fire as Justice's people began reaching the sweeper. Outnumbered now, the bandits went down quickly, the last one raising his hands high, Justice smiling at the man just before he blew his head off.

He looked up at the bridge, a flight of metal stairs above, and began charging in that direction. "Bring everyone over . . . quick!" he called to Bergman, who'd fought like a madman in defense of his charges.

Justice took the steps three at a time until he reached the bridge deck, the man firing from within, windows busting out as Justice charged past them. He hit the door without hesitation, diving immediately, the man's shot going where the crazy man had been a second before. There was no way a bullet could catch up to Justice now. He tucked and rolled, springing to his feet and slamming the Zoner in the chest, the man going back hard into his instrument panel and sliding to the floor, the fight gone out of him.

"Oooh, my man," he whispered harshly, grabbing the punk by the lapel and jerking him to his feet. "I would hate to be you right now."

"Please don't k-kill me," the punk pleaded, Justice stripping the gun easily from his hands and sticking it in his belt.

Justice smiled. "Have I got a deal for you." Then he turned and unplugged the mike from the pilot's radio, sticking it in his pocket.

He moved to one of the broken windows and called down to the deck. "Hurry it up!" he yelled. "Time's run out!"

Bergman waved up to him and began barking orders as Gail Compton sent people over on the pulleys, children first, then the elderly, then the women. It looked as if she had rounded up close to thirty people.

Justice walked out on deck to watch the spectacle, keeping a loose eye on his bridge captive. The Queen was going down for good, its aft already a third under water, as more explosions bubbled up from beneath in white foam, a beautiful lady with beautiful memories going less than peacefully to eternal rest.

The remainder of the rescue operation took less than ten minutes, but even in that short a time the balance had begun to get treacherous as the Queen threatened to roll over and go belly-up.

"We'll get sucked down with it!" the pilot said from inside.

"Hurry!" he called across the decks, Gail waving and

taking the last ride herself, the other lines already severed. Justice turned to the pilot. "Get us away from here."

The man didn't need to be told twice. He spun the wheel as Bergman's people rushed to raise anchor and crew the thing.

They broke off and eased away just as the *Queen* roared like a dying prehistoric beast and rolled, going down hard, the ocean swirling crazily around it in a whirlpool, sucking everything down, covering the brutality with its own kind of peace as all the bodies swirled down the whirlpool like dirty water down a drain.

As they moved off, Justice watched in fascination as the mighty Pacific buried every single remnant of the bloody encounter.

Now it was time to get even. For everything.

XVI.

SANTA MONICA GENERAL HOSPITAL—LOS ANGELES 10 APRIL 1983—THE MIDDLE OF THE NIGHT

Justice lay on his back, staring at the darkened ceiling and listening to the late-night sounds of the hospital filtering up and down the hallway outside his partially open door. He'd pleaded with the ambulance crew not to bring him to this place of death and memories, but they didn't listen. He had been, after all, paralyzed.

Ed Barkes rode with him to the hospital, crying, babbling in a way that made Justice wish he could do the same thing and get the grief out. But he knew he wouldn't be able to—ever.

The doctors had examined him and tried to console him. They questioned him at length about the scars on his back, but he never answered. Then they got their X-rays back and gave Barkes a hard time for acting as if a paraplegic had been walking at all. It was cruel and a waste of everyone's time, they had said, to play such a horrible joke.

Poor Ed. He'd never understood what they were talking about, explaining at great length how Justice had been walking right up to a couple of hours ago. Impossible, they'd said, with a severed spinal cord and a bullet lodged in it.

Justice had briefly considered explaining to them the power of mind that allowed him to walk, or the fact that the bullet was the electrical conductor to his brain synapses—but they wouldn't have understood. Allie hadn't understood until . . . until . . .

Allie.

His life had fled with her. Everything he'd been had been a direct result of her love and compassion. She'd been all give and no take, and finally she'd given everything. And here he lay, in a place very much like the place where he'd first met her, except this time there was no Allie to rescue him. There was no hope.

Movement had returned, slowly, after he'd willed it to return. He wanted to die, and while a hospital might be a nice place to accomplish that, he didn't feel it would be fast enough. So he'd willed movement back into himself, and it was time to go.

He stood slowly, his limbs stiff and sore. The hospital gown came off easily, Justice changing back into the sweats he'd been wearing when they brought him in. After he got into his shoes, he crept to the door, peeking out. The nurses' station sat at the end of the hall, but which of them would recognize him in a vertical position?

He took a long breath and pushed the door open, striding into the hall and turning immediately toward the nurses' station and the elevators that lay just beyond. He passed the station, a nurse looking up quizzically, but returning to her charts when she saw him casually push the elevator button half a hall distant.

It amazed him that no one could tell he was a walking corpse. He was surprised that no one noticed the decaying death in their midst. It had to be a measure of the human being's stupidity, for he had no more connection to this land of the living than a statue had to the pigeons who shit on it. He was walking, festering madness, a man brought to the brink one too many times. It was time to bring the foolishness to an end.

The elevator arrived, Justice taking it down to the lobby. He crossed the carpeted floor and went out the front door, looking for a car.

An old MG sports car caught his eye—burnt orange, a nice color. He walked up to it and looked inside. It had a good stereo.

He glanced around and, seeing no one else in the lot, swung out hard with an elbow, smashing out the glass on the driver's side, cutting his arm in the process.

The handle opened easily through the window space,

and he cleaned out the larger pieces of glass before climbing behind the wheel and hot-wiring the thing to roaring life. He turned on the stereo, changing stations until he found rock and roll, then cranked it up full, squealing out of the lot.

He drove, aimlessly at first, his mind alive with screams and fires, Allie's face already mixing with dark Indian faces, all of them dead, the light gone from all their eyes. He was beyond consolation on any level, a brain caught in conundrum, spinning a never-ending circular track, always leading back to the same place.

A traffic light, red, roared up in front of him, Justice plowing through without seeing it, lines of cars screeching to avoid a collision. It woke him up enough to make him realize where he was—Olympic Boulevard—and that it wasn't fair to the rest of the world to make them die along with him.

He came to an intersection and looked south, seeing the ribbon of the Santa Monica Freeway just blocks distant, set above the roadway. He realized that he was barely five miles from home. Zeroing in on the freeway, he reached it quickly, taking the ramp up with his gas pedal flat out, hitting the highway itself at seventy-five.

The road was practically deserted as he hit straightaway and gunned it, the needle pressing a hundred, then beyond, Justice reaching down to crank up the stereo even more—the Rolling Stones, "You Can't Always Get What You Want." Laughing and screaming along with the song, he reached up and unsnapped the convertible top, the wind grabbing the thing and ripping it right off the car, Justice watching it for a second in the rearview as it floated like a parachute above the road. And then he had distanced it.

He'd thought plenty about death when he'd lain on the ground at Volcán Barú, but he'd never had the guts to face it totally. Now he embraced it gladly, racing the speedometer to the end of the scale. Whatever death was, he hoped that it was peace.

The end of the freeway was racing up on him, the monstrous interchange where Interstate 10 and Highway 1 intersected in a mix-master of overpasses and bridge abutments—the perfect place to crash out.

He left the pedal on the floor and aimed for the overpass pylons, his blood racing as the scenery blurred past him.

You can't always get what you want.

Visions of Allie filled his head, her years of patient therapy, her undisguised virtue... all for a lost cause.

You can't always get what you want.

Beauty crushed by ugliness. Did it mean there was no beauty, no compassion, no goodness? Was it all a lie? God, he wished he had her capacity for striving toward good, even in the face of the overwhelming.

But if you try sometime
You just might find
You get what you need.

Up close the pylon flew at him, and whether it was him or some force within him put there by Allie, he jerked the wheel at the last second, the bridge rushing past just as the car flipped up into the night sky.

He was flying, a bullet whizzing into the darkness, aware somehow of the car, far below him, twirling over and over across the breadth of the highway in a symphony of crashing glass and rending metal, and his body, conditioned by years of training, reacting on its own, tucking, preparing for flight's end.

He came down in a roll, hard, harder than he could have possibly imagined, and when he came out of the roll, barely touching earth, he was still moving at a hundred miles an hour, his tumble continuing as the car, now far distant, exploded in fury all over the roadway, its pieces strewn everywhere; and as he continued his tumble down the median, his mind crystallized the stupid hope that the owner of the thing had insurance.

He stopped, finally, his out-of-control tumble, and lay on his back on the median. Everything hurt, but he could tell that nothing was broken. He stood slowly, painfully, and looked back at the highway. The car had disintegrated, its twisted pieces over a hundred yards distant, a line of burning gasoline blazing the whole roadway bright orange.

He had survived again, despite the death of everything around him. His curse was, apparently, to live. He hobbled off the road, cars beginning to back up at the accident scene, and when the flashing lights of the highway patrol flared the night, he hid in the bushes as they passed, sneaking away, finding himself on Highway 1 going home.

He limped down the same road he had jogged earlier

that same evening, the path familiar enough that he could take it without thought. He was beginning to realize that he was totally insane, totally removed from life the way others understood it.

The walk home could have taken hours or minutes. Time held no meaning for him. He was a bundle of anger and remorse, guilt and indignation—contrasting emotions with a similar root. If only Allie were around to help him, to tell him what to do. He turned his thoughts to the men who'd killed her, but couldn't put names on them. He'd made enemies in powerful places. Any one of thousands could have torched the house, but that didn't stop him from wanting to *do* something, to lash out with his anger and cause the same kind of pain that ate away at his own gut.

Without realization, he was standing before his home. There was nothing left except collapsed, blackened rubble, still smoking, pieces of Allie probably still burning within. He let it wash over him, continued to take the pain onto himself in ever greater doses as if he could explode with it. Then he walked around the back and down the hill to the beach.

The deck was gone, burnt and collapsed, leaving only the leafless forest of pylons that had once supported it. He moved into the supports, climbing over the rubble until he reached the place he'd been looking for. Bending, he began clearing away rubble, working faster and faster until the area of sand was exposed beneath.

He fell to his knees and began digging with his hands, scooping sand away and tossing it over his shoulder until his fingers scratched the top of the box buried there. He pulled it out with trembling hands, opening it to expose the automatic still residing within.

He took it out, cradling it reverently, transferring all his anger into its molded contours. He couldn't keep it inside any longer. His heart and his conscience had been burned away, and he would no longer control the vengeful demon he had trapped there. He had seen the death of enough innocents. He intended for the guilty to die.

XVII.

PANAMA'S PACIFIC COAST—
ABOARD THE MINE SWEEPER
20 FEBRUARY 1988

Justice stood drinking coffee on the bridge of the sweeper, nicknamed *Vulture* by its late, unlamented crew, his eyes scanning the distant coastline as they cut through the rapidly brightening waters of the Gulf of Chiriquí. The pilot, a Zone cop named Thompson, stood at the wheel, his face drained bloodless. Captain Bergman, his own face cleaned up and dressed, and Gail Compton stood with him. All of them were exhausted physically and emotionally. All of them knew that they weren't finished yet.

"There's a lagoon . . . over there," Thompson said, "near the fishing village of Pedregal. We'll drop anchor there and be met by several boats."

"Then what?" Justice asked, taking a sip. He was tired and battered, but still serviceable. Gail had also managed to get the remnants of the handcuffs filed off his wrists, leaving him considerably lighter, both physically and emotionally.

"I don't know much at that point," the man replied. "The boats reload the cargo onto trucks that pull up to the pier. Usually an escort copter follows."

"Where do they take the stuff?"

The man shrugged. "Nobody tells me," he said. "We divide the bags in half. They go with theirs. Though Pedregal is only a couple of miles away from the city of David on the Pan American Highway."

Justice had tagged a map of Panama up on the bridge

wall. He walked over to study it. It had been pretty easy convincing the Zoner to tell what he knew. With the amount of trouble he was in already, cooperation was his only hope. Justice would just as soon kill the son of a bitch, but he needed him alive for very specific reasons.

The map told the story. Volcán Barú was a straight shot up the highway from the drop point, barely a fifty-mile trip, equidistant from Bocas del Toro on the Atlantic side.

He turned back to the man, shaking his head. "Why the hell did you do this?" he asked.

Thompson shrugged. "It was Portilla's idea," he said. "He wanted the cash to increase his personal power over the Guard. There were a lot of promises and a lot of money involved, and a lot to lose if we didn't go along. Since the treaty days, we've been at his mercy."

"At his mercy!?" Bergman yelled, jumping on the man, beating him, Thompson putting his hands up to fend off the blows. "Don't you know what you did? All those people, all those . . . children!"

Bergman pummeled the man, Justice letting him go for a time before stepping in. When he finally pulled the captain away, he just looked up at Justice, his face strained in remorse.

"What in God's name is wrong with this world?" he asked, desperate for an answer.

Justice looked deeply into the man's eyes. "The jungle," was all he could think to say. Then he took the man's shoulders. "Hold it together for a while. We've got shit to do."

Bergman breathed deeply, settling back to the place without thought. "I'm all right," he said. "You can count on me."

Justice nodded. "I know. I think I'll need you down in the engine room now. There's no one else."

The man nodded once, then walked out. Justice turned and shared a look with Gail Compton, both of them jumping when the radio squawked to life.

"Vulture One, this is Indio. Come in."

The voice was heavily accented. Thompson looked at Justice, who nodded and took the microphone out of his pocket, handing it to the man. "Make it sweet," he whispered.

Thompson plugged it in, took a deep breath, and made contact. "This is Vulture One. I read you, Indio. Over."

"Vulture One, we have confirmed you visually. Did all go well? Over."

"Roger, Indio. Cargo large and intact. Over."

"Bring it in. Out."

Justice unplugged the mike again, setting his coffee on a map table. "Do as the man says," he told Thompson, then looked at Compton. "I'm going for some air."

"Sounds good," she replied, following him out of the bridge and down the metal stairs to the bloody deck. He hoped that the loaders wouldn't want to come aboard. As was customary on these trips, according to Thompson, the bags of personal effects were lined up on deck. There were thirty of them, the gleanings that pigs like Thompson thought were worth all the horror and pain and death. Man's callousness never ceased to amaze him. Humans loved to think of themselves as being above the animals of the jungle, yet the most they could think of to do with their brains was invent new ways to hurt things.

Justice moved to the siderope, looking out into the bright, hot morning. The shoreline had grown larger as they approached, the lagoon coming into view. He sat on one of the sacks and rubbed his eyes.

"Tired?" she asked, moving behind him to massage his shoulders.

"It's this place," he said. "This... atmosphere."

"You sound as if you've been here before."

He looked up at her, not able to talk about the madness that had been steadily creeping over him, the pull toward the void. "One hellhole's pretty much the same as the next," he responded.

"You know," she said, sitting on the sack next to his, "if this is a joint operation with Medellin, then Portilla's working with them."

"Just good politics," Justice responded, straightening somewhat, scanning the horizon. "It's an investment. You back both sides, then you've got the winner in your pocket no matter who it is. The Medellin people are smart enough to see the crush of history and know that, one way or the other, Noriega's on his way out. The only constant is corruption."

"What happens when we get to the lagoon?" she asked.

"I'm going with them," he said, "to Volcán Barú."

He stared straight out at the choppy waters of the bay, but he could feel the weight of her eyes on him. "You're serious," she said after a moment.

"Dead serious."

"What about your people?"

"They're all grown up," he said. "They'll have to take care of themselves."

"But what if they don't show?"

He turned and stared. "Then they don't show. As far as I'm concerned, that doesn't change a thing."

"You *are* crazy," she breathed low.

"Just cursed," he said, "cursed with life."

He stood. They were entering the mouth of the lagoon, several large powerboats sitting idly two hundred yards distant. "Look," he said, pointing.

A long pier made of steel sat amid a profusion of small wooden docks. A helicopter sat on the pier's end, its rotors beating air.

The ship jerked slightly, the engines shutting down, then reversing. "Drop anchor!" Thompson called from the bridge through the broken window, several of the survivors hurrying to knock the brake out of the take-up wheel, the anchor falling with a loud rattle of chains across the deck. The engines stopped completely, the cargo skiffs starting up like angry mosquitoes and moving toward them in heavy wake.

"You'd better get below," he said. "They might get suspicious if they see a woman aboard."

She stood without an argument and walked off, Justice wondering just what was on her mind. He turned and walked back toward the bridge, Captain Bergman intercepting him before he went up the stairs. "What should I do?" he asked.

"Watch our friend up on the bridge," Justice said. "When everyone leaves, I want you to lower a lifeboat and take everyone ashore. You're very close to the village. Go there and find a phone. Call Albrook and ask for General Thurston. . . ."

"Thurston," Bergman repeated.

Justice nodded. "Don't talk to anyone else. Tell the general your story. Don't leave anything out, and tell him you are afraid of the local authorities. He'll probably understand.

I've checked him out. He's a decent man. They'll send a cutter out for you."

"What about you?" he asked.

"Our association ends here," Justice said. "Don't worry about it."

"But..."

"Enough," Justice said. "You'd better get upstairs and watch Thompson. He might just get a wild hair up his ass and decide to start screaming."

Bergman smiled. "Just let him try," he said.

"Good," Justice said, shaking hands with the man. "Now you know why I let you beat on him before. You've already gotten his attention. Good luck."

"I think you're the one who'll need the luck," Bergman said. "Good-bye, Mr. Lambert. I'd like to say that I won't forget you, but I hope I forget everything connected with this horror."

"Just get yourself another ship, Captain," he returned. "You're a good man. You did everything humanly possible."

"Except I had you locked up."

Justice shrugged. "I'd have probably done the same," he said, and the boats had reached them. "You'd better get up there."

The captain climbed the metal stairs, Justice turning to the gunwale and looking over at the ten boats grouped thirty feet below him. He waved.

A shirtless man in a straw hat waved back. "How many bags?" he called.

"Thirty-one," Justice called back, the men in the boats cheering and applauding loudly. Apparently this was a commission job.

"You know we get the odd number?" the man asked.

"Fine with me," Justice responded. "You want me to toss them down?"

"Yeah... yeah... like always," the man called.

Justice looked around him. Five men were on the deck. "Drop sixteen sacks," he said.

The men moved to the gunwale and one at a time began dropping the sacks into the boats as they'd maneuver up against the *Vulture*. It seemed odd to Justice that they'd take the sacks sight unseen. A good way to get cheated. He walked to the port side and looked over at the helicopter. A fat, dark man with a black mustache and a permanent frown stood beside his chopper, an old camouflage-green Bell Kiowa, a rifle with scope cradled in his arm as he watched the proceedings.

He moved back starboard. Several rope ladders lay rolled up on deck. He picked one up, hooked the ends to the corresponding notches on the gunwale and watched it unroll itself down the side of the ship. The lagoon was calm and peaceful all around them, palm trees drooping along the rocky shore, a village of mud and thatch evident in the sleepy distance, its inhabitants already hard at work though the day was still young—the way of those who live close to the earth.

He had felt the pull of Volcán Barú ever since they'd spotted land. It grew stronger the closer he got. His heart and soul lay there. He would reclaim them or die trying. Thompson's Beretta was still stuck in his waistband. It would be enough for now. He stuck a leg over the sideropes and began climbing down, surprised when he looked up to see someone else climbing down with him.

It was Compton, her hair stuck up under her ball cap, her face smeared with lines of soot to distract attention from her feminine features. She'd put on a heavy leather jacket and had an M16 strapped on her back. He took a breath and ate his anger. There was nothing he could do about her now.

He flagged one of the boats over and climbed aboard, the woman following seconds later. "Take me over to the chopper," he told the man. "I've got something to show him."

The Indian pilot started the engine up again, loud, whiny, and buzzed them toward the pier, Justice smiling over at Compton. "Pretty pleased with yourself," he said.

"It's my job," she said.

"Okay," he said. "I'll play, too. Give me the gun."

"Why?"

"I have a plan. Give me the gun."

Her eyes narrowed, but she did as she was told, Justice slinging the weapon over his own shoulder as the pilot cut his engine and bumped them up against the pier, Justice looking up to see the fat man staring down.

"What you wan'?" the man said, low, guttural.

"I'm coming up," Justice said. "Got something to show you."

With that he climbed up the metal ladder attached to the side of the pier, the woman following right behind him. He reached the top, the fat man holding his rifle, a Steyr-Mannlicher SSG outfitted with a ten-round magazine, a little tighter. His face was bloated with abuse, his eyes just dark, angry slits.

"That's close enough," the man said, in barely recognizable English, his voice just loud enough to be heard over the rotor sound.

"I want a ride back to Volcán Barú with you," Justice said. "Got something to show the big boys."

"You show me first," the man sputtered through thick lips.

"Okay," Justice said, turning to Gail and pulling off her ball cap, her long hair spilling down to her shoulders. "Underneath all this crap is an heiress, my friend. Not just any heiress, but a Kentucky Fried Chicken heiress. She's probably worth a hundred million. I recognized her from *People* magazine when we were going through the *Queen*. We could ransom this bitch for twenty million bucks."

"Fuck you," Compton spat in a rich-girl way, being forced to play along. "My bodyguards will hunt all of you down and kill you before you know what's what."

"Right," Justice said, winking at the fat man.

The man laughed, getting into the spirit of the thing.

"I think there could be quite a reward in this for us if we bring her in together," Justice said.

The man leveled the weapon. "Or for me if I bring her in alone."

Justice pointed a thumb over his shoulder toward the boat. "And my friends blast you right out of the sky."

The fat man saw logic in that. "I think we got a deal," he said, motioning them into the chopper, Justice taking the copilot seat, Compton taking the thirty-five-foot craft's passenger compartment just behind.

They sat for a moment, watching the final loading of the boats; then the man throttled them off the pier, water beneath swirling under the rotors' manufactured wind, and headed them north—toward the past.

"Did you have a good time this run?" the fat man asked, as a landscape of jungle growth and green foothills floated beneath them, the ribbon of the Pan American Highway visible far below.

"It was okay," Justice replied.

The man shook his head, chuckling. "I'd give almost anything to go out with you once and see the faces on those rich bastards when you blasted them away and took their women. Those motherfuckers eat shit, all of them."

Justice turned and shared a look with Compton, the woman making a face at him, angry that she was being used as the guinea pig. As far as Justice was concerned, she was getting what she deserved for interfering.

"How far?" Justice asked.

"Fifteen minutes," the fat man said. "Maybe twenty." He turned and stole a glance at Compton, leering. "How come you put that shit on her face."

"So people wouldn't recognize her and get any ideas," Justice replied, winging it.

"Hey," the fat man said. "You fuck this bitch before you brought her out?"

"Sure," Justice said, stealing another glance at Compton, the woman's eyes wide with anger and indignation. "Twice."

The fat man looked at her again. "How was it? Maybe I'd like to get a piece before we sell her upstairs."

"Not worth the trouble, my man," Justice said, watching Compton the whole time, her face red with anger. "I bet they got women at your camp. I'd spend my money on them and get some decent ass. This bitch hasn't got any heart."

"You're just a faggot, that's all," Compton said. "The son of a bitch couldn't even get it up."

The fat man laughed loudly, the funniest thing he'd heard in years. The radio crackled, cutting the joke short.

"Unidentified aircraft... please identify yourself. You have entered authorized airspace. Over."

They weren't close enough to Volcán for visual sighting yet. It meant they had radar.

The fat man picked up the mike and responded. "Base camp... this is Eagle One... repeat, Eagle One, returning to base with good news. Over."

"Confirmed, Eagle One. Bring her in on visual."

"God . . . we must be close," Justice said.

The man grunted and pointed out the windshield. "There," he said. "Volcán Barú."

Justice looked, his insides lurching. There, in the distance, its peak shrouded in haze, sat a giant among midgets, a towering peak whose presence seemed to pull directly on his mind and heart. Volcán Barú. A monstrous sentinel, marking his folly for all time. He felt as if he'd been slapped, and he had to take several deep breaths just to calm himself enough to continue the charade.

"Say," the fat man said, glancing again at Gail. "If she was such a bad piece of ass, how come you done it to her twice?"

Justice nudged the guy. "Just trying to get my money's worth," he said, Compton gagging in the backseat.

The fat man threw his head back and laughed, Justice swinging out a rigid left hand and chopping him across the throat. The man doubled over, gagging. Justice threw a hard right to the temple, putting him out cold.

He slid away from the stick, the chopper going into steep decline.

"God!" Compton screamed. "I hope you know how to fly this thing."

"We'll find out," Justice said, as he took his own set of instruments and controls and eased the bird back into the flight path. Reaching over, he unsnapped the fat man's seat belt and jerked him off the seat, dropping him between. He looked back at a still furious Gail Compton. "Here. Do something with him."

"With pleasure," she said, grunting, dragging the bulk back with her and opening the door. Bracing herself, she began shoving with her legs, sliding the punk toward the doorway, the man tumbling silently out of the chopper and falling into the inscrutable jungle below.

The woman moved up into the fat man's vacated seat. "I'll get even with you for that," she said.

He turned hard to her. "Stop gaming me," he said. "We're both going to get killed if you don't."

"From the way you're approaching this thing," she spat, "I think you *want* to get killed."

He stared evenly at her. "There're worse things than being dead," he said, and checked the instruments.

They were cruising at 117 mph, clicking off the miles. Volcán Barú had grown larger in his sight, its presence drawing him in like a magnet. She was talking, but he couldn't focus on her words. Too many memories were pushing conscious thought away and filling his head with a babble of voices. He shook his head, forcing himself to think.

"Are you all right?" she asked, and her voice seemed to hold real concern.

"Fine," he said, pulling his eyes from the volcano to stare down at its base. His voice was a whisper. "My goodness."

Below them sat base camp, a small city of roads and houses, whose apparent purpose was to help keep the fortress above functioning. There was a large motor pool and a landing area set aside for helicopters. A cable car was running from ground level, its gondola just then swinging as it made the climb into the haze bank that covered Barú's peak. A great deal had happened here since Justice's last visit, but that wasn't his major preoccupation. On the edge of the base camp sat a tent city, aligned in neat, precise military rows that stretched far off into the foothills. There had to be between two and three thousand of them, troops in uniform moving around the campsite, filling the entire area with thousands of people.

They were flying the Cuban flag.

XVIII.

OAK CLIFF—DALLAS, TEXAS
20 APRIL 1983—SUNSET

William Justice sat behind the wheel of the rented Camaro on the residential street, taking one last look at all the paperwork he'd put together before shoving it into the manila clasp envelope, licking the bitter-tasting envelope glue, and sealing the thing.

It had been ten days since Allie's murder, ten run-together days of depression and anger and remorse, interspersed with frantic attempts at getting his affairs in order. His mind was a jumble as he found it nearly impossible to dwell upon any one thought for very long. The only thing he did know was that if he didn't strike out at something soon, he would surely explode. It had taken several days of thought, but he'd finally decided on this town, this street, as his place of retribution. It was time for the guilty to pay, and since he didn't know specifically whom to blame for Allie's death, he blamed the systematic dehumanization of all people by greed and self-interest, and he determined to take out the worst animals when he found them.

He had one now.

He turned the envelope over and read the address. Wouldn't Ed Barkes be surprised when he went to his mailbox and found William Lambert's power of attorney made out to him? He'd gone through everything he could think of and had just given it all to Ed to do with as he saw fit, liquidating enough to give himself a great deal of money in the process. He knew Ed well enough to know that the man would simply hold Lambert Enterprises in trust for his eventual return, but that return would never come. William Justice was tired of the lies of the world. He didn't have the heart for it anymore.

He climbed out from behind the wheel and walked to the mailbox on the corner. It was a swank neighborhood, bulged large with Dallas's oil income, the lawns meticulous and well kept, the gardens weeded and lush—the orderly exterior covering the swarming snakes beneath the surface.

After one long moment with the envelope, he dropped it into the mail slot and turned toward the business at hand. He walked slowly across the street, three children on bikes whizzing by, yelling happily to one another as the last few weeks of school got them pumped for a hot summer. He took note of them but couldn't connect them with any kind of life he could understand. He reached the sidewalk and stood, watching his prey.

The man was slightly overweight, his paunch hanging over the plaid bermuda shorts he wore, his white T-shirt stretched across his stomach. He was a little older, a little balder since the day Justice had met him in the VA hospital in '78, but it was definitely the same man.

Justice scouted the terrain. Like most gangsters, this one lived on a corner lot with good visibility up and down the street. There were no dark corners anywhere on the property, no bushes to hide in, no trees hanging down. A nine-foot stockade fence enclosed the backyard and the snarling chow dog that reigned supreme there.

"Excuse me!" Justice called to the man over the sound of his mower.

The man looked at him with narrowed eyes and a hand cupped to his ear.

"Excuse me!" Justice called again, the man shutting down the mower and walking over to him.

"Sorry," the man said. "I couldn't hear you."

"I'm looking for Rolling Brook Road," Justice said. "I can't find it anywhere."

The man smiled and pointed farther down the block. "It's only a one-block street," he said, "about three blocks farther on."

"Up that way," Justice said, pointing also.

"That's it," the man said, then looked around. "Guess I'm through anyway."

"This is a nice neighborhood," Justice said.

The man agreed. "Too many damned kids, though," he replied, then shrugged. "Guess you can't get away from it." He looked at Justice with a practiced eye. "Don't I know you from somewhere?"

Justice smiled. "Don't think so," he said. "I must remind you of somebody."

"Yeah," he said, suspicious. "Wish I could remember who."

"You sound like a man with a past."

"Me?" the man said, pointing to himself. "Naw. I'm just a pencil pusher transplanted from Cleveland. Nothing doing in my life. Well, good luck to you."

"Sure," Justice said. "You, too."

The man walked casually away, but Justice could tell something was bothering him. He turned and looked back darkly, forced a smile and a wave, then pushed the silent mower off the lawn and into his long driveway toward the open garage in the back.

Justice looked both ways, then followed him back. The garage was lost in shadow in the deepening twilight, the man barely visible in the rear as he put up the mower, the smell of cut grass, old wood, and motor oil heavy in the thick atmosphere.

"John Bignell," he said low, the man jumping at the sound of his name.

"Wha—"

"Dirty-work man," Justice said. "Did you always hire your killings, or did you ever have the guts to do them yourself?"

Bignell took a step toward him. "That voice . . ."

"Far enough," Justice said, pulling the .45 out from behind him, the man stopping immediately. "Remember the voice? Remember the face connected to it that you thought was blown to pieces?"

"It *is* you," he said. "You changed your face. Listen, Justice, I had to do it. You were a security risk. I dealt with you by the book."

"Then the book is inhuman."

"My God, you can't blame me!"

"I blame you," Justice said.

"What are you going to do?" the man said, his voice weak, cracking. "For the love of God, Justice. I'll do anything. Money...I'll get money. I can help you in a lot of ways. Please, just tell me what you want."

"I want you to die like a man," Justice said.

Bignell started whining. He fell onto his knees there on the oily garage floor. "Please," he begged. "Please, don't..."

"My man," Justice said, the fires raging in his head. "It's that time."

He pulled the trigger once, the gun popping loudly in the enclosed space. Bignell's head exploded with the impact, his body dropping heavily to the floor. Justice stuck the gun back in his waistband and strolled casually out of the garage. The report had been loud, like a backfire, the neighborhood sounds immediately taking over again as if nothing had happened. He moved easily down the drive, listening to the wind blowing through the cottonwood trees and smelling someone's backyard barbecue several houses down.

Nothing was going on around front as he crossed the street and got into the Camaro, driving slowly back out of the neighborhood and along Interstate 30 to the Dallas–Fort Worth airport. He turned the car in at Avis rental, then put his .45 into the one suitcase he'd packed, checking the thing to Houston.

As he made the flight, he tried to sort out his tumbling mind. The killing of Bignell had given him a kind of grim satisfaction, allaying somewhat the feelings of helplessness that tended to overcome him since Allie's death. But it hadn't taken the hurt away, just as he'd feared it wouldn't. The thing that was odd to him, though, was the feeling of rightness. He'd despaired the taking of a human life, but he'd never considered Bignell human. The man was a vicious animal passing as human among the ranks of real people. He'd been a cancer to be eliminated from the body of mankind, and in fulfilling the role of pest controller, Justice felt himself doing the world a favor. But the pain remained constant, a wall always between him and the rest of the world. It was no way to live.

He deplaned in Houston, checking into the airport Hilton for the night. The next morning he took a cab down 225 to La Porte, where the *Lutine* was docked. As he carried his bag on board and cast off, he never even looked back once.

The harbor was busy, sailboats breaking the monotony of sky and water with splashes of color, elegance, and grace. He cleared the harbor checkpoints on inboard, puttering slowly out to the sea lanes before attempting to unfurl the sails and get under way without a crew.

He moved through the traffic and finally the sparse traffic. The *Lutine* was packed with food and charts and fresh water. If need be, he could stay out to sea for nearly six months without taking on supplies or seeing another human being. He made open water and fought for two hours with the mainsail before getting himself set and heading south by east, just letting the Gulf waters take him, hoping to shoot the gap of Florida straits between Key West and Cuba.

On a ship the size of the *Lutine*, rough waters would kill him without help. He was alone, just he and God's waters, and God would decide if he should live or die. He lashed down the helm and worked the jib.

He headed into the void to test out his curse of life.

XIX.

VOLCÁN BARÚ
20 FEBRUARY 1988—0738 HOURS

There may have been thirty choppers in the roped-off and guarded landing area, Justice and Gail Compton climbing out to stare around them in amazement.

"This is incredible," the woman said as they walked through a forest of helicopters. "Have you noticed the flags on these things?"

"They're from all over," Justice said, looking up. The sky was beginning to cloud, thunderheads rolling in from the north. "Something's up."

They walked down the long rows of African-, Arab-, and European-marked helicopters. There were even a couple of American corporations represented by choppers and one sporting the red star on the rotor. The volcano dominated the landscape all around them, its presence towering over everything, as the base camp was tucked into its folds, but Justice tried not to look at it. He was a churning machine right now, an exposed nerve tingling with pain and longing. He had to control himself if he was to do the job.

They made their way to the impromptu gate, the Medellin guard taking no notice of people going out. It was only the ones trying to get in that concerned him.

"I didn't expect this," Compton said as they made their way into the city proper.

"Me neither," Justice said. "It looks like Mardi Gras."

To their left and in the far distance was the tent city of

the Cuban troops, separated enough from the camp to maintain discipline, but close enough for R and R. The dusty street they walked on was jammed full of people—soldiers certainly, but many others as well: Medellin, Chiriquí Indians, blacks, Arabs in fezzes, and Orientals in dark suits with cameras. It looked like a United Nations cookout. The street was plowed dirt, its edges filled with trailers, vendor stands, and bars made of warped plank wood. Cooking food, tortillas and beans, filled the streets with heavy odor as Justice realized that he hadn't eaten for nearly a day. Women called from windows up and down the block, displaying their own brand of wares while Medellin people—mostly Panama City hoodlums with family connections—kept an eye on the streets. Crowd control, Justice supposed.

The smells of defecation were also strong, sanitation a real problem in a little town swelled to unnatural size. A small, naked boy ran across the street in front of him, his Indian mother giving chase, calling out in unknown dialect. There were gun stores and clothing racks and a post office. A sign on a shack proudly announced a telephone within, for "reasonable price." God only knew what passed for reasonable in this place. Water was being sold midblock, but there were no signs about the prices being "reasonable" here, water the world's most valuable commodity when you didn't have any. All around them men shouted and sang, occasional fistfights breaking out that were quickly broken up by the makeshift law enforcement. A mariachi band filled the air with music as they stood before a ramshackle bar, attracting patrons.

"I'm starved," Justice said. "You got any money? We threw all mine out at Panama City."

The woman shook her head. "That handsy nurse cleaned me out back on the boat," she said. "Serves you right for not saving up. What are we doing, by the way?"

"Reconnoitering," he said as they made the end of the block, an outdoor movie theater set up there for after dark. Beyond the street, under a grove of trees, lines of connected adobe houses bustled with activity, children running and playing as their mothers ground corn into meal on the rocks by their doors. And beyond that another shanty town of thatch and mud, its inhabitants black and Indian. Base camp was a real city, all right. It even seemed to have its class divisions.

A National Guard jeep roared by, its driver plowing down the center of the street, people jumping out of the way as it passed. Two Arabs wearing checked ghutras sat in the back, talking animatedly, gesturing as they spoke. Justice turned and watched them pass. They screeched through the main street, then turned north, heading in the direction of the cable car. Whatever was happening, it was happening up in the castle.

The woman stood with her hands on her hips, looking around. "Well, we've seen the town," she said. "Now what?"

"Now we wait," Justice replied.

"Wait for what?"

The man smiled and pointed. A white '65 Cadillac convertible roared into the main street, carrying a dust cloud behind it. A man stood up in the backseat with his arms outstretched. "Where's the party?" he cried loudly—Bob Jenks.

"Over here!" Justice called, waving them to him, Jenks letting out a war whoop when he saw who it was.

The car roared over to them, Victor Ibanez behind the wheel wearing a cowboy hat and a bow tie. Sardi and Jorge sat beside him in the front, with Jenks, Kiki, and Kim in back.

"We looked for you," Ibanez said.

"I came a different way," Justice said, noticing Sardi staring at his forehead. "Oh, this..." he said, reaching up tentative fingers to touch the bandage on his forehead. "I ran into a door."

"I see you have a friend," Kim said, looking at a soot-streaked Gail Compton.

"Cohort," Compton replied. "A friend is somebody you go to the movies with." She reached out a hand to Kim. "Gail Compton."

Kim just looked at the hand, then shook it reluctantly. "William a bad man," she said.

"I know," Compton replied. "It's nice to know all of you."

"Good," Ibanez said. "We're all good friends. That's nice."

"Is there any decent food in this place?" Justice asked the man.

"Are you kidding?" Ibanez asked. "Though I know a place where you can maybe get a table to eat on."

"Fair enough."

The man pointed across the street to a building that had been made by piling up bags of cement, then hosing them down. A makeshift sign on the top of the thing advertised: Beans and Beer. Close enough.

"You go eat over there," Ibanez said. "And I will call up to the mountain and see when you may go up."

Everyone piled out of the car, Jenks lugging the aluminum suitcase full of money out of the trunk. They moved across the crowded street to the café. The place was a large, covered space and nothing much else—kerosene lamps, a simple wooden bar with a kitchen stuck on the end. They pushed several wooden tables covered with butcher paper together by a large, glassless window space that overlooked the main drag. Ibanez had pulled the car onto a side street facing their vantage point and had gone into an unimposing cinder-block building that seemed to have no connection with the other buildings in the makeshift city.

They sat and ordered in accord with the sign out front. The food came immediately, beans and tortillas, Justice waiting until they'd been served before speaking.

"You made it out okay," he said.

"The police came with their sirens," Sardi replied. "We evaded them on the stairwells. I brought you an extra change of clothes."

"Good."

"What the hell happened to you, Will'um?" Jenks asked around a bottle of warm beer.

The sky had darkened considerably outside, nightlike. Justice told them the story briefly, eating as he did, the food, as usual, killing his hunger but not his pain. When he'd finished talking, he could see the hurt in all of their eyes and knew why they were there with him.

"Have you given any thought as to how we handle the present situation?" Jorge asked, as Justice finished the last of the beans.

"Not completely," Justice replied. "Obviously we'll have to adjust to the environment."

"Ah," Kiki said. "Then it behooves us to know as much as possible about the ambience of base camp."

"You have any ideas?" Sardi asked him.

"Indeed," Kiki said. "Communication is a specialty of mine." He stood. "I will go have a little chat with some of my less fortunate brothers who live on the outskirts of town."

"By the way," Justice said. "Did you bring anything... dynamic with you?"

The man smiled and unbuttoned the bottom of his shirt, revealing a large utility belt stuffed with C-4 plastique wrapped around his middle.

Justice nodded. Good. "We don't have a lot of time," he said. "The best thing you could do for me at this point is to get me an idea of the layout of the fortress."

"Certainly," Kiki said, tearing a section of the butcher-paper tablecloth off and holding out his hand. "Anyone have a pencil?"

Sardi produced a ballpoint pen from inside his jacket, Kiki taking it and disappearing immediately.

"What is our basic objective, William?" Jorge asked, as rain began to fall outside, light at first, turning rapidly into a deluge.

"Our objective," Justice said, his mind filled with fires and screams, "is to get into the fortress and kill everything that moves."

"Judging from the size of its support camp," Jorge replied, "I'd have to say that might be a formidable task."

"Yeah," Justice responded, watching Ibanez charge out of the building a hundred feet distant. The man bustled around his car, yelling, as the rain sheeted down on it. He finally got himself together enough to fight with the convertible top, pulling it up and hooking it as the rain washed around the brim of his cowboy hat to pour like a faucet in front of his face.

"You did see all them troops out there, didn't you?" Jenks asked.

"Yes, I did," Justice said. "I surely did. And just like before, if you want out, take a walk. I won't hold you here."

Jenks smiled. "Hell," he said, "ain't nobody lives forever anyway, right?"

"Spare me," Jorge said, standing. "While macho boy here is getting ready to arm wrestle the Cuban army, I think I'll scout around a little myself and see what's what."

"Good," Justice said. "We'll be right here."

Ibanez came driving up to the front of the café, climbing out to run inside. Jorge moved to the doorway, stepping aside to let the man pass. He pulled a fold-out umbrella from inside his suit coat and opened it, moving off into the rain.

"Senor Lambert," Ibanez said, taking off his cowboy hat and holding it to his chest. "My superiors wish me to extend to you their greetings, and regret that they cannot visit with you today. They are in executive session up on the mountain and won't be free to speak with distributors until tomorrow morning."

"That will be fine," Justice said, needing a day's planning and a night's sleep anyway.

"They also said that you are free to use one of our dignitary houses for the night at no charge to you," Ibanez said. "I told you . . . very good people, my bosses."

"Extend my thanks to them," Justice said.

"Would you like to go there now?" he asked. "We can leave word here for your associates."

"Certainly," Justice said. "Lead on."

They left the café, the rain not so much falling as crashing to the ground. Justice had forgotten what a hard rain really was. They climbed into the wet Caddy, the dirt street now a river of red mud that ran like blood in large channels to lower ground or pooled in giant puddles in the middle of everything.

Ibanez sloshed them through the mud, the trip ending at the grouping of mobile homes he had seen when they'd left the helicopter holding area. The trailers were old, but they looked dry, and that was something. Ibanez led them to a rusted white twelve-wide with no steps up. They had to climb up to the door. There may have been twenty mobile homes in the grouping, some of them looking lived-in, while the others appeared to remain vacant in order to accommodate visiting dignitaries like himself. Justice began to think it oddly interesting that what Medellin was doing here didn't seem, in its own way, much different than what he was doing at Haven. But in that small difference lay volumes.

The mobile home wasn't really furnished, except for a wooden table and four chairs, a great many ashtrays, and a number of sleeping bags piled up in the corner. Luxury on a budget. The place smelled vaguely of vomit and dank sweat. He moved himself into a corner and sat heavily, sinking in. Ibanez left then, promising to come get them first thing in the morning.

Justice drew his legs up, wrapping large arms around them. He hadn't recognized the area at first, but the vacant field that the mobile homes occupied had been a grazing pasture once for the Indians of Hate del Volcán. The dead city was close, probably no more than a mile or two from this very spot, a touch more around the base of the volcano to get the morning sun. He wondered where they had been buried, for when things got quiet, he could swear they were calling to him from close by.

Jenks produced a deck of cards, he and Kim moving to the table in the kitchen area to play gin and wait out the rain while Compton took one of the sleeping bags farther back into the guts of the thing, an idea that looked good to Justice, too. In a while, after the demons left him alone.

Sardi came and sat beside him, the only person able to interrupt the kind of reverie that held him. "Are you all right?" the man asked.

Justice shook his head. "No," he said. "Not really. I'm having a difficult time getting far enough beyond my emotions to think."

"Are you a danger to the mission?"

"Probably. Staying alive is not uppermost in my mind right now. I almost *expect* this place to take me, to bury me."

"And the rest of us?"

"I've used all of you," Justice said. "I never thought beyond myself. I don't know, maybe I lied to myself, told myself I could handle it. I don't know anymore. I'm always professional, always in charge . . . not here."

"You've got good people," Sardi said. "Perhaps you can lean on us this time."

Justice turned and stared at him. "You think we can pull it off?" he asked.

The man smiled. "I think you have cards you haven't played yet," he said. "Haven't you?"

"Suspicions," Justice said. "Some thoughts I'm not ready to share."

Sardi nodded. "This place has taken your confidence because you have failed here before," he said. "It's perfectly natural. I once thought that it would be a bad idea ever to come here. I don't think that anymore. You *must* face this. I don't think I ever realized just how tied to the past you were until we came here. There was a time when you could have stopped this. That time is no more. To save yourself you must face this."

"But not the rest of you," Justice said. "You didn't sign on for my personal nightmare. You could still take everyone away, you . . ."

"No, William," Sardi replied. "We are all of a mind, all facing the same eventual consequences. Let us join you with dignity."

"Dignity," Justice said. "I think I've gone insane."

"Everyone's insane," the man answered. "Look around you and show me sanity anywhere. The trick is to be functionally insane, to channel it. Do you think the pact we made on Haven Island back in eighty-three was sane? I followed a dream to you, a vision. I wanted to change the world. I still do. Now *that's* crazy. Let me tell you about sanity, though. When you came here, you instinctively knew to bring us with you. All of us are the best at what we do. All of us owe our lives and our hearts to you. You can't carry the whole world on your shoulders alone. This is the time for you to reach out to those who owe you so much. Let us help you. Conquer this demon, and the world can be yours."

Justice sat a little straighter, leaning his head back against the wall. "It's just a little tough when you dig down into yourself for a reality check, and there's no reality there."

Sardi stood and pulled a sleeping bag off the pile, tossing it to him. "There's no such thing as reality," he said. "You know that."

"Something must be real."

Sardi squatted down, getting right in his face. "Your quest," he said low, "your mission in life. It's the most real thing any human being has ever undertaken. You are the transitional link between the jungle and civilization, you and no one else. The planet is yours to save."

Justice laughed without humor. "If I can just keep from going totally psychotic. That's funny."

"Merrily, merrily," Sardi said, the childhood rhyme. "Life is but a dream." He stood. "Get a little sleep. Deprivation leads to paranoia."

Sardi stood, going into the kitchen to watch the card game. Justice unrolled the sleeping bag and crawled in. He lay with his eyes open, listening to the rain pounding on the tin roof and watching it run down the windows. After a time he closed his eyes, the sounds lulling him to sleep, his dreams inexplicably centering on his father's attempts at getting a church built in the northern Vietnamese jungle. Every time they'd get close to finishing, the local communist sympathizers would burn it down, his father greeting it all stoically, then beginning the task all over again. He did get the church finished, finally, Justice getting the letter about it at Yale just two days before the Red Cross notified him of his parents' deaths.

He awoke with a start, to someone touching him. It was Kim, bent over, gently washing his forehead where he'd taken the stitches. Her face was set in deep concern as she concentrated on her work, Justice's pain her own.

"What time is it?" he asked.

"Late afternoon," she said. "You sleep good. Everybody back now. You lie still. Let me bandage you."

He did as he was told, waiting patiently as she rebandaged his head from her own first-aid kit, the others filtering in as they heard his voice, everyone taking up positions around the empty living room, most on the floor, Sardi and impeccably dressed Jorge bringing chairs in from the kitchen and sitting.

The rain had finally slowed down outside to a trickle, early-evening light beginning to filter through, brightening things somewhat. Justice sat up straight, leaning his back against the wall. He smelled coffee, his eyes widening. His head was momentarily clear, his thoughts lucid. It wouldn't last. He needed to handle things now, while he still could. "Coffee," he said.

"I'll get you some," Compton said, leaving the room.

"You all stuck," Justice said. "I'm glad. Tomorrow night

at this time we'll either be celebrating a victory or we'll be dead."

The woman returned with the coffee in a paper cup, Justice accepting it gratefully as she took a seat near him and folded herself into the lotus position.

He tasted the coffee. It was rancid and hot, but not too hot, and he drank half the cup in one long swallow. "As near as I can figure," he said, putting down the coffee, "we've got two necessary ingredients for success here. First, we've got to be quick. If we can't take care of our business within a couple of hours after undertaking it, we'll just have to hang it up. Second, we've got to isolate the fortress from base camp. What kind of luck did you have, Kiki?"

The man smiled graciously and stood. He was dressed in khaki shorts and a white button-up shirt, looking like the blacks he'd seen on the streets earlier. The man reached into his pocket and pulled out a piece of paper, folding it open in the middle of the floor. "I spoke with my oppressed brothers," he said, "and learned many things. Here is the fortress."

Everyone got closer, getting a good look. Kiki's drawing was beautifully rendered, professional looking even in ballpoint pen. It showed the top of the volcano transformed by the hand of man. There were three main highpoints encompassing the fortress: one describing either side, and a center place built up with stone—a castle with spires and turreted walls reaching into the sky. His father would have called it the Tower of Babel.

Kiki pointed to the outer peaks. "Antiaircraft installations," he said. "My sources don't know anything about configurations, but from my discussion with them I believe we are dealing with American-made twenty-millimeter Vulcan systems. The tactical application is ideal, since the volcano is generally shrouded in haze, needing only sporadic protection anyway." He pointed to the center peak. "The keep, where the hierarchy reside like tramp kings. This is where you will find the specific men you are looking for. This area here"—he pointed to a long stretch of similar peaks between the keep and the most distant turret—"is where everyone else stays."

"Everyone else?" Jenks asked.

"The Medellin people live up there as a defensive force.

Their families stay below at base camp, the men getting leaves and furloughs to come down and visit."

"So," Justice said, "the fortress itself houses only combatants."

"Just so," Kiki replied. "Barracks have been erected along a narrow stretch of rock, widening here to an area of warehouses and laboratories gouged into the rock itself. Excavation goes on continuously as they try to burrow more and more deeply into the mountainside for absolute protection."

"How many men live up there?" Compton asked.

"Between four and five hundred," Kiki replied, rolling his eyes. "Lots of gangsters in one place. I hear they are like animals."

"How many ways up?" Jorge asked.

"There are three ways up the mountain," the prince said. "First the long way."

He traced a line up the side of the volcano, wrapping around it on a slow upgrade. "It takes three hours to climb this way. Some of it on the outside of the mountain, some of it through caves honeycombed in the side. Generally supplies are brought up this way by bearers picked from a pool from the shantytown. The bearers are paid almost nothing and spend all of that just for survival in the base camp. You've already seen the cable car. That is the second way up. The third is by helicopter. There are two chopper landing ports atop the fortress. One in the courtyard of the keep, the other a platform that is set atop the keep. Usually a helicopter is kept there all the time for escape purposes."

"Interesting," Jorge said.

Justice looked at him. "What?"

"Isolation," the man replied. "The cable car is the most vulnerable and should be relatively easy to put out of commission. But the choppers will be much more difficult...."

"Destroy them on the ground?" Kim offered.

"And if we get caught there," Jorge said, "it gets no further, or we leave people on the mountain to die. No. I was thinking about those antiaircraft guns. If we could take one of those installations, we could blast the choppers out of the sky from the fortress itself."

"You know," Kiki said, "the beauty of the Vulcan system is that it can be operated by one man."

"I'll take care of the cable car," Justice said, "on my way up in the morning. Jorge, I want you and Bob to handle the installation. . . ."

"Not with that son of a bitch," Jenks said.

"Surely, William . . ." Jorge began, Justice cutting him off.

"We either work as a team or end it right here," he said. "It's the mission that's important, not your petty feud. You're both good men. Hell, the reason you don't get along is that you're too much alike. Find the common ground. *Comprende?*"

The two men shared a look, their love for Justice overcoming their mutual distrust. They acquiesced.

"Good," Justice said. "That leaves the path up. I'll bet that it could be traversed a lot quicker than three hours in a forced march situation."

Kiki nodded grimly. "Cut the time in half or less," he said. "I will go up the mountainside with my brothers in the morning and secure the trail."

"You can do that?" Compton asked.

"I am a most persuasive gentleman," the prince replied modestly.

"Good," Justice said. "It's settled then. Sardi and I will go up in the cable car in the morning. Jorge and Bob will try to secure a chopper to take the gun placement. Kiki will go up with the bearers."

"What about me?" Kim asked. "How I get up?"

"For what it's worth," Jorge said, "they are setting up for a huge party tomorrow night. Apparently some big deal is supposed to be concluded and they want to throw a bash. They'll be taking a great deal of food and drink up by helicopter."

"So what?" Kim said.

The man shrugged. "They are also taking women up with them, you know . . . working girls. I heard several of them talking about it. . . ."

"So *that's* where you've been," Jenks said.

Jorge flashed pale eyes at him. "You have your sources, I have mine," he said. "Anyway, the girls are excited about the whole thing because a man is coming to choose the best of them to take up. Apparently a great deal of money is involved."

Kim smiled wide. "Hooker, huh? I never been paid for it before. You think they'd want Asian girl?"

"Honey," Jenks said, "if they got eyes, they'll want you."

"Good," she said. "Then I go. We'll kill them all, then get drunk."

"Simple eloquence," Sardi said.

"You'll probably need someone back here in base camp to keep an eye on things," Compton said. "I guess I'm elected."

Justice looked at her, not believing a word she said. "Good," he answered. "Which only leaves us with two problems: two thousand Cubans down here and four hundred killers up there. Unfortunately, we'll have to take that one on the fly as it comes. Any questions?"

"Yeah," Jenks said. "What's the capital of South Dakota?"

Vanderhoff stood. "I'm going outside for a smoke," he said. "The rain's stopped."

Jorge stood and moved out the door and into the deepening twilight. Justice stared at those still sitting with him. He wished he had words to say to them, something that would make it go better—but he didn't. It had been the unspoken word on everyone's lips. Every one of them knew they were going up the mountain to die, and the fact that they were doing it without complaint said more than words ever could. Maybe that's why Gail Compton offered so readily to stay behind. Perhaps her tastes didn't run to suicide.

They were an extended family, all of their futures hinged upon the emotional inconsistency of one man. He hated himself for what he was doing. Even as the hot blood of vengeance pumped through his veins, he hated himself.

The front door flew open, Vanderhoff poking his head inside. "You'd better get out here," he said, Justice jumping up and hurrying to the doorway.

The man pointed into the distance. "Look. The sky has cleared."

Justice saw, his mouth going dry, his knees weakening, threatening to buckle. He grabbed the door frame and stared. The rain had cleared the haze around the peak of the volcano, the incredible fortress coming into view.

Even from eleven thousand feet down it was impressive as it towered over the landscape, dominating it, an evil eye controlling all it surveyed. The structures were built right into the crater's lip like stone scabs, the whole a remarkable combination of man and nature. Lights burned all over the thing, thousands of lights, as the continuously running cable car climbed the side of the mountain, nestling into its cradle on the castle walls. The sun was setting behind the fortress, making it stand out in bold relief, its wall cutouts like jagged, hungry teeth against the pink-streaked sky. The trail down was evident, also, marked with burning torches.

Justice watched the burning lights and could think that most people would find the spectacle a thing of beauty. But to him it was the ultimate ugliness, the grisly spawn of his perverse union with Frank Merriman, a towering monster child conceived in blood and bloated full on death. And he actually felt he could *see* Merriman at one of those distant castle windows, calling to him, mocking his parenthood.

He jumped from the trailer door, sloshing in mud. He began walking, his eyes fixed on the castle and its burning, burning lights like tiny perpetual flames on a grave site. He was aware of people calling to him from behind, but he couldn't stop himself, the magnetic pull of Volcán Barú finally trapping his soul for good and all.

He was lost.

His feet pulled him in a direct line through town, Volcán Barú a monstrous, beckoning presence, all-pervasive, a sight commanding all attention. He could look at nothing else as he continued moving, faster now, out of the city traffic, the vibrant green jungle plain just a haze around him.

He was running now, through a level field full of moving khaki shirts and bright lights. He stopped, looking around frantically. Lines of troops marched all around him, going in different directions, the ground around them dazzling white, trucks with spotlights parked around the field's periphery, blinding the night. It was crazy . . . crazy. He spun a wide circle, the volcano grabbing him again, impelling.

His legs pumped beneath him, running again, through the sunshine drill-field lines of marchers in formation, the landscape undulating beneath him as he ran into darkness over the monstrous roots Barú had sunk into the ground when it grabbed hold and starting sucking so many millions of years ago.

And it was there, so close he couldn't look up and see the top even if he stared straight up. And still he ran, until the lights of base camp became tiny pinpricks in the distance and the drill field sparkled like a diamond facet.

And suddenly he stopped. A wave of pain tore through him, and he began to cry. He looked around through the wet-window vision of tears.

The barest remnants of what had once been a village were spread all around him. Nature had done her best to disguise the horror but hadn't completely succeeded. Here in this place of neither man nor nature, trees and tall grasses grew up around the burnt-out frames of old houses, stone stairways and foundation blocks supporting beds of weed and frond. He looked up into a young tree that had grown up where he remembered his friend Francisco had lived. A small cast-iron kettle was lodged in the highest branch, perfectly sealed with bark on two sides. It had grown up there, the area of the massacre untouched since that time.

He walked to the center of town and found the communal well under a tangle of ground vines. He sat, crying, his outstretched hand hitting something that rattled. He looked, clearing more vines, reaching in for a flash of bright white and coming out with—a human skull.

He stared at it. God, the bastards hadn't even had the decency to cover over their own vileness. Was there no end to it? Was there no one to pray, no one to mourn?

He fell to the ground, cradling the skull to his breast. They had died alone and disappeared without a trace, while Merriman lived, a king in his castle of flesh and bone. And the hatred burned in his gut, and the guilt burned beside it, and he *felt* the fire of Volcán Barú, he felt it in his gut and in his soul, and when he held out the skull, it had become the head of an old man, attached to a body oozing bloody bullet wounds across the chest.

He let go of the dead man, jumping, fire raging all around him as the Dobermans torched the village, laughing as the orange flames leapt from their flamethrowers and arced delicately across the huts and hovels of Hate del Volcán.

"No!" he screamed, running toward one of the men with the flamethrower as villagers fell all around him under the relentless pounding of automatic weapons.

He grabbed the Guardsman, ripping the nozzle from his hand and turning it on an advancing squad, the fire setting them all ablaze, then going out, the men laughing, advancing again.

Yelling, he shoved away the flamethrower, turning to see another soldier violently raping a young girl. He grabbed the man, throwing him away from the girl, only to turn and find another man had taken the first one's place. He pulled that one away, another quickly taking his place. He turned, running, stumbling.

"Please stop," he said over and over as he walked through the burning village. "Stop...please, stop." Before him a mother screamed as she was being raped not ten feet distant. "I'm so sorry," he told her. "I didn't know. I'm sorry...sorry."

He stumbled back through town, his hands covering his ears, trying to keep out the screams that only seemed to get louder. What could he do to stop it? He ran from the village, from the searing heat and light. But the sounds never diminished. He stared back at the village in the distance, now just a raging fire storm, then his eyes traveled up, up to the peak of Barú and the blazing castle lights, and he *knew* they were the extensions of the flames that had burned the village, the fires still burning brightly. He could never find peace until those lights had been extinguished for good and the people of Hate del Volcán put to rest.

"William," came a soft voice behind him. He twirled to see a figure just visible in the distant firelight. A woman. She stepped closer, and he could smell patchouli.

"Allie," he breathed, and she was there before him, her presence a balm even in this place of death.

She opened her arms to him, and he went to her eagerly, years of tensions melting away immediately with the contact. "Oh, Allie," he said. "God, how I've missed you."

"I know," she said, stroking his hair.

He drew her close, their bodies pressed together, a sensation like none other in the world.

"You're so troubled," she said.

"There's so much..." he sobbed. "So...much to tell you. So much pain."

"Yes," she said simply, and she was drawing him down to the ground with her, touching him, arousing.

"Here?" he said. "In this place?"

"Yes," she answered, and her face in the firelight was so beautiful, so comforting, and she was helping him with his clothes, spreading them beneath their bodies as he was getting lost in her softness; and for once he let go and gave the control to someone else, abandoning himself completely.

And he never knew how much it had hurt until it stopped.

And then an odd thing happened as he lay on the ground beside Allie. She changed somehow, reformed. He sat up, staring down in confusion at Gail Compton.

"You," he said.

"You needed someone," she said, her eyes sad. "I was handy. Are you okay?"

"Just a little . . . confused," he said.

"I've never seen anyone in so much pain. Who's Allie?"

"Nothing," he said, rubbing his hands across his face. "No . . . body."

He looked toward the village and saw only darkness.

"You're really acting strange," she said. "Are you sure you're all right?"

"Fine," he said, standing, shaking his head. He looked at the village again, found he could look at it without feeling its pull. His eyes traveled upward, taking in the castle lights, the hatred a strong, white fire.

He still had the hate, but the guilt was gone, burned away somehow. Even in the midst of mental carnage, life would have its way. Nothing he could ever do would change the tragedy of Volcán Barú, and feel bad as he might, it wouldn't alter one second of what had happened that horrible night. What remained was the mission. What remained was that son of a bitch Merriman.

He heard the woman get up to dress behind him. He stared at the mountain, whispering to it. "Tomorrow I avenge you or die trying," he said. "Either way I'm free of you."

He itched for the fight, the bloodlust a physical presence inside him. He could picture the image of Frank Merriman in his mind's eye and rip the arms and legs off him like a bug. He wondered if all madmen saw with such crystal clarity.

XX.

VOLCÁN BARÚ
21 FEBRUARY—DAYBREAK

The hard-eyed mestizo looked Kiki Anouweyah up and down before bringing up the coiled whip he carried to rub the stubble growth of whiskers on his left cheek. "You're a new one, huh?" the man said.

"Yeah, boss, I'm new," Kiki said, grinning with all his teeth. "New and strong. And I very much want to work and earn some money."

"Did you hear that?" the man said to the assembled group of Chiricanos and blacks. "Here's a man who understands the value of hard work. I'm going to make him my foreman."

The dawn had come up soft that day, with just a touch of coolness in the air. The men all stood in the dusty yard of shantytown, hollow-eyed women and children watching from the open doorways of their hovels, hoping their husbands would get enough work to keep the children fed. Life was very elementary in shantytown.

"Thank you, boss!" Kiki called out loudly. "I will make you proud of me."

The mestizo's lips curled into a cruel smile. "Sure, you will," he said. "I like your spirit. Tell you what, you pick the crew. We're carrying dynamite today and canned food. Get me twenty good men. We leave in ten minutes."

"Sure boss," Kiki called to the man's retreating back as he moved under the shade of a group of palm trees to talk to the women grinding cornmeal. The man turned once to look at Kiki, who smiled widely, waving in return.

When the man's back was to him, the smile faded, Kiki spitting loudly on the ground and turning to the assembled bearers. "I want twenty men who would kill boss man if they had the chance," he said, fire in his eyes. "I want twenty men who wish to control their own destinies."

The beauty shop consisted of five chairs set up under an open-sided tent, with three mestizo women who went from chair to chair clipping and styling heavily with hair spray since nothing else was available. Kim Bouvier sat patiently, trying to steady her hand-held mirror so the woman wouldn't cut off her ear.

Young women were lined up waiting their turns, a large group of men standing just outside the tent area watching and pointing, laying bets on which women would be chosen to go up. Also under the tent several racks of dresses had been lined up, selling for prices that would make Paris designers proud. And all around the women giggled and chattered, the excitement high.

Kim took it all in with a callous eye. Life was very simple to her—human beings were entitled to live their lives as they chose. Willing servitude to someone else's needs was a concept beyond her understanding, and the fact that all the women around her accepted so little for themselves rubbed her raw. They were little sheep, happily dancing off to be slaughtered, and it simply made no sense. How much better to stand up and fight for yourself, to take what you needed from those who would take from you. If you died, so what? Everything dies. What good was life if you had to live it in a pigsty.

A large lock of her sleek black hair snipped off and fell into her lap, Kim picking it up angrily. "Take it easy, bitch," she spat. "Don't cut too much."

"Then hold still," the plump mestizo snapped.

"I *am* holding still," Kim replied angrily. "You just got the shakes like a drunk."

"Go to hell," the woman said, jerking her hair too hard, Kim coming up out of her seat to swing out with a hard right, connecting with the woman's chin. The attendant's eyes glazed over, and she fell immediately, out cold, the other women yelling, angry that the pool of barbers had been trimmed by one-third.

Kim stared down at the unconscious woman. "I told you," she said. "You wouldn't listen."

She looked at herself in the mirror, turning it every which way to check the job on her hair. She nodded happily. "Not bad," she said, then looked down at the woman, who was moaning low, coming around. "Good work." She took a twenty-dollar bill out of her pocket and leaned over, sticking it in the woman's hand along with the mirror.

She shoved her way through the crowd of women. Most of them looked drawn and tired from a hard night's work. Kim had had the advantage of a full night's sleep, and it would help a great deal. She wandered over to the racks of clothes and began looking through them.

"I'll bet you look *wonderful* in black," a male voice said from behind her.

She turned to see a lean albino man dressed in a white silk suit and rose-colored glasses, a wide-brimmed panama hat sitting oddly atop his head. He wore a great deal of jewelry—gold chains and rings on most of his fingers. "I look wonderful in anything," Kim said. "I'm a classy broad."

"Yes," the man smiled with thin lips. "But black . . ."

He reached into the rack and pulled out a low-cut, slinky black evening gown shimmering sequins up and down its tight-fitting length. He smiled and held it up against her.

"You like?" she said.

"Very much," he replied. "So much so that I believe I have a job for you."

She let her eyes drift up in the direction of the fortress. "Up there?" she said, a smile stretching her full lips.

He nodded slowly. "Up there," he said.

William Justice straightened the knot on his black tie and ran his hands once more over his hair. Sardi stood behind him, helping him into the pale blue blazer with the gold buttons and black display handkerchief. He looked like the rich boy that he was. He had taken the bandage off from the night before, replacing it with a skin-colored Band-Aid so as not to draw too much attention to himself.

They stood in the kitchen of the trailer, Justice dipping his head from time to time, checking out the window for Victor Ibanez.

"You look good," Gail Compton said as she sat with them at the table, drinking coffee. "You're quite handsome when you're all fixed up."

"Yeah," Justice answered. "Handsome is just one of my many disguises."

His feelings about the woman were totally up in the air. She had been a life giver to him the night before, helping him through a deep and enduring grief in ways she'd never understand. But he couldn't help but feel, deep down, that it had just been another of the games the two of them had played continually since his arrival in Panama. She had yet to play the last of her trumps, even though the hand was running itself out. And despite everything that had happened, he really had no idea of where Gail Compton's loyalties lay.

"I guess the next few hours will tell the tale," she said, and the tone of her voice was off center, making both Justice and Sardi turn to stare at her.

"I guess," Justice said. "Look... if things don't work out up there today... don't waste any time around here. Steal a car and get the hell out of Dodge." He laughed without humor. "Victor's car will be parked by the cable car."

"Don't worry about me," she said. "I can look out for myself."

"I know that."

They shared a look, Justice trying to see through the control in her eyes to the feelings beneath. He thought there was sadness there, perhaps pain, but he also saw the flat stare of dogged determination, the kind of emotion that had gotten her a job with the Company and kept her in it for over a decade. All she made him was nervous.

A car roared up outside, Victor honking loudly, and slowed to a halt just outside the door. "Well," Justice said. "I guess this is it." He looked at Sardi. "Last chance to back out?"

The man responded by picking up the big aluminum suitcase and moving to the door. Justice looked at the woman again, and she moved into his arms, resting her head against his chest.

"You're a strange man," she said, then raised her head to look into his eyes. "I wish..."

"Wish what?" he said when she didn't finish the sentence.

She shook her head. "Nothing," she said, and stood on tiptoes, kissing him deeply. "Be careful."

"If I was careful," he replied, breaking from her and moving to the door, "I wouldn't be here."

At the door Sardi looked at him, Justice nodding once. The man opened the door, stepping right from the door space to the car door, then onto the seat, tossing the suitcase in the back. Justice followed suit, not looking back at the woman, not wanting any more baggage with him than he could handle. His mind was clear today, his purpose crystalline and pure. If insane hatred was what moved his blood through his veins, then his blood pressure had to be reading off the scale, so great was his desire to get up the mountain.

"Good morning," Ibanez said, as Justice slid down in the front seat beside Sardi. "Are you ready for a beautiful trip up the mountainside?"

"Indeed," Justice answered. "I can hardly wait."

"Good. We go now."

The man backed up, taking them the way he had just come. The dirt road led them back through town. Crowds already filled the streets, the bars and restaurants running around the clock. A number of people slept by the roadside, and maybe more than one of them was dead.

"Should we eat before we go up?" Sardi asked as they traversed the main drag.

"No...please, don't," Ibanez replied. "Save up. The food in the fortress is much better."

They passed the restaurant where they'd eaten the day before, Bob Jenks and Jorge Vanderhoff leaning up against the wall there, watching. Jenks saluted casually as they passed him, his eyes wary, following every move.

At the edge of town they passed a large semitrailer truck that hadn't been there the day before. A group of shantytowners were unloading exotic foodstuffs and cases of champagne from the back of the thing and onto military trucks that were driving to the helicopter holding area. An albino in a silk suit was checking off cases on a clipboard as they came out of the truck. Ibanez waved to the man as he passed the truck, the

266

albino's eyes just flicking him, then dropping once again to the clipboard.

They followed the dirt road past the choppers whose numbers had increased remarkably since Justice's arrival yesterday morning, the makeshift fence expanded to enclose the larger area. Guards were placed at intervals of ten feet all along the rope border.

The sun was struggling over the foothills surrounding them as they approached the cable station at the base of Barú. The haze was light, but already threatening to sock in the fortress within a couple of hours.

They pulled up to a parking area beside the gondola housing. As they walked up, the car descended toward them carrying a number of Medellin people who were, apparently, coming down the mountain to visit their families.

A large number of men in suits were waiting for the ride up, but Ibanez had apparently made some connections earlier, and he got them on as the Medellins exited. They were frisked thoroughly by two burly guards, then whisked aboard. The car was bright red, with two facing seats, holding six comfortably. Two men speaking German and a Japanese man got on with them. Justice told the operator to hold the car for a moment. He looked at the men.

"Do you speak English?" he asked, all of them nodding. "Good. I really want to take the ride up by myself. I'm a . . . stickler for privacy."

"That is too bad," one of the Germans said. "We've been waiting for two hours for this car, and we intend to go up in it."

Justice reached into his inner jacket pocket and pulled out several bundles of money. "Would five thousand dollars each make you change your mind?" he asked, waving it in their faces.

The men smiled. No self-respecting crook in his right mind would ever turn down free money, taking it being the ultimate form of self-gratification, the hoodlum's raison d'être.

Within a minute the gondola started up the incline, without its extra passengers.

"You are an amazing man," Ibanez said. "You get exactly what you want."

"Exactly," Justice said, watching through the window

cutout as base camp began to recede in the distance, its filth and odors washing out, leaving quaint splashes of color and movement, like a Christmas garden. "This meeting here . . . is this an annual thing, or what?"

"In a way," Ibanez said. "Our distributors come from all over the world once a year, but this time it's different."

"Different . . . how?"

The man shrugged. "No one knows," he said. "They are making some sort of announcement or something. It's all very hush-hush, as you Americans say."

"Interesting."

"How long does it take for the gondola to reach the top?" Sardi asked, as he stood, balancing himself in the shaking car, and moved to the vacant seat opposite, pulling up the seat cushion to find storage beneath.

"Fifteen minutes, give or take," the man said as he watched Sardi curiously.

Sardi pointed to the storage section, then put the cushion down, sitting.

Ibanez, his eyes narrowed suspiciously, turned to look at Justice. "But Mr. Lambert . . . *why* did you want to ride up here alone?"

"Witnesses, Victor," Justice said, reaching out powerful hands. He grabbed the man's head, twisting violently, the neck snapping, Victor's eyes fluttering wildly, his tongue hanging out as he slid to the floor.

Justice stood, grabbing Victor's lapels and dragging him to Sardi's bench, the man lifting the cushions. Justice hauled the dead weight up, stuffing it into the storage area beneath. Sardi closed the cushions and sat, Justice moving to the other seat and unlacing his right shoe.

"Something happened to you last night," Sardi said. "You're somehow . . . different today."

"Don't worry about it," Justice said, removing his shoe and turning it over in his hands. "Just keep your eyes open when we get up there. If we're going to cowboy, we're going to cowboy better than anybody else."

"Your confidence seems to have returned."

"It's not confidence," Justice answered, sliding off the sole of the shoe to expose the plastique explosive contained therein. "It's pure meanness."

He peeled the C-4 from the shoe and wadded it into a ball. He replaced the sole and popped off the heel, bringing out the small timing device connected to the watch face. He jammed the two electrical connectors into the ball and stood, lifting up the cushions on his own seat. "I'm setting it for three hours," Justice said, placing the plastique into the storage and clicking on the timer.

He sat, looking out, enjoying the view. They were two-thirds of the way up the rock face, the base camp now far distant. From here he could make out the narrow trail leading up the face of Barú, a small caravan of bearers and mules partway up the ascent.

"I don't trust the woman," Sardi said.

"Neither do I," Justice replied. "We'll just have to keep our fingers crossed with her."

"An unusual attitude for you, William," the man told him, Justice flashing his eyes in return.

"You know me too well," he answered.

He looked up, at where they were going. The castle drew closer, the gondola angling toward a port that cut through the imposing gray stone, seeming to grow directly out of the natural, dark rock. The place was medieval looking, but jagged, bending in and out along with the prevailing contours of its environment. He could see the keep well from here, a large square base going up three stories, topped by several squat towers that had a vague twisted-bread-dough Arabian Nights look to them. In the center was a large tower, the spire that Kiki had shown on his diagram. It rose perhaps another five stories, widening out to a flared, flat top. A black helicopter, unmarked, hung somewhat over the edge of the platform, its rotors tied down with rope. He could also make out the antiaircraft placements—one close to the keep, the other two hundred yards away. The peaks were natural and jagged, but a narrow stone road led up to them, the same stone and design as the rest of the castle making up the placements themselves. Several men bustled around the nearest placement. Taking one of those was going to be tough going, even for Jorge and Bob.

He sat back, settling into the gaming mode. Sardi sat lotus style on the seat across, his eyes closed, his hands, palms up, resting on his knees. So much the keep reminded him of Diamond Rock, so similar were the goals of Medellin. Both groups realized that life could be controlled, and both had a purpose. But the similarities ended there. Justice fought for life. Medellin fought for money and power as an end in itself. Medellin reaffirmed the jungle rule that Justice hoped to break. They were the animals, the man-eaters entering the dens of civilization to maim and destroy innocence. Justice was the hunter come to beat them back to the dark obscurity of the forest they clawed their way out of.

The gondola reached the walls, Sardi opening his eyes immediately and looking around. They rode through the cutout section, swinging slightly as they came to a stop within a small station just within the confines of the courtyard.

A man wearing crossed bandoliers and an AK47 slung over his back opened the door for them.

"Watch your step," he said, as Justice stepped out onto the small platform by the door, Sardi right behind.

They stepped out onto a flat stone yard a hundred feet on a side. As he looked out, directly across, he could see over the wall the distant peaks of the far side of the crater. To his right sat the keep; to his left a road about thirty feet wide ran out from the courtyard for a distance. Both sides of the road were lined with barracks. That roadway opened a hundred yards distant into another courtyard, this one cutting directly into the rock of the volcano. A huge crane sat at the end of this section, a squat water tower just at the end of the barrack's road. A large number of men mulled around the barracks area, many of them in the far courtyard, watching a soccer game being played there. The castle walls rose thirty feet tall around the courtyard, with stairs leading up and a narrow pathway leading around the top of the wall. Fifty-caliber machine-gun mounts were set directly into the stone cutouts of the tower's edge.

"Quite a place you've got here," Justice told the man as he pulled the suitcase out of the gondola.

The man was frowning, looking at a clipboard. "Wasn't a Mr. Ibanez supposed to come up as your escort?" he asked.

"He got sick at the last minute and didn't come," Justice said. "I hope there's not a problem."

"No sir," the man said. "We just like to make sure our guests are well taken care of."

"Well, don't you worry," Justice told him. "Victor did a wonderful job with us. He really stuck his neck out, you know?"

The man grunted, motioning over several uniformed Cubans who were standing in a holding area just out of the booth. "You go through that door, there," the man said, pointing to a large casement door leading into the keep. "You will tell the man who you are and that you want to visit with Colonel Gomez."

Justice looked at Sardi. Gomez himself, Desechado. He felt his blood rise, his jaw muscles clenching. "Thanks," he said, forcing affability, he and Sardi exiting the station as the Cuban soldiers took their place.

It was a lot cooler up here, the wind a force to contend with. Wild falcons perched on the walls, watching the human zoo with detached ennui. Several Medellin punks stood around the courtyard smoking cigarettes and marijuana, all of them loose. Who would expect trouble up here?

They moved across the courtyard, Justice no longer human. He was roving eyes and a clicking brain. He was watching, memorizing, trying to let the atmosphere become a natural part of his psyche.

They opened the heavy wooden door and walked into a large reception. The castle entry was a square, two-story room with steps leading up on both sides to a mezzanine. Perhaps a hundred men in suits moved around the large room, taking drinks from trays served by naked Indian women. A huge tableful of food sat room center, the crowd mulling around it, talking loudly enough to be heard above the jazz band that played in the corner. The cold gray walls had been enlivened somewhat by red-and-green velvet hangings, and candles burned everywhere, dripping wax in a place without electricity. A man in a white tuxedo and red hair walked up to them as soon as they got in the door.

"And you might be..." he said in a clipped English accent.

"Well I might be Teddy Roosevelt," Justice said, "but I'm not. My name is Lambert."

"I see," the man said through strangled adenoids, pulling square reading glasses out of his breast pocket to stare down his nose at a small list he held. "Yes," he said after a moment. "And you must be Mr. .... Sardi, is it?"

"Sardi . . . yes."

The man stared down at the suitcase. "Will you be staying with us long, Mr. Lambert?"

Justice shook his head. "It's my lunch," he said.

The man frowned. "This way please," he said, leading them through the party and up the stairs to the mezzanine. He opened a door for them. "The colonel will be with you in a moment."

"Charmed," Justice said, cold.

The man fixed him with curious eyes, then moved on, closing the door behind him. The room was of average size, with a beautifully carved table of heavy wood in its center, a crystal candelabra on the table. It was a conference room of some kind, chairs set all the way around the walls. A bow-slot window was cut through the stone, overlooking the valley below. Justice walked up and looked out, watching the cable car descend, mentally picturing the timer counting down on the C-4. He was ready, more than ready.

"Mr. Lambert!" came a voice from the doorway, Justice turning to see a face that had been burned into his brain with acid. It was the Doberman killer, Gomez, his depravity all closed up in a purple smoking jacket and gold ascot. He looked like a punk's idea of a gentleman, with a pencil-thin moustache and plucked eyebrows, his hair greased back and hanging down his neck.

He wanted to choke the life out of the man. Instead he said, "Colonel Gomez . . . how wonderful to meet you." He crossed the floor and shook hands with the man, immediately wiping the hand on his pants. "I want to thank you for being such a gracious host."

"Not so gracious," Gomez said, in an affected tone of voice. "No one has gotten you a drink."

Justice put up a hand. "Not for us," he said. "Business first."

"Good," Gomez said, leading them to the table. "Our time at the moment is relatively limited. Please . . . sit."

They all sat, Gomez smiling at them like a snake with a gutful of mouse. "I'm so sorry that I was unable to meet with you last night. Were your accommodations acceptable?"

Justice stared hard at the man, wanting to knock his

fucking teeth down his throat. "Most acceptable," Justice said. "We needed the rest anyway."

"Quite so. My associate, Mr. Ibanez, has informed me that you are interested in acquiring our . . . services in a rather large way."

Justice nodded to Sardi, who pulled the suitcase up on the table and opened it, shoving it across to Gomez, the man's eyes lighting up.

"I guess you'd call this earnest money, Colonel," Justice said. "The people I represent in the United States are prepared to invest a great deal more with the . . . right party. Go ahead, pick it up. It's real."

The man made a gracious gesture. "Of that there is no doubt. We are all honorable men here." He picked up several bundles of cash anyway, flipping through them with practiced eyes. He pulled a bill out of the stack, held it up to the light, and said, "You have a familiar look, Mr. Lambert. Do we know one another?"

"I don't know," Justice said. "I had a friend around here once. Maybe we met through him. His name's Frank Merriman."

Gomez lowered his eyes. "Frank Merriman," he said.

"Yeah, you know him?"

"Perhaps our paths have crossed," Gomez said with evasion. "How long since you've seen your friend?"

"Oh, it's been a long time," Lambert said. "I dunno, eight or ten years."

"If you run into him, you may find that he's . . . changed somewhat."

"Changed?" Justice asked.

All at once the door flew open, banging against the wall, Gomez closing the suitcase quickly and latching it. A dark man in a dark suit filled the doorway, a Colombian with a thick black mustache and nothing but death in his eyes. "You will come and make the presentation now," the man said, then walked off without closing the door.

"Sure, Tomas . . . Mr. Guerrero," Gomez said nervously. "I'll be right there!" He looked at Justice. "That is one of my . . . associates. I must go. Please join us in the main conference room, if you will. We are unveiling our plans for the coming year to our distributors, and since we're almost partners, maybe you'd like to go, too."

"We'll be along in a minute," Justice said. "I want to freshen up first."

The man stood hurriedly, staring longingly at the suitcase for a moment before setting it back on the floor. "I must go," he said. "We'll speak after." He hurried to the door, turning at the last second. "Just ask any of the servants for whatever you want. They'll help you." He was out the door, still talking as he went down the hall. "Mention my name...."

"Fascinating," Sardi said.

"How much time we got left?" Justice asked.

Sardi looked at his watch. "Two hours, thirty minutes," he replied. "What do you make of our friend, Gomez?"

"First," Justice said, standing and walking to the doorway, "it's obvious that Gomez has no real power here. The Medellins reserve that for themselves. Second, Merriman is here. I'm convinced of it. Though I'm not sure why he's not taking a part in the proceedings."

"Perhaps at the presentation," Sardi said.

"I'm betting not," Justice said. "If he was down there, I'd smell him."

He peered out the door, down at the party below. Everyone was being herded out of the room through double doors on the side, the naked servers hurrying to clean up. He walked back in, shutting the door behind him.

"I'm going to go down and check out the presentation and see who's there," Justice said. "I want you to poke around, make the defenses, and see if you can find Merriman. With so many people here, they're probably expecting sightseers and lost souls."

"I will do as you say," Sardi replied, as Justice walked to the door. "What about the money?"

"Leave it," Justice said, opening the door again. "It's just paper." He turned hard to the man. "And Sardi..."

"Yes, William?"

"We need weapons. Find some." Justice turned and strode from the room, his mind lost in darkness.

They struggled up the hillside, Kiki bringing up the rear, squinting up into the sun. The trail was no more than a foot wide at best, covered with loose gravel and eroded places. It was dangerous for anyone, but nearly suicidal if you carried a crate on your back. He carried no crates; he was the foreman. It was his job to push from the rear, to hurry the men along as the mestizo boss did with his whip from the front. At first he'd wondered why they didn't exclusively use the mules for the caravan work, the answer becoming appallingly obvious right away—the people were more expendable than the mules.

The mules carried only the canned goods, the bearers being forced to carry the sweating boxes of dynamite, sweating because of deterioration—the sweat deadly, unstable nitro that could go up at any second.

"Bring 'em up!" the ramrod called from the front of the line, unseen behind mules and crates, the sound of his whip cracking.

"Coming boss!" Kiki called back, the man in front of him teetering dangerously on loose rocks. "Easy, mon." Kiki grabbed the box, steadying it, a drop of nitro sweat falling to the gravel to hiss and smoke.

"Thanks," the Chiricano said over his shoulder.

"Mon, why do you take this from them?" Kiki said. "You don't need to live like their oxen."

"We got trapped here by the promise of money," the man returned. "Once we left our fields, it was too late. We can't go back and plant now. What will we do for food?"

"Take *their* food," Kiki said. "All men are entitled to respect and decent treatment."

"But they have the guns, my friend."

"Bring 'em up!" the ramrod called.

"Yeah, boss!" he called, then lowered his voice. "But they don't have the brains."

"Ha!" the man said. "They were smart enough to get us here."

"But not smart enough to keep you happy," Kiki said. "A fatal mistake. How far to the next cave?"

"Just a few hundred yards up," the man said. "It's called Thirdway because it's a third of the way up. We will get water there and a chance to sit for only a moment."

"Is it a wide cave?"

"Wide enough for all of us to sit in."

"Good. That is the place then."

"The place for what?"

"The place to teach that boss the proper respect."

There was a yell from farther up the line, one of the bearers losing his footing and going over the side, screaming as he fell, his crate exploding on impact with the mountainside, the force of the blast shaking all of them as loose gravel fell from above. Kiki watched the body of the man continue its descent over three thousand feet down, the man dead long before he hit bottom.

"Get 'em up!" the ramrod yelled, the sound of his whip snapping loudly, Prince Kiki Anouweyah staring up the line with deadly intent. He would bide his time—for now.

Bob Jenks wandered with Vanderhoff up near the chopper compound, keeping a loose distance, not trying to arouse any attention. Jenks wasn't much for this covert shit; he far preferred meeting trouble head on, dealing with it out front. He didn't much like secrets, which was probably the root of his problem with Vanderhoff. The man was nothing but secrets, all closemouthed and snaky, never coming out and saying what he meant. Will had been a fool to pair the two of them. They could never work together.

"See anything you like over there?" he asked the man as they retreated to an outdoor café under a grove of palm trees.

Vanderhoff picked a table off by itself that still afforded a good view of the compound. "They've got an Arab ship over there," he said, "a Hughes AH-64."

"Sleek lookin' ain't it?" Jenks said. "I test-flew one back in seventy-six. Got a thirty-millimeter chain turret underneath. Kick some ass with that baby."

A waiter came up. They ordered two beers and waited until they were served before continuing the discussion. "I have an idea about how we can get it," Vanderhoff said, "but I'll need a toolbox."

"Toolbox, hell!" Jenks said, taking a long pull from the bottle. "When we want the damned thing, let's just knock that fuckin' guard on his ass and take it. We don't need none of that undercover shit here."

"There's no use arousing undue suspicion," Vanderhoff said. "Why make trouble when we don't have to?"

"'Cause it's fun, you idiot!"

"You're a fool!" Vanderhoff said loudly, then lowered his voice to a harsh whisper. "Why don't you just go announce yourself to them and let them shoot us now? It's going to happen sometime today, anyway."

Jenks stared cold fire at the man. "Will'um needs us," he said, and for Jenks that summed it up. "He needs us and we're goin'."

"Let's at least give ourselves a fighting chance," Vanderhoff said. "Stop being stupid for just five minutes."

Jenks stood and cocked a beefy fist, but before he could throw it, a procession passing by caught his eye. "Look," he said.

All the men in the area had gathered, cheering as the albino came by with the line of women—fifteen of them, dressed to the teeth, waving to the appreciative crowd.

"There's Kim," Vanderhoff said, pointing near the front of the line. "She's made it."

They watched from fifty feet as the women were taken to a large Chinook helicopter, its front and rear rotors already whipping the oppressive air. The women climbed in, holding down their hair against the beating of the props, their fancy dresses flying up over their hips to the delight of the crowd.

"That's four up, counting Kiki," Jenks said, as the chopper lifted off, the albino moving away. "We can't be left behind now. Tell you what, partner. I'll give it a try your way."

Vanderhoff looked to the heavens. "The light dawns," he said.

"Don't push your luck," Jenks replied, darkening. "When do we go?"

Vanderhoff took a drink of his beer, meticulously wiping his mouth on a handkerchief when he was through. That was the other thing Jenks disliked about the man. He was prissy. He hated a prissy man. Vanderhoff looked at his watch. "William's been gone for an hour and a half," he said. "I believe we should start up in an hour."

"I'm gettin' itchy," Jenks replied, wiping his own mouth on the back of his hand and looking around, his eyes locking on a figure moving through the shadows of the trash dumps behind the buildings. "Who the hell is that?"

Vanderhoff narrowed his eyes suspiciously, then reached into his suit pocket, pulling out a small pair of binoculars and holding them up to his face. "My God," he said. "It's that woman who's been dogging us . . . the Company bitch. What's she up to?"

"I'll be damned," Jenks said. "Looks like she's makin' her way around to where they're loading the supply choppers."

"But why? She's supposed to be giving ground support."

Jenks followed her with his eyes. Thirty feet from her position, several stripped Hueys were being loaded with the supplies from the party truck, the albino moving over to supervise that. She was inching closer, keeping to cover, but casually, in case she was being watched. "We've got to stop her," he said.

At that instant she broke for the nearest of the choppers.

Gail Compton ran hard, the sound of the choppers covering her approach as the albino counted cases of champagne with his back to her. Several of the African bearers saw her as she slipped the Huey between herself and the albino, but it was nothing to them, and they didn't speak. She was dressed in khakis purchased from the Company store, blending in, the Beretta she'd swiped from Lambert's trailer stuck in the waistband of her pants.

She moved slowly along the side of the chopper, her eyes constantly roving, looking to see if anyone was taking notice of her, but there was simply too much activity in the area for her to be singled out.

She moved up to the open bay of the thing, peering through, seeing the back of the albino's head through the bay opening on the other side.

As he tried to hurry them along, one of the Chiricanos dropped a case of champagne, the man yelling and dropping down to save what he could, Compton taking the opportunity to scoot up into the bay and slide back.

The tail section was already full of piled-up boxes of caviar, crackers, and canned meats. She shoved the stack of boxes as far to the side as she could and jammed herself in, the shadows closing her up. It was unbearably hot back there, the sweat pouring from her, drenching her shirt immediately, her hair dripping, hanging plastered to her face.

The loading continued, more and more boxes being shoved into the bay, as the pilot sat forward, barely visible through the open crack of his door, running preflight. She could hear herself breathing, and the breath was ragged.

She removed the gun and set it before her, safety off, to keep it dry. She was getting nervous, her fear of closed-in places nearly as oppressive as the heat. Damn, she hated this. She hated everything about it.

But she had a job to do.

The surface cave had at one time probably been a bubble in a monstrous, plopping cauldron of running lava. As the lava slowed and began cooling on the mountainside, the bubble burst, leaving a perfectly round hollow of smooth cave wall, a circular entrance on either side of the fifteen-foot cavern. It would have been an event unnoted in the annals of history, except that it happened to be placed exactly one-third of the way up the highest elevation in the country of Panama and was for these men, at this moment, the most beautiful spot on planet earth. And if Prince Kiki Anouweyah had anything to say about it, it would soon be a scene of high drama.

He stood with the ramrod at the mouth of the cave, the bearers sitting, already exhausted, on the smooth floor within. The vast jungles of Panama stretched out all around them, a magnificent patchwork in shades of green, tied together with blue, flowing ribbons—a portrait in lavish green. It reminded the prince of home.

"I'm gonna scout the trail up ahead," the ramrod said, spitting over the edge. "See if anything shook loose when el stupido fell over before." The man shook his head. "They'll take that out of my pay. Another one falls, and I take it out of *your* ass. Got it, nigger?"

"Sure, boss," Kiki said brightly.

The man spit again. "Give 'em three more minutes, then move 'em out. They don't get no water until they pass out the door."

"Right."

The man's eyes twitched for just a second, Kiki smiling because he knew the bastard had gotten within an inch of having a thought about him. But—not to worry. He watched the man walk off, then turned to the men on the floor.

"Look at you," he said. "Frail little cubs who sit and whimper on the floor while that slimy thing you call the boss walks on you and treats you like something other than men. How can you let your wives and families suffer while you slave for these monsters?"

"You got no right to say that," one of the blacks said, standing. "We need to feed our families... that comes first. But there's no food with no money, we..."

The prince waved it off. "Money, money, money," he said. "Cry, cry, cry. You say you need money to be men? How stupid you make yourselves sound. I suppose that if you had the money, you'd throw over these hyenas in human skin and be men again, huh?"

"You don't think we want to work for these men?" the standing man replied. "We are... bonded to them only because of what we get. No one would take this treatment for less."

"Bring 'em up!" the boss called from farther up the trail.

Kiki walked right up close to the man's face. "No one should take this kind of treatment for *anything!*" he said. "You're going to show me what men you are."

He reached into his pocket and pulled out a wad of money, all hundreds, the universal magnet. He threw it on the ground. He pointed to it. "There's more money there than you'll ever know in your lifetimes," he said. "Take it. It's your ticket to manhood."

The men reached down, tentatively at first, then with greater urgency as they grabbed up the bills, stuffing them in their pockets. All but the standing man. He simply turned his gaze at Kiki. "What are we supposed to do for this money?" he asked.

"Do?" Kiki said, smiling with his eyes.

The ramrod's dark form filled the cave mouth, his whip dangling from his right hand. "I told you to bring 'em up!" he shouted.

"But boss," Kiki said, moving up to the man. "I thought it'd be easier if I brought you down."

"Wh—"

The man raised his whip hand, Kiki grabbing the arm,

jerking it down hard over his raised knee, the bone snapping loudly. The man went down, gagging, his arm quivering wildly. The prince walked around before him, kicking him with force in the stomach, the man's breakfast coming up.

He looked at the men. "You've got your money," he snapped. "Come get your self-respect."

Just as with the money, they moved tentatively at first, then urgently, charging the man, going at him with feet and hands, finally using the whip itself until Kiki put a stop to it and put a bullet from the man's own gun through his head.

They had tasted blood. They were ready for the rest.

XXI.

VOLCÁN BARÚ
21 FEBRUARY—MORNING

Kim Bouvier sometimes found that when she pretended not to understand English, she could learn more than if she talked with people for two days and two nights nonstop. She thought it was funny how the world worked and decided that she'd try playing dumb this time, too.

The helicopter brought them down right inside the castle walls, into the courtyard. She looked around as she climbed out, taking note of the lax security. No operation she ever ran would be so shoddy. They assumed that superior position meant superior ability—never assume.

They marched her and the other girls into the castle, Kim noticing that the albino hadn't made the trip with them. They moved into the entryway. She made four armed guards, also not security conscious. They had taken up positions more for comfort than defense. They would go down easy—the two on the mezzanine first. There were no security cameras or any electronic surveillance gear present at all. It was going to be a numbers game.

They marched her upstairs, skirting the mezzanine to walk up another flight, the highest this part of the building went. She counted the stairs up as she climbed, in case she had to back down, then wondered if she should take out the two men who were leading her and the others and get them out of the way right at first.

She decided against it, simply because it was too far from

the time to go. Disposal of the bodies would be the problem with advance hits. She filed that note and began looking for windows.

They were all taken into a room where a number of important-looking men sat chatting and smoking cigars. The room was full of hunting trophies—a boar's head, jaguar and tiger pelts on the wall, a huge elephant tusk hanging above a fireplace. It disgusted her, little boys playing games. Killing was no game to Kim Bouvier.

Of the ten men in the room, she made eight different nationalities. Two of the men looked American. One of them, a square-jawed, tall man with cowboy boots and a wicked eye, kept looking at her.

An older woman with silver hair and a long blue evening gown stood before them. "This is our board of directors," she told the girls. "These men come from all over the world and are the most important clients you'll ever have in your lives. If you are fortunate enough to be chosen by one of these men, you will do whatever he requests of you. Understood?"

The girls giggled excitedly, Kim looking around as if wondering where she was. Then the woman went down the line, asking each girl her name. When she got to Kim, Kim pretended she couldn't understand what the woman was saying. The woman kept talking to her, Kim looking at her, then speaking in Vietnamese.

"Gentlemen, I'm sorry," the woman said. "We appear to have ended up with a girl here who doesn't speak a word of English. . . ."

"That's fine with me," the square-jawed man said, standing and moving toward them. "I like them quiet." He took her roughly by the arm. "How about it, chink?"

Kim smiled up at him, the man jerking her toward the door.

"Well," the woman said. "It appears that Mr. Russell has made his choice!"

All the men laughed, the laughter muffling as soon as they reached the hallway and the door closed behind them.

"Oh, you sweet little slant," the man said, pushing her through a doorway farther down the hall, a bedroom with French doors opening to a balcony. He threw her on the bed and took his sports jacket off. "Are we going to have a time. We'll fight the Vietnam war all over again."

"You l-like me?" Kim asked in halting English.

"Yeah, I like you," he said. "You understand me?"

She cocked her head and smiled at him.

"Well, I'll tell you," he said, unbuttoning his shirt. "Here's what I'm going to do to you. I'm going to fuck the shit out of you, twice maybe. Then I'm going to beat you till you're almost dead, then maybe I'll fuck you again. Then I'm going to take you over to that window over there and toss you out and watch you bounce on down that mountain."

He pulled his pants off, his penis already erect as he talked excitedly. "Then I'm going to go on home to my sweet wife and kids and my important firm and never give your slanted ass another thought."

"Me Kim," she said, pointing to herself.

"And me Tarzan, baby," he said, grabbing her by the wrist and pulling her to her feet. He jammed himself against her, squeezing his arm around her hard, hurting. He kissed her roughly, bruising. She gave him that one back full measure, the man backing off a step.

"Come on, gook," he said. "Get your fucking clothes off."

She tugged questioningly at her black gown.

"Yeah," he said. "Yeah. Get it off."

She bent to her skirt with one hand, caressing his penis with the other. She slid the skirt up to her thighs, slipping the K-bar out of the top of her garter. "Don't worry," she whispered in his ear. "I'll get it off."

She leaned back, jerking his penis out straight, her right arm snapping up with the razor-sharp knife. He fell back on the bed, screaming as he held his bleeding crotch. The screams didn't bother her. She'd already discovered how sound muffled in there.

She threw his penis on the bed beside him. "There you go, sport," she said, then jammed the knife into his throat and rolled him off the bed.

She ran onto the balcony. Down was a sheer drop with nothing to break the fall for a thousand feet. She turned and looked up. If necessary, someone could stand on the balcony rail and hoist himself up onto the flat roof. She tried it, getting up far enough to look out over the rooftop. No guards up here. A large tower sat in the center of the roof with a door leading in.

She noted it and climbed back down, quickly searching the room for weapons. Nothing. She wiped off the blade of the K-bar and stuck it back into her garter. Then she tore her gown up the front and back all the way to the crotch for ease of movement. Her next step was to find weapons. Her next after that was to find William.

She moved to the door and peeked out. The hallway was wide, with closed doors on both sides. The stairs down were fifty feet distant to the right. To the left was another twenty feet of hallway ending in a blank wall. The hallway was empty. She kicked off her high heels, pulled off her hose, and charged into the hallway at full speed.

She ran for the stairs, a man cornering into the hall just as she reached it. She braced for impact and ran straight into the arms of—Sardi.

"Come," he said. "I've found weapons."

She followed him down the stairs without question.

Justice sat in the great hall with a hundred of Medellin's "distributors" and felt the pressure build within him like the molten pressures that churned deep within the bowels of Volcán Barú. He listened to an incredibly lengthy business meeting conducted by Gomez that detailed a year's worth of drug profits, to the tune of billions, that the people in that room had earned. They were business people and political leaders who used legitimate enterprise to turn an illegal buck at the expense of the rest of the world. They felt secure in themselves, and calm. They were good men who attended church on Sunday and belonged to the country club. They simply trafficked in blood and tears a little on the side, no harm done. He wanted to kill them all, and today, if he had his way, he *would* kill them all.

Cara piña was here, several rows down in the theater-style room, surrounded by several of his men. He was dying to get at the man but held himself in check. Finally, when Gomez opened the floor to new business, Noriega stood and addressed the man at the podium.

"My friend, Manolito," he said. "What is this business

with the sinking of the boats? This is bad business . . . bad for the canal, bad for tourism, bad for the country."

"But good for us," said the Medellin brother from a table onstage, the one Justice had seen in the conference room earlier.

"No, this isn't right," Noriega said. "I have a country to run."

"You have what we give you," the Medellin punk said. "Sit down and shut up."

The room got quiet then, Noriega looking around nervously, then sitting. Gomez leaned down beside the lectern and picked up a box. "Actually," he said, "the sinkings have ended. We received the last shipment from them this morning. And they are part of the reason why we wanted to talk to all of you today."

He poured the contents of the box out on the lectern, various pieces of identification tumbling out—driver's licenses, passports, credit cards, passbooks.

"Identification," the man said in his affected voice. "Why do we need so much identification? Simple. We will soon be going out of the exporting business."

A gasp went up from the crowd, Justice sitting up, listening carefully.

"We are preparing," Gomez said, "to take the risk and the guesswork out of the drug business." He held up a bag of white powder. "Anyone know what I've got here?"

Everyone laughed. "Cocaine," somebody called out.

"Wrong," Gomez said. "*Synthetic* cocaine, made from our own perfected formula. And believe me, it's better than the real thing." There was scattered applause.

"What about the IDs?" somebody called out.

The man put down the bag. "Since we can make the cocaine anywhere," he said, "it would be foolish to make it out of country and import it. We've decided to use these pieces of identification to help us establish identities for our own people in the countries from which the identification comes. That way we can produce the synthetic cocaine without giving up our formula, and you, my friends, can continue to disseminate it through your usual channels with greatly lessened fear of exposure. Just think, no cocaine lost to border patrols, no middle men with wagging tongues captured bringing it in, no waste, gentlemen. Increased profits for everyone!"

The hall burst into loud cheers and applause, the Medellin cartel in their dark suits standing at their table and waving to the appreciative crowd.

Now Justice knew why Medellin didn't bother checking what the pirates had brought them. They didn't care about the valuables. They wanted only the part that most self-respecting crooks would throw away.

He forced himself to stand, his back hurting badly, and walked out of the hall. He couldn't take anymore. He looked at his watch. Just under an hour until the fun.

Gail Compton was finding it difficult to breathe, her lungs heaving as the chopper made its ascent. There was no air. Nothing to . . . she put a hand to her chest. Her head got light, and she swayed to her left, knocking the boxes, something falling.

"Who is it!" someone called in a German accent, and she struggled for consciousness, her hand groping for the gun before her.

Boxes were being moved as she held the gun up, weaving badly.

All at once a rush of cool air hit her in the face as obstructions cleared away, and she was staring into the face of the albino, a gun coming out of a shoulder holster before her.

In a haze she squeezed the trigger, the gun exploding loudly, the albino's white, white chest exploding red. He screamed and fell backward out the open port, the pilot kicking open his compartment door from the inside and blasting away at her with a .45, glass shattering, champagne popping pressurized foam all over the inside of the cargo bay.

She fired back on auto in a champagne rain through the open doorway, the man groaning loudly as his insides blew all over his windshield and the chopper pitched violently to the left.

Cargo went everywhere, most of it sliding out the bay. She grabbed a support strut as the chopper tilted, her weapon slipping from her grasp and out the port, castle walls just below her and coming up—fast!

They hit the inside of the wall, an incredible jolt that

bounced her off her beam and dropped her to the wall beneath. Seconds later, the bird slid off the wall and came to ground in the courtyard, the thing crying loudly, then catching fire.

Compton lost consciousness for just a second, then came back around at the smell of gasoline. She moved. Nothing broken. She crawled painfully along the wall, an open bay just above her head bleeding black smoke into the blue of the afternoon sky.

Standing on shaky legs, she pulled herself up to the opening with her remaining strength and tumbled out onto the courtyard, rough hands pulling her seconds later, dragging her away from the burning chopper.

They had her under the arms, pulling her toward the keep, her mind spinning in and out of consciousness. She looked up and saw Lambert standing by the front door.

Then a familiar voice called her name. She looked up to see his face in a high window.

"Bring her up to the tower," he called, the ring of triumph in his voice.

She passed out.

Jenks and Vanderhoff were still sitting in the outdoor café when they saw the black smoke rising from behind the walls of the keep.

"That's it," Jenks said, lifting his shirt to pull out and check the load of the long-barreled .38 he had carried when still a lawman. Vanderhoff drew the all-plastic Glock 17 from its shoulder holster and looked around. Then he took the nine-millimeter clip from his jacket pocket and slowly pushed it into the butt of the thing. He primed it to readiness.

"My way up," Vanderhoff said.

"Yeah, yeah," Jenks replied. "Just do it. But no toolboxes."

Vanderhoff stood, hiking up his pants and putting the gun away. He rebuttoned his jacket as Jenks stuck the .38 back in his pants and pulled the checkered shirt down over it.

"Your move," Jenks said, the men striding across the field toward the chopper compound. The soldiers were gathered together, talking and pointing to the smoke coming out of the distant stronghold.

"We're nothin' if we ain't subtle," Jenks said, bending to

pull out a long stem of grass. He stuck the thing in his mouth, chewing on the end.

They approached the gate guard, the man eyeing them nervously, bringing his rifle up before him.

"Excuse me," Vanderhoff said to the man, "but I seem to have left my compound pass... back on my helicopter." He pointed into the holding area, the man turning to look. "You remember me, don't you... the... white Hughes model way in the back."

The man frowned at him.

"My dear sir," Vanderhoff said, reaching into his pocket and withdrawing some cash. "Surely you recall me coming through here before with my pass. You know that..."

"Ah hell, Jorge," Jenks said. "This is stupid."

Jenks reared back and gave the guard a hard right to the forehead, the man going down immediately.

"You asshole," Vanderhoff said, the two of them running into the compound, dragging their hardware into the open.

The lid was off and Jenks loved it!

There was shouting behind them, a horn blaring loudly through the camp—an alert from the trouble at the castle. They wove in and out of the machines, following the vision of the solid white chopper.

Gunfire behind, Jenks turned to give them his side as he aimed, left hand on his hip, firing fluidly, taking two of the fuckers off their feet, two more diving for cover.

Vanderhoff worked ahead, firing on single shot with the Glock, keeping a nest of them at bay behind the front of a Chinook. "I ought to blow your fucking head off!" he screamed at Jenks.

"That's it, Jorge... open up!" Jenks called, running to catch up, then turning to fire behind again. "Let it all out! You need to loosen up—you're too tight!"

"And you're a stupid shit kicker!" Vanderhoff said, as he fired from a crouch, taking the face off one of the punks behind the Chinook.

"Aw... you don't hafta get personal," Jenks said, reaching the sleek white chopper and ripping open the pilot's door. The tail of the thing was green and fixed with the Saudi flag, a scimitar. Jenks climbed in. The pilot's compartment smelled of cardomom.

He hit the controls immediately, running through the luminescent green panels to try to familiarize himself with the operation.

Vanderhoff stayed outside, keeping them back. "Come on . . . hurry!" he yelled.

"Yeah . . . yeah," Jenks said, calmly running through pre-flight. He reached out and juiced the rotors. He fired them, the engine turning over right away—the Arabs must have an American mechanic.

As the engines kicked, the rotors building up torque, Vanderhoff was in the passenger door, dropping a clip from the Glock and jamming another in its place. "I'm going to do you sometime, Jenks," he said low. "And I'm going to enjoy it."

"You could ruin a rainy day, you know that?" Jenks replied, gunfire dicing the side of the ship, the windshield shattering before them, blinding them.

"Fuck," Jenks said. "One damned thing after another."

He worked his foot out from under the controls and kicked out at the windshield, knocking its remnants away. Then he opened up the engines, the ship lifting straight up, twisting as it rose.

"Whooee!" Jenks called as they spun gloriously up into God's country, air whooshing in through the broken windshield, the gunfire diminishing below until it was lost in the rush of the rotors. He steadied the spin, keeping it open full, rushing up the mountain.

"Reload me!" he called to Vanderhoff, the man reaching across to take his gun, Jenks pulling an automatic loader out of his pocket.

Vanderhoff ejected the spent shells, the side of the mountain quickly blurring past their window. He finished the load, snapping shut the chamber as they crested the fortress walls, the vast stronghold spread out beneath them.

Jenks reached down and juiced the thirty-millimeter cannons, the TV screen sighting fading in as the cannon turret dropped out of the bottom of the ship and locked into position beneath.

"That one!" Vanderhoff called into the teeth of the wind, pointing to the most distant gun placement, men scurrying up the stone roadway to the gun.

"Just for you, Jorge," Jenks smiled. "Just for you."

He swooped, the throttle open full, his fingers squeezing off on the fire controls, the belly cannons opening up with the death rattle.

Justice had frozen at the doorway when they dragged Gail Compton out of the wreckage of the chopper, had heard the voice when she heard and knew the sound of Frank Merriman. He stood weaponless and alone and tried to separate his growing feelings for the woman being dragged up the steps of the castle wall from the contingencies of the mission itself. Why was she there? Whose side, indeed, was she on? But he kept seeing her as Allie, their faces blending in the muck of his brain, and when the white chopper crested the wall, he knew that he had held himself in check long enough.

As Jenks and Vanderhoff soared above him, he tore open the castle door, running back inside. The doors to the auditorium were just beginning to open. He charged them, grabbing a free-standing candlestick and jamming it through the handles, locking them in.

A downstairs guard challenged him. He simply turned and charged the man, gunfire rattling outside, crossing the twenty feet that separated them before the man could raise his weapon. He hit the man hard, going over with him. Snaking out with a rigid palm, he jammed the man's nose up into his head, the cartilage driving straight into his brain—instant death.

He was below the mezzanine, the guards there unable to get to him. But the other downstairs guard, a fat man in a jumpsuit, brought his automatic to bear.

Justice grabbed his guard's M16 and rolled as the other man opened up, the carpet tearing up behind him. The man emptied the clip in his haste, Justice jumping to his feet and taking the man out with a single shot to the chest.

There was firing from above, and a body fell heavily from the mezzanine to the floor beside him. One of the upstairs guards. He ran out near the table, Sardi and Kim waving to him from above, both of them carrying multiple weapons on their backs and in their belts.

"They've taken Gail," he said. "It's begun."

"Where first?" Kim asked.

Justice pointed with the automatic toward the doors of the auditorium, a furious pounding coming from within. "Get down here," he said, the woman hurrying down the stairs to stand beside him.

The candlestick was beginning to crack as they pounded the door with their bodies. Justice took two of her automatics and slung them over his own shoulder. "I want you to empty your guns in there," he said. "Shoot everything that moves and don't stop shooting until you're out of ammo."

She looked at him and snorted. "Bad guys, huh?"

"Yeah," he said low. "Bad guys."

The doors burst open, six or eight men stumbling out with them. Justice and Kim opened up on automatic, the first wave of men going down hard, driving the others back.

They charged in over the bodies of the fallen, firing at will into the crowded auditorium, Justice operating with an almost mechanical precision, moving in surgical, controlled bursts, aiming head high, trying to erase the evil from their brains.

The punks yelled and charged around like animals in a forest fire, none of them armed, a precaution he approved of. He emptied one gun, then threw it down and worked on another, men crumbling under the withering fire in bloody heaps, too late Justice seeing the Medellin people and Gomez getting out through a back door.

He dropped the second gun and started in with the third, walking into the crowd, stepping over bodies, looking for Noriega. It bothered him that he saw no uniforms. Men lay dead everywhere, the firing now slowing to take in occasional movement, he and Kim walking through the auditorium together in silence, doing the job that had to be done. They were knee deep in bodies, and still he couldn't find the ones he sought.

"You're finished here," came Sardi's voice from the doorway. "Let's go."

Justice threw down the last of his spent weapons, hurrying back to Sardi, taking an M16 from the man and a .45 for close quarters.

"Where?" Kim asked, reloading from a utility belt slung across her shoulder.

"The tower," Justice said.

"There's a way up from the mezzanine," Sardi said. "I found it earlier."

"Let's go!"

They ran back out of the auditorium, Medellin punks now coming through the front door. Both Justice and Kim opened up as they ran, taking turns keeping them back while the other made distance. Justice knocked over the table, food going everywhere, firing back through the front door as Kim and Sardi ran up the stairs, Kim then returning the compliment from the mezzanine so Justice could join them. Once up, they ran.

Quickness and decisive action were their only friends now as they ran a long hallway, firing at anything moving, not so much trying to kill as to keep their way clean. Sardi took them down a narrow, blank hall, a large wooden door at its end. Locked.

"This is a siege tower," Justice said. "It's going to be barred from the inside."

"I know a way," Kim said. "Quick!"

They charged out after her, taking fire as they crossed the mezzanine, then charging up the stairs three at a time. They came out into the upper hallway, Medellin's board of directors, in various stages of undress, running the hall. Kim opened up on them with pleasure, watching the big shots fall, squirming and pleading. Then she was through the door to the American's bedroom, the two men following her out onto the balcony.

They threw their weapons up first, then hoisted themselves up to the flat roof, all of Panama spread out around them. Justice looked down at base camp. Choppers were taking to the sky like mosquitoes, all coming for them as the sky clouded up for its daily outpour. He looked out over the castle, hundreds of men out of their barracks and charging. It was up to Jenks and Vanderhoff now.

Jenks took the chopper down at head level, going right at the men charging the antiaircraft gun, trying to take out the men without damaging the ADS. Twin cannon fire churned up the cement pathway, eating up the symmetrical trail behind the men, two of them going down, the chopper on top of the third in another second, Jenks having just an instant to appreciate the look on the punk's face as he turned and saw them there before he was bumped off the wall and into oblivion.

Their momentum took them past the gun, Jenks making a wide turn and coming back. A fourth man had reached the gun and was trying to bring it to bear. But they were on him too quickly, the man unable to get them in the bite of sights. Jenks hovered above. "Take him with your sidearm!" he yelled, Vanderhoff aiming through the window space with the Glock as Jenks tilted the bird for him.

Vanderhoff took the man out with one shot, Jenks leveling and hovering directly over the placement. "Nice knowing you, pal!" he said, Vanderhoff kicking open the door and staring down the fifteen feet to the placement below—a postage stamp two miles up. If he missed, he was gone. No time to think—instinct!

He slid down, sitting on the edge of the door space, his feet dangling.

"I can't hold it in this wind!" Jenks yelled behind him, Vanderhoff jumping right away, coming down hard atop the man he had just killed and jumping to his feet.

He moved to the weapon, realizing firing sequence hadn't even been started. He looked to the other placement. It was fully manned, the crew already bringing it to bear on him. He looked up. Jenks saw it too, the man a sitting duck hovering there.

He waved Jenks off as he juiced the system, but the man didn't leave. Instead, he flew out thirty feet and placed the chopper in a direct line between Vanderhoff and the other placement.

Damn him! The son of a bitch was screwing him with loyalty. He bent, turning on the lead-computing gun sight and the range finder radar mounted on the side of the thing. He released the safeties, setting the operator control for thousand-round-a-minute bursts as the other placement began firing, bullets ricocheting off a chopper hull able to withstand twenty-three-millimeter cannon fire at any point. But not for long.

Vanderhoff set the mechanism for sixty-round bursts, engaging the 1,100 rounds of linked ready-use ammo—the system up-loaded and ready. He swung the turret on its outrigger platform, bringing it around to the other placement. Jenks's bird was shaking slightly, but holding, smoke bleeding from somewhere inside to dissipate quickly on the wind. He locked eyes with the man for just a second, sharing something deeper than words. Then Jenks gave him the thumbs up and angled away with a jerk, Vanderhoff opening up with the air-cooled six-barreled cannon on the other placement, firing three bursts of sixty, the men falling away under the intensity, the cannon falling to point straight up. He fired two more bursts at the gun itself, disabling it, then swung away just as the choppers from below crested the walls and came at him.

Kiki Anouweyah and his people broke through the walls at the excavation sites just as Jenks's chopper bore down on the gun placement and dropped Vanderhoff into position. He turned to his second in command, the man who had stood up to him in the cave. "Take five men," he said. "Secure the pathway and hold it."

"Why don't we just blow it here?" the man said.

The prince was looking up at the storage caves that layered above him and the huge crane that dominated the landscape. "Because it might be our only way down, my friend," he told the man. "Look above. Five men with rocks from up there could keep a whole army off that trail."

"Got it," the man said, picking his men and hurrying off.

Men were beginning to pour out of the barracks just across the yard, while right before him a soccer game had been interrupted, men running everywhere. Hundreds of men. They were his responsibility. Ten crates of decomposing dynamite had made the trip up along with five mules. He had fixed each crate with a blob of C-4 from the belt around his middle, the timers sticking out of the plastique.

"Quickly!" he told his people. "Fix five of the crates to the mules. Five of you carry the rest out to the barracks. Fix one beneath that water tower. Set the fuses for two minutes." He still had ten men. They had broken one crate down on the trip up and fixed the sticks with fuses. "The rest of you, take out the warehouses . . . hurry!"

They had rehearsed this on the way up, Kiki keeping

them scheming, working with their heads to keep them from thinking of their plight. They were caught in the excitement now, moving with it.

He looked up again at the crane. That was where he needed to be. He moved to one of the mules as a crate was being strapped to its back. "I'm sorry, my friend," he said, "but you must give your life for the cause."

He slapped the animal on the rump to start it off and ran, scurrying up the partially excavated mountain on all fours, climbing rapidly, making the crane, panting, within a minute. He climbed up into the cab of the thing, looking down at the tableau.

Men charged in all directions as helicopters screamed up over the walls, firing wildly at Vanderhoff's placement. Mules ran through the crowds on short fuses, and bearers turned mercenaries charged about, crates of nitro on their heads. On the distant castle walls a pitched battle was taking place.

He looked down at the controls. He had never operated a crane before but reasoned that if one pushed enough buttons on a mechanical object, that object would eventually respond. He started pushing buttons.

The thing groaned to life in his hands and he found the levers to make it go up and down and cut a transverse course. He turned the machine toward the action, then shoved forward the lever that brought down the neck of the thing and the heavy iron bucket on the end.

He was amazed at how far it reached as it came crashing down in the center of the barracks area, scattering men, smashing some. He started laughing at the sight, swinging the arm back and forth at ground level, punching through barracks and walls behind, sending stone and men down the mountainside as Jenks brought the white chopper to bear on the ones who'd made it into the castle courtyard, strafing them with his belly cannons.

Kiki brought the arm up again, retracting it somewhat and letting it fall atop the barracks. He rooted the thing back and forth as he had done earlier, clearing a huge gap in the walls on either side.

And the explosions began.

All over the yard crates of dynamite blew with orange-and-black fury, men and machines flying, tumbling in pieces as the mountain rumbled beneath him and a helicopter fell into the castle courtyard under the relentless pounding of the Vulcan's cannons.

The base of the water tower blew at the edge of the courtyard, the tower itself creaking, then falling, dumping thousands of gallons of water into the barracks area, washing men and buildings right over the edges that he'd created with the shovel. Scores of men were tumbling down the side of Barú in a cascade of bright water and stone.

The courtyard below was so thick with bodies that he couldn't see the ground, and the men left were charging for the path down, Kiki's people chunking huge rock slabs on them from above, peeling them off the mountainside.

Another chopper went down atop the barracks still intact, orange fire bursting from its full tank and spewing out in a wide arc all around itself.

He heard distant sounds and turned to look. An army was rumbling toward base camp from the east, led by a flotilla of helicopter gun ships. But whose?

Vanderhoff stayed on the gun, taking them out as they crested the wall, Jenks buzzing the courtyard, trying to hold the Medellins back from the keep.

A chopper went down under his tracers, explosions going off from the far courtyard—Kiki!

They came over the wall in twos and threes, swarming. He swung the gun quickly, taking out another, the thing going down in flames as one came around behind him. He whipped the turret violently, blasting the son of a bitch head-on as he swooped, deck guns blazing. He hit it with three bursts, the thing exploding fifty feet before him, hanging for a second, a ball of orange fire, then falling into the crater.

He came back around, gunships everywhere. He bore down on the closest, then saw more, a bunch of them flying the Panamanian colors. He hesitated for only a second—but it was long enough.

The ship was on him. He fell back as the breech exploded in his face, his world turning red, then black . . . the void closing in around him.

* * *

Jenks saw Vanderhoff's placement go up as he strafed the yard, his guts tightening with anger, and he angled up, turning the cannons loose on the bird that had hit Jorge. He came up from beneath, dicing the thing's belly as his guns ran dry, the enemy chopper doing a flip and disappearing over the edge of the crater upside down.

He tried to come around again, but the quarters were too tight, his rotors tangling with another chopper's, snapping off to pinwheel into the men below, and he fell like a rock, bouncing into the courtyard and falling sideways.

A sharp pain gouged his side, but he pushed himself out of the wreckage and jumped to the ground in the middle of the courtyard, his .38 in his hand, his side covered with blood. He began firing at anyone approaching the door.

As hell raged around him, William Justice moved with the calm of a saint, totally removed, absolutely goal oriented: crouching, firing, advancing, crouching, firing, reloading, firing. Moving, always moving, inexorably toward the tower door and his destiny. He noted the carnage around him but didn't relate to it. Kim and Sardi moved with him, supporting, acting as his eyes and ears. The Medellin choppers buzzed the tower like bees on the hive.

"Those birds will finish us!" Kim said, moving her attentions to the choppers, firing on them.

"Just wait!" Justice called.

"For what?" Sardi said.

Justice looked up from his gun. "For Portilla's people," he said. "Behind you."

They turned and looked. Below, the Panamanian National Guard had engaged the Cuban troops, their choppers bearing down on the castle.

He jumped to his feet, firing from the hip and spraying a wide area, charging, finally making the tower, the others behind him. The door was locked, but it was metal, malleable. He blasted it at the handle, the door pocking, then springing open.

"How'd you know they'd come?" Kim asked him from the doorway.

He poked his head around the door frame, looking for the stairs. He slid inside, pulling them in behind him and closing the door. "They *had* to come," he said low. "We blew their scam yesterday. Portilla's only chance is to come out here and solidify his position by taking absolute control of the Guard. The only way he can avoid a firing squad is by being in charge."

"But Noriega runs the guard."

"Not if he's dead," Justice grinned.

"I don't get it," Kim said.

Sardi spoke up as they inched slowly up the twisting staircase. "Portilla told the troops they were coming out here to save Noriega, when he actually hopes to accomplish just the opposite, then taking control because the top dog's out of the way."

"Isn't life grand?" Justice said.

They reached a window cutout, Kim pointing out. "The cable car!" she said.

Justice looked out, the Medellin brothers just passing their vantage point, taking the car down. Kim raised an M16, Justice looking at his watch and pushing her gun away. "Save the ammo," he said, the gondola exploding white and pale yellow, flames shooting long streamers through the windows as the bottom fell out of the thing, several burning bodies plunging into the valley.

They heard voices from above, the sound of many footsteps charging down the stairs. Justice shrugged and held the M16 like a baseball bat, ready for the men to curve down the stairs in his direction.

The men ran into them on a dead run, ten of them, Justice and Kim lashing out with their guns, Sardi ducking and weaving on light feet, almost a dance, using the soldiers' own aggression against them. They slammed into walls and fell down stairs as he bent and bobbed, never landing a punch, just staying out of the way. And in half a minute, the three of them were heading back up the stairs again, walking quietly. Justice took a deep breath. Two of the men on the stairs had been wearing khakis—the mother lode.

The stairs terminated at a single door that was just slightly ajar. He set the rifle down gently on the stairs and pulled the .45 out of his belt, priming the thing as the battle continued to rage outside.

He took one look back at the others, then hit the door,

rolling into the room and coming up in a crouch. Everything froze.

The room was round with a thirty-foot diameter. A short flight of stairs led through the far side and out to the chopper pad, which was just visible through the door space. The place reeked of opium, its walls covered with erotic art interspersed with stuffed human heads, mounted like trophies. The floor was covered with pillows, the only extant furniture; several cutouts let in light, though the sky had darkened completely, thunder rumbling ominously.

Three men occupied the room. Manuel Noriega stood motionless midway up the stairs to the pad, a box full of bundled dollars in his hands. Gomez stood in room center, stupidly holding a load of gold bars. And then on the floor...on the floor fondling a barely consciously Gail Compton sat a near-human creature.

Justice didn't recognize him at first, a blob of skin with hands, wrapped in a silk robe. The thing had to weigh five hundred pounds, the skin sagging and sallow, almost yellow, the face bloated, swelled up like a balloon and splotched with large crimson sores. But the slit eyes, barely visible through layers of fat were still the eyes that he remembered from that night so long ago. Frank Merriman sat before him, a product of his own disease, a long curl of smoke drifting from the stem of the tall hooka between his lips. Merriman was the physical embodiment of the gross excess of Volcán Barú, the living symbol of the jungle gone mad through the perverted imagination of the human animal and its capacity for cruelty.

"Take your fucking hands off her," he said low, waving the gun slowly back and forth.

Merriman looked at him, narrowing his eyes even more, and Justice realized that the man was there, but just barely, his brain so eaten up that he couldn't relate to even the simplest of situations. He was a walking vegetable—*if* he could walk.

Noriega began talking. "Look, senor. We'll share this money. There's more than enough to—"

"Shove it, *cara piña*," he said. "Just keep your fucking mouth shut and speak when you're spoken to."

Compton had squeezed out from under Merriman's huge bulk, sliding over to where Justice still crouched.

"Kill them," she said. "Do it now."

"Not until we've sorted out a few things first, sweetheart," he said. "I'm all confused."

An explosion rocked the tower, half the room collapsing in a shower of stone and mortar from a direct hit. They all went down, debris blasting through the room as a huge section of outer wall imploded, shaking the tower, rocking them. Justice was hit by fragments, going down in a haze of dust and smoke, the bulk of a Panamanian helicopter visible passing the large gap in the wall.

He struggled to rise in the fog of dust, his weapon lost in the confusion, other dark forms also emerging from the haze. He stood on shaky legs, his clothes ripped, shredded by blasting frags, blood oozing from dozens of small wounds. But there was no pain, none at all. It was lost in the place of anger. He pulled off the remnants of jacket and tie.

He staggered out from under the debris in time to hear the sound of boots charging up the stairs, a small squad of Zone police in combat gear and helmets pouring in the door followed by a man he'd hoped he'd meet again.

"Excellent!" Colonel Portilla said as he picked his way into the rubble, his men freezing the room with M16s. "Mr. Justice, you've done a wonderful job!"

The dust was settling. Justice looked around to see everyone shaken but unhurt, all picking themselves up. His eyes began searching for his gun.

"Congratulations," Justice said, smiling into the teeth of the enemy. "Looks like the United States has itself a new ally. Have you seen my gun anywhere?"

"Good afternoon, General," Portilla said, smiling at a dust-covered Manuel Noriega crouching on the stairs up to the platform.

"Colonel," Noriega said. "You've rescued me."

"No, no," Portilla said. "I've come to bury Caesar. You see, Mr. Lambert has cut off my options. There has been some . . . distasteful business, and I must redeem myself. But I may now be the hero of Panama and a friend of the United States of America. I have not only destroyed the evil dictator, but I've routed the Cuban presence from our land and eliminated the drug trade all in one afternoon." He looked at Justice, who had spotted his .45 on the floor and was inching toward it. "I believe that your government will forgive my small indiscretions regarding the sinkings of the boats after all of this. Don't you agree, Mr. Lambert? What would you call it . . . the lesser of two evils? I will be a *very* democratic ruler and a shining jewel in the tiara that is Central America."

Justice smiled. "The government has chosen worse," he said, reaching down to pick up his gun, blowing the dust off.

"I'll admit," Portilla said, "that I was angry with you at first, Mr. Lambert, but judging from the way things are working out, I couldn't be happier."

"Besides," Justice said. "Now that Porras is dead, you'll need someone to intercede for you. Someone to take all this wonderful news back to the United States."

"Quite true," Portilla said.

"Only one problem," Justice said, leveling the .45 at Portilla's chest. "I don't work for the American government."

"Put the weapon down," Portilla said, his face turning hard. "My men will kill you."

"Not if they've got any brains they won't," Justice said, looking at the men who surrounded him. "Because if what you say comes to pass, you'll be in charge of the National Guard with all the power in the world. About the last thing you'll need around you is a bunch of foreign nationals who have something to hold over your head. . . ."

"Shoot him," Portilla said coldly, the American cops holding firm on the weapons raised to their shoulders. But they didn't fire. "Shoot him!"

"I'll bet," Justice told the men, "that you've got a considerable sum tucked away from all those sinkings. How much of it do you think you'll ever see if Portilla walks out of here alive? You guys are meat. If you have half a brain in your heads, you'll walk right now, get your cash and get to Rio, because you're going to be dead or wanted by the entire world otherwise. You've got no options, boys. Your friend has been using you."

"Kill him now!" Portilla said, voice strained. "Don't listen to him!"

"They don't have to listen to me," Justice said, locking

eyes with the man. "They've got their own minds and know a last chance when they see it."

"Kill him!"

"Take a walk boys," Justice said. "Take the trail down. If you take the choppers, I'll blow you out of the sky."

One of the cops lowered his rifle slowly, the others following one after another.

"No," Portilla said, grabbing at their arms as they filed out one at a time. "We've got it all . . . just like we'd planned. Don't you understand? He's just using you . . . telling you . . . he's . . ."

They were gone, Justice left alone with Portilla and the others.

"Please," Portilla said, his hands shaking wildly, his face white as paint. "Can't we make an arrangement? There's lots to share here, we . . ."

"My man," Justice said, shaking his head. "It's that time."

He pulled the trigger, the gun coughing twice in his hand. Portilla fell to his knees, his khaki staining dark on his chest, his mouth working furiously without words as he pitched face down onto the rubble.

A door slammed behind him, Justice turning to see his way barred to the outside platform, Noriega and Gomez—gone.

He charged up the debris-filled stairs to the door. It was heavy wood, barred from the outside. He could hear the sound of the chopper firing up on the platform. No time.

He rushed back down the stairs, thunder rumbling outside. Sardi and Kim, covered with mortar dust, had retrieved their weapons and held Gail Compton and a bleeding Frank Merriman in check.

"Kim!" he said, moving quickly to the blasted-out wall, a hole ten feet around looking out over the landscape. "Get downstairs and make sure they don't take those choppers!"

"Got it!" she charged out of the room as Justice ran to the place. He threw the gun down and walked to the edge. The roof was several stories straight down as he tentatively reached a leg outside the bombed-out place, looking for hand- and footholds on the outside of the tower.

He found a ledge several inches wide with his foot. Hugging the wall, he eased out of the tower, into the high wind, the beginnings of rain lashing at his face as lightning flared the dark sky.

He hugged the wall, creeping, his ability to balance the only thing holding him up on the three-inch ledge. His mind was all centered on Noriega as he kept moving, the battle sounds at the foot of Barú drifting up to him through the cloud layer that now obscured everything below.

He rounded the curve of the tower just as the camouflage-painted Huey lifted crookedly off the high platform to swoosh past him. Without thought, he released his precarious balance and pushed off from the wall, jumping at the thing.

He grabbed just the base of the runner as it slipped past him, fingers like steel grabbing hold, barely hanging on as the ship tilted slightly with its now-unbalanced weight, Gomez at the controls.

The rain began sheeting down as he pulled, straining, his arms working his weight up the runner, lightning flaring. He was a directed brain, going for Noriega. Below, bodies lay scattered everywhere, the remnants of the battle, small fires mixing black smoke with the dark clouds.

The runners got slippery, Justice swinging his legs up to wrap around the skid. He came up, kneeling on the runner, and ripped open the pilot's door, Gomez kicking him in the face, knocking him back.

He slipped down, falling, his fingers scrabbling again for a handhold as the chopper veered away from the tower, pain shooting through his arms as he hauled himself up again, moving, always goal directed.

He swung back up on the skid and grabbed the door again. This time when the boot kicked out, he let go, grabbing the leg it was attached to.

Screaming, Gomez came out of his seat, Justice falling backwards with the man, Gomez plunging into the raging storm, falling, his legs on the runner breaking his own fall as the man disappeared into the cloud bank.

The chopper banked sharply with no pilot, Justice swinging upside down from the runner as Noriega grabbed the controls and tried to steady the craft that was swinging back, nearly sideways, toward the tower.

Justice reached up, his fingers grasping the slippery runner. The tower rushed up at them, then past, as Justice pulled himself up again and reached, muscles quivering, for the pilot's door, his strength ebbing.

Yelling, Noriega kicked the door into Justice's face, the thing snapping his head back, darkness fighting with light for his conscious mind. He was losing it, his mind reeling from the blow as he fell backwards, just pulling himself up at the last second, and he reached for the door again.

Noriega kicked out again, the door smashing Justice on the temple, knocking him back, his legs sliding off the runners and he was falling, his mind drifting, floating with his body.

He hit something hard and bounced, the first instinct of the infant taking over, and he grabbed, his mind spinning, as he fell again. His fingers locked in mesh, his body snapped hard as he went down, the fingers cramping with the weight as he shook his head, trying to bring back full consciousness.

He looked up through a haze of blood to see he was just holding onto the edge of a satellite dish attached to the side of the tower, the chopper circling as Noriega got control of it. Reality sank in and he yelled, pulling himself up into the bowl of the dish as the chopper dropped below him, moving off into the clouds.

He looked up, into lashing rain. The platform was above him. He found finger-size cracks in the stone of the tower and started climbing sheer rock face, scurrying up the side of the tower. He made the platform, pulling himself up and grabbing rock debris, throwing it at the retreating Huey, growling like an animal.

He hit the rotor with a large chunk of rock that shattered to dust on impact. But the chopper tilted, smoking as it disappeared into the clouds. Justice stood on the platform, raging in a primal language at the sky as the thunder rolled around him, and suddenly he turned and looked at the platform door.

Merriman.

He moved to the door in an adrenal haze, lifting out the heavy iron bar and throwing it over his shoulder to clang loudly on the wet, slippery platform. He tore open the door and moved down the stairs, his mind lost in passion as he went for the man who had made him what he was.

And the thunder called to him as he moved to the man,

who was standing, his robe askew, his hand to his bloody head. And the lightning strobed through the missing wall place, Justice grabbing Merriman by the throat, fingers tightening, and every instinct screamed in him for blood.

"W-who... are you?" the man choked, his slit eyes now bulging, his thick tongue protruding from his lips.

"Don't recognize me, Frank?" he said. "Remember... college boy... remember, Hate del Volcán?"

"J-Justice," the man rasped, and went to his knees, his head lolling.

Justice knelt with him, squeezing slowly, enjoying. He could stretch this out for an hour.

"William," Sardi said softly from behind him. Then louder. "William."

"Remember shooting me, Frank?" Justice said loudly. "Remember laughing?"

"Kill him and you kill yourself," Sardi said. "Stop."

Justice turned, trying to comprehend the man through the instincts that were driving him. He could barely focus on rationality. "W-what?"

"Don't you understand what's going on here?" Sardi said. "Medellin used Merriman as a control rod against the U.S. government. As long as they had him to tell the world about the government's involvement in drug trafficking, the U.S. could never invade Panama. Do you understand what I'm saying?"

"B-blackmail," Justice said, easing his grip somewhat but holding the man tightly by the throat. "That's why they told me Merriman was dead so many years ago. He'd simply gone deep cover to work with Medellin and Noriega, financing Noriega's loyalty in-country."

"Then there was a power struggle between Medellin and America," Sardi said. "The cartel controlling Noriega and making him break with the U.S., and with Merriman as the trump card, the U.S. couldn't do a thing about it."

"Except hire me to solve their problems for them," Justice replied. "This was all about Merriman, not Noriega."

"And William," Sardi said, moving up to put a hand on his shoulder. "You now hold the trump. Merriman alive could keep the U.S. Navy out of Haven just as it kept them out of Panama."

306

"No!" Justice yelled. "I've waited...waited, so...long for this, I..."

"Is it the animal talking, William, or the civilized man?" Sardi asked him. "This is the decision of your life."

"You can't ask me to do that," Justice said softly. "This man has to pay."

Sardi pointed down at the pitiful creature on the ground, the man blubbering incoherently under Justice's grasp. "It looks as if he's made his own hellworld to me. No, William, your choice is very simple. Leave this man alive, and your mission remains. Kill him, and you lose it all. The symbolic gesture, the difference between light and darkness. Are your passions for revenge more important than your dharma? If so, then you are no better than those you fight against. Your life has been reduced to this moment."

Justice stared down at Merriman, the hatred a tangible commodity thick in the air between them. But he knew that Sardi was right. He'd lived for vengeance, but for the vengeance to be an end in itself negated everything positive he'd ever stood for, everything that Allie had ever stood for. He couldn't tarnish her memory that way. He couldn't let down all the people who depended upon him. The civilized man took over from the animal. William Justice walked out of the jungle and into the daylight. Opening his fingers, he let Merriman go.

"You should have killed him," Gail Compton said from behind them, Justice turning to see her across the room as she held his .45 with both hands out in front of her. Her voice was quivering. Justice held out his hands and took a step toward her.

"Stay a distance from me!" she screeched. "I've seen you in action."

"You were here to kill Merriman," Justice said, "and probably me."

"Your name is J-Justice?" she said, distant. "I've already k-killed you once."

Justice smiled, confirming what he'd already believed. "It *was* you that night at the hospital in Dallas." He took a step toward her.

"Stay back!" she yelled.

"Was Frank your superior?" he asked, taking another step.

She nodded. "Until Noriega walked, he was," she said. "We couldn't do a damned thing here with him renegading."

"They'll have to kill *you* now, too," Justice said, moving closer. "Don't you see? All criminal organizations work the same way. They take new people and make them commit a crime, something to hold over their heads. With you, they had you kill somebody. In criminal organizations, they also move up through assassination. You took my place."

"It was my f-first assignment," she said. "They said you were a t-traitor. I got so confused. I couldn't find the right room . . . then the elevator wasn't working when I left, I . . . I've been in ever since."

"You don't want to kill me, Gail," he said, reaching out a hand. "You're better than those people."

She looked into his eyes, and he let her see the truth of his mind and heart—let her see *real* truth. She dropped the gun and fell into his arms. "I-I just wanted to do the right thing," she said. "And then . . . then . . ."

"They used you, Gail," he said. "Just like they used me. We can walk away from it."

He turned to Sardi. The man was staring at him, the slightest smile turning the corners of his lips, Justice mouthing a silent thanks, Sardi nodding in return.

Kiki came running into the room, staring around at the devastation without reaction. "Chopper's up," he said. "We need to go before the rest of the charges go up."

"The whole basement of this place is an arsenal," Sardi said.

Kiki smiled. "I know that, mon. Come on."

"Then let's go," Justice said, Kiki pointing to Merriman on the floor.

"Him, too?"

"Yeah," Justice said, walking over to pinch the man's cheek. "We're going to castrate him and put him out to pasture. Would you like that, Frank?"

The man just looked at him, working his thick, purple lips.

They moved down the stairs, Justice beginning to feel the pain now that the rush was over. He walked with his arm around Gail's shoulder, his right eye swelling closed from the blow of the helicopter door. "What do you do now?" he asked her as they hobbled down the stairs.

"I don't know," she said. "I'm finished with the Company."

"They're going to kill you, you know."

"Not if I'm faster."

He hugged her closer. "Why don't you come out to Haven and live with us?" he said. "We could use a hand on the pimento harvest."

She looked up at him, smiling. "Sounds a little slow moving for my tastes," she said. "Maybe I can take a rain check. I really need to be out on my own for a while . . . figuring things out."

"I understand."

They made it down to the courtyard. Bodies lay everywhere, strewn amidst the wreckage of a half dozen helicopters. Kim sat at the controls of the Huey that had brought Portilla to the castle, the rotors already beating the air, the rain slowing to a drizzle.

The helicopter bay was full of people, Kiki's men and several of the servants and musicians. Bob Jenks knelt on the floor, tending to Jorge Vanderhoff who was unconscious, swarthed in bandages.

Justice climbed into the bay, crawling to Jenks and Jorge. The man was near death, the left side from hip to head chopped up and bloody.

"My God," Justice whispered, taking the man's limp arm.

"He's lost an eye," Jenks said. "Maybe a hand . . . but if we can get him some help . . ."

"Yeah," Justice said. "We'll get him help."

He stood and moved to the pilot's compartment, Kim already lifting them into the lightening sky. "Get us to Bocas del Toro," he said. "I have an infirmary in the cannery that is fully staffed. Quick. Then raise the American embassy in Panama City and tell them to pass along the message to the State Department that *we've* got Merriman and the same deal is in effect."

"Got it," she said, swinging them to the north, Justice sliding to a sitting position there in the bay as people talked excitedly all around him, Sardi now bent over Jorge as Bob

Jenks hovered protectively. Gail Compton crawled up next to him, sitting beside as Merriman blubbered like a baby in the back.

"Did Noriega get away?" she asked, as they swung completely around, Volcán Barú evident through the open bay.

"Yeah," he said.

"That leaves him in charge," she said. "He'll just make more contacts and start all over again."

"That he will," Justice smiled. "But not here. And not with *those* assholes."

At that moment, Volcán Barú went up in a huge explosion, from the warehouses to the keep, orange flowers blooming high into the morning sky, rumbling far louder than nature's thunder as the castle collapsed, tumbling down the mountainside like lava, a powdered snow of cocaine raining over everything.

Kiki was crouching in the bay. He turned to Justice with wide eyes and a huge smile. "We did good today, boss man," he said.

"What about the trail down the mountain?" Justice returned.

Kiki shrugged. "We blew that, too."

Justice smiled and thought about the Zone cops. "Yeah," he said. "We did good."

And he brought cramped fingers up to gently rub the rough, swollen places on his face. The pain felt good, the pain of hard work well done. He stared into the sky through the bay and saw life instead of death. And after so many years, the ghosts of Hate del Volcán knew a peace that only the settling of his own troubled mind could bring them.

It was over.

XXII.

THE CARIBBEAN
15 JUNE 1984—AFTERNOON

William Justice swung out hard with the machete, severing the stem that held the large bunch of green bananas to the tree, the bunch falling into his arms.

He set them on the ground and hacked the next one off the tree, his workers running behind him, picking up the bunches and carrying them to the distant truck. The harvest was going well this year. The plantation might even turn a profit—not the kind of profit that would mean a thing to Ed Barkes or the consortium, but enough to make him feel good and keep his employees working and happy.

This is where the winds of God had brought him. In the middle of a storm three months out of Houston, he'd run aground here and chosen it for his home. He enjoyed the jungle, the primal challenge of sun and rain forest, and had managed to lose himself in the soil, returning to something basic and finding, if not peace, then at least a lessening of the constant pain.

He sat on a stump, wiping his forehead, his T-shirt soaked through, sweat glistening from his arms and chest. He stuck the machete in the ground before him and ran powerful hands through his wet hair.

"Mr. Lambert!" one of his people called from farther up the trail. "Someone comes!"

Justice stood, watching down the path as sun slanted through gaps in the trees, casting small spotlights onto the emerald green shade of the jungle trail. A vision was floating toward him, a tall lean man, dressed completely in white, a turban perched atop his head.

The man moved fluidly, his body in total concert with its surroundings as he moved through darkness and light, his determined step taking him ever closer to William Justice.

Justice blinked several times, but the vision was still there, and within a minute it stood before him. A dark man, perhaps an Indian. His eyes were deep pools of liquid brown.

"Are you William Lambert?" the man asked in sonorous English, and he was holding a newspaper out in front of him. "Publisher of this paper?"

Justice looked down and saw an old copy of the *Watchdog* in the man's hand. He laughed. "You came a long way to ask that question," he said.

"My name is Sardi," the stranger said. "I've been searching for you."

"Why?"

"I have a dream to share with you."

Justice looked into the man's eyes and saw real power. "I've lost the ability to dream," he said.

"You are the dharma," the man said. "I'll help you provide the form."

"I don't know what you're talking about, my man," Justice said. "But you've come sniffing up the wrong tree."

Sardi just smiled, his deep eyes twinkling. "I don't think so," he said, and sat on the ground, spinning a marvelous tale to capture the heart of a madman.

ABOUT THE AUTHOR

Before turning to writing, JACK ARNETT led a varied and interesting life in Southeast Asia and the Orient working for the U.S. Department of Defense. Disillusioned by the system, he left the government and became a political organizer and speechwriter before expatriating in the early eighties to pursue his own visions. The BOOK OF JUSTICE comprises the bulk of his message to the world.

Arnett is forty-two years old, single and living somewhere in the Caribbean, where he writes sporadically and lives the life of a beachcomber.